'This is an impressive book. In writing it the author demonstrates great talent, as well as great courage.'
Mario Vargas Llosa

'No one that reads this book will be able to look at their family in the same way again.'
Gabriela Wiener

'An extraordinary family story … Renato Cisneros delivers here the captivating narrative of a strange and disturbing filiation. A loving and lucid puzzle.'
Le Monde (France)

'People should read this novel to learn more about themselves.'
Jorge Edwards

'Cisneros is a phenomenon in Latin America today.'
Jesús Ruiz Mantilla, *El País* (Spain)

'A book so intelligent and moving, you wish it would never end.'
Libération (France)

'*The Distance Between Us* is the story of a villain told from love. It dwells in the humanity hidden behind the themes left by war. It also narrates that other war: the one which all of us wage against our parents to become the persons we are.'
Santiago Roncagliolo

'*The Distance Between Us* goes far and appeals to the reader exactly because there is so little distance between what is written and what was lived.'
Alberto Fuguet

'"Just as a father is never prepared to bury his son, a son is never prepared to dig up his father"(…) It is within this tension that this magnificent novel lies, full of drama and suspense from the very first page.
Edmundo Paz Soldán

THE DISTANCE

BETWEEN US

CHARCO PRESS

First published by Charco Press 2018

Charco Press Ltd., Office 59, 44-46 Morningside Road, Edinburgh EH10 4BF

AUG 2 0 2020

Copyright © Renato Cisneros 2015

English translation copyright © Fionn Petch 2018

Photo courtesy of the author

A CIP catalogue record for this book is available from the British Library.

ISBN: 9781999859312
e-book: 9781999859367

www.charcopress.com

Edited by Robin Myers
Cover design by Pablo Font
Typeset by Laura Jones
Proofread by Fiona Mackintosh

This book has been selected to receive financial assistance from English PEN's 'PEN Translates' programme, supported by Arts Council England. English PEN exists to promote literature and our understanding of it, to uphold writers' freedoms around the world, to campaign against the persecution and imprisonment of writers for stating their views, and to promote the friendly co-operation of writers and the free exchange of ideas. www.englishpen.org

Printed and bound in Great Britain by Bell and Bain Ltd, Glasgow

Supported using public funding by
**ARTS COUNCIL
ENGLAND**

ENGLISH
PEN

LOTTERY FUNDED

Renato Cisneros

THE DISTANCE
BETWEEN US

Translated by
Fionn Petch

CHARCO PRESS

Renato Cisneros with his father
(1980)

Contents

To my brothers and sisters,
who had a father named like mine.

'I am a man of sad words. Why did I feel so guilty? If my father always brought absence, and the river brought perpetuity.'

The Third Bank of the River
João Guimarães Rosa

Chapter 1

I'm not here to tell the story of the woman who had seven children with a priest. All I'll say for now is that her name was Nicolasa Cisneros and she was my great-great-grandmother. The priest she fell in love with, Gregorio Cartagena, was a high-ranking bishop in Huánuco, in the Peruvian Sierra, in the years before and after independence. Over the four decades of their relationship, both did what they could to avoid the repercussions of the scandal. Since Gregorio could not or would not acknowledge his offspring legally, he passed himself off as a distant relative, a friend of the family, so he could stay close to them and watch them grow up. Nicolasa reinforced the lie by filling out the baptism certificates with false information. This is how she came to invent a fictitious spouse, Roberto Benjamín, a ghost who played the role of legal husband and father. The day the children found out that Roberto had never existed and that Father Gregorio was their biological father, they resolved to break with their past, with their bastard origin, and made their second, maternal surname the only one, relegating Benjamín to a middle name.

Nor will I say anything here about the last of those illegitimate children, Luis Benjamín Cisneros, my great-grandfather. Nothing except the fact that his school friends nicknamed him 'The Poet'. And that he was such a single-minded character that at the age of seventeen, he decided he was going to win the love of Carolina Colichón, the mistress of President Ramón Castilla. What's more, he succeeded. By the time he was twenty-one they had three daughters together. The five of them lived hidden away in a squalid room in the middle of Lima, fearing retaliation. Early one morning, at the urging of his mother, who had just discovered the beleaguered life he was leading, Luis Benjamín left Peru and set sail for Paris, where he wrote romantic novels and guilt-ridden letters. Two decades later, he returned to Lima as a diplomat, married a young lady of fourteen, and became a father again, producing five further children. The next-to-last of these, Fernán, was my grandfather.

Fernán became a journalist and at the age of twenty-three was hired as an editor at *La Prensa*. After just two years he became the editor-in-chief, following the imprisonment of the entire editorial board under the dictatorship of Augusto Leguía. He too suffered harassment from the regime and in 1921 was exiled to Panama, although he ultimately took up residence in Buenos Aires. By then, he already had five children with his wife, Hermelinda Diez Canseco, as well as a new-born baby with his mistress, Esperanza Vizquerra, my grandmother. Both women followed him to Argentina, where Fernán managed to support both families, while avoiding any contact between them.

But this novel isn't about him, either. Or perhaps it is, but that's not my intention. This novel is about my father, Lieutenant General Luis Federico Cisneros Vizquerra, 'El Gaucho' Cisneros, third son of Fernán and Esperanza, born in Buenos Aires on 23 January 1926, died of prostate cancer in Lima on 25 July 1995. It's a novel about him or someone very like him, written by me or someone very like me. It's not a biographical novel. Not a historical novel. Not a documentary novel. It's a novel conscious of the fact that reality occurs only once and that any reproduction made of it is condemned to adulteration, to distortion, to simulacrum.

I have tried and failed several times to embark on this novel. Everything I wrote invariably ended up in the bin. I couldn't figure out the right texture for the copious material I'd collected over the years. It's not that I've clarified everything by now, but spitting out these first paragraphs anchors me, gives me purchase, provides an unexpected solidity. The doubts haven't dissolved, but somewhere in the depths I can make out the glimmering granular light of a certainty. All I know for sure is that I'm not going to write a novel about my father's life, but rather about my father's death: about what that death unleashed and revealed.

To do that, I have to go back to April 2006.

To what was going on in my life then.

I'd been avoiding psychoanalysis for months. The end of my relationship with Pierina Arbulú – five years together, two years living together – had devastated me. I was struggling to admit that my depression called for treatment. I'd come and go from the newspaper office where I worked. I'd come and go from my apartment. I'd get up in the mornings, think, sleep. Especially sleep. And I was barely eating.

A friend put me in touch with Elías Colmenares, a psychoanalyst who received patients in a two-storey house on La Fuente Ave., near the corner of 28 de Julio St., in Miraflores. Since I lived just three blocks away, I agreed to try him out for purely geographical reasons. That was my excuse, at least. The day I saw him for the first time, Elías had just turned fifty. He had broad, rosy cheeks. His lively eyes, blue as mouthwash, stood out between his nose and the black line of his eyebrows. We entered a room, he closed the door, we sat down. Despite all his hyperactive tics, Colmenares conveyed an oceanic calm. His speech, varied and comfortable, resembled the room where he saw his patients: a portrait of Lacan, a yellow satin couch, puppets of Freud and Warhol and Dalí suspended from the ceiling, a gladiolus in a pot, a cactus, copies of Picasso prints, a chessboard with two armies of wooden gargoyles lined up facing each other, a glass jar full of lollipops, miniature lamps, tourist guides to Athens, Prague, Rome, novels by Kundera and García Márquez, LPs by Dylan and Van Morrison. Depending on the details that caught a patient's attention, the room could have been the sanctuary of a restless adult or the refuge of an awkward adolescent. In our first two sessions, I was the only one to speak at all. Elías invited me to explain why I'd come, and I felt a moral obligation to summarise my relationship with Pierina. I barely talked about anything else. I didn't mention my family or my tedious job. I briefly mentioned my father's death, but I focused on Pierina: on how she'd entered and exited my life, altering it, splitting it in two, like a bullet piercing a body and destroying its vital organs. From the leather sofa that served as his throne, Colmenares watched me, nodded, cleared his throat, completed the sentences I couldn't finish with teacherly aplomb. It wasn't until the third session that we had something resembling a real conversation. I was in the middle of a monologue about how horribly jealous I'd become in my last months with Pierina, and I was blaming myself for having caused the break-up by harassing her, attempting to trail and control her. I'd stopped acting like a boyfriend and become more like a police officer, I admitted, not looking at Colmenares, my gaze buried in the terracotta-coloured rug that covered the parquet floor. I was getting fed up with my own narrative, leading me as it did to reconstruct the fights that wore away at our relationship, the silences that hurt more than the insults, the insults that hurt more than the slammed doors, the slammed doors that recurred like bells tolling the hour. Suddenly, a silence fell that seemed to last an eternity. Colmenares broke it by

4

changing the subject altogether.

'Tell me something. Your parents – how did they meet?'

'Weren't we talking about something else?' I responded, interlocking my fingers in my lap.

'I think the change might be useful,' Colmenares pressed, crossing one leg over the other.

'Well, I don't know, let me think,' I said. I glanced upward, as if scanning the air for information that I should have been able to find in my memory. 'They met at the Ministry of the Economy when it was still known as the Treasury.'

'Could you be more specific? What were the circumstances? Who introduced them?'

'My mother was a secretary in the office of Minister Morales Bermúdez. My father was the deputy minister or advisor. I suppose it must have been Morales who introduced them. My dad was still married to his first wife at the time.'

'What was her name?'

'She was called Lucila. Lucila Mendiola.'

'Was called? You mean she's dead?'

'Yes, she died a few years ago.'

'Did you know her?'

'Barely. I saw her twice: at the wake for my father's mother, Esperanza, and at my father's wake.'

'Do you remember what she was like?'

'She was a very difficult woman. She came from an influential family from Sullana. That's where she met my father. They say that when he once fell ill with appendicitis, she looked after him with such devotion and he felt so grateful that he married her out of a combination of love and duty. I don't really know. They married and had three children. My three older siblings.'

'Who's the *they* who told you all this?'

'My mother, my aunts and uncles.'

'Go on.'

'The problems began over the years. When my mother appeared in my father's life, his marriage to Lucila was already in pieces. But she refused to sign for divorce, no matter how many times he asked her. My parents married outside of Peru, in the United States, in a registry office in San Francisco.'

'And why wouldn't Lucila have wanted to grant him the divorce?'

'Resentment, spite, pride, something like that, I guess. Seeing her husband in love with another woman, a younger woman, she must have felt, I don't know, humiliated or ridiculed. I'm speculating. What's certain is that she wouldn't give in. For us she became a kind of witch, the villain of the story. Perhaps she believed she could hold on to my father if she didn't sign the papers, but she was wrong. Lucila never forgave him for leaving home, abandoning her, abandoning their children. I think she underestimated his feelings for my mother; maybe she thought it was just another dalliance, the whims of a womanising military man. She didn't imagine he'd dare to leave altogether, much less that he'd remarry and have three more children.'

'If they never divorced, then Lucila was still officially his wife when she died…'

'In the legal sense, yes.'

'So how were your parents able to marry? Why San Francisco?'

'I don't know. All I know is that a relative who was an ambassador helped them sort it out. It was a question of opportunity. It could have been Canada, Panama or anywhere else. In any case, it was a very quick, small ceremony, a formality. No guests.'

'And witnesses?'

'None. I don't know. I'm not sure.'

'Have you ever seen a photo of this wedding?'

'Never.'

'But do you know if there are photos from that day?'

'As far as I know, no. No photos.'

'What about the certificate?'

'The certificate? I have no idea! It never occurred to me to ask my parents for their marriage certificate. Is that something people do?'

'What I mean is, is there any record of this marriage?'

'What else do you want me to say, Elías? I've never seen a photo. It'd never even crossed my mind.'

Elías Colmenares uncrossed his legs and leaned forward to sit on the edge of the sofa.

'There's the link. Don't you see?' he asked.

'What link?'

'Think about it. You're the product of a marriage that emerged amid uncertainty, that was formalised only under great strain, far away, under another country's laws, perhaps even in another language, without witnesses, without announcements, almost in secret. A marriage without evidence. There are no files, no photos, nothing to prove what happened in that registry office. What I'm trying to say is that your parents' marriage has all the appearance of a myth. You're the child of a myth. To some extent, we all are. What you've described surely happened, but there's no proof. As the product of this union, there's a root of uncertainty planted in your unconscious. Isn't that what you said you felt whenever you read Pierina's emails – uncertainty?'

'Let me see if I've got this right. I was jealous because I've never seen a photo of my parents' wedding? Is that what you're trying to say?' I asked.

'No. The point is that there's a connection – a symbolic one, if you like – between what happened to your father

7

and what you feel is happening to you.'

'Why my father and not my mother? She was there too, she took part, she agreed to things.'

'But it was your father, not your mother, who took the decision to build a second marriage on shifting sands. Look, even when a person comes into the world through maternal desire, he structures himself on the basis of identification and transference with the paternal figure. It's the father who determines his identity. Leaving the mother's womb, he's incorporated into culture through the father. It's the father who sets him on his path, who grants him language. The mother generates love, trust, but the father gives him the tools to occupy a place in the world, you see?'

For a moment it annoyed me to hear Colmenares talking about my parents as if he knew them better than I did, but his logic struck me. It jolted me from scepticism into astonishment. It was as if he'd suddenly shed light on information that was lodged within me without my knowing. I couldn't grasp everything that was fragmenting and coalescing in my mind; I only remember feeling exhausted, overwhelmed. I was experiencing something like a mental cramp. His words caused a shock, a tremor in me that – I sensed – would become a breaking point. Once the session was over, back in the street, delaying my return home, I went back over Elías' theory and thought about all the other links that might exist between my father's unexamined life and my own. I felt rising panic. The one thing that calmed me was realising that the oppressive memory of Pierina had abruptly loosened its grip on my throat. The ghost of my former girlfriend hadn't been banished altogether, but it had been displaced by the scale of the new task before me. For that was what I now felt: that I had a task. I didn't know what it involved, but I was ready to find out.

Chapter 2

One day in 1929, during a lunchtime break at San Marón School in Buenos Aires, nine-year-old Juvenal Cisneros beats a fellow pupil in a maths quiz. The other boy accuses him of cheating and gives him a shove. Juvenal pushes back, and soon their fists are swinging – a trifling incident that would soon grow serious. Someone pulls them apart. But as the other boy moves away, bitter with defeat, he yells over his shoulder 'At least I don't share my dad, like you do!' For minutes afterwards, once the youngsters returned to their classrooms and peace has been restored, these words continue to ring in Juvenal's ears. In fact, he'll continue to hear them for the rest of his life. 'At least I don't share my dad, like you do.' The next morning, he gets up and decides to follow his father. Fernán's teaching jobs and his work as a journalist at *La Nación* have secured a more comfortable lifestyle for the family. Gone are the dingy hotels and rented rooms of his early years as an exile: the flat at 400 Suipacha St.; the room with the shared bathroom at 330 Cerrito St.; the tenement at 2200 Paraguay St. Now they live at 865 Esmeralda St., in flat number 20 of an old sand-coloured mansion house with cold tiles and exposed pipes in the entrance hall. Juvenal tells his mother, Esperanza, that he has to be at school early and descends the chipped marble staircase. He passes through the front gate and spots his father on the corner. He follows his route for one, three, six, seven, ten blocks, trying not to lose sight of him. Heading down Córdoba Ave., he crosses Maipú, Florida, and San Martín before turning right on Reconquista. Then he turns again on Corrientes before zig-zagging across Sarmiento, then Rivadavia. He's not sure what he's doing there or what he hopes to find. It feels foolish to be chasing the silhouette of this man who now seems more mysterious than ever. Yet it also feels urgent. Could there be any truth in what the boy yelled at him? Who do I share my dad with? If he had a secret, wouldn't he tell me? Of course he would, Juvenal answers his own question, and he quickens his step to keep sight of that patch of blue advancing unhurriedly down the pavement. Juvenal watches as his father stops before a shop window, perhaps considering a gift for him or his siblings – and he feels like an idiot for doubting him, for being swayed by the blethering of a spiteful kid. But as much as he wants to believe that this pursuit is senseless, a stronger force impels him to keep playing detective. Rounding yet another corner, Juvenal tries to talk himself into abandoning the mission – What am I doing here? What will they say at school? Won't they have called my mother already? – and gradually slows his pace, but without taking his eyes off the target. Just two more blocks, he tells himself, ashamed now, wishing he could run to catch up with his father and embrace him, apologise for questioning the exclusiveness of his love, beg for forgiveness. So he allows Fernán to pull further ahead and starts to feel like the danger has passed. Then, turning the next corner, at the junction of Tacuarí and Moreno, Juvenal sees what he most feared – or what, deep down, he had hoped to discover. He will never be able to erase the scene from his memory. There, on the other side of Belgrano Ave., his father is leaving the pavement and entering a house, holding hands with two children. A boy and a girl, older than Juvenal. The boy must be about 14, the girl 15 or 16. Frozen behind a newsstand, Juvenal watches as these total strangers kiss and hug his dad as blithely and spontaneously as he himself does every night when he gets home to Esmeralda St., and he feels something collapse inside him. The scene is a revelation. Perhaps too much so. The front door closes behind them, and only then does Juvenal notice how much bigger the house is than where he lives, and he is filled with a rage beyond his years – a heat and a pain that immediately turn into tears, no matter how hard he tries to hold them back. 'Hey, kid, you ok?' the newspaper seller asks. But the kid is too distressed to answer, and he sets off at a run, in every direction and none, cursing himself for not having gone straight to school that morning. And as he runs, his face crumpled, tears flowing freely, he wonders who these other children could be. He doesn't know that their names are Mincho and Rosario. He doesn't know there are three more inside: Fernando, Moruno and María Jesús. All are his father's children with Hermelinda Diez Canseco. He doesn't know that he, Juvenal, is actually the first of the seven offspring born to a beautiful but impure relationship. But he does understand something, he makes a connection – and suddenly, as he runs, he thinks of Lima, of the room where he was born, in a yard beside the ghostly Matusita house, at the junction of Sol and España streets, a bedroom where his mother was always alone, and now, on the streets of Buenos Aires, this past solitude suddenly makes all the sense in the world. Juvenal keeps running aimlessly; there's no way he's going to school now, and he wonders how long his father has been going to that big house, the sight of which he wishes he could expel from his mind, but cannot.

Juvenal said nothing about what he had seen until many years later, far into adulthood. He kept it to himself, and only he knew how deeply the discovery had changed him.

When his brother Gustavo, at the age of sixty, discovered

their father's hidden letters and all the echoed truths they contained – the existence of the priest, Cartagena; Luis Benjamín's illegitimacy; Fernán's adultery – he proposed to Juvenal that they write a book together. It made sense: Juvenal was the older brother, the only one who had studied literature, and he had become a much loved and respected intellectual in Peru. If there was anyone in the family who had been called to illuminate these centuries of darkness, it was he. From the outset, though, Juvenal responded to his younger brother's investigations and discoveries with unwavering disinterest. He wanted nothing to do with the past. Undeterred, Gustavo kept insisting that they collaborate on the project, until one day Juvenal cut him off with a curt statement that he wouldn't fully understand for many years: 'To me, our father was nothing more than a man who came home at midnight and left at six in the morning.'

* * *

When my uncle Gustavo first told me the story of the pursuit across Buenos Aires, I was stunned. I couldn't stop thinking about my uncle Juvenal, about his reticence to discuss certain details from his childhood. The image of the boy secretly making his way through the city streets, ultimately glimpsing his own father's hidden life, made me feel both astonished and empty. Thanks to the letters Gustavo later entrusted to me, I was able to reconstruct those years when my grandfather Fernán – out of fear, out of his inability to express himself – perpetuated this gruelling strategy of conjugal survival: he'd spend the night with my grandmother Esperanza; leave the house on Esmeralda St. early in the morning to spend the first part of the day with his wife Hermelinda and his older children, taking advantage of the fact that the younger children were at school; and then he'd go off to work at *La Nación* before returning to his lover and their children late at night. These younger children, these hidden children, grew up with my grandfather's endless stories about Peru. He never stopped reminding them that they were Peruvian, even though they'd been born in Argentina, and he made clear that the family's mission was to return to Lima someday. They understood that their father had been forced out of the country, that they were foreigners, and they grew up waiting for Leguía's dictatorship to fall so they could avenge their exile and see their homeland at last. Meanwhile, they had to talk like Peruvians. Esperanza pulled their ears every time she heard them say *che* or *vos* like their Argentinian schoolmates, and she warned the boys not to fall in love so they wouldn't suffer when it was time to leave. My father, 'El Gaucho', was to disregard this last piece of advice.

From Esmeralda they moved to 3104 Avellaneda St. and two years later to an upper-floor flat at 611 Boyacá St., an apartment with two huge windows.

My grandfather had employed Fernando, the oldest of his 'official' children, as his personal secretary when the Peruvian government assigned him a diplomatic post in Argentina. Every night, Fernando would accompany his father to the corner of Boyacá and Méndez de Andes. He would usually leave him there and continue on home. One night in 1936, he changed his mind.

'Can we go all the way to your doorstep?' Fernando said, not entirely sure of his own next move.

'Sure,' Fernán replied naturally. He didn't sense what was coming.

They walked in silence for a few more steps until they reached the front door of number 611. Fernán moved towards his twenty-nine year old son to kiss him goodnight. Fernando drew back.

'Now can I come up, Dad?' he asked.

His voice tore apart the night.

'What for?' said Fernán, his jaw tense, his eyes incredulous.

'Do you really think I haven't worked it out?'

'What do you want to come up for?' Fernán repeated stubbornly, trying to postpone the moment of truth, his gaze now fixed on the bunch of keys clinking in his clumsy hands.

'I want to meet the rest of my family!' Fernando shouted and pressed the bell.

Esperanza was observing the scene from a window, and when she went down to open the door a minute later she found them in each others' arms, sobbing uncontrollably. My uncle Gustavo recalls what happened next as if it were a movie. Fernando, the older brother, whom the Cisneros Vizquerra children had never seen, climbs the stairs. From the living room he hears the footsteps on the wooden treads. They sound like shots. Esperanza, nervously drying her hands on a tea towel, receives him at the top of the stairs and opens her arms in welcome. Behind her, hidden among her skirts like shy dwarves, are Carlota, Luis Federico – my father – and Gustavo, their eyes as wide as plates. Further back, Juvenal is curled up at one end of a sofa, concealing his curiosity behind a comic book. In another room, Reynaldo is asleep in his cot. They all stare at the apparition with a mix of terror and curiosity. The children have never seen this man before, but they sense that they know him or should know him. Fernando's eyes shine moistly in the dim, almost orange light of the single bulb hanging in the centre of the room. Fernán says something, Esperanza says something in reply. Everything is brief and stiff. Then the visitor moves his lips, addressing his siblings. His words, awkward and imprecise as they are, hit with the force of an earthquake.

A year after this encounter – after Hermelinda Diez Canseco had died and several of her children had moved to Peru – Fernán and Esperanza felt at liberty to marry in Buenos Aires. My aunt Carlota and my uncle Gustavo served as acolytes in the church where the ceremony was held. There is just one photograph of that day in 1937, a photo in which my grandmother Esperanza wears the benevolent smile of someone receiving a much-delayed reward. Flanking them are two couples, their friends and witnesses, the Arriolas and the Pancorvos. Father López, a Franciscan priest who lived in Argentina, completes the group. The exact date is uncertain, but it was summer, that atrocious summer of 1937 when Buenos Aires suffered a plague of locusts that swarmed in from the pampas, where they'd devastated the crops; descending on the city, they darkened the sky and caused panic on the streets. This horde of voracious, battle-hardened insects took over downtown Buenos Aires for days. On the day of the wedding, Fernán had to repeatedly use his cane to shoo away the locusts that were blinding him.

The years following their marriage were perhaps the most memorable of their exile. With nothing left to hide, Fernán dedicated himself to his children. He educated them, took them to school, led them on walks through the city and the countryside. The children would always picture their father as the man who took them shopping, rode trams, drafted documents for the Chaco Peace Conference, shaved in front of the mirror wearing his long-johns, and always carried around the youngest, Adrián, when he was an infant. Fernán recited French and Spanish poets to them, taught them to comb their hair in a side parting, and composed improving verses that he'd frame and hang on the bathroom door – ditties that my father and his siblings would recite from memory whenever they met for lunch, years later, in a display of gratitude for a period filled with discovery and upheaval.

If the fair Cisneros lass
and the fine Cisneros lads
don't give their hides a scrub
every morning when they wake,
she'll never be a lady,
and gents they'll never make.

Around this time, Fernán purchased a shortwave radio so he could listen to Peruvian National Radio broadcasts and follow the ins-and-outs of the General Benavides government. The apparatus became a kind of family pet. Everyone took care of it, taking turns to manipulate its various buttons and dials, and making sure nothing scratched or damaged it. The Cisneros Vizquerra children spent hours huddled around that radio, as if it were an oracle or a bonfire. The news would transport them to distant countries they'd quickly locate on the globe that spun on a metal axis at the corner of their father's desk. This device also brought them news from the Spanish Civil War, which they followed attentively, though they were predisposed by the political views of Fernán. He distrusted the communists and admired Francisco Franco and Colonel José Moscardó, who had preferred to sacrifice his own son over surrendering the Alcázar de Toledo – a story my father would tell me with tears in his eyes fifty years later, at the dining table of our home in Monterrico, and which so moved me that I felt a sudden respect for Colonel Moscardó and pity for his son, Luis, who at the other end of the telephone tells his father not to worry about him, that he knows he's going to be shot, but the Alcázar won't surrender, and so the colonel asks him to commend his soul to God, to cheer for Spain, and promises him he'll be a national hero as he bids him farewell, saying goodbye, my son, I embrace you.

* * *

My grandfather Fernán returns to Peru on 12 August 1951, during the administration of General Odría, thirty years after having been forced to board a ship bound for Panama. He returns in his sixtieth year, thirty of them spent in exile. He returns as a diplomat, but he still identifies as a journalist and poet. He lives with the Cisneros Vizquerra children in a house in the Pardo district. From there, he heads into central Lima every day, walking down the street now known as Jirón de la Unión, along the stretch previously known as Baquíjano that was home to the offices of *La Prensa*, traversing the streets where a retail store now stands in the place of the former Palais Concert, and crossing at the corner of Mercaderes and Plateros, opposite Casa Welsch, the building where my grandmother Esperanza had worked as a young lady.

Fernán subsequently moves his whole family to a house on La Paz St., near the Quebrada de Armendáriz avenue that cuts down to the sea, where decades later I would live with my parents and siblings. There, Fernán resumes writing lectures and essays that would never be published. In early 1953, returning from one of his walks, he feels tired and dizzy – symptoms of pulmonary emphysema, which will render him bedridden and dependent on an oxygen cylinder the shape and hue of a naval artillery shell. His son, my father, sees him arrive home that first afternoon and senses something worrisome in his face, an expression of fear or bewilderment. It's the same expression I'll see in his own face much later, in 1995, after his first heart attack.

On 17 March 1954, Fernán answers a call from Pedro Beltrán, editor of *La Prensa*, who invites him to his house opposite the San Marcelo church. In his haste, my grandfather leaves an article unfinished on his desk – only the title is legible: 'This Time, the Real Crisis' – and asks his son Mincho to accompany him. Beltrán welcomes them in and offers them cognac; over the course of the conversation, he formally invites Fernán to return to writing a column for the newspaper. Fernán is overjoyed. Little does he know that within a few minutes this joy will kill him.

There he is, trading ideas on possible names for the new column (*Disappearing Lima, Eminent Peruvians, Luminaries of Lima, Landscapes*) and discussing the frequency and length of the articles with Don Pedro – when he suddenly struggles to breathe and feels a stabbing pain. It's his heart, which has begun to burst. Beltrán lays him on the floor. Seeing that his left arm is stiff, he runs to call a doctor who lives nearby, who arrives only to confirm the severity of the heart attack. At his side, Mincho sees his father's leg shudder in a spasm, and all he can do is cross himself.

Beside me is a folder containing the front pages from the following day, Thursday, 18 March 1954. 'Cisneros died yesterday. His life was a paragon of civic values,' *La Prensa*. 'Fernán Cisneros is dead,' *El Comercio*. 'The poet of noble causes has died,' *Última Hora*. 'Fernán Cisneros passed away yesterday,' *La Nación*. 'Deep sadness at the death of Cisneros,' *La Crónica*. The headlines continue in further cuttings: 'Journalism is in mourning across the nation.' 'Just as he returned to writing, Cisneros left us.' 'Sudden demise of the former editor of *La Prensa*.' 'A life dedicated to Peru.' There are cables from newspapers in Uruguay, Mexico and Argentina announcing his death, as well as a series of reports from the wake, held in the editorial offices of *La Prensa*, and about the burial in the Presbítero Maestro cemetery.

I also have photographs of the ceremonies held on the centenary of his birth, in November 1982, at the Academia Diplomática and in the Miraflores park that bears his name: Parque Fernán Cisneros. I appear in some of these photos, aged seven, alongside my father, siblings, cousins. I still remember that sunny day in the park and the unveiling of the commemorative plaque and bust, which describes Fernán as a 'poet, journalist and diplomat'. Further down, the plaque quotes the verse that we would repeat at countless breakfasts and lunches: 'Birth, life, death – these are not the worst. True tragedy is to live without smiling. Everything grows beautiful with love. Birth, life, death.' A sweet, sad verse that cloaks more truthful would-be epitaphs: the worst is not to die, but not to know; tragedy is not failing to smile, but remaining silent.

It is precisely because of the things that Fernán failed to do or say – far more than those he did and said – that I acknowledge myself as his grandson, and as the son of that other silent man, the Gaucho, who admired and loved his father in the same way that I loved mine, with the same love shot through with mystery and distance that is the only way to love a man of over fifty who indolently brings you into the world, uninterested in really accompanying you, and then imposes himself as the guiding force of your universe, the architect of everything you touch, everything you say, everything you see – though not everything you feel. And it's precisely because I can feel something that he was unable to show me that I can tolerate the thousands of questions spawning in the space beyond the limits of the world he designed for me. Questions that arise in the darkness he never knew how to explore, perhaps because he'd inherited the very same from his own father too: discipline and distance; protocol and absence; awareness of duty, of force of will, of conduct. A responsible vision of the future, and beneath all of this a failed or clumsy love forged of letters and dedications, of verses and songs, of pompous and rhetorical words – but empty of affection, of closeness, of any warmth that might leave a visible trail a century later.

Chapter 3

Mexico City, 14 July 1940

M*y darling Esperanza,*

I'll begin by asking once again for a letter from our little Gaucho, in case that helps persuade him. And tell him I don't want any old letter, but an account of everything he thinks, wants, and does. I think it's time for a father to understand his son's mind.

As a result of the nervous condition he suffered in his early years, our dear son has an understandable and painful inferiority complex that must be eradicated from his spirit. My impression is that he has often held clear intentions to return to formal study, but he is troubled and embarrassed by the belief that he has no knack for it. It's a common situation. He is proud, so he doesn't admit it, and since he won't admit it, his spiritual confusion discourages him. He doesn't study because he doesn't like it, and he doesn't like it because he doesn't think he's up to it. So he doesn't attend school and deceives us all. Now, skipping school might be innocent enough today, but tomorrow it could lead him down the road to ruin. Therefore, I believe that you should return him to a boarding school, on my orders – but darling, allow him to choose which one. Or at least let him believe that he is choosing it. Talk up the virtues of the military college, for example. Don't let him suspect that it is about punishing him or putting him on the right path. That way, he can enter the school with his head held high. Of course, this is my preferred choice of college because it will teach him love for discipline, for structure and for work. But may God guide your decision, my dear, and may it be your heart and not your sternness that seeks this end. If the autumn of my days is to be a happy time, we must all make an effort to save this child, while remembering that his difficulties are simply a matter of timidity and confusion. You probably think that his violent reactions are far from timid. But they are, my dear. By virtue of his timidity, he says nothing, and so he explodes, without knowing why. Write to me, my dear, and don't fall silent, for life far from you is painful. Kiss my children and keep hold of my heart.

When I uncovered this letter my grandfather Fernán sent to my grandmother Esperanza about my father, he, my father, the Gaucho, had already been in his grave fourteen years. But in 1940 he was fourteen years of age and displayed personality traits that would never have fitted the man I knew.

It was a great surprise for me to learn, for example, that as a child my father had suffered from a nervous illness. My siblings and my mother knew nothing about it either. Curiously enough, my teenage years were marked by nervous attacks, allergies and acute asthma attacks that ended in exhausting nebulisation sessions in a cold room at the military hospital. No one knew where I could have inherited such weaknesses. The family history was there, but nobody was able to establish the link.

My grandfather believed that this illness left my father feeling insecure. Reading this was like discovering a new continent. From my point of view, my father was the most impenetrable person on the planet. A wall. A fortress. A bunker. His whole life expressed certainty: his words, his actions, his morals, his identity, his decisions. Everything about him expressed his certainty of never being wrong. Fear and doubt were faint shadows that flitted by in the distance.

Nevertheless, in the X-ray analysis of the Gaucho that Fernán conducted over the course of this letter, he is a confused, timid and violent child with an inferiority complex. The extraordinary thing about this description is that it matches that of the fourteen-year-old boy I was or believed myself to be: the boy who feared family mealtimes, who felt abandoned and powerless due to his inability to communicate with his father.

In the text, my grandfather refers to the need for everyone to join forces to 'save that child' that my father was. I wonder if my father ever read this letter. But more importantly, I wonder if he ever felt entirely safe from the childhood torments, so similar to mine, that we never managed to talk about.

Another letter from my grandfather, addressed to my father in the same year, reveals the conflicted sense of love that underlay their relationship, and the affectionate but subtly manipulative tone Fernán employed to try and win over his son:

You must tell me everything you want, everything you feel, everything you think with the frankness of good men and with the hope that your father will come up with what you need: help, encouragement, remedy or reward. I carry you in my heart like a sweet burden, my son, and I want this burden to become joy as soon as it can. I kiss you dearly.

A sweet burden. This is what my father was to his father. Was I too a sweet burden for him? If this was the case, he never said so. Or did he, and I failed to pay attention? Why have I lost the letters my father wrote to me? How could they possibly have got lost? I remember two in which he addressed me with a tenderness and emotion so out of character that I had to check several times if it was really he who had signed them, if the signature was authentic. I think about these letters – his neat handwriting, the texture on the reverse of the page from the pressure of the pen – and I realise that this was the only way my father was able to communicate with me.

There are people who can only express their feelings in writing. My father was one such person: for him, written words were the site of emotion, the region where the feelings denied in everyday life emerged and took shape. In these letters he could be himself, or at least that was how I saw it. He wrote what he didn't say, what he couldn't say to me in front of the others, in the dining room or the living room. In the privacy of these letters he was my friend; in public, less so. Almost like an imaginary friend who appeared from time to time, not in the real world, but in the world of writing. Outside of it, he imposed his firm will and his icy authoritarianism. I'm not even sure whether he was aware of who he was in his letters, but what I do know is that I came to love the man who wrote them far more than the man he was outside of them. In these letters – even if they only amounted to two or three – he stopped being the Gaucho Cisneros and again became the lad whose cracks and deficiencies so worried my grandfather. Outside of his letters, his love was silent and therefore confused, painful; a repetition of the love his father deposited in him, an arid love in which it was necessary to dig deep to find the diamond of those few words that could be studied on the surface.

Nor did I know that my father had been sent to a military boarding school. What I had always understood to

24

be his natural vocation turned out to have been imposed. He was forced into it. He wasn't allowed to choose because he was an errant child – when he was little, my grandmother tied him to a leg of the bed if she had to leave the house alone – and because he skipped school. Instead of attending classes in the British school where he was enrolled, he would head for the Buenos Aires docks to watch the ships and steamboats loading and unloading.

Indeed, it was a prank he played at the age of eleven that earned him the nickname he bore until the end of his days. One morning he assembled his siblings and friends in the large courtyard of the house at 3104 Avellaneda Street. At the time he was a devoted magic fan, and dreamed of becoming a magician.

'Silence!' he commanded the tame group of kids, spreading an aura of false mystery around him. 'You have been called here to witness the final and most astonishing trick of Mandrake the Magician.' 'What's the trick called?' asked a shrill, dubious voice. 'The dead hand!' my father replied, and with his left hand he pulled out a sharp kitchen knife with a wooden handle that he had concealed in his belt, and slowly moved it closer to the palm of his right hand. He held it there for a few seconds, creating tension among his audience with their shorts, socks around their ankles, and dirty shoes, before emitting a theatrical howl and slashing up and down at his hand, to the horror of the children, who began to scream at the sight of the blood flowing ornamentally from the hand – which remained where it was, evidently neither false nor a prop, but all too real. My father, his eyes wide, the bloodied knife still held firm, smiled with pain. My grandmother Esperanza rushed out from the house like someone possessed. When she saw the damage he'd done, she dragged him by his hair to the nearest emergency clinic so they could patch him up.

The doctor was struck by the behaviour of my father, who kept that morbid smile on his face and didn't wince as he received, without anaesthetic, the fifteen stitches needed to sew up the wound in his hand, leaving the long scar I always confused with a lifeline.

'Madame, your son is a real *gaucho*,' pronounced the doctor upon completing his work, unaware that he was not only imposing an unforgettable sobriquet on the boy, but also naming a character trait that was starting to emerge. The *gaucho* – the cowboy forged on the southern pampas in the 19th century – meant the robust man who tolerated the cold of Patagonia, the horseman who grew in strength in the solitude of the barren plains, the nomad who took refuge on remote ranches and was used to living in the border lands. In that last sense, my father was indisputably a *gaucho*. He always got used to borders. He got used to his father's exile, which forced the family to move on multiple occasions, and also to his own, when he had to leave Argentina and start over in a country he didn't know but had been assured was his. And, of course, he got used to the inflexible environment of the military college, where he learned rigor and slowly accustomed himself to being something that others had chosen for him.

I think that perhaps, if it had depended on him alone, he would have decided to be something else. Something more artistic – why not? Perhaps a magician, like Mandrake. Or perhaps a dancer. Didn't Aunt Carlota, his older sister, say that my father accompanied her to ballet classes? First to protect her from a suitor who would harass her as she left the school; later, to seduce Mirtha, the daughter of actress Libertad Lamarque; and finally, behind his father's back, to dance, having become fascinated with those elastic, tip-toe steps, those tight Axel turns, the bodily harmony that demands such concentration and power in the legs.

Was he not after all an amateur tango dancer, one capable of the most complex choreography I ever saw: dancing with Carlota, foreheads pressed together, hands on each others' backs, switching their legs back and forth like swords in a forest? Perhaps he doubted or repressed his own abilities, not wanting to risk giving them full rein. Or perhaps someone persuaded him it was too feminine, and he ended up a soldier out of sheer stubbornness, so that no one could look down at him, obstinately proving to anyone who doubted his skills that he was perfectly capable of mastering even things that didn't interest him in the least. If his parents believed that his lack of discipline had no remedy and that he would refuse to enter the military college, then he would show them just how wrong they were. When in April 1941 his father learned that he had enrolled, he wrote from Mexico: 'However happy you may feel, your absent father is even happier.'

My father did not choose to become a soldier, but once he joined the Army he found the lifestyle to be compatible with something he'd always sought from the domestic sphere during the exile of my grandfather Fernán: order. An order that would quell the chaos. An order that would restore authority. He embraced the Army with an unfaltering dedication because he needed something to order his head and his life. Nevertheless, in the barracks he found a way not to entirely abandon the artist he carried within, to open up a tiny source of sustenance: joining the cavalry. It made sense. After all, the horse demands of its rider the same as ballet does of dancers: correct posture, strong calves, balance, a sense of space and serenity. A serene dancer never loses the rhythm. A serene horseman controls not just the steed he mounts, but also the wild animal he carries inside. And that's what my father was: a wild animal. His character drove him to escape, flee and disappear into the plains, like

27

a dispossessed *gaucho* who rides off until he is no more than a trembling point of light in the distance.

★ ★ ★

After his third year at the National Military College, in September 1942 he received another letter from his father in Mexico, the final one I uncovered in my Uncle Gustavo's files.

Serene and strong, you have embarked on a course determined by fate, and I will always follow your steps closely in my heart, as I accompany you now from afar with a deep emotion that is both born of my affection for you and mindful of my responsibility. I am certain that we will continue loving and understanding each other in life not only as father and son, but also as best friends, with a shared interest in maintaining the tradition of integrity, seriousness and patriotism that marks our family name.

The father declares to his son his responsible affection and promises his friendship. But it's a friendship based on our most well-tested family tradition: that is to say, a rhetorical friendship defined by geographical distance. The letter confirms as much with the expression: 'You have embarked on a course determined by fate.'

In 1943, only four years remained before my father left Argentina to pursue this course. Ever since they were little, he and his siblings had all adopted a mandate: to return to the country where their parents were born and from which their father had been exiled. And that was the word they used: to return, even though they were talking about returning to a country they had never visited. How do you return to a place you have never been? They never felt the weight of this contradiction because they accepted that they lived in a kind of imaginary Peru, a bubble made of the countless references provided by their parents; of their grandfather Luis Benjamín's lines of poetry; of the pages of the history books that reached their hands; of the postcards sent from Lima by relatives they had never met; of the voices of cousins, uncles and aunts who visited Buenos Aires and told them about everything they'd see in Peru.

Soon these mental pictures of the country would come to an end: in 1947, one by one, the Cisneros Vizquerra siblings returned to Peru. Once they had settled in Lima, while maintaining the family fraternity and solidarity, they began to dedicate themselves to their own very different fields: Juvenal studied Medicine and Linguistics; Carlota, Psychology; my father continued his career in the Army; Gustavo became an industrial engineer; Adrián a civil engineer and Reynaldo – oh Reynaldo! – uncle Reynaldo, the wildcard uncle, the one who studied Tourism, who became the king of public relations, a frustrated designer, and ended up a *bon vivant* always ready to live large, even if he didn't have a penny in his pocket. Everything they'd seemed to share during their childhood in Argentina changed during their adulthood in Peru. While they lived in Buenos Aires, they were bound together by the future. Peru was a shared goal. Once they had reached it, their greatest similarity would be their past.

* * *

The Gaucho was twenty-one when he had to leave Argentina. How hard it was to put Buenos Aires behind him. Not only because he was leaving behind his childhood friends – Pepe Breide, Tito Arenas, 'El Chino' Falsía – or because he was interrupting his Army training, but because it meant he would be dangerously far from Beatriz. Beatriz Abdulá.

This is a name that I heard around the house since I was very young. An almost mythical name, even though it only belonged to – my father claimed – 'a lass I knew in Argentina', an account my uncles and aunts echoed in chorus when I asked them, overcome with curiosity at the idea of my father in love for the first time. Even my mother spoke of Beatriz without jealousy, almost fondly. But no one offered many details. Instead of placating my desire to know, this laconic response made it more acute. What was this Beatriz like? What kind of relationship did they have? Why did it end? Who broke up with who? The Gaucho said she was just a lass he'd known, but the emptiness in his eyes when he spoke contradicted his words. I didn't trust his story, like with everything he said about the feelings that marked his childhood and adolescence. He was always editing events, cutting and pasting them so that his children wouldn't see what he concealed behind the montage. He didn't like losing, either in life or in the account he presented of his life, and so during his lifetime Beatriz Abdulá was just that: a childhood crush, a girlfriend of no real importance, a scant memory that it wasn't worth turning over or digging into.

A year ago I went to the Peruvian Army's Permanent General Archive, located in a pavilion of the general headquarters known as the 'Pentagonito' (or Little Pentagon) of San Borja. There I was received by a tall, brown-skinned, heavily mousta-chioed colonel who pulverised the bones in my hand with his greeting, asked me a series of irrelevant questions and told me just how much he admired the wonderful, exemplary man General Cisneros Vizquerra had been. He then allowed me to examine my father's personal file. Sitting behind his desk in his office with its tinted windows, he warned me that I must maintain total secrecy with regard to the confidential material I was about to see.

'This is the intellectual property of the Armed Forces. If anyone finds out you've been here, I'm the one with his neck on the line.'

'Don't worry, colonel. I won't say a word,' and I pulled an imaginary zip closed over my lips.

'That's what journalists always say, and then they screw us.' Now the colonel was laughing.

'Take it easy, I'm not here as a journalist.'

'Hmm.'

'I'm very grateful for the opportunity.'

'One more thing, Cisneros. Since your father was a Minister of State and Chief of Staff of the Joint Command, his file is kept on a special shelf and it's not supposed to be moved without orders from higher up. I'm turning a blind eye to this, you understand?'

'I understand. I just want to see the papers, perhaps make a few copies.'

'Copies? Impossible! They told me you just wanted to take a look.'

'Alright, alright, forget it. I'll just read the file, that's all.'

'Don't try and pull the wool over my eyes, Cisneros,' he warned. His nose flared and the tips of his moustache stood erect for a moment.

In the adjacent room, on a small table set up for the purpose, a thick file was waiting for me containing a series of classified documents relating to my father's career. Standing beside the table, a deputy intelligence official, Paulo Pazos, was waiting to greet me. He had been given the task of keeping an eye on me to make sure I complied with the colonel's instructions and I didn't exceed the permitted time. 'You have two hours,' Pazos informed me. Shit, I thought, two hours to go through the documents that summarise the thirty-two years, four months and twenty-four days my old man was part of the Army.

The room was humid and cold, like a kitchen in the early morning. There was no one but the deputy official and me. To my good fortune, he was sensitive to the needs of journalism – as a kid he'd wanted to be a reporter, but his family didn't have the money to send him to university or the journalism college – so when I told him I could get hold of a press pass from the newspaper I worked for that would help him pursue his undercover intelligence missions, he whispered: 'You can't use the photocopier but you can take photos of the papers with your mobile. I saw nothing.'

I set about leafing through and taking pictures of the hitherto unseen documents for many long minutes. There, for example, were my father's report cards from Argentina, both the San Martín military high school and the National Military College, where he studied between 1942 and 1947. He got top marks in Maths and Spanish, average in History, poor in Geography, and a fail in Languages. I was surprised to see he scored highly in Music, Drawing and Singing. I can't recall ever having seen him draw anything. Nor hear a complete song emerge from his mouth. He would mumble boleros, tangos, ranchera songs, a few waltzes, but didn't sing them, or only sang them when accompanied by his brothers or old Army friends. He did like whistling. He was always whistling. In the house, the car, the office, walking along the pavement. I remember how the sound of his whistle traversed the windows like a flying insect, penetrating our bedrooms on weekend mornings. We could tell from his whistle if he was in a good or bad mood. My mother and he had a special tune they would whistle to call and acknowledge each other, borrowed from *The Song of Forgetting*, one of my grandfather's favourite operettas.

His average score in exams was 6.35 out of 10. A normal score, slightly above the median. In all his school workbooks, however, there were exercises marked as fails. Two or three in each, the score written in red. I wished I could have had these reports in hand years later to compare them with mine, to gather strength in the face of the punishments he imposed on me, demanding the outstanding performance he'd never delivered himself. When I would bring home a marked exam for him to sign, he would immediately clench his fist and box me round the ears the same number of times as the number of points by which I'd fallen short of the maximum, 20. Regardless of the subject. If I got a 13 in Chemistry or in English, he'd thwack me on the head seven times with his knuckles. If I got 15 in Literature or in Sciences, that was five thumps. If I'd failed an exam in History or Civics, as well as the beating, I was grounded for a month. And as if that wasn't enough, he'd dole out tasks to complete at home, from washing the cars to polishing his twenty pairs of shoes.

Thinking about how he might react caused me such anguish that I once stole the exam paper of a kid in my class who had got 20 in chemistry. I'd failed it, with a score of 7. When I was handed my paper, I started to shake. I didn't think twice: the bell rang for break, I waited until the classroom had emptied, pretending to make a start on an exercise. I made sure I was alone and then crept over to Gustavo Verástegui's schoolbag to take the exam paper from his folder. He was the best student, a real swot, plus our handwriting was similar, or at least I copied his, I don't remember. Verástegui always got 20. He must be fed up of getting 20s, I thought. I tried to make something noble of the crime; I wanted to believe that this 20 would do more for me than for him. That afternoon, at home, I carefully erased Gustavo's name, put mine in its place, and ran to my dad to wave the paper in his face. Without even looking at the score, he received me with a rap on my forehead. 'But why did you hit me if I got a 20?' I complained. 'My children don't get 20, they get 21,' he growled, grim-faced.

Nor did my father make concessions when he disciplined us. Between the ages of ten and fourteen, he would punish me by giving me lines to copy. I remember two in particular: 'I must not answer back to my mother' and 'I must not fight with my brother and sister'. Each phrase three hundred times on lined sheets of paper. I could only go out to play with my friends if I completed this forced labour, the purpose of which, according to him, was to make sure I thought twice next time I was tempted to engage in these domestic misdemeanours. But instead of reforming, I was left with a desire to get my own back, to relapse just to see him get angry again. As soon as my father would issue the punishment, I'd shut myself up furiously in my room to write the line over and over, like Jack Torrance in *The Shining*. I almost always completed the task but on a few occasions I left it half-done, whether because my hand went numb or because my self-esteem rebelled. On these occasions I went to seek out my father to humble myself and ask for a pardon, but I never succeeded in moving him. 'If you want to go out, it's up to you,' he would say, deceptively, without looking up from the newspaper he was reading, and I'd shut myself up again, my eyes red with impotence, resigned to continue covering the paper with my handwriting, filling pages and pages with promises I would inevitably break. That may have been when I felt the first stirrings of a conviction that has stuck with me ever since, and which I indirectly owe to him: that my freedom depends on writing. The more I write, the closer to freedom I will be.

I was never able to confront my father. I didn't have the balls. His shouting, his stare (Christ, his stare!) immediately left me undone. I can only recall one occasion that I was stubborn enough to answer back to him. It happened in the house on La Paz St. in Miraflores. I can't have been more than eight years old at the time. I'd said something he didn't like and he started after me to give me a walloping. He chased me through my room, the living room, the dining room. With nowhere left to run, I dodged into the kitchen and saw the best place to hide was the larder, but I failed to notice that the latch was missing. From inside, sweating, I grabbed the door handle with both hands. He did the same from outside and we started to wrestle with the door. I pulled with every muscle in my body. I pulled to save myself. But he was pulling too. I began to sob, knowing that there was no way out, that there was no way to beat him. If I strain my memory, I can still feel my screaming forearms, my burning wrists, my shoes scrabbling on the floor tiles. Then my father said something that's still engraved on my subconscious. A phrase both approving and wounding. Or just wounding. 'The little cockroach has muscles.' That's what he said. And it broke me.

The ironic or unfair thing was that he punished my misdemeanours without looking in the shattered mirror of his own unruly youth. He not only bunked off school to watch the boats come and go in the port of Buenos Aires, but skipped classes to watch the daughter of Libertad Lamarque dance in the theatre, until my grandmother Esperanza was obliged to go and drag him back to college. He was rebellious and even seditious. On the morning I spent looking through his file in the Little Pentagon, I came across a memo from 1946 addressed to my grandmother by the head of Argentina's National Military College:

I write to inform you that according to Directive No. 229 of the eighteenth day of October this year, this office has imposed on your son, cadet LUIS FEDERICO CISNEROS, a disciplinary sanction of 45 days of suspension of duties for:

holding a meeting to propose disobeying the orders of a senior cadet because these were believed to be arbitrary, without – as he should and could have done – seeking recourse to regulatory procedures; and deciding at this meeting to collectively disobey and subsequently fail to comply with these orders, with the mitigation that the order involved a non-regulatory punishment.

Yours sincerely,

Juan Carlos Ruda

Director

This was not to be the last time – by any means – that my father would rise up to conspire against a superior because he objected to the course of action being taken. He would do so repeatedly throughout his career, and even after it was officially over. He spent many nights of his retirement from the military in his study with generals who were as retired as he was, or more so, with their furrowed faces and some disease or other eating away at them, seriously conspiring against the governments of Alan García or Alberto Fujimori. Entire nights spent in that room, which ended up stinking of tobacco and strong liquor, distilling the dream of overthrowing the president of the day, taking the Palace of Government and setting the country on the right course: one final but necessary phase of the already extinct military revolution. Long nights in which they shuffled tentative cabinets, dealt out the ministries among themselves, filled out dozens of A4 pages with a master plan for government. For my father, nothing was more thrilling.

He had no qualms about mutinying before a superior or upsetting hierarchies whenever his ideas so demanded, and maintained the dark conviction that he was destined to be the leader of a political cycle in history, the all-powerful military man, the omnipotent caudillo, the uniformed head honcho of the republic, able to impose order where it was lacking and of sending the regime's traitors and the disloyal to prison, silencing them, or exiling them.

This deep-rooted theory of justice, however, clashed with his domestic tyranny. He was capable of defending his ideas before any audience, but he wouldn't allow me to express mine, or to argue with his categorical decisions. He disregarded my reasoning and continually forced me to acknowledge him as the highest authority, developing a sophisticated series of exemplary punishments. The thing that most confused or angered or depressed me was seeing and feeling how his implacable severity was directed solely at me, and not at my siblings. Valentina, his favourite, was never rebuked with the heavy-handedness, coercion and psychological manoeuvring that sometimes bordered on aggression; and Facundo, the youngest, born when my father was already 56 years old, was treated in the amiable and benevolent manner of a grandson. Nor did my older siblings from his first marriage – Melania, Estrella and Fermín – have to brave the snare of his authority when they were younger. Though their situation had been different. The father they had was a thirty-something Army captain who was progressively promoted to major, lieutenant colonel and then colonel. A man who armed himself with ideas, knowledge and self-composure in order to shake off his core insecurities. That man was a soldier whose uniform acquired new badges year after year; a good military cadre who hadn't yet come to know his limitations and who lived on a salary that could best be described as lean. A Gaucho who was not like the Gaucho I had for a father: a man in his fifties, set in his ways, hard, impenetrable. An unvarnished man who was not only at the peak of his career, but firmly believed he was better prepared to lead than any other and represented a particular type of power in a country that, in his view, needed people like him. It's not the same to be raised by a lieutenant colonel as by a lieutenant general. It's not the same to have as a father a middle-ranking official with justified professional aspirations, as a Minister of State with clear political ambitions. The father of my older siblings was not my father. He just shared the same name. But even if the young Lieutenant Colonel Cisneros Vizquerra had been just as severe and dominating with Melania, Estrella and Fermín as he was with me, he wouldn't have won the respect of his first children. And if he had done, he ended up losing it altogether the day he left the house he shared with them and Lucila Mendiola: chalet 69 in Villa de Chorrillos. They were aged 17, 16 and 13 at the time. At that age – at any age – how can you respect a father who goes off with another woman with whom he will later, not much later, build another family? How can you respect this other family that has been imposed on you? How were my older siblings supposed to understand this behaviour as anything other than a moral shadow-play that would soon be undone by the events that followed?

Perhaps, I think now, my father's obsession with moulding my character – by shouting so loud that my mother sometimes felt obliged to snap back at him things like 'We're not in your barracks here' or 'My son is not your whipping boy' – perhaps this obsession arose from a need to test himself and to show others that he could set boundaries for at least one of his six children, and could inspire respect in one of the younger ones, having failed with the older set. I was the male child who held the winning ticket in this dubious lottery. And though my father did win my respect – or fear – in the long run, his need to dominate me left a deep fissure in our relationship.

My reaction to this was hardly intelligent either: I

withdrew into myself, refused to communicate and blamed my sense of insignificance on the rest of my family. As for my father, my foolish way of punishing him was to filch his military campaign caps: I would wear them back-to-front, put on my oldest, baggiest and most frayed jeans, which he hated, and head out like that, transformed into a scruffy soldier. This was a time when I was writing my father letters filled with furious questions that would lie unanswered in a drawer, letters I rediscovered during the first house move after his death, and which I tore to pieces in tears, crushed by a terrible urge to stuff them down my throat and choke myself on them.

* * *

When he was a cadet, my father suffered a horse-riding accident. It happened on a training ground, near the city of El Palomar, where Argentina's National Military College stands to this day. After forcing a manoeuver, he slipped from the saddle. As he fell, one of his boots became trapped in the stirrup. The horse took fright at the jolt, reared up and set off at a canter, whinnying, dragging my father along a rocky path for several minutes, causing him injuries that would afflict him for the rest of his life.

He spent just over a month in the college infirmary with a fractured hip and all his teeth broken. As I write this I can't stop thinking about the incessant aches in his waist that would draw muffled groans of pain, or about his false teeth at the bottom of a glass of water in the bathroom. When he stretched his lips to smile, he didn't reveal his teeth, just a thin white line. The only way to see the shape, size and colour of his teeth was when the prosthesis was floating in the glass at night. From within this glass receptacle, my father always grinned.

As a consequence of the dramatic fall, it became very difficult for him to qualify as a horse-riding instructor. In a dispatch of July 1947, the head of the Cavalry School at the National Military College states: 'Due to a riding accident that kept him away from instruction for most of the year, the progress in this activity by Cadet Cisneros has been practically nil. As a result, his performance as an instructor is barely satisfactory.' And an academic report from 1953, when he was already a lieutenant, contains the following observation: 'He needs to dedicate more time to sports, above all horse-riding, for he is a hopeless rider.'

To be labelled mediocre must have triggered a wave of frustration together with an obsessive desire to come back stronger. That's what setbacks did to my father. He fed on them, redoubling his energy. Instead of knocking him down, they motivated him to carry on, to persist in his objective with unwavering determination. It was not something he'd been born with: he had learned to be that way, to transform the enemy projectile into a boomerang, to return the sword swipes of his opponent with a single thrust. That was his thing: the most refined fencing match, the cerebral counterattack.

Thanks to the horses, he acquired the brutal elegance that allowed him to always come out on top, and his air of constant silent reflection. 'We cavalrymen are accustomed to battling the monotony of long rides, and since we have adventure in our blood our thoughts are constantly roaming far afield. For each sorrow there is a residue of joy in us; for each grudge, cordiality; for each betrayal, affection. The horse prevents you being confused with the foolish mass of people around you.' That's how my father talked about riding. He wrote it in a magazine article. Despite adoring horses, and owning two foals in a sunny paddock somewhere whose names were Valour and Tetchy, which I

40

only remember seeing in photographs, he never took an interest in teaching his children to ride regularly. Only my sister Valentina, behind his back and with my mother's complicity, became a serious rider, reaching a level at which she could enter competitions with jumps of up to a metre in height. When my father found out, he was furious. Perhaps he didn't want to be reminded that he'd done the same thing to his father when he was a boy: deceiving him to take ballet classes with the connivance of his mother. In the end he resigned himself to the idea that Valentina was a kind of Amazon, and even accompanied and encouraged her in tournaments at the Military Riding Club or the Huachipa Club. Once he himself approached the winners' podium to present her with the first prize pennant in a newcomers' contest. That day, without knowing it, the two, or rather, the three of them – my father, Valentina and the sorrel horse she rode – avenged that toothless horseman who would wander the house at night with his shattered hip, bow-legged, the startled whinnies ringing in his ears.

* * *

Yet that morning in the Little Pentagon it wasn't my father's report cards or the remarks from his military superiors that most disconcerted me, but a letter he wrote on 30 October 1947, a month and a half after his arrival in Peru. When I finished reading I had to sit back in the chair in order to breathe easily again. It was a letter with an Army insignia at the top left corner, yellow around the edges from damp, typewritten and addressed to Brigadier General José del Carmen Marín, Minister of War at the time, requesting permission to travel to Buenos Aires to marry Beatriz Abdulá.

'What's wrong?' deputy official Pazos asked me, seeing

my white face and my tense neck, my eyes moving from the letter to the ceiling and back again to reread the lines that triggered a mental image of my father over sixty years earlier, a cigarette in his mouth, striking alternately with hope and anticipated disappointment the heavy black keys of a borrowed typewriter.

'I just discovered something.'

'About your old man?'

'Yeah. He wanted to marry his Argentinian girlfriend soon after he came to Peru,' I said, my voice a slender thread that vanished in the air.

'Seriously? And you didn't know.'

'I had no idea.'

'That's crazy.'

'It sure is.'

'And why didn't he marry the girl?'

'That's what I'm trying to find out. The answer from the ministry must be here somewhere.'

'Wait 'til you find out you've got a long-lost brother somewhere.'

Deputy official Pazos then embarked on a lengthy soliloquy about the bitter stories of sad old widows who, when they came to collect the pension of their deceased husbands, suddenly discovered that they had other children, other women, other families, other homes, sometimes even other names. They would go crazy and cause grotesque scenes, uttering howls of rage that echoed down the halls of the military headquarters. Pazos carried on talking, but my ears no longer heard him; his words blurred into a monotonous symphony. My senses were focused only on the name that flashed in my head like a film title on the marquee of an abandoned cinema, still announcing one final show. Beatriz. Beatriz. Beatriz. Beatriz Susana Abdulá. It was now clear that she was not, as I had believed, just a youthful girlfriend now lost in the mists of time, but the woman he had promised to marry, to whom he pledged 'the prestige of his honour' and his 'good name', as he had written in the letter. What exactly had occurred? Why hadn't the marriage come to pass? The file would provide an answer a few minutes later.

★ ★ ★

There is a photograph that shows that the Gaucho and Beatriz had met as children at a birthday party in Buenos Aires, but neither of them remembered this on the summer morning in 1945 when they became aware of each other for the first time. They were at the beach in the resort city of Mar del Plata. He was 19, she was 15. That morning the sun reverberated over the seashore like a great fiery bell.

The Gaucho was dragging his feet in the coarse sand alongside two friends, Tito Arenas and El Chino Falsía. Three bodies with neither cares nor muscles, wearing diminutive swimming trunks, with pencil-thin legs, fresh out of the sea, traces of foam still glistening on their shoulders, stomachs, knees. A couple of hundred yards away, under a two-toned parasol, Beatriz was arguing with her sister Ema about exactly where to lay out a huge red towel that resembled the flag of Morocco. The boys approached. Who knows which of them spoke first. Most likely it was El Chino Falsía, who never lost a second when it came to girls, unlike with his schoolwork. Or perhaps it was Tito Arenas, whose smile – more roguish than sensual – awoke a tenderness in girls that he found hateful and depressing. The last to open his mouth was undoubtedly the Gaucho, but all it took was a glimpse of Beatriz' eyes for him to fall in love as if struck by a hammer blow. He would never recover from the vision of those two pupils, dark as grottoes, their depths pierced by the incipient beam of an unblinking lighthouse. The gaze, the perfect arcs of the eyebrows, the pointy, mouse-like nose. There the cadet Cisneros Vizquerra stood, paralysed, shredded by this girl wrapped in the clarity of daylight, who was now saying her name was Betty, addressing them with gracious gestures from the centre of that African flag. He found her so expansive, so fragile and so proud that he immediately longed to adore her to the end of his days.

Over that summer the three of them would pay regular visits to Beatriz's parasol. The three boys would take her to dance at the Casino dance hall, to eat ice cream in cafés on the seafront promenade, to watch boat races from the top of the stands at the nautical club, to walk to the far ends of the resort's less popular beaches, where the sea broke against the shore with greater power, to watch the latest films at the Ambassador or Sacoa cinemas, from which Beatriz always emerged teary-eyed and upset, sure that she would have played the leading role better than the actress in question. On one such afternoon the Gaucho must at last have opened his mouth to seduce her, to make her his girlfriend and kiss her against the walls, the rocky outcrops, the revolving doors, the trees, the boats pulled up on the shore, and to tell her that he wanted life to stop right there, because what would come later, however good it might be for both of them, would always be inferior, as it would lack the sparkle of that summer. To Beatriz – who at the age of fifteen had never lacked for male attention – this primitive and uncon-ditional emotion was something new and different. Used to her beauty attracting a different kind of approach and endless frivolities – which she had been known to cultivate – she had never imagined that she could inspire a kind of love that was tinged with religious adoration. The Gaucho told her: 'A woman like you shouldn't sleep in a bedroom, but in a sanctuary.' And some nights, in the darkness of the bedroom she shared with her sister Ema, Beatriz would smile as she imagined that her little room was actually a jewel case or a music box, and she would quickly fall asleep to the thought of herself as a miniature dancer who stood up tall, stretched her arms, took hold of one calf and raised her leg into the air, revolving before the bejewelled sea of the mirror.

The relationship between the Gaucho and Betty continued after they returned to Buenos Aires. The Abdulá family lived in Villa Devoto, a neighbourhood close to El Palomar, the headquarters of the military college. The Gaucho would visit her there on weekends when he had leave. He'd take the first tram on Saturday morning and after forty minutes – passing through the stations of Caseros, Santos Lugares and Sáenz Peña – he'd reach Villa Devoto, where he'd remain until evening fell at about seven. Juvenal and Gustavo, the only brothers who knew about the existence of Beatriz, covered for him whenever their mother, Esperanza, asked out loud where the devil the Gaucho had got to. Their father, Fernán – at that point the Peruvian Ambassador to Mexico and shortly after- wards to Brazil, appointed by President Bustamante y Rivero, fully occupied by the organisation of a conference at which the countries of Latin America would establish a continent-wide position in response to Germany and Italy's defeat in the Second World War – remained wholly oblivious to the small events that marked the inner lives of his children in Buenos Aires.

The Gaucho would speak to his friends in the Army not only of Betty, but of the Abdulá family; above all her father, a Syrian-Lebanese man who was very strict or at least pretended to be in order to frighten off his eldest daughter's suitors. Any allusion to Arab culture or symbols made in the classrooms of the military college provided an excuse for the cadets to tease the Peruvian about his girlfriend. 'He's got Peruvian blood, a *criollo* soul and wears the local garb, but he has the heart of a Turk,' they ragged him. The school's annual magazine, *Centauro*, published a profile in its 1947 issue:

The Peruvian's favourite dance is *Arabian Boogie* and he has found his love in the land where God is God and Mohammed is his prophet. We are told that the first time he went to tea, his future father-in-law asked: 'What'll you have, Luis?' Seeking to find favour, he replied: 'Croissants, please, sir, croissants.'

According to the first account I heard of the break-up between the Gaucho and Beatriz, Abdulá senior opposed his daughter pursuing a romantic relationship with a young soldier, one who – worse still – was the son of a couple of exiled Peruvians. It was her family's disapproval and the agony of not being able to carry on with Betty that had brought about the Gaucho's journey to Peru.

Now I know that this version distorted the facts. After two and a half years, the Gaucho and Beatriz had decided to marry. They took it very seriously, aware that if they lacked determination, if they wavered even a little, everyone else would try to convince them they were crazy. And perhaps they were, but they were set on upholding their right to be crazy.

The plan was as follows: the Gaucho would go to Peru and wait for a month or two before informing his family of the decision. Then he would ask for permission from his superiors, return to Buenos Aires to speak to Betty's parents, and following a religious ceremony they would travel to Lima to set up home. The plan, however, failed to reckon with one detail. Not long after arriving in Peru, the Gaucho became aware of an Army regulation that prohibited officers from changing their marital status during their first five years of service. Five long years. Sixty months. Two hundred and sixty weeks. One thousand eight hundred and twenty-five days. Let's not even go into the hours or the minutes. Regardless of how in love Betty and he were, it would prove too long a wait. The distance, or the physical absence of the other, or the parental pressure to abandon the engagement would cause them to falter sooner or later. That's why the Gaucho wrote the following to the Ministry of War:

I, Luis Federico Cisneros Vizquerra, second cavalry lieutenant, having graduated from the Argentinian National Military College on 22 July this year, an institute I joined as a cadet on 25 February 1944, having travelled to Peru on 2 September this year and currently being deployed as a deputy officer at the Chorrillos Military School, address myself to you with due respect on account of the following:

That having formalised my engagement to be married on 30 August this year in the Republic of Argentina, not having been notified before this date by any of the Senior Officers who held the position of military attachés at our Embassy of the law prohibiting marriage for officers of the Armed Forces during the first five years of service, I entreat you to consent to have the necessary authorization granted to me in order to contract this marriage, in the understanding that only in this way will I uphold the prestige of my honour and my good name. In the hope that my request meets with a just response from your dignified office,

Second Lieutenant Luis Federico Cisneros V.

Beneath its veil of solemnity, this letter concealed a cry for help. My father needed to return quickly to

Buenos Aires, marry and put an end to this oppression that prevented him from studying or sleeping. Requests such as his, however, were not resolved directly by the Minister of War, but by the subordinate body, the Inspectorate. Upon learning this, he hastened to seek the intervention of the Director of the Officers' School, who promised to call the Inspector General and ask him to give special consideration to his request. Meanwhile, letters travelled back and forth between Lima and Buenos Aires: they left the house on Paseo Colón where the Gaucho was staying with an aunt and uncle, and six or seven days later arrived at the door of the Abdulá family in verdant Villa Devoto, before beginning the return journey a short time later.

The Gaucho also wrote to his brothers Juvenal and Gustavo, whom he begged to take care of Beatriz in Buenos Aires, to keep her occupied, to invite her to lunch or to take her to hear Leo Marini sing their favourite bolero, 'Dos almas', and to talk to her about him while everything got sorted out. But there was to be no solution. The response of the Army took a month and arrived in the form of a circular, almost a telegram, in which the Inspector General communicated the following:

The request presented by second lieutenant Luis Federico Cisneros Vizquerra, of the Chorrillos Military School, is dismissed. Pass this document to the cavalry office to be appended to the personal file of the abovementioned officer.

That day in the Little Pentagon sixty years later, the missive's curtness remained intact. Its harshness hadn't aged. The revelation led to a storm of speculation on my part. Did my father renounce Betty, given the impossibility of abandoning his military education? Or was it she who ended the engagement, upon learning of the Army's response? Did they try to carry on? Did they make any promises to each other? Where might those letters be? Did the family get involved? How long did they remain in touch? Did they ever see each other again? Which of the two was the first to embark on a new life?

I felt that I was peering into a ravine at night, blindfolded. I took a few further pictures of the file, swapped numbers with deputy official Pazos and left the headquarters building as fast as I could. I decided to walk home. I suppose there must have been cars and people on the streets, but I remember nothing. I can just about picture myself advancing down the narrow, tree-lined streets that run parallel to Angamos Ave., then crossing under the Primavera bridge, turning the corner onto El Polo Ave., thinking about the randomness of this story, of the direct repercussion its conclusion had on my existence. What would have happened if the Inspector General had woken up in a better mood that day in 1947 and, persuaded by the Director of the Officers' School, given my father the green light to marry? Would the plan with Beatriz have come together? Would they have married? Would they have had as many children as they ended up having with other people? Who would I be? In which of these imaginary children would I have been incarnated? Would they have divorced, or grown old together, looking at those photos of their summer in Mar del Plata from time to time? Were there even photos of their summer in Mar del Plata?

As these questions piled up in my head, I was suddenly moved by a sense of sadness at this frustrated marriage, as well as shame or anger at discovering like this – snooping – the reasons why it had never taken place. I also felt I was betraying someone with all this digging around, though I wasn't sure who. From the moment I left the military headquarters I was obsessed with Beatriz Abdulá. Before

I rang the doorbell at my mother Cecilia Zaldívar's house, where she was waiting for me to have lunch, I had enough energy left to fire off another burst of internal questions. Is Betty still alive? Is she in Buenos Aires? Perhaps in Villa Devoto? What if I were to look for her? What if I were to write to her? What if she were to reply to me?

Chapter 4

Twenty years can pass since you buried your father without asking yourself anything specific about the ravages caused by his absence. But just when you think you've grown used to it, just when you're certain that you've got over his disappearance, an ache begins to eat away at you. The ache awakens your curiosity. The curiosity leads you to ask questions, to seek out information. Little by little you come to realise that you're no longer convinced by what you've been told for so many years about your father's life. Or worse: you realise that what your own father said about his life no longer seems trustworthy. The accounts that always sounded accurate and sufficient become confused and contradictory, no longer add up, collide noisily with the questions that have been amassing inside you since he died. Once these emerge and rise to the surface, they eventually form a solid islet on which you find yourself washed up, a sole survivor of the wreck.

The thing that gets to you is not knowing. Not being certain and yet suspecting so much. Not knowing means you lack refuge, and a lack of refuge leaves you exposed to the elements: which is why it troubles you, slows you down, leaves you cold. So you start digging things up. To find out if you really knew your father or only glimpsed him in passing. To find out just how inexact or distorted your scattered memories – your family around the table, chatting after lunch – really are. To find out what is concealed in those oft-repeated anecdotes, recounted as smooth parabolas precisely charting the surface of a life, but never revealing its intimate workings. What sawn-off truth is hidden behind these domestic tales whose sole purpose is to forge a tired mythology that no longer serves its purpose, because it can't keep countering those stark, stifled and colossal questions that now torment your mind.

Where are the authentic stories and photographs of the traumatic, aberrant passages that don't belong to your father's official history, but are just as important – if not more so – to the construction of his identity as the moments of glory or triumph? Where is the album of negatives, of the veiled, shameful or unspeakable acts that also took place, but which no one bothers to recount? As a child, your family lies to you to shelter you from disappointment. As an adult, you no longer care to ask, accustomed as you are to the family's version of events. You yourself circulate, repeat and defend events in your father's life that you never witnessed, studied or verified. Death alone – inflaming your restlessness, multiplying your doubts – helps to correct the lies you've always heard. It allows you to swap them, not for truths but for other lies, lies that are more truly your own, more personal, more portable. As sorrowful as death may be, it can provide glimpses of a wisdom that, in the right minds, proves illuminating, fearful, anarchic. Death is more alive than your own life because it penetrates it, invades it, occupies it, eclipses it, suppresses it and studies it, calling your life into question, ridiculing it. There are questions death provokes that cannot be answered in life. Life lacks the words to talk about death because death has consumed them all. And while death knows a great deal about life, life knows absolutely nothing about death.

★ ★ ★

I know that I'll never find peace if I don't write this novel. How can I be sure that what my father passed on to me wasn't first passed on to him? Were his surliness and reserve all his own, or were they implanted in him before birth? Did his melancholy belong entirely to him, or was it the trace left by something bigger, something that preceded him? What ancestral wellspring fed his rage? What was the root of his arrogance? We often blame our parents for defects we believe are theirs alone, without considering that they might be geological faults, constitutional failures: ulcers that have persisted for centuries or generations without anyone trying to extirpate or to cure them; the ghosts of long-dead starfish that have clung to a rocky undersea outcrop for aeons, and remain there, invisible, demanding our touch.

If I wish to understand my father, I must identify where we overlap, shed light on the areas of darkness, search for contrast, solve the riddles I had once set aside. If I succeed in understanding who he was before I was born, perhaps I'll be able to understand who I am now that he's dead. These two vast questions underpin the enigma that obsesses me. Who he was before me. Who I am after him. This, in short, is my goal: to bring together these two half-men.

At the same time, I must also explore his relationship with his own father, whom he rarely mentioned and only through tears. What peculiar electricity moved between them that atrophied his affection and stunted his spontaneity? I'll have to travel up that blind, muddy ravine until I find something that starts to make sense. How hard have generations of Cisneros children struggled to discover something, anything real, about the father they had? How much did they undergo as children that they never forgave as adults? How much did they see as sons that they never fully metabolised and then suppressed when it was their turn to be fathers? How many of them have gone to their graves still harbouring bitter suspicions without ever confirming or untangling them, without attributing them to anyone or anything in particular?

I must exhume these piled-up corpses, bring them out into the light, dissect them, perform a general autopsy. Not to know what killed them, but to understand what the hell had animated them.

* * *

Monday 9 July 2007 was marked by a frenzy of events that seemed to have been arranged or rigged by some sort of cosmic plan. I was a few days into my first visit to Buenos Aires, as part of my incipient family research. I had travelled there with a friend, Rafael Palacios, who was also new to the city. Over the previous week all Argentina had experienced a dramatic drop in temperature. According to the National Meteorological Service, the cold – which was also affecting parts of Uruguay, Paraguay and Brazil – was reaching polar extremes. That Monday, which was also Argentina's Independence Day, was no exception: we were at zero degrees Celsius. Bundled up as if heading into the foothills of the Himalayas, we left the hostel on Maipú St., guided by a folding pocket map, and went looking for the address I'd written down in my notebook: Flat 20, 865 Esmeralda Street. The flat where my father was born.

We followed Sarmiento until we reached Esmeralda and then headed north, crossing Corrientes, Tucumán, Viamonte and Córdoba at the brisk pace maintained by the locals even on public holidays. If we spoke, we did so through our scarves, not looking at each other, focused on dodging the crowds walking in the opposite direction. Suddenly the eighth block of Esmeralda opened up before us like a rift valley. We drank a coffee in Saint Moritz, the patisserie on the corner. It was a quarter past three.

We walked down to number 865. To my surprise, the mansion house where my father was born over eighty years earlier remained unaltered. I had seen the façade in photographs, so I recognised it straight away; when I peered inside, though, it looked more like an ordinary apartment building than a converted mansion. It was the only building of any age on this street bristling with office blocks, restaurants, bookshops and general goods stores, a wedge of the past that pertained to me amid an irrelevant modernity. Hearing the doorman's voice on the interphone, I began to stammer. He must have got bored of listening to me because the buzzer sounded and the outer gate opened while I was still trying to explain the reason for my visit.

Walking into the entrance hall felt like plunging into a tunnel in time. Everything was sepia-toned, humid, peeling: the faded floor tiles, the relief of the majolica wall tiles rubbed down by repeated passage, the skylights, the jerry-rigged pipes, the water valves, the precarious electrical fittings, the rusting apartment windows, the frames of doors you didn't have to open to know that they creaked like coffin lids. The high ceilings of the corridors were hung with wrought iron lamps that swayed like decapitated heads. The apartments were distributed over two four-storey buildings. Each building had a courtyard and each courtyard a palm tree. The bark of both trees bore a few traces of incisions that could have been carved there years ago by long-dead occupants. Everything felt old. Even the tricycle parked on a landing. Who did it belong to?

As I observed the scene, I progressively unwound my scarf and removed the layers of warm clothing: the woolly hat, glasses, gloves, cravat, and the first of the two jackets I was wearing. Rafael was photographing everything from all possible angles, as if he was planning to recreate the building in model form.

Soon we heard slow footsteps. A very old man appeared and raised his cap to us in greeting. I approached him to ask how long he had lived there. 'All my life,' he replied. His breath smelled of stale oats. I asked him if by any chance he recalled a large family from Peru who had lived there some eight decades ago. The Cisneros Vizquerra. The parents were Fernán and Esperanza, and their children were Juvenal, Carlota, the Gaucho, Gustavo, Pepe, Reynaldo and Adrián. His face remained blank for a few seconds, as if trying to fit these names to the countless faces that ran through his memory, before he said yes, he remembered them well, but he couldn't say more because he had to hurry so as not to miss his four o'clock train. 'Could I take your telephone number, sir?' I asked. 'I don't have one,' were his last words before he faded into the cold air.

I then decided to look for the stair that led to flat number 20. I climbed the same sixty marble steps that my father must have tired of ascending and descending as a child. I put my ear to the white door as I rang the bell, encouraged by the sounds of dishes and cutlery from inside. No one came. The clattering continued, accompanied now by a clacking of adult voices I couldn't quite make out. I rapped on the door with my knuckles and spent a few seconds admiring the elegant two numerals of the number 20 inscribed in black ink to one side of the great window that dominated the landing between the third and fourth floors. The box for the fire extinguisher was empty. No one answered the door. I was about to knock one more time when I was struck by how implausible the speech I was planning to give would probably seem, how absurd my intention was going to sound. What exactly did I hope to achieve? To go inside and search a surely refurbished flat for the hardships into which my father had been born and raised? Breathe in the thin air of my grandfather's years of exile? See the kitchen and imagine my grandmother Esperanza preparing dinner for her children – and also for her husband's legal family? I felt a sudden unease that caught in my throat like a stuck walnut. I understood that I was forcing the experience in order to make it, I don't know, more literary somehow, more worthy of consideration, when it was obvious that this place no longer represented anything at all. It was just an old flat in a crumbling tenement house. There was nothing romantic, quixotic or worthy about bursting in like this. The ghosts that once inhabited the building had long fled.

I told Rafael it was time for us to go. After closing the front gate and stepping back onto the street, we entered the adjacent second-hand bookshop. It was called Poema 20. Rafael wanted to buy a present for his brother. I left Rafael talking to the man at the counter and stretched out an instinctive hand to take a book at random from the first shelf I stopped in front of. I don't want to suggest that the book I picked up was a sign, but in some sense it must have been. Or at least, that's how I want to remember it: a subliminal synchrony. The book, with its distinctive white and red cover, published by Escorpio, was by Andrés M. Carretero and its title was *The Gaucho: Distorted Myth and Symbol*. I held it up to show Rafael, and he crossed the length of the bookshop to embrace me. This scene must have been disconcerting for the bookseller, to whom I handed a banknote in lieu of an explanation. A few minutes later, at four o'clock precisely, with one foot back on the pavement – perhaps the left – I felt a light, cold brushstroke against my cheek as if a substance somewhere between cotton and spittle were falling from above. I then saw that the black asphalt of the street was gradually being covered by a kind of white foam. It took me several seconds to realise that these soft, wind-blown icy blades were splinters of a miraculous snowfall over the city. We mingled with the crowd of people running towards the Obelisk to marvel and celebrate no longer just Argentina's independence but also this natural phenomenon that – as the evening news would confirm – had not occurred in the capital for eighty-nine years. The survivors of that ancient snowfall watched the spectacle from behind the windows of their homes. The rest, conscious of how rare an event this was, left their buildings to wander the broad, frozen avenues that gradually began to resemble Siberian steppes. Euphoric pedestrians tried to catch snowflakes in the air. The older men, clumsier, rubbed them into their faces or swallowed them as if they were a manna or an elixir. The women caught them delicately in their hands, improvising songs of delight. A few younger folk filmed the experience on their mobile phones while others leapt around half-naked, their football strips clinging to their backs. The children, meanwhile, forgot the cold to solemnly build plump, once-in-a-lifetime snowmen. Rafael stayed by the Obelisk shooting photos until the early hours of the morning.

By that time I had abandoned the snow party to go and meet the poet Fabián Casas, whom I had emailed before leaving Lima. The poet welcomed me with a Cossack hat on his head and a neat whisky in his hand. We swapped books, talking about who we were and what we liked to do, and I allowed his dog Rita to mount my leg beneath the kitchen table. Night had fallen when we said farewell three hours later, but it was still snowing in the street. A few minutes later, huddled beneath a bus shelter waiting for a taxi, I felt like a writer. More like a writer than ever. As if the drinks and the talk with Fabián, combined with the snow that was blanketing Buenos Aires for the first time in a century, had yielded a poetic circumstance I deserved to belong to, I already belonged to, even though at this hour of the night there was not a single damn passer-by in the

avenue to witness this fact. So I leaned against the illuminated sign on the bus shelter to read the book of poems
Fabián had gifted me. I opened a page at random and read:

Not all of us can escape the agony of our time
and so, in this moment,
at the foot of my old man's bed
I too prefer to die before I grow old.

Thick flakes of slantwise-falling snow were covering
my shoes. I felt a desire to let myself be buried by the snow
right there, to greet the dawn transformed into one of
those expressionless figures the children had been building
around the Obelisk. Perhaps from this new compartment, I
thought, I could better understand something of what had
happened on this fabulous day that was already dying, already
thrashing like a fish on the damp ground. So I thought
about the verse by Fabián Casas, about the distorted man
my father was, about how there never was and never would
be a way of getting free of him, though the years passed as
swiftly as the snow fell, became a crust, and melted away.
And just as I was starting to sink into the hole of this sorrow
that resurges in me even now, deliverance appeared in the
form of the lights of a yellow taxi, its windscreen wipers
tirelessly battling the murky layer of slush, the driver's sleepy
face barely visible behind the glass.

* * *

Now it's 2014 and I'm on a bus heading for Mar del Plata
to meet Ema Abdulá, Beatriz's younger sister.

The strange memories of my last trip to Buenos Aires,
seven years earlier, project themselves like a short film on
the black screen of the bus window. On the other side of

the glass I don't know if there are shacks, fields of crops or cliffs. Only at daybreak do I realise that the highway is lined by trees of different sizes. In the sky I distinguish a constellation of compact clouds that roll along like tumbleweeds in Western movies.

Two months ago I set about tracing Beatriz, my father's first girlfriend. I had no idea where to start, so I wrote to at least forty people with the surname Abdulá on Facebook. Not one replied. I asked for recommendations on websites dedicated to searching for people and spent whole mornings browsing the ones that appeared most serious or professional. In the end they always asked for money to complete the investigation, with no guarantee of success and no promise of a refund if the search was fruitless. I even got in touch with an Argentinian friend, a well-known journalist by the name of Cristina Wargon, to start a local campaign to find Beatriz Abdulá.

One afternoon, during lunch, my uncle Reynaldo claimed he'd once heard my father say that Betty had got married in Buenos Aires to a man with a Basque surname, a difficult name he couldn't recall just then. A few days later it came to him. 'Etcheberría! Etcheberría! That's what Betty's husband was called,' he told me triumphantly over the phone before spelling out the name, which sounded more like a sneeze than anything else.

The next day, I asked a Buenos Aires-based friend to send me a list of the full names and telephone numbers of all the Etcheberrías living in the capital city who appeared in the phone book. It didn't take him long: there were only sixteen. I started to make long-distance phone calls. One of them must be able to provide a clue about Beatriz, I thought. After two weeks I had contacted Ana, María, Tadeo, Alfredo, Mariana, Celia, Fernanda, Corina, Carlos, Máximo, Nélida, Alberto, Mercedes, Teresa, Carmen and

Bernardo Etcheberría. Not one could give me any precise information about Betty. A few had heard tell of the Abdulá family in the past, but they didn't think any remained in Argentina. Others said they had a more or less distant relative in Córdoba or Santa Fe who knew a woman of Arabic origin who, if they remembered rightly, might be named Beatriz. None of the answers were encouraging. One of the women I contacted, Celia, was an ailing old lady who could barely speak anymore. As she struggled to tell me something, her young carer took the phone off her and said she couldn't help me, offering only to note down my details, or to say that she would.

I had just resigned from the morning radio program I'd been hosting. It was no easy decision, because I enjoyed the work, but I needed the four extra hours to write. After arranging my departure with my boss, I carried on for one more week.

On the morning I was scheduled to say my farewells on air, I felt overwhelmed by doubt. I announced that this was my last program, but I had to force out the words, as if they refused to be spoken; I had to push them, like pushing a child into the dentist's chair. I availed myself of a musical interlude to leave the studio and lock myself in a stall in the washrooms on the fifth floor to ask myself, bluntly, my eyes damp, if it was really worth leaving the radio station, the wonderful people I worked with, the regular paycheque, the public recognition, the provincial fame, in exchange for a dubious novel – a novel that might be of interest to no one but myself, a novel that would cause trouble with my family, that would lead to accusations of ingratitude, injustice or betrayal. Perhaps, I thought, the moment had come to leave my father be, to admit that my determination to narrate his past and his death was futile.

I returned to the studio ready to retract. I wasn't going

anywhere. Even though I had trumpeted my departure mere minutes before, now I would declare my resolve to carry on, and I would beg forgiveness for my outburst from our thousands of listeners. I would say something like 'I don't know what the hell I was thinking when I said I was resigning because I needed to write a novel; there's no damn novel.' Yes, that's what I'd say. After all, the radio was real, the other thing wasn't; the other thing was a pipe dream that would never become reality. I only had to wait for the red light to come on again; for Cindy Lauper to finish singing 'Time After Time'; for the operator to give me the nod to shout out that, in a flash of insight, I had decided that everything was going to carry on as before. There would be canned applause, a silly sound effect and that would be that. It would be like nothing had happened at all.

At that moment I noticed an alert on my mobile: a new email pinged into my inbox. As I opened it, Cindy was singing her last lines: *If you're lost you can look and you will find me, time after time. If you fall I will catch you I'll be waiting, time after time...*

Hello. This is Ema Abdulá, sister of Beatriz, your father's girlfriend. I'm writing to you simply because I learned that you called Celia Etcheberría's home looking for clues about my dear sister. Let me tell you something. I met your father. She missed him very much when he went back to Peru. She wanted to marry him. My sister argued a lot with our mother about the marriage, but there was nothing to be done. She told me a lot of things and I cried with her too. But those were different times, you couldn't just do what you liked.

About twenty-five years later, your father came to visit Beatriz in Buenos Aires. They met and went out to dinner, and your father, as smitten as ever, gave my sister his military baton. They spoke of the possibility of seeing each other again, but it never happened. When we learned of the Gaucho's death we were deeply saddened. And look what a coincidence: I am writing to you now to tell you that my sister, my dear Beatriz, died of cancer one month ago. I wish you all the best in your search. If I can help you with anything further, please don't hesitate to write.

Warm wishes,

Ema

'We're live on air!' The console operator, whose nickname was 'Pechito' because of his highly-developed pectorals, started to wave at me through the thick pane of glass that separated his cabin from mine.

His voice reached me distantly through the headphones. I understood what his gestures meant, but I found myself unable to respond. Ema's email was still open on the screen of my mobile phone.

'...'

'We're on air! Talk!

'...'

'Come on, man, what's up? Are you ok?' Now he was sounding worried.

'...'

'Can't you talk? What do I do?'

'...'

'Play a song, damn it, play a song!'

'...'

'Play "Creep" by Radiohead! I've got it here! Quick! Play it.'

'...'

That same night I got in touch with Ema. Her voice sounded so warm: it was like talking to someone I had known for years. Through Ema I contacted Gabriela,

Beatriz's oldest daughter, whose first email was another shock to my system. She told me that just a few days earlier, emptying her dead mother's drawers, she had found some photographs of the reencounter between Betty and the Gaucho in 1979, which my father had inscribed on the reverse. She had been there, had seen with her own eyes something I could barely imagine: my father – he was already my father in 1979 – visiting the woman who could have been his first wife, the woman he may have never forgotten, from whom he separated against his will, who nevertheless he learned to mention as if she were a minor player in his biography, keeping to himself the tremors that undoubtedly overwhelmed him every time her name crossed his lips. Gabriela had also found among Beatriz's belongings the military baton that my father had given her at the same reunion; it had hung on her living room wall right up until the end, a sentimental relic that awakened the curiosity of guests. For two weeks I exchanged intense emails and phone calls with them both, and I understood how deeply the recent death of Beatriz had influenced this sudden escalation in affection, trust and companionship. It was because she had just died that Ema and Gabriela allowed me to get so close to the delicate territory of her private life, displaying a generous availability that may not have been possible under other circumstances. They found it implausible but also magical that the son of the Gaucho, a man she had once loved, should appear right on the heels of Betty's death, quite literally out of nowhere, like a friendly ghost anxious for details of a shared history that represented a sacred heritage. They assured me that I was a miracle for them. They were wrong. They were a miracle for me.

A few weeks later, I arranged a trip – this trip – to see them in Argentina, to meet them and interview them. And now that I'm finally here, that I'm getting off the bus at the Mar del Plata bus station, taking a taxi to Ema's house and checking that the batteries of my voice recorder are working properly, right now, I sense a strange power, a force that makes me aware of the anxious enthusiasm I'm giving off. For some reason I spend several seconds watching a flock of birds gliding past, setting a course over the vast dominion of the Atlantic waters. And while the taxi wends its way along the coastal boulevard of Playa Chica before turning into the tree-lined streets of Los Troncos and finally slowing down and coming to a halt towards the end of Rodríguez Peña St., I feel proud of having come this far, of having picked the locks of a chapter in my father's life that was crying out to be recounted. Whatever the eighty-year-old woman waiting inside ultimately tells me, I know it will forever alter the Gaucho I have known up to now, and I know that I'm seeking out this story so I can put an end to my father once and for all: so I can tear him from my spinal cord, from the centre of the visceral anguish that hounds me, and relocate him to some immaterial place where I can learn to love him again.

★ ★ ★

What Ema told me that day, added to what Gabriela told me two days later in Buenos Aires – in a café on Libertad St. whose side windows offered a perfect view of the wrought iron canopy of the Colón Theatre – helped me fill in the gaps in the story. As they spoke of their sister and mother, Ema and Gabriela came to realise that they too needed to find a name for certain circumstances that had been silenced out of shame, fear or respect for Beatriz. They realised the importance of unblocking the sealed valves and sluice gates to irrigate a long-abandoned memory, dried up and covered with thorns and weeds. These talks gave way to sudden monologues that they continued insofar as they judged them useful, and it was during these minutes that the story I'd been seeking began to take shape before my eyes like a complete image, with no more blanks.

★ ★ ★

One day in 1947 Beatriz arrived home, sat down in front of her parents and swallowed hard before telling them that she had got engaged to the Gaucho. After the wedding, we'll make arrangements so that we can go and live together in Peru, she continued. Beatriz, who never spoke, who was used to hiding both her feelings and the events that motivated them, suddenly opened her mouth to present this ultimatum.

From her room, Ema heard their voices and noted how her sister's resolve slowly opened up an abyss of silence. Within seconds the house seemed to be collapsing around them. Stunned, Mrs Abdulá buried her face in her hands, weeping as if the imaginary aeroplane on which Beatriz would travel to Peru was already waiting on the tarmac. Mr Abdulá, terrified by the determination in his daughter's voice, stood up to counterattack and refuse permission – not only because she was too young to marry, but because it was madness to leave for a country they had no connection to. The fighting and weeping continued for days. According to Ema, her father's refusal, rather than disheartening Beatriz, merely granted her lunacy a thicker layer of poetic vindication.

The couple's plans evolved. Before returning to Peru, the Gaucho entrusted Ema with a series of cards he asked her to hide under her older sister's pillow. One per night. 'Your father wrote pure poetry. For one hundred nights I had to place those romantic cards under Beatriz's pillow.

They smelled of him,' Ema now tells me, as she sips a spoonful of soup under the thin Mar del Plata sunlight. Listening to her, I'm convinced that my father appropriated the poems written by his own father or grandfather to fill these cards. Traveling back in time, I think of how ironic it is that in 1869 the parents of Cristina Bustamante gladly gave up their fourteen-year-old daughter's hand in marriage to my great-grandfather Luis Benjamín, who was not only much older than her but also father to three illegitimate girls – while almost eighty years later the parents of Beatriz Abdulá would reject my father, despite his impeccable military education. Luis Benjamín broke all the rules, but still won approval. My father had no such luck. The moral transgressions of a distinguished diplomat who has lived in Europe are forgiven in any century. Not so the feelings of an unworldly young soldier without money or prestige.

Beatriz kept her hopes alive even after learning that the Army refused the Gaucho permission to return to Buenos Aires and marry her. She compensated for her fiancé's absence by gazing at the photographs they had taken together, realising only then that they were very few: just three, in fact. One taken at a New Year's party alongside two other couples, all kids dressed as grown-ups, beside a table with an ice bucket and uncorked bottle of champagne in the centre. A second at a reception of some kind, Beatriz swathed in a fur coat, her eyes bright, with her beaver-toothed smile; the Gaucho wearing his gala uniform, lips tightly pressed together. The third photo is the one that looks most like a movie still: the two of them are seated on a rocky outcrop above a beach one afternoon, their backs to the waves as they break over the rocks, their hair tousled by the sea breeze; Betty wears a pullover and trousers that reveal her skinny calves, while the Gaucho sports a summer shirt and those striking, prominent ears, outlined against the white foam running up the shore.

Now they were no longer inside but outside the photos, very far outside them, far enough away for the couple to wonder whether these images showed a life that now belonged to the past. For a month and a half their correspondence flowed punctually back and forth, sustained almost entirely on the hope that the situation would take a sudden turn for the better.

But it didn't. Their communication was met with obstacles and disruptions, and the missives began to dwindle. Abruptly, Betty stopped writing altogether. Her exhaustion in the face of what to all eyes seemed a fruitless wait was exacerbated by a smear campaign against the Gaucho, orchestrated by none other than his old Buenos Aires friend José Breide – Pepe – who had long held a candle for Beatriz. He set about filling her head with untruths, seeking to persuade her that the Gaucho would never return from Lima, denouncing him as a traitor, claiming that his ingratitude and neglect were such that he had already set up with another woman.

'Pepe started to turn up at the house not long after your father left. My sister didn't love him, but she felt lonely. Breide was very persistent: he followed Beatriz from Buenos Aires to Mar del Plata every summer. He offered her everything under the sun, and because he was well-off and from the same Arabic community, our mother supported his suit. In the end she was the one who arranged their engagement,' Ema revealed to me in a choked voice, fulfilling my request not to keep any details to herself, however painful they may be.

The final letter the Gaucho received from Betty was the letter breaking off the engagement. Three handwritten pages on slippery paper that end with a bolero, 'Nosotros', a hymn to devastated love whose lyrics well describe the arduous battle that must have been waged inside Beatriz throughout 1947.

Listen, I want to tell you something
that perhaps you don't expect,
something that may hurt.
Hear me, for though my soul aches
I need to speak to you
and so I shall.
The two of us,
who have been so sincere,
who since we first met
have been in love.
The two of us,
who made of love
a wondrous sun,
a romance so divine.
The two of us,
who love each other so much,
and yet must part;
ask me no more.
It is not for lack of feeling,
I love you with my soul;
I swear that I adore you
and in the name of this love
and for your own good I bid you farewell.

This letter tore the Gaucho apart. A tear that would reopen every time this bolero came on the radio or record player, whether in the voice of Los Panchos, Sarita Montiel or Daniel Santos. With the first few notes, my father would trail off mid-conversation and stare at the ceiling, smoking one cigarette after another, lost in painful memories.

He didn't deal well with the break up. He abandoned himself, got drunk, lost control. Even though he didn't drink at the time, one afternoon he shut himself up for hours in a bar on the road down to Baños de Chorrillos. Once all the other customers had left, the owner told him he was about to close, if he would be so kind as to pay up and be on his way. My father gave no reply. Ten minutes later the man repeated his request. My father ignored him once more. From behind the bar there emerged a huge figure who approached the Gaucho and urged him to settle up and leave. One more whisky, my father ordered, without looking at him. The figure refused with his hand and warned him forcefully that he had to go, now. I can visualise the scene. My father, his voice distorted, his tone defiant, his face fixed on the wall in front of him, informs the man that he is a second lieutenant in the Army, that they're inviting disaster if they refuse to serve him. The other – taller, larger, more lucid – picks him up by the scruff of his neck and drags him out of the establishment. My father, hanging in the air like a doll, waves his arms and legs uselessly in protest. Once in the street, on his knees on the pavement, the sound of the bolts being locked sends him completely out of control. He pulls the hidden pistol from his belt and unleashes the promised disaster. Four bullets riddle the door, which then opens by itself like in a haunted house. The owner, shaking, emerges with his hands in the air. Now he is all acquiescence. The bruiser stands by nervously, an iron bar in his hand. One more whisky, dammit! my father stammers, his eyes full of tears of rage.

A few weeks after this event, which undoubtedly cost him more than one warning back in the barracks, my father learns that Beatriz has a new suitor. He doesn't yet know that he has been betrayed. The news leaves him so low that he asks his superiors for immediate transfer to any province in the country. I don't care where, he replies dejectedly when they ask him if he has any preference. The only thing the Gaucho wants is to leave Lima, where his desolation leaves him exposed every day to the intrusive questions of family and friends. He can't deal with their pestering any longer.

He needs a change of air, to grapple with himself. He needs hard work, retreat, countryside, distance, solitude. They send him to northern Peru, to the heat and light of Sullana, as platoon commander of the 7th cavalry regiment. During the more than fifteen hours the journey north takes – alternating his thoughts with the views of the flat, leaden outlines of coastal cities like Chimbote, Chiclayo, Piura – the Gaucho decides to erase Beatriz, to remove her memory as if it were an enormous mound of earth that obstructed the sole window of his house, preventing the light from entering. The indignation of knowing she was with another man somewhat helps in this task. He takes up the challenge, without melodrama, a question of pure mental effort, like when he confronted mathematical problems deftly at school. But since he also suffers from pride and arrogance, he sets himself an additional feat: to find a substitute, someone to cover the hole left by Betty. Hadn't she done the same? It wouldn't be too hard, not when there were always so many women around soldiers, excited by the boots and the epaulettes of the uniform – and even more so in the provinces, thought the Gaucho. It was during the final leg of the journey to Sullana that he persuaded himself of this: he had to find another woman. He never imagined he would find her so quickly.

* * *

Lucila Mendiola fulfilled the fundamental characteristic that my father sought in women: she was difficult to win over. An aristocratic and pious young woman, she was the daughter of Ildefonso Mendiola, twice mayor of the city of Sullana. A girl who wouldn't go out with just anyone. As soon as he caught a glimpse of her on his first stroll around the city plaza, he was disarmed: her eyes the colour of every shade of the sea, the gypsy skirt, the heavy necklaces that hung against her bony chest. If my father had read the poetry of Federico García Lorca, he would have felt that this woman had escaped from his verses.

'Who's that skinny lass with the green eyes?' he asked the man walking beside him, Captain Miranda.

'Don't even look at her,' Miranda replied curtly. 'She's the mayor's daughter.'

'So?'

'She won't pay you any attention. In any case, she's engaged.'

'Since when?'

'Since two weeks ago.'

'In two weeks' time, she'll be mine.'

In the end it took not two but seven weeks for him to execute his boast. The last thing the Gaucho needed was a woman who was already engaged, but he stubbornly pursued Lucila Mendiola and did everything he could for her to break off her engagement to an estate owner from a neighbouring town. He even deceitfully seduced a friend of the betrothed couple, little Brígida Garrido, so little that from afar she resembled a sparrow.

Faking an interest in Brígida secured him direct access to Lucila's inner circle. That was how he managed to start talking to the young Mendiola, to beguile her with his Buenos Aires accent, to flatter her with the poetry he borrowed from the books penned by his own father. When he finally won Lucila's full attention and began to promenade beside her around the central plaza, poor Brígida Garrido understood the wretched role she had played and shut herself up in a convent, never to leave again.

As the months passed, once his obsession with finding a

mate had been satisfied, the Gaucho learned to love Lucila and her family. The Mendiola family received him in Sullana as the Abdulá family had never done in Buenos Aires. They made him feel welcome, appreciated, and even took care to make his convalescence more comfortable following an operation for appendicitis.

All this despite the fact that Don Ildefonso Mendiola, the mayor, had hated the military ever since a lieutenant by the name of Lizárraga had left his eldest daughter Norma stranded at the altar. With second lieutenant Cisneros, this prejudice faded. Such esteem, such domestic affection amid that pastoral setting, served to deepen and strengthen the Gaucho's initially uncertain sentiments towards Lucila.

I still have in my possession a series of little cards from my father on which he wrote messages to Lucila, all infused with florid rhetoric.

May we commemorate together many thirtieths of the month, my love. Yours, Lucho. 30 July 1948.

God willing, I may come to be worth something in this life, if only that I may lay it at your feet as the greatest proof of my adoration and idolatry. Yours, Lucho. September 1948.

All I ask of you, my love, is that you never take from me the blessing of adoring you for the rest of my life. October 1948.

For my adored Lucila, my love, my life, my hope, my world, my obsession. You are everything to me, but above all you are mine. February 1949.

In those same days, however, the immaculate name of Beatriz still sent shivers up his spine.

★ ★ ★

There is a photograph someone took of us in Piura in 1980. A while back I removed it from a family album. I like to look at it. You're standing at the end of the swimming pool in the enormous house we lived in that year. You're wearing a bathing costume patterned in blue and white squares (I still remember the texture of the damp suit hanging in the garden). The hairless legs, the wet hair, the blurred moustache, the blurred nipples. The sun throws slashes of light across your milky skin. Your muscles still evoke the robust horse rider you once were. Poised on your shoulders like a child acrobat on a giant, I'm just about to dive into the still waters of the swimming pool. My arms are outstretched, my eyes fixed on the tiles. Our shadow appears against the faded green background, and it trembles where it crosses the water. I'm five or six years old. My blue swimming costume has a red waistband and a fish embroidered on the left hand side in the same colour. The elaborate dive is about to take place. After my body pierces the water, causing the minimum disturbance to its calm surface, you'll dive after me, producing a thrilling tsunami; without resurfacing, advancing like a slow submarine or tame shark, you'll swim the length of the pool. We loved putting on this show for an audience. I felt so good up there, so essential, so brave, a leading player. That was our ritual, perhaps the only one we shared in those years. I'd climb up your back like a steep stairway of vertebrae, and once at the top, on the broad platform of your shoulders, holding onto your hands, your wet hair between my ankles, I'd prepare myself for the dive straight into the pool. Click! You'd follow straight after. We'd hear the distorted echo of the applause from under the water.

That year, the Army sent you on a tour of several northern cities as General Commander of the First Military Region. We moved to Piura. Your office was adjacent to the house, so you were your own neighbour. Your daily commute took ten steps. If I were to return to that house I might find it had shrunk, but at the time it seemed huge. It had two floors connected by a wooden staircase with a banister and very broad bottom steps. There was always a bustle of people around: drivers, butlers, staff. The photograph shows the sliding glass doors that led from the terrace inside, where the chairs of the informal dining room can be glimpsed, and its mosquito-screened windows. Everything exudes the tarnished hue of the 80s. Behind us is a large pot with plants, undoubtedly placed there by my mother, Cecilia Zaldívar. I think I already said how much I like this photo. It's an X-ray of our complicity. My body looks like a prolongation of yours. An appendage emerging from it. Your half-naked body is an autonomous engine, the machine that assembles me, supports me and then thrusts me into the world. The parabolic leap is only made possible by the strength and determination of your grip on me. It's hard to say whether you're the one who lets go of me or if I'm the one who breaks free of the organism we comprise together. However it may be, there's harmony in the structure and beauty in the manoeuvre. For years this photograph has stood on a shelf of my bookcase, leaning against the spines. It's like a postcard freezing a moment that has the duty to remain unforgettable.

One afternoon in 2006, as I was reading Paul Auster's *The Invention of Solitude*, I glanced at the photo. There it was, within the sphere of my gaze. In two separate passages in the novel – parts seven and eight of 'The Book of Memory' – Auster narrates the marine exploits of two characters who are engaged in a search for their respective fathers: Jonah and Pinocchio. One biblical and one literary figure. I'd always felt sympathy for both, for their rebellion against their nature, for aspiring to become more than they were born to be. Jonah didn't want to become just any old prophet. For Pinocchio it wasn't enough to be a living marionette. Jonah refuses the mission God entrusts to him – preaching to the pagans of Nineveh – and flees from Him by boarding a ship. During the crossing a great storm is unleashed. Jonah knows it is the work of God and asks the sailors to cast him into the sea in order to calm the waters. They do as he asks. The storm ceases and Jonah sinks beneath the waves, until he finds himself in the stomach of a whale, where he remains for three days. Amid the resounding echoes of this solitude, Jonah prays for his life. God hears his prayers, forgives his disobedience and orders the great beast to vomit him up onto the shore. He is saved. Something similar occurs with Pinocchio. In Carlo Collodi's novel, Geppetto's boat is overturned by a huge wave. Half-drowned, the old carpenter is dragged by the current towards a great asthmatic shark that swallows him 'like a piece of pasta'. The brave Pinocchio searches for Geppetto unflaggingly. Once he finds him, he lifts him up on his shoulders and waits for the shark to open its mouth so he can swim to safety in the darkness of the night. Jonah is rescued from the waters by his father. Pinocchio rescues his father from the waters. Auster asks himself, or I ask myself: is it true that you have to dive into the depths and save your father in order to become a real man? Since I read *The Invention of Solitude* the photograph of Piura is no longer just the photograph of Piura. It has become a talisman, the kind of photo that's taken at a certain moment in time, but whose significance isn't revealed until much later. Now I understand far better the watery ritual enacted by that child of five or six. Every time I look at the photograph, that child charges me with the same inescapable mission: dive into the water. Find your father.

My dear brothers and sister,

This time I am the one to write, given your silence. Though I take up my pen only rarely to scribble a few lines and send proof of my fondness for you, this time I am doing so to offer you a more detailed account of my life.

I was released from Piura hospital two days ago, having left my appendix in a glass jar. If one day, in the not too distant future, I become president of Peru, this diminutive organ might be exhibited like a museum piece. It was something so swift and violent that I've still not got used to the idea that it's been taken out of me. The first sign something was wrong was in the early morning of the 18th, the first and final such attack in my whole damn life, and six hours later I was marching to the gallows of the operating theatre, where a murderous hand awaited me. I fell asleep in an instant. After the operation, performed by Commander Núñez, I slept for eighteen hours straight.

All of this happened and I'm now back in the barracks with thirty days of sick leave. Fortunately I had my savings, which have now been drained. Apart from this, life continues with the same monotony as usual. Colonel Gómez wrote to me and I have answered him. I also received a letter from our mother. I frequently correspond with El Chino Falsía and we have promised to keep in touch.

As for my Betty, she has replied to me, but in such different terms than I had hoped. She tells me that I am wrong to blame her mother for losing my letters, that it is true there is another man in her life, though she does not dare to tell me who he is. She also asks me to return all her letters. I, meanwhile, still as enamoured of her as I was four years ago, have answered her

77

with a letter that I fear leaves me playing the wretched role of the fool. I don't know what to do. So many things can happen before the year's end…

The leather jacket and the shirt have still not reached me. When you send them, please also send some bed sheets, and nothing else.

Remember me to the rest of the family. If I start to mention everyone, I'll need four more sheets of paper and that would be a sacrilege. A big, big hug to you all. My heart remains with you.

Disillusioned, the Gaucho pushes forward his proposal of marriage to Lucila. Suddenly, he wants to be married as soon as possible, and furiously embraces an illusion marred by silent contradictions. On 28 January 1950, the day of his engagement, he writes to Lucila:

Today one of my greatest desires has started to become a reality. I want you to know, my sweet maiden, that I shall spare no effort until my utmost dream comes true.

The first to congratulate him on his engagement are friends from Sullana, the captains Miranda and Ritz, both of whom are married to cousins of Lucila. They would go riding at weekends and share the small successes and anxieties of a military career constantly subject to the sway of political events.

The Gaucho's brother and sister Juvenal and Carlota travel to Sullana to meet their future sister-in-law and establish relations with the new family.

From Rio de Janeiro, where he remained as ambassador, Fernán Cisneros exchanges cables with the Mendiola family to formally request the hand of their daughter Lucila in his son's name. A few days later he writes to the Gaucho to tell him: 'My son, the lines written by your fiancée have convinced us that she is a good girl, conscientious and serious, and ready to share in your destiny.' My grandfather added a few further solemn thoughts on married life – which sound rather ridiculous, coming from a man who secretly maintained two parallel households over a period of two decades.

The religious marriage between the Gaucho and Lucila takes place at eleven o'clock in the morning of Saturday 21 June 1952 in the church of Our Lady of the Pillar of San Isidro, in Lima. There is a photo album containing at least fifty photographs of this day. My father boasts his military gala uniform and Lucila a pearl-coloured dress. They look happy as they emerge from the tunnel formed by the crossed swords.

I had heard that on the morning of his wedding my father was sombre, downcast, and that my grandfather Fernán had said 'My son is not marrying happily' after seeing him tying his shoelaces with an air of sadness that ill-suited the union about to be celebrated. However, the photographs of the day speak for themselves, radiating a bliss that promises to endure. The Cisneros and Mendiola families appear united, surrounded by friends from Sullana and from the Army. Like multi-coloured birds, the guests' faces shine with a happiness both delicate and bold.

Only one person seems to remain apart from the general atmosphere of celebration. A slim, elegant, frowning woman. A woman wearing a hat with a large, up-turned brim in a shade of grey that matches her necklace and earrings. It is my grandma Esperanza, who deigns to arrange her haughty face into courteous expressions, though they fail to mask her annoyance and discomfort. If there is anyone who doesn't bless this marriage, it is she.

A few months before Lucila and the Gaucho's wedding, Beatriz Abdulá had become engaged to José Breide in Buenos Aires. Did my father learn of this? Did the decisions taken by Beatriz in Argentina come to influence those taken by my father in Peru? Or perhaps she was the one who found a way to stay apprised of the love life of her Peruvian former fiancé, taking steps in accordance with the information she gathered? Could there have been a long-distance tussle of pride between them? A contest of egos? A silent challenge that intimated, if you can get married over there, then I can here too; if you can be happy with someone else, then why can't I?

* * *

What Gabriela tells me in that hot café on Libertad St. is that her mother left Breide shortly before their wedding date, breaking off the engagement and sending tremors through the conservative Syrian-Lebanese community in Buenos Aires. Virtually overnight, she married a man by the name of Federico Etcheberría, Gabriela's father.

Betty had never much liked Breide, her daughter recalls. She wasn't enthusiastic about her engagement to him. 'She let herself be carried along by the current, but it was no great love story, I've no doubt about that. She met Federico, my father, and broke off with Breide, even though they were engaged.'

While Gabriela untangles details on the voice recorder, I sip my cappuccino and ponder Beatriz's actions over time. I suddenly feel or want to feel that everything she did after my father left for Argentina was in reaction to his departure, and that she tried to remain close to the Gaucho however she could. Perhaps, I consider, getting engaged to one of his best friends was, however perversely or misguidedly, an allegorical way of staying close to him or to the space imbued with his presence while he lived in Buenos Aires. Leaving Breide to marry this Federico – my father's second name – may have been another act of unconscious nostalgia, an irrational desire to appropriate a name that had once meant so much to her. And when this second Federico died years later in a car accident, what did Beatriz do? She secretly married the brother of her dead husband. Was this reflex action not an exact repetition of what she had done years earlier with Breide? Letting yourself be loved by the friend of the boyfriend who has left – wasn't that the same as letting yourself be loved by the brother of the husband who has died? Is it a coincidence that, in both situations, faced with an abrupt abandonment, Beatriz rushed into the arms of the most inconvenient character on the scene? As if betraying the absent person was the only possible way to pay homage to them.

Many years later, the Gaucho and Beatriz would see each other's faces again. The encounter took place in Buenos Aires in October of 1979. He was fifty-three years old, a Lieutenant General and Chief of Staff of the Joint Command of the Armed Forces. He was no longer married to Lucila Mendiola. He maintained an affectionate distance with his older children, and for almost a decade had lived with Cecilia Zaldívar, with whom he had two children by then.

He travelled to Buenos Aires to attend a ceremony for the anniversary of the creation of the Argentinian Army, to take part in a series of military conferences and to receive a tribute from his former classmates in El Palomar. He stayed for eleven days altogether.

Beatriz was forty-eight and had been a widow for just a few months. One morning she received the most unexpected phone call of all. It was the Gaucho, her Gaucho, who only after a few minutes of exchanging greetings and nervous laughter told her he was in the city. Before they hung up, they agreed to meet at the Plaza Hotel where he was staying, adjacent to the Military Club and looking over Plaza San Martín.

Gabriela tells me that her mother was happy at the thought of meeting my father again. Her desire to see him, however, was neutralised by the self-control with which certain women protect themselves from the past. She was the only one of the two who accepted the reality of their new roles. Beneath his military attire, the Gaucho, by contrast, was the same excitable little boy who had kissed her eagerly at the door to her house in Villa Devoto thirty years earlier, in 1947, before leaving for the airport on his way to discover Peru.

After his marriage to Lucila Mendiola had fallen apart, the Gaucho had fallen in love with Cecilia Zaldívar, a young woman of twenty-two in whom he believed he had found the physical and spiritual twin of Beatriz. To his eyes, Cecilia was Beatriz reincarnated. If the latter's subsequent relationships were a kind of distorted refraction of her love for the Gaucho, his had been formed with Beatriz firmly in the centre of his gaze, whether in order to bury her or to resuscitate her. He had been very fond of Lucila Mendiola and he loved Cecilia Zaldívar – 'two good women who don't deserve to come to any harm', he would say once – but for Beatriz, or for what she had been and still represented, he maintained a love whose purity, weight and endurance were directly proportional to its degree of mythification.

As soon as he saw her enter the lobby of the Plaza Hotel, my father regressed to adolescence. His actions were all out of synch, as if he was unable to understand that he had grown old, had five children, that he was no longer a cadet engaged to this girl – who, by contrast, treated him solely with affection, a melancholy affection at best, continuously marking the boundaries that destiny had laid down between their lives. My father refused to acknowledge that gap. He acted just like his great-grandfather, the priest Gregorio Cartagena, who in contravention of his Church vows had loved Nicolasa so many years earlier; or like his grandfather Luis Benjamín, who had taken off with the mistress of President Castilla; or like Fernán, his own father, who had seduced Esperanza on afternoons in the centre of Lima, overlooking his legitimate wife. It was centuries-old behaviour. Imprudent, egotistical, but doubtless enchanting behaviour. My father, like three generations before him, didn't care about the consequences. He had abandoned Brígida Garrido to court Lucila Mendiola. He had abandoned Lucila Mendiola to court Cecilia Zaldívar. And now he was abandoning Cecilia Zaldívar to court Betty all over again. His heart was a vicious circle. His impulsive romantic conscience was inhabited by a macho predator: once the target was identified and the field of operations drawn up, there was no space for moral doubt. It was a matter of acting, nothing more.

Gabriela pauses the conversation to pull an envelope from her handbag. It contains photographs from that October of 1979. As she delicately slips the contents from the package, I realise that I feel torn. Torn between my desire to see them and my desire not to. Then the photos begin to move from her hands to mine and each one of them is an explosion that only I can hear. Four bombs. Three were taken in Beatriz's house, the fourth at a Susana Rinaldi tango show in San Telmo. Gabriela was present on both occasions. 'On the night of the show', she recounts in her neat, meticulous manner, 'your father's body language expressed how captivated he was by my mother. I was struck by the way his tears flowed. He was deeply moved, as if he had been frozen in the past.'

The first thing that hits me is my father's face: his usual hardened features have been replaced by two small, melancholy eyes, a limp, placid expression and a smile so broad it creases his face: two or three lines expand like sound waves between the corners of his mouth and his ears. His teeth, which were rarely on show, are prominent in the image.

I had never seen photos in which my father appeared so devoted and vulnerable, so engrossed and happy. I stare at them again and again, then pause for a few seconds to look up at the couples seated around the café, and wonder if they might be confessing secrets to each other that could compete with Gabriela's revelations. I feel both satisfaction and emptiness, the same sensation of pride and shame that assaulted me on visiting Ema in Mar del Plata, the feeling that I'm killing that man who was my father with each new story and photograph I obtain – and composing, in his place, a version of him in which I can see myself for the first time. And before I can even reach a single conclusion about the old images that burn in my hands like deadly weapons, Gabriela speaks again: 'Turn them over, they're inscribed.'

And then it's no longer just the Gaucho smiling in this new, effusive way, but also his handwriting, his perfect left-handed calligraphy I tried to copy as a boy so that something in me would resemble him, the writing that forms phrases perhaps even more eloquent than the photos themselves. On one he writes: 'For Gabriela, with sincere life-long affection.' Another reads: 'With the nostalgia for a family portrait that will travel with me always.' The third: 'For my Beatriz of yesterday, today and always.' And on the final one, which shows just the two of them at the San Telmo tango show, my father simply wrote on the back: 'No words.'

It is these words, the ones he couldn't find to describe what he was feeling that night, that now pour onto my computer screen; all the language that slipped away from my father in his attempt to name that specific circumstance now washes over me, fragmented but abundant. And here are these words, this language, to say what he avoided saying, perhaps because it was so obvious or inappropriate or timeless: that Beatriz Abdulá was the great love of his life; a love whose roots determined how he would behave with all the other women he loved or tried to love in the future; a historic, truncated love that he sought desperately to reproduce in other bodies, other names, other identities.

If they had married and lived together, perhaps the dream would have faded, but this is something we will never know, Gabriela is saying now, aware that if this had come to pass, neither of us would be here today. After all, seen from one perspective, Gabriela and I are both the fruit of a thwarted story. We are the children that the Gaucho and Beatriz would have wanted to have together and ended up having with other people whom they also loved, but who now get in the way of the story we are trying to reconstruct. The two of us, her and I — not her siblings or mine, but the two of us — by the mere fact of being here in this café, implicated in this situation brought about by me and accepted by her, in a scene both symbolic and thrilling, in asking each other these questions, have the right — by this mere fact — to speculate that our parents have channelled themselves through us, and our mission is to recount all of this to each other because it's the last encounter that they would have wanted to have. I am certain that Gabriela is terrified by the same thought now flitting through my head: that our parents would have been very happy together, perhaps happier than they subsequently were with her father and my mother respectively. This hypothetical happiness, as I can confirm in Gabriela's blue, deep-set eyes, gives us joy just as it wounds us. We are who we are because they stopped being what they were. Their separation was our vital breath. We are rendered siblings by absence, by failure, by what never came to pass. We are the proud dead children of a marriage that never was.

When they reunited in 1979, Beatriz found my father's attitude somewhat disproportionate, even mawkish, but she put up with his impulses because she felt protected, loved, desired. My father called her on the phone two days before returning to Lima. He insinuated that he wanted to spend the night with her. No, he didn't insinuate: he told her so. A general never insinuates. But Betty – perhaps because of the recent death of her husband Federico or because she was simply operating on a different frequency – refused. The morning he returned to Peru, in order to keep this inopportune proposal from distorting the nature of his feelings, the Gaucho appeared at Betty's front door, kissed her on the forehead and presented her with his military baton, the baton of a recently promoted lieutenant general. I want you to keep this, he told her. And she took it in her hands like a sceptre intended to honour her beauty or her past.

Gabriela recalls that her mother kept this baton hanging on the living room wall, in a central place, impossible to miss. And now, after paying for the coffees and juices and toasted sandwiches, she invites me to her home to see the baton, which she has salvaged from her dead mother's belongings. And so here I am now, in Gabriela's living room, holding my father's wooden baton, running my fingers over the gold handle, on which I recognise the coat of arms of Peru. I examine it closely; I mime marching with it. My mother, Gabriela says suddenly, was very imaginative and always embellished the stories she told, but she truly loved your father, really loved him, and always told me about her Peruvian fiancé. I connect these words to something Ema had said to me two days earlier: that in her final days, when the cancer was at its most aggressive, Beatriz remembered my father in sudden flashes and spoke about the engagement that was never to be, gazing for minutes on end at the photographs of Mar del Plata. I think about these testimonies and I think about how every child imagines, trusts or desires that the relationship between their parents is the most important or essential one they have ever had. Every child hopes that no man has had a greater impact on their mother than their father, and that no woman has broken and repaired their father's heart better than their mother.

What materials forged the love between my parents? I wonder on the flight back to Lima. And since I don't have an immediate answer I become distracted, and focus on the image of the military baton in the middle of Beatriz's lounge, like the founding rod of an empire, like both inheritance and plunder. And suddenly I regret not asking Gabriela if I could have it. And I wonder if it would be fitting for me to have it. Then the plane lands and when I switch my phone back on I find an email has arrived from Gabriela Etcheberría that reads:

You must be on the flight back to Lima by now. I wanted to tell you that it was wonderful to meet you and have the opportunity to talk with you. Your quest seems so meaningful to me, and I truly hope that new and fruitful windows have been opened up on the past; they have for me, inevitably and without even looking for them. All of this has been a revelation. Today I was thinking, rather angry at myself for not having thought of it sooner, that I should have given you your dad's military baton to take with you. It's a very symbolic object. It's much more yours than mine. If you like, I'll hold on to it for you until you come back to Buenos Aires to present your novel.

Gabriela

Chapter 5

The hands of the Cartier wristwatch Lucila Mendiola hurls at the Gaucho come to a halt as soon as it hits the bedroom wall behind him. The blow damages the mechanism. This is the only time it will display from now on: twelve minutes past seven p.m., Saturday, 11 September 1971. Crouched down, the Gaucho cradles the fallen timepiece in his hands like a diminutive metallic corpse. Only when he notes the hour does he realise just how long they've been tangled in this argument, their shouts and sobs forming a musical accompaniment to the aerial trajectory of the objects Lucila has been throwing at him. The Cartier was preceded by a candelabra, three books, a cigarette case, a wooden spoon, a fly swatter and at least two bowls from an antique set that now lie in smithereens on the parquet. As for the expensive watch the Gaucho had given her on her last birthday, Lucila never wants to wear it again, and so she has flung it in his face, peppering the offensive with a string of insults and threats of which only angry fragments can be heard: 'you're not leaving me', 'that two-faced whore', 'you want me to die of a heart attack', 'think of the children', or just isolated but easily linked words like 'wimp', 'drunkard', 'wretch', 'hate' and again 'whore' and again 'heart attack'.

When Lucila runs out of projectiles and affronts, she approaches her husband. Behind a furious, liquid mask her eyes announce the arrival of a cataclysm. Her right hand held rigid against her body looks like it could conceal a knife. Her jaw clicks, shifted out of place by the tension. In a rage, she raises her arm and cracks her hand full across the Gaucho's face. A sharp, violent slap that would resonate for days and years. He touches his face to staunch the burn, feeling his body fill with humiliation, stares at Lucila and retreats to the bedroom, where without thinking he takes a suitcase from the wardrobe and hurriedly begins to pack, as if the Army had just sent orders for an urgent transfer to the warzone. Lucila tries to stop him, but to no avail. She rebukes him for his cowardliness, demanding that he take responsibility instead of running away. She tries to punish him by pummelling his back with her fists, which does nothing to distract the Gaucho from his course of action. And so Lucila weeps her last tears and takes refuge in a final flurry of wild cries that shatter the ears of her children, who all suddenly emerge from their rooms as if fleeing an earthquake, wanting to know what's going on. What's going on is that their father is leaving. Leaving home. This time it's not a warning nor a theatrical display nor a bad dream. This time their father has packed his suitcase and is walking to the door of chalet number 69, determined to stay away for who knows how long. Melania, at seventeen the oldest, understands the magnitude of this action, as if she'd been expecting it, and within seconds she has taken her mother's side. She embraces her, cries with her and stares resentfully at her departing father. It is because she loves him above all else that she despises him with all her power during these endless seconds. The younger two, Estrella and Fermín, throw themselves round their father's legs like human chains or snares. The Gaucho advances blindly through the wreckage, by force of inertia, as if he'd torn out his own heart so as not to feel the pain around him, and carries it steaming in his hands like a blood-soaked bird, still beating hotly. When he crosses the threshold he turns, casts a last look back at this interior scene – now a bitter tableau, a painting of outsize sadness – and he feels shaken but above all cruel, indifferent, responsible for the animosity his children will show him from this day on. But his steps don't falter, and he swiftly disappears down the corridor that leads to the staircase and from there out to the street.

Just minutes later, as he drives down the nocturnal Costa Verde in the direction of his mother's house, he wonders where he'd tapped into such a titanic force of will that he was able to abandon his family. And he imagines – or at least I imagine now in front of this screen and ascribe him this thought – that his dead father has acted through him. Or not precisely his father, but rather the memory of his father's cowardice. For his father, Fernán, never dared to leave his first wife, Hermelinda Diez Canseco, for his lover Esperanza Vizquerra, and kept up two parallel households, following the demented routine of sleeping in one house only to wake up in the other, and vice versa, and slowly sank into a nightmare in which furtive, forbidden activities became confused with a natural part of the scenery. All to avoid the recriminations of those around him, the social scandal, the shame. An indelible stain appeared on the skin or rather in the minds of Fernán and Esperanza's children when they discovered who they were, and their place in their father's life. Over time, some of them managed to erase the memory, but the stain of illegitimacy never went away.

My father, the Gaucho, has no desire to pass this stain on to the children he might one day have with Cecilia Zaldívar, the woman he's now in love with, the woman who is asleep, unaware of what is going on, in her parents' house in a middle-class development in Pueblo Libre. The Gaucho wants Cecilia to be his wife, publicly; he doesn't want to hide her away as his father hid his mother. He wants to remedy the past, and to do this he needs to leave Lucila

Mendiola and keep a distance from his children, though he has sworn he will never abandon them. He acknowledges his weaknesses as a man – he's a womaniser, he spends long nights drinking with old friends, he's a workaholic – but he has been a model father and intends to remain one, however impossible or at least remote this resolution may seem right now. He tells himself all of this as he drives along the coastal highway, smoking one Dunhill after another, one hand on the wheel, and he pictures Cecilia Zaldívar's young, smiling, freckled face in an effort to temper the rage and guilt that are already eating away at his mind.

★ ★ ★

He had met Cecilia two years earlier, in March 1969, five months after the coup d'état led by General Juan Velasco Alvarado against President Fernando Belaúnde. This had marked the start of the Revolutionary Government of the Armed Forces, which was just a euphemism for military dictatorship.

Velasco's pretext for overthrowing Belaúnde and marching him out of the Palace of Government in his pyjamas in the middle of the night was the – undoubtedly scandalous – disappearance of a page from a contract signed with a US oil company: the mysterious page eleven. The document supposedly implemented changes to the conditions for the extraction of oil reserves, but the loss of this page – the very one on which the new prices were established – triggered conspiracy theories claiming that Belaúnde was handing over the oil to the gringos behind the backs of the Peruvian people.

When the coup occurred in October 1968, the Gaucho was a lieutenant colonel and head of the 15th cavalry regiment operating in the district of Las Lomas, in Piura province.

His boss, General Artola, was the one who called to inform him of the coordinated uprising of the Armed Forces and to deliver two startling pieces of news: the Gaucho was expected in Lima, where he would be promoted to colonel and assigned a position as head of the Army's Department of Research and Development.

What he would have given to stay a little longer in the heat of the north, far from the noise and troubles of the capital. The Gaucho despised Velasco's revolution and hated the idea of serving the government that had defenestrated a democratic gentleman like Belaúnde. Nevertheless, in March 1969, when General Francisco Morales Bermúdez, known as Pancho Morales – his friend and the new Treasury Minister – designated him inspector and advisor to his department, the Gaucho began to warm to the revolution. And when, a few days later, he met the enchanting secretary Cecilia Zaldívar and had a presentiment about her, he started to think that luck was on his side and perhaps 'El Chino' Velasco wasn't such a bad guy after all.

Cecilia clearly remembers the morning she saw him enter the great hall of the Treasury office for the first time. He was in civilian attire: thick-framed dark glasses, a turtleneck mahogany sweater under an antelope suede jacket, brown cashmere trousers, freshly polished pointed shoes, a cigar between his fingers and a manly aroma, a mixture of cologne and tobacco that floored the secretaries gathered there. He looked like an actor. A slightly shorter double of Omar Sharif. Even Major Romero Silva, a pettifogger employed by Morales Bermúdez – a boorish little fellow who liked to boss janitors and butlers around, and whom the secretaries found so ugly they called him 'Pot Face' – dropped his usual devious expression when confronted with the light radiating from Colonel Cisneros. It took him several seconds to shut his mouth and restore his usual brown-nosing simper. A few days later, fed up with the advances of Romero Silva, who would hassle her and the other girls in the office toilets, Cecilia requested a transfer to another department. She wanted her old job back in the tax section, where her best friends still worked. Hearing of this transfer and annoyed that he hadn't been consulted, the Gaucho called up the head of personnel and told him in no uncertain terms – chewing on a cigarette or perhaps a cigar, rapping his index finger on the desk – that he needed that Zaldívar girl back in the Treasury office, and that it was actually the cretinous, inept and deceitful Pot Face who should be sent to rot in the Archive, that cold basement where employees either fell ill from the humidity or went mad with boredom.

From that moment on the two of them had direct and daily contact. Sometimes the Gaucho would ask her to eat lunch with him in the office while they dealt with internal ministerial issues and checked over draft legal bills and supreme court rulings. Cecilia would hurry through these sessions to avoid the discomfort of being alone with the colonel, but he'd prolong them with every mouthful, deliberately taking conversational detours, interrogating her about her personal life; she'd respond awkwardly, her head lowered, limiting herself to the task in hand.

'Meeting you is the only good thing that's come out of this revolution for me,' the Gaucho would tell her months later at one of these in-office lunches, gazing at her from the other side of the desk, in an effort to disarm her shyness and show his hand.

These glances must have been like a solar storm for Cecilia. She wasn't indifferent to him, but she knew he was married with three children, and she fought against her youthful nature – she was twenty-one at the time – by taking refuge in her Christian moral upbringing to ignore these pleasant and melodious words no one had ever spoken to her before. It was impossible to expect such gallantry from her boyfriend, Lieutenant Marcelino Álvarez, whose language was rather more rudimentary and whose manners could at best be described as vulgar. If it hadn't been for a certain provincial charm and his unconditional loyalty, Cecilia may never have accepted Marcelino the day he declared his suit with a bunch of dead carnations, blinking rapidly as if he had sand in his eyes.

Although she didn't try to compare them, she quickly noted the astronomical distance between the young Lieutenant Álvarez and the mature Colonel Cisneros. The former was an insecure, kinky-haired lad who knew nothing of life, who would come to pick her up at Pueblo Libre on Friday afternoons, smelling of the same cheap aftershave, wearing the same baggy trousers and the same faded coat, to go to the same cinema, to drive his Volkswagen around the same streets of the Jesús María district, making the same jokes and stopping at the same anonymous street stall to eat the same bland sandwiches. Cecilia scolded him every time he indulged his persistent habit of digging in his ear with his little finger, or when he slapped down her slightest conceit. The colonel, on the other hand, was a dandy of forty-three, enveloped in a cloud of Paco Rabanne, Royal Regiment or English Leather, seasoned in the fine art of conversation, full of wisdom and ideas on the most varied subjects, and who spoke with an attractive Argentinian accent: lilting, full of alluring sh-sounds. But he was married, and the mere fact that he wore a wedding ring made him a forbidden man, at least in Cecilia's eyes. Which is why she'd try to ignore him whenever he found an excuse to enter the office of Minister Morales; she knew he did it to see her, and this brought on a nervous perspiration that distracted her and made her hit the wrong keys on her Olivetti

Valentine. The Gaucho liked to observe her there, sitting up straight behind that red typewriter, silhouetted against the geometric pattern of the office wallpaper, and revisit the sensation that something about her left him overawed. It wasn't just her appearance – the fall of her wavy copper hair, the triangular smile, the spilled constellation of freckles, the shapely legs beneath a suede miniskirt – but something that emanated from her, something guileless and innocent and incorruptible that cried out for protection. He wanted to give her this protection and drink deep, in exchange, of her youth and her energy and her virginity – to rediscover the joy that used to be inseparable from him, but which at Lucila Mendiola's side had turned dry as a pumice stone. Cecilia also possessed a compassionate halo that reminded him of Beatriz Abdulá, and this only served to increase the Gaucho's directness and his desire to get to know her better, to make her fall in love with him, to take her prisoner, to never let her go.

The more he talked to her, and above all the more he listened to her and showed he understood her, Cecilia stopped seeing him as an advisor to the Treasury Minister and began to consider him a work friend. A very special friend. An extremely attentive friend. A friend who would call her into his office every twenty or thirty minutes. A friend who would take her out to lunch or sometimes dinner twice a week, always somewhere new, in search of particular and distinctive dishes: the *lomo saltado* at the Military Club in Salaverry, the smoked trout prepared by Señor Hans on La Marina Ave., the royal hamburgers in the Central Park on Olaya de Miraflores, or the *chupe verde* soup at El Molino de Magdalena. A very considerate friend who would open the car door for her, pull back her chair in restaurants, absent-mindedly take her hand in his until she modestly withdrew it onto her lap. A friend who asked for too much information about her boyfriend, Lieutenant Marcelino Álvarez, who in turn suddenly found himself transferred to a post in the province of Juanjuí, in the jungle beside the Huallaga River, even though he was supposed to remain in Lima for at least another year. A friend who once had her Toyota Tiara removed from the Ministry car park so that she would be late and – anxious about the mysterious disappearance of her car and the impending nightfall – allow him to drive her back to her parents' house. It wasn't till the next morning, discovering her car parked exactly where she'd left it the day before, that Cecilia realised it had all been another trick contrived by Colonel Cisneros.

When she'd ask about his family, the Gaucho would produce embellished lies containing a grain of truth. He'd talk of a wrecked home, of an irritable and uncomprehending wife, of children who grew more distant from him every day. Only for them – he assured her – did he stay with that bad-tempered woman.

However, one Sunday when Cecilia took her mother, Doña Eduviges Berríos, for a ride in her car around the centre of Lima, she was heading down the Paseo de la República boulevard when she caught sight of the colonel's unmistakable green Malibu on the other side of the road, and in the passenger seat she saw a woman who bore a great resemblance to Lucila Mendiola, recognising her only from the family photographs that adorned the colonel's office. 'I had to take her to visit one of her sisters, as a favour,' he would say the next day, by way of unnecessary explanation.

Cecilia was flattered by the Gaucho's special treatment, but she was suspicious of his intentions. Her friends – whom she always referred to in the diminutive as Anita, Carmencita, Martita, Cuchita – advised her not to get caught up in a game that could only leave her hurt and in disarray. They all complained about military men: the more stripes they had, the bigger the womanising liars they were. It was in response to this advice that Cecilia began to cool her tone of voice whenever she heard the colonel at the other end of the telephone, and to gracefully turn down his invitations. He'd invite her to come for lunch at their old places, to drink a few vodka and oranges at the Ebony, to dance to the boleros of Puerto Rican star Tito Rodríguez at the Sky Room in the Crillón hotel or to listen to the piano from the sofas of Seniors on Pardo Avenue. She'd diffidently refuse and the Gaucho could sense her hesitation, recognise her caution, smell her fear – but instead of backing off and leaving her in peace he doubled down on his strategy. He'd fill letters with verses and place them on the windshield of Cecilia's Toyota; he'd leave anonymous boxes of chocolates on her typewriter; he'd send flowers to her house in Pueblo Libre from multiple addresses, leading her father Eleuterio Zaldívar to scold her for leading on so many suitors. Finally, overwhelmed by the insistent attention, Cecilia agreed to talk with him for a few minutes outside of the office. She went to meet him at the Desamparados station café, where the Gaucho awoke her sympathy, professing his sorrow at how distantly she was treating him, and then she gave in and let him embrace her, and only then did she realise that the colonel's mouth was on her mouth.

Throughout 1970 and part of 1971, on the few occasions Cecilia had cause not to turn up at her desk in the Ministry because she was running an errand for Morales Bermúdez, the Gaucho would lose focus on his work, wondering where she could be. The piles of official papers, decrees, memorandums and communiqués he was supposed to be reviewing advanced across his desk and he did nothing to halt them. Her unexplained absence would plunge him into a melancholy that quickly led to stress, dark moods and chain-smoking. On such days, pacing back and forth across his office, he again blamed the military revolution and cursed Velasco for leading it, but he also cursed himself for getting into this convoluted sentimental cul-de-sac. He felt ashamed of chasing after a young woman. At the same time, he laughed at himself because he knew he was in love with her, and this is how he behaved when he fell in love: he became reckless, shrewd, foolish and passionate. His thoughts then turned to Lucila Mendiola and to his children and his household thrown into chaos, until the image of Cecilia – 'Where is she now?' he muttered between puffs of smoke – returned to the centre of his mind, accompanied by a vague but imminent sense of hope, of freedom and of countless second chances.

They fell in love in this hazy, clandestine way, and rumours of their relationship flooded the gossip mill that was the Treasury. One morning Lucila Mendiola made an unexpected appearance in the office with her children. The secretaries all froze when they saw her. She advanced down the carpet between the desks, gazing at them in turn as she passed as if casting an evil spell on each. Then she shut herself up with the Gaucho in his office for almost two hours. When she emerged she walked straight to Cecilia's desk, stretched out a hand that was more calculating than courteous, bent down and whispered in her ear, something like 'I'm leaving because I can see that you're a decent girl.' Cecilia felt like dying where she sat. Lucila's words would resonate inside her for days.

The same week she decided to speak with the colonel to put an end to their relationship and tell him that he should forget about her, that it was better to leave things as they were, that she was sure something bad would come of it. He responded with steadfast opposition, and with a few mysterious and eloquent phrases succeeded in calming her, making her retract, persuading her to stay. It was true that he couldn't stand his wife any longer and that he wanted to leave his home and start over, but it was still too soon. Cecilia heard him, believed him or wanted to believe him, while at the same time remaining sceptical. These were times in which her friends were talking of their future marriages to their long-term boyfriends, of the trousseau, the churches where they might celebrate the wedding. They would pass the time imagining guest lists, decorations for the reception party, honeymoon destinations. Hearing them, Cecilia became depressed and asked herself what she was doing entangled with a man twice her age, a forty-something who passers-by confused with her father or even her grandfather. A relationship in which she was playing the role of the other woman, the substitute, the intruder, a situation that would never give her the chance to dress in white and recite her vows at the altar. On top of that, she had to put up with not only the gossip in the corridors of the Treasury, but also with comments as openly offensive as those made by the head of the National Accounts department, a repressed woman with the aspect of a Nazi sergeant who one morning, upon seeing her pass by distractedly on the staircase, hissed at her: 'Now that you're Colonel Cisneros' flavour of the month you think you're the bees' knees, don't you?' Why did she have to flee such scenes to hide weeping in the toilets, beset by humiliation and injustice? She'd listen to her girlfriends' plans and think of Marcelino Álvarez and other young men who had made their feelings known and whom she had rejected, and she'd imagine herself marrying one of them. In these reveries she saw her parents and sisters beaming with pride, and she felt a tug of desire to return to that false life, which at least gave her something to dream about.

Then just as she was losing heart, she would receive a sign from the colonel – a letter suffused with his cologne, a single glove, a flower plucked from a pot, anything that served as a reminder of what they had together – and she felt encouraged once more, felt that she was in love and determined to overcome the setbacks and transform this burdened romance into a victory that all would be obliged to acknowledge, accept and applaud.

This is how they went about it. They were cautious and discreet lovers, keeping up a façade of reserve in the presence of others before reuniting in the Malibu, whispering together as if they'd met backstage to congratulate each other on their daily performance. Everything went reasonably well until the rumours reached the ears of the minister himself, Morales Bermúdez. One afternoon he called them both into his office. His face was that of a dried-up mummy, and his breath suggested several whiskies had passed his lips.

'Colonel Cisneros, Miss Zaldívar. I don't really know what this is about, but it must be resolved because it has become unbearable. Over the past two weeks I've been receiving complaints from the wives of senior officials. They have nothing better to do than gossip. I wish I didn't have to take any notice of them but I can't feign ignorance any longer. What are we going to do?'

'If I may just say, General,' the Gaucho began, 'that Cecilia is entirely innocent in this whole misunderstanding. If it's necessary, transfer me elsewhere, but I don't want her to lose her job.'

'General Morales,' Cecilia interrupted, 'please don't pay any attention to the colonel. He has a career to think of – please don't damage it by sending him to another post. Send me back to the Tax Department instead, that's where I belong. Things have grown very tense in the office. If the others are going to carry on talking behind our backs, I'd rather not be here to listen to them.'

'No, General, I should be the one to go.'

'No, General, I'm the one who should leave.'

'No, me.'

'No, me.'

'Shut up the pair of you, dammit!' Morales barked. 'No one is going anywhere. If there's something going on between you, that's your business. But please, deal with it without causing a scandal, without all this racket.'

'No, General, it's not what you think...'

'Cisneros, you're free to do whatever the hell you like! All I ask is that you keep me out of it!'

That same night, as the Gaucho drove Cecilia back to Pueblo Libre, they discussed Morales' attitude. The minister was on their side, was letting them off – perhaps because of his appreciation for the Gaucho, or perhaps because he had his own little affair with Teresa Tamayo, the longest-serving secretary in the Treasury pool.

The prevailing sense of tension and impending catastrophe in the country caught up with the Gaucho and Cecilia in early 1971. Lucila Mendiola knew about her husband's romance with his secretary. Initially she claimed it was just a passing weakness – 'One of those infatuations that Lucho sometimes has' – but gradually she realised this was no mere fling, and that they were falling in love more deeply every day. It was then that she began to scheme against this happiness that conspired directly against her own and that of her children. Cecilia's mother, Doña Eduviges Berríos, began to receive disturbing calls in which unfamiliar voices warned that her daughter was a husband-stealer, a home-wrecker. Three, four and then five letters appeared under the door, declaring that Cecilia was a nobody, a little whore who would never be able to marry Colonel Cisneros. Doña Eduviges demanded an explanation from Cecilia. Amid floods of tears, her daughter first denied everything, but then she told her about the Gaucho and confessed that she loved him, and that his wife was a spiteful witch from whom these vicious attacks, and worse, could only be expected.

On one occasion, a nun from the Belén School turned up at their house in Pueblo Libre on the instructions of Lucila Mendiola, introducing herself as Sister Margot. Since Doña Eduviges was very pious and recited the rosary every day, and liked to talk to the priests in the doorway of the Magdalena church, she had no qualms in allowing the nun inside, believing she represented the local parish; she even served coca tea to enliven the conversation. However, when the nun began to tell her that she had to 'open her eyes to her daughter's immoral sins', Doña Eduviges was quick to chase her back out the door.

Cecilia reacted to this intimidation by calling the Gaucho at the chalet in Chorrillos. As soon as he heard a woman's voice he slammed the phone down.

The hostilities waged by Lucila continued throughout the summer of 1971, and given that the Gaucho did little or nothing to keep his wife from hassling Doña Eduviges, Cecilia broke off from him in his office one morning, calmly asking him – and her serenity was what most astonished the colonel – to rebuild his family, to return to his children and forget all about her. She also told him she would ask to be transferred out of the Treasury. He was instantly transformed: he began to shake his head and threatened to commit suicide if she left him. 'I swear that I'll kill myself, I'll throw myself out the window right now,' he warned her with damp, startled eyes, their tiny veins visible.

He didn't say this only to her, but also to the few people in the office who shared the secret of their affair. Martita Rodríguez was one of them. 'You have to talk to Cecilia, Martita, she says she doesn't want to be with me any more, and if she leaves me I'm going to put a bullet in my head, you hear me? I'll shoot myself right now, you understand?' And Martita understood, because she watched as the colonel took out his revolver and raised it to his temple in an act of desperation that she couldn't confidently identify as love, madness or manipulation.

The final straw was the letter that his children, Melania, Estrella and Fermín, under pressure from Lucila, sent to Cecilia. Perhaps, deep down, they did want to say something to this woman they had never met – though surely not with the kind of words they wrote down at their mother's instigation. Perhaps they did want to protest against her intrusion and blame her for something, but not necessarily by telling her that she was 'a gold digger who was only interested in their father's stripes and money' and 'the best thing for everybody would be if she disappeared'. These belligerent words were Lucila's, a hostile missive provoked by the betrayal that was overwhelming her, ventriloquized through her children's handwriting.

When the Gaucho heard about what his children had done, prompted or otherwise, he sat thinking in his Treasury office for a long time. Then he wrote out five sheets of paper by hand and spent hours transcribing them on the typewriter. That night the Dunhills followed one another at a greater speed than usual. That night his window, a vertical rectangle on the sixth floor of the concrete monstrosity, was the only one to remain lit until dawn broke across the city, dispelling the nocturnal dominion of electric light.

My darling children,

I must break my long silence in order to tell you the truth. I have decided to take this step for several reasons. Firstly, the constant sadness I see in your eyes. Secondly, the misunderstandings about the problem I've been facing for several months now. Finally, the letter you have sent to Cecilia. All these reasons lead me to ask you, not just to forgive me, but to grant me an opportunity to be understood.

I have to tell you that there is another woman in my life. It is Cecilia. But just as honestly as I confess these feelings to you today, I want to tell you how it came about and explain the real nature of our relationship. I know that all three of you are grown up enough to understand me and draw your own conclusions.

My marriage to your mother has never been as happy as you have believed. I was never an ideal companion to your mother. In the early years my friends almost always came before the home; later, social commitments and drinking sessions often kept me away; and now it is these feelings that cause my distance. All of this has a fundamental cause. Your mother and I have different upbringings, different views on most problems and different ways of reacting to them. I have always admired the boundless care she shows for you, her constant devotion to the home and her desire to give you all the very best. But at the same time, she has always expressed a lack of trust in me. She has doubted my loyalty and fidelity. Her head was filled with an endless parade of women's names she insisted on linking to me. Her actions were hurtful and offensive. I don't need to describe these reactions as you have witnessed them yourselves, but you may be sure that she has never been right to rebuke *me for a disloyalty that might have caused me to forget my responsibilities towards the three of you.*

Cecilia slipped unnoticed into my life without my even registering a physical attraction for her that might have awoken my instincts. I believe that I have been in love with her since the day I met her and I nevertheless spent more than a year unable to say anything to her. I spoke to her of this for the first time in December last year, and although she too confessed her love to me she has never accepted my feelings precisely because I am married. She has forced me to think everything over a thousand times. She is the one who makes me think of you, of our home. She is the one ready to sacrifice her feelings for me in order to spare you pain. She has repeatedly asked me to stop pursuing her, and this is the greatest proof that she is not interested in my current situation, nor in my status in life. These – you must acknowledge – can only be the actions of a person of honourable feelings and a noble spirit. You cannot imagine how hurt she felt on reading the letter you sent her. She suffers to think that, through no fault of her own, you might take her for a woman of evil intentions, for someone who seeks to rob you of something that is not hers, or who is interested only in exploiting my success or my future career. She doesn't care about the age difference between us, and nor does she care about my money, money you know I do not possess.

Cecilia is, if you will allow me to say so, a good woman. She comes from an honest home, one that is neither poor nor well-off. She is a sensible young lady who thinks that everyone has good intentions, and her moral upbringing allows her to distinguish good from bad, right from wrong. Perhaps her upbringing could be your best ally: she will never do anything that might cause you harm.

As a consequence of the letter she received – which she has shown to her parents – she wishes to leave her job in my department and move as far away as possible, a solution I do not share or support. In fact, I will do everything possible to prevent this from happening.

I know, better than anyone, how much I want to see you grow up at my side, working to provide you with everything a father wants for his children. I am proud of you all in every respect. We have been friends and companions, and I hope we will remain so, even when we follow different paths.

With regard to your mother Lucila, I have to tell you that I married her more out of a desire to make her happy, than with the certainty of having found my own happiness. I have to acknowledge that I have failed in this regard, and I blame no one but myself. She deserved a better life and I was unable to give it to her. I gave her all I could, and never spared any efforts in offering her my support, but it was not enough. The heart of the matter is love and this love has been frittered away in sterile arguments, irrational jealousies and inexplicable reactions. In all this, I beg you to believe me: Cecilia is not at fault. This has been our daily bread for many years now; more than a decade I would say.

Please don't think, my children, that I am exchanging an older woman for a younger one, nor that I am leaving a woman who gave me everything for one who has given me nothing, and still less that I am abandoning a tired woman for one who is full of life. I'm not swapping a pair of old shoes for a pair of new ones. If I have fallen in love with Cecilia, if I truly aspire to joining myself with her in legal matrimony, it is because the human soul cannot resign itself to passing through life trying to please everyone else only to wind up alone in the end. I have a right to my own happiness, just as you and your mother do. Today I can no longer be the source of Lucila's happiness because I cannot sincerely and honourably offer her the affection that she seeks from me. It would be an *act of baseness on my part to deceive her with something that I do not feel. But please don't think that the affection she lacks today is enjoyed by Cecilia. I don't visit Cecilia in her home, and nor has she agreed to be mine. I am in love with her and she has confessed that she loves me too. Nothing more. The only certain thing is that no one is happy as things are: not your mother, not Cecilia, not me, and none of you either.*

Faced with this situation, I must take a decision and I only have two alternatives: to stay at home or to leave. To stay means that I must distance myself from Cecilia, that is, physically separate myself from her and not see her. But do you think that a physical separation can break the bonds of feeling? Do you believe that if I left home the bonds that tie me to you would disappear? Of course not. And if I were to take the other course, do you think that my physical presence at home would be signal enough that your mother and I are united in our feelings once again? This wouldn't be true either. The proof is our situation today: I am physically there, at home, but isn't my emotional absence actually the cause of all our conflict? Do you believe that I don't suffer, thinking of you all?

This is my position. These are my thoughts. Leaving is the most honest course of action, as I see it. Please don't think that moving out means going to live with Cecilia. Until I can find a legal solution, I wouldn't be capable either of proposing it to her or of insinuating it to you. When I leave, because no other path remains, I will go to my mother's house, if she'll have me.

In view of all this, I want to ask you one thing only. If you truly love me and love your mother, whom I hope you can give all your affection and understanding, please don't share the contents of this letter nor the name that appears in it with anyone. The only people I have entrusted with the truth of my life are yourselves, and Cecilia. Please don't disappoint me. Please try to understand me and to remain my best and

*most loyal friends. I'm not asking you to support me or to
take my side, and I certainly don't intend to set you against
your mother. All I ask is that you believe me, and I invoke the
memory of my father as witness. With this truth in your hands,
each of you can form your own sense of my perspective, and ask
me anything you like.*

*I send you kisses with tenderness in my heart, and with
tears in my eyes, but also with the relief of having fulfilled a
duty imposed by my conscience. I cannot live like this anymore.*

*I do hope you can understand me, my little ones. Yet if you
cannot, I won't love you any less and I will always feel proud
to be your father.*

L.C.V.

Naturally, the letter reached Lucila's hands, and it was
during the subsequent hours that the fight took place
involving the flying objects, culminating with the slap and
the Gaucho's departure from chalet 69. The following days
saw him holed up in his mother's house, waging daily combat
with Lucila over the telephone and exchanging ever briefer
letters with Cecilia, the vertigo of the unknown overtaking
his whole being, setting up residence inside him like a
foreign body. Despite his older brother Juvenal's insistence
that he act sensibly, calm down and return home, the Gaucho
was determined not to go back to his wife, and brusquely
truncated these fraternal chats. I'm not consulting you on
my decision, he told Juvenal, I'm communicating it to you.
Juvenal was disconcerted by this stubbornness, attributing
it to the dumb primeval character he saw in his brother. It
may have been around this time that to admonish him for
his negligence Juvenal began to reference him indirectly in
the grammar classes he taught at the Catholic University,

using an example that would became a classic illustration of certain theories on the linguistic sign: 'My mother has two sons: one intelligent, the other a soldier.'

The only thing the Gaucho wanted was to get Cecilia back and to explain to his children – in person this time – why he had left the house in Chorrillos. If you want to help me, he told Juvenal, organise a meeting with them at your house. They respect you; invite them, and I'll turn up later. Thinking it over carefully first, Juvenal agreed to prepare the ambush and called up Melania, Estrella and Fermín.

That afternoon, with the four shut up in Juvenal's study – a carpeted room stuffed with books – the Gaucho asks for their forgiveness and speaks of his unhappiness with Lucila, of the feelings he had gradually developed for Cecilia, of his unconditional love for his children. Fermín and Estrella are disposed to hear out his unconvincing excuses, but they can hardly concentrate between their sobs. Melania, by contrast, isn't even listening. With her deliberately apathetic gestures and slouching posture, she does all she can to show her father that he will never receive her blessing, that the separation has only exacerbated the stress and pain of this period between the end of high school and the start of university. 'You decide to clear out just when I need you most,' Melania tells him with a disdainful look, the rage and disappointment tangling up inside her like barbed wire ensnaring her bones. 'Are you done, Dad?' she asks him at the first break in the Gaucho's monologue. 'Yes,' he responds, awaiting a round of questions or recriminations. But there are no recriminations or questions. Melania stands up, takes her brother and sister by the hand as if they were dolls and leads them out of the room, expressionless, slamming the door behind them.

It is around this time that Cecilia, brought up to date with the news, begins to believe once more that they have a future together. For the first time, moreover, she feels like a part of the colonel's family thanks to the intervention of Esperanza, who not only answers her calls in a friendly manner, but also shows concern for her situation and a readiness to be of assistance.

The Gaucho's mother becomes Cecilia's greatest ally because she sees her own story repeated in her. Over the course of her own lengthy affair with Fernán, from those distant dates at the Palais Concert in Lima to the constant ups and downs of the Buenos Aires period, she had spent over twenty years with the anguish of having to contain herself. She had learned what it means to subject your love to volatile circumstances beyond your control, and to bear the frustrations and aggravations that first tormented and then hardened her. Encouraging her son to leave Lucila and begin a new life alongside Cecilia is her way – not wholly unwittingly – of retrospectively correcting the story she endured with Fernán, as if the present and immediate future were an editing table on which all prior errors could be laid out, an inexhaustible laboratory for improvising experiments and developing formulae so that others may improve on the errors of the past.

Putting into practice her declared support for Cecilia, Doña Esperanza erects an impenetrable barrier between the Gaucho and Lucila, ordering the staff to tell anyone other than Miss Zaldívar who tries to contact the Gaucho by telephone or comes to the door that he isn't home. Despite this barrier, which Lucila Mendiola finds deeply unjust, she views the Gaucho's presence in the house of his mother as a kind of lesser evil. She believes that the familiar surroundings will help him to clear his head before retracting his decision and rebuilding what he has shattered. She trusts that they will once more establish, if not the same, then something similar to what they had in those first years up north, in Sullana, when their marriage was or seemed indestructible, when there were no risks nor anything on the horizon to announce the coming ruin. However, when at the end of 1972 Lucila learns that Cecilia is pregnant and that she and the Gaucho have moved into the second-floor apartment of a building on Aljovín St., her faith vanishes and she unleashes a torrential hatred.

One morning she turns up at their new address and screams the whole street down. When the Gaucho appears at the window, Lucila lets off a tirade of expletives and tosses him a threat like a live grenade, her eyes shining and her mouth twisted: 'I'll have you done for bigamy!' The colonel, in his night-shirt, dishevelled, bleary-eyed, takes the bait and gives as good as he gets, shouting back: 'Go right ahead, all you'll achieve is sending your children's father to prison!' Inside, concealed behind the half-drawn curtain, Cecilia observes the altercation with her six-month belly and a line of sweat on her upper lip, and prays for it to end soon.

The scene repeats itself two or three times during the summer of 1973. On one such occasion Lucila Mendiola rings their doorbell with Fermín by her side. The Gaucho descends the stairs and reproaches her harshly for using their child as blackmail. Fermín never forgot the word 'blackmail', nor the sheer fact of finding himself there, against his will, exposed to the gaze of onlookers, like a helpless notary obliged to testify to the end of his parents' love. Fermín may well agree with Lucila's complaints, he may think the Gaucho is behaving like an imbecile or a narcissist, but he knows he shouldn't be there, knows that he is an unnecessary bystander at this adult spectacle. And it hurts. And this pain will stay with him.

Days later, in an act so lacking in self-respect that it comes off more like the desperate flailing of a drowning woman, Lucila Mendiola informs the colonel in a letter that she is prepared to accept his affair with Cecilia if he will return to live in the Chorrillos house with her and their children. The request elicits no response. From then on, she is increasingly consumed by the sense of having been replaced, plunging her into an anguish that gradually transforms into a vengeful misery. She decides to call or meet up with the wives of other military men to tell them how her husband has run off with his secretary, and rants and raves against the both of them, in an attempt to lower the Gaucho's standing in the Army and to establish a collective animus against Cecilia.

The smear campaign lasts for years and to some extent achieves its goal. At get-togethers of the Gaucho's cohort in the Military Club or in private houses, Cecilia notes an atmosphere of intrigue fostered by a group of women, always the same five or six, who shoot her dirty looks, give her the silent treatment or whisper behind her back.

One morning, Gladis Hoffman calls through the bathroom door to her husband, General Eduardo Mercado, president of the council of ministers at the time and one of the most influential men when it comes to drawing up military promotion lists: 'How can it be that the Gaucho became a general after leaving his wife?'

'I pay no attention to gossip. All I care about is his service record,' her husband replies, as he buttons the collar of his uniform in front of the mirror.

'Are you saying you think it's fine for him to have abandoned his family?'

'What are you on about, Gladis? What does it have to do with you?'

'Come on, my dear Eduardo, everyone knows.'

'I don't know. And I don't give a damn.'

'What's more, he's gone off with his secretary, Miss Goody Two-Shoes.'

'For God's sake, enough! You're like one of those harpies who've nothing better to do than talk about other people!'

'Don't talk to me like that!'

'Then stop pestering me about it!'

'It's just that I don't think a general should...'

'Don't you understand that I don't care? I'd thank you for keeping your opinions to yourself, unless I ask for them!'

'Or what? Are you going to leave the house like the Gaucho did?'

'I'm not going anywhere. If you carry on like this, you'll be the one who's leaving.'

* * *

As Valentina's birth approaches, the colonel feels more deeply involved with Cecilia and with the idea of establishing a second family. Meanwhile, the distance grows between him and his existing children. A thick fog envelops them. The Gaucho doesn't want to lose them, but he does. One night he forgets to pick up Fermín and take him to his graduation party, as he had promised. This is a serious fault, just below the worst mistake he'd ever made, in his son's view: having left the family home four days before his thirteenth birthday. Before that, the Gaucho had forgotten to attend Melania's high school graduation, despite his promise to be in the front row, in the seat finally occupied by uncle Juvenal. The humiliation of that absence shapes the anger that has hounded Melania for some time, and that will remain with her for several years to come. Though she will patch things up with her father before leaving to study and live in France, wounds will remain that are not fully healed. For Estrella, the greatest surprise is to see her father wearing hippy-style shirts, jeans, broad flowery ties and ankle-length boots. None of these would previously have been found in his wardrobe, which used to contain boring clothes in shades of dark grey. 'What discotheque are you taking us to for lunch?' she asks sarcastically one day when he arrives in this attire. Estrella thinks at times that the man who picks them up some Sundays isn't really her father, as if the new garments don't fit with his former personality.

The older children feel that their father is changing too fast, in a clumsy attempt to appear young; and that he is too easily shaking off the past represented by them and their former life together. Which is why they back Lucila each time she refuses to go to the lawyer's office to sign the divorce papers, and they enjoy hearing her on the phone inventing asthma attacks or twisted ankles – it's always the right ankle – that prevent her from getting up to deal with the matter. The older children blame all this chaos on Cecilia, and unintentionally on Valentina, who has just been born. They see her as a blunder, a miscalculation, a gaffe on the part of their father, and they mistrust her because her birth is proof that the Gaucho will forever more have a second family.

As the years pass, however, they grow curious to get to know her. They share the same blood, and they wish to sound out this new trace of their father in the world. What is Valentina like? What gestures do they share? Could they ever get used to her? But despite entering into contact with the little girl, despite taking her on camping expeditions in the mountains organised by their father, despite Valentina's proud habit of gathering photos of these trips into an album and despite the fact that she grows up feeling that she loves and is loved by these siblings, the loss of their father many years later would return her to the only place that had ever truly belonged to her in Melania, Estrella and Fermín's eyes: the place of discord.

Chapter 6

My parents were lovers. They were never legally married. Valentina, Facundo and I are illegitimate children. I could never say it before, but now I find pride and pleasure and satisfaction in using these words, in writing them without shame and without judging or victimising anyone. I had no way of knowing it before, but now I do know that my parents' story, like that of Nicolasa with the priest Gregorio Cartagena, or Luis Benjamín with Carolina Colichón, or Fernán with Esperanza Vizquerra, is the story of a triumphant passion, a passion that goes against the established order. It succeeds in transforming, at least for me, a group of morally and culturally dirty words – 'infidelity', 'adultery', 'bigamy', 'illegitimacy' – into something friendly, clean, dignified, sensitive and human. I feel like embracing these words, gathering them in my arms as if they were beggars or stray dogs. I feel like speaking them aloud and reaffirming them against every occasion they've been done down, every time someone chose to bury them in the depths of their personal biography in order to surround themselves with better-accepted nouns and adjectives. These scorned words, evaded like the vilest insults, the most infectious skin disease, the most abominable sin; these words equated with vermin; these words that millions of lips and hands have avoided out of a dumb fear of contamination by their supposed perversity; these words, I declare, are my inheritance, are part of my heritage or simply are my heritage. They name what has fallen to me; what inhabits me, though I never chose it; what I can neither escape nor ignore, because it has nourished and underpinned my presence in the world.

Let's talk about my presence in the world. So accidental on the one hand, so hard-sought on the other, so unexpectedly and serendipitously located in the middle of a triplex of siblings. Being the second child saved my life, though it may have ruined my childhood. The second of three, the middle one, tends to be the most introverted, withdrawn, sickly, shy. A fibber, inquisitive, maladroit, a reader. Long-memoried, resentful, selfish, laconic, vigilant, dramatic, a tormentor. As a creature of the middle I wasn't interested in extremes, but in the chiaroscuros, the folds of ambiguity harbouring other people's light. I never felt attracted to the moral absolutes of my father nor the functional practicality of my mother. There had to be something in between these two visions of the world, and whatever it was, I wanted to grab it, hold it close, make it my own – because I was the middle: that was my origin. One who is in the middle must dig deep into the very thing that forms his birth mark, his birth wound, so as not to crumble away in the pendulum's swing of being no one, of knowing nothing about himself, not to swing on endlessly with nothing to hold on to. One who is in the middle must delve into the intangibility at his core because something happens there: at the centre of the mind, at the centre of the body and at the centre of the will. Something happens there and I've always needed to know what it is.

If as a boy this was a position I despised, if I observed with envy or arrogance how my parents treated Valentina and Facundo as more likeable or more deserving of affection or care, I now celebrate that this was how things were. It's because I was in the middle, between two bright-burning flames – because I saw things from an irregular orbit, and felt that painful distance without realising its benefits – that

I can stand here today and offer this overview of my investigation to my brothers and sisters too, and even some kind of answer to or ordering of everything we've felt since our father's death. For ever since that terrifyingly imperative man died, we've all stored up some form of rage, rancour, or madness, and we've marked our distance from the axis that once kept us in a tight orbit. No one can emerge unscathed from such a capital death, the effects of which only grow and expand over time, and we are no exception.

The same year we buried my father, Valentina married, throwing herself into the arms of an older man who, like my father, was a soldier, a horseman. She couldn't stand losing our father; we couldn't stand losing her as well, so soon afterwards. In a matter of months we went from being five to being three in that vast Monterrico house. We hated my sister then. Or at least I hated her. About the same time, my younger brother Facundo was transformed – or it would be better to say we transformed him – into a shrinking violet. We feared that the loss of his father would be the end of him, and so we overprotected him and arrogantly sought to guide his steps. In response, he sought refuge in a bunker of isolation, where he took up every kind of activity: piano, poetry, acting, photography, yoga, dance. He was trying to tell us something, to flee an enemy that was stalking him from somewhere he couldn't yet name. Or perhaps he could, which would have been even sadder. We were his enemies. We, who had watched him grow up, were suddenly harassing him mercilessly, obliging him to follow a discipline it wasn't up to us to teach. Taking on the role of surrogate father, I began to correct his behaviour, to offer him a model of authority, and I stifled the natural spirit of our friendship. Facundo not only lost his dad at the age of thirteen, but also his sister and his brother, who had become a scion of his father. It took him several years to escape from the madhouse, but he got out eventually, fleeing that toxic air to convalesce in the mountains, the rivers and the jungle, taking in the energy that his own family had drained from him.

A calamity came down around our heads when my father died, and the fact that we survived it is something we owe to Cecilia Zaldívar. With his death, my mother changed, morphed into a different woman, a better woman, I would say: a stronger woman, divested of ingenuity. A woman with priorities. 'The day your father died was the day I was born,' she suddenly declared to me, over one of those therapeutic lunches that have become our confessionals. At first I didn't know how to interpret this, but I thought her words gave off the echo of a liberating rebirth rather than a resigned emancipation.

Cecilia Zaldívar was a creature shaped by the Gaucho, tailored to fit him. Her social conduct – her way of dressing, how she crossed her legs, the amount of perfume she wore, how she did her hair – was always determined by the macho standards of that totalising man, that man twenty-two years her senior who loved her but inadvertently made her invisible, too. He'd show her off in social settings, introducing her as his wife, festooning her with all the perks and paraphernalia that his military rank and political positions entailed. But then he'd make her just another member of the audience for his monothematic perorations amid the scenery of the cocktail parties, receptions and social events they attended. At these gatherings, if she managed to get the general to pay her any attention and join her on the dance floor even once, it was an out-and-out victory.

My mother lavished affection on the Gaucho, following his suggestions and adapting to his criteria, but she also had a voice and opinions of her own. Setting their stories alongside each other, I realise that there were major decisions they took together, could only have taken together – like the decision to stage their wedding in 1972.

They staged it so that her parents, my grandparents Eduviges and Eleuterio, would allow her to leave their home in Pueblo Libre in peace with God, in peace with the patron saints and with all the provincial deities who appeared in laminated images displayed in niches around their living room. Since Cecilia was secretly pregnant with Valentina and the Gaucho could do nothing about Lucila Mendiola's refusal to grant him a divorce, they had no other choice but to perform a miniature theatre show at my grandparents' house. Innocently believing the ceremony to be real, they wept real tears and waved off the newly-weds with very real happiness.

The performance took place on 18 August and was overseen by an Army administrative official by the name of Romaní, who played the role of the registrar for the municipality of Magdalena. He appeared that day with an ordinary school jotter under his arm, claiming it was the official marriage registry. Mr Romaní was the only attendee who knew it was all a ruse – he and the two witnesses, my uncle Reynaldo and my aunt Rudy. All the other guests were taken in.

There is a splendid photograph from that night – a photo I struggled to get my hands on – showing the happy couple as they celebrate with their guests. There are streamers, mood lighting, glasses of champagne. My father is slim, clean-shaven, wearing a dark three-piece suit with a red tie and unforgiveable cream-coloured socks. Cecilia Zaldívar is heavily made-up but radiant, a purple orchid pinned to her black dress. I love the fact that my mother is wearing a black dress in the photo of her wedding night. It's a statement. I love the fact that my parents staged a fake wedding. I like being the son of that performance. Sometimes I feel like

I'm acting more than living. I suppose I owe this to them.

Years later, they would once again be joined in symbolic matrimony; twice more in fact. They genuinely enjoyed fake marriages, now that I think about it. The second wedding was staged in Mexico, in the vast gardens of a house my aunt Carlota had in Cuernavaca, and was accompanied by a shamanistic ritual of which no record remains. The third wedding took place in the Peruvian consulate in San Francisco, taking advantage of the fact my father had come to attend Army courses in the United States, and at the insistence of his cousin Carlitos Vizquerra, the Peruvian consul in California at the time. He promised to furnish them with a document that would greatly resemble a marriage certificate without exactly being one. Carlitos also suggested my father choose as a witness one of his military friends from Argentina or Chile, who were also attending these courses. My mother set a great deal of store by the San Francisco marriage because it was the only one that would enable her to salvage her honour, with an official-looking document she could produce on the day someone turned up to claim that she wasn't the real wife of General Cisneros.

When we were little, Valentina, Facundo and I organised a wedding for our parents. It was a Saturday, in 1985 perhaps. We waited for them to go out shopping and locked ourselves in their bedroom to decorate it. When they arrived, they discovered a red carpet made from crêpe paper (which my father's shoes tore as he advanced), leading to one of their bedside tables, transformed into an altar. My sister placed a sheet on my mother's head like a veil while I pressed play on the stereo, releasing the strains of Wagner's wedding march. A flower was thrust into my father's hands. Standing on a chair, Facundo played the priest, raising a glass of wine as if it were a chalice and pronouncing the words we had coached him to say. When my five-year-old brother declared my parents man and wife, one of us threw confetti over them. Everything was going well until my mother tired of the game, or felt that it was a farce, and left the room in tears, angrily tugging the sheet from her head.

I grew up believing that the United States marriage was the real one. That was the one I meant when Elías Colmenares asked me to talk about it at one of our first psychoanalysis sessions. It was as a result of this conversation with Elías, of this kind of awakening – noting the lack of photographs of my parents' wedding, the sense of a mystery there, and the realisation that I cared more about solving it than I'd understood – that I decided to embark on what became months and then years of research.

Two years ago I travelled to San Francisco and walked the length of Market St. until I found number 870, before ascending to office 1075, still occupied by the Peruvian consulate. To my surprise, their archives contained no record of that marriage whatsoever. The officials working there recalled Carlitos Vizquerra, but they knew nothing of the document. It appears to have gone missing. Or perhaps it never existed. And that too is why I'm writing this book. Because I need to shout to the world that my parents married three times and that even if none of them counted in the eyes of the law, all of them were valid to me. And also because I need my mother, Cecilia Zaldívar, to understand that the papers don't matter and never mattered in my eyes, that she doesn't need the witness of any court or the approval of any Church or the services of any consul, just as Nicolasa or Carolina or Esperanza didn't, and that this book might be the document they were all looking for, that these pages are the only pages that matter. Here, all of their stories, or my versions of their stories, are safe. This novel is my parents' lost marriage certificate.

* * *

'Yes, your parents were lovers,' my sister Melania told me one night in September 2012 at her Paris apartment, in a peaceful condominium in La Défense. To get there I had had to take line 4 of the Métro at Saint-Michel in the direction of Porte de Clignancourt, change at Les Halles for line A, the red line, and get off at the Nanterre Préfecture stop. To my disoriented brain, this operation felt like connecting aeroplanes with cruise liners and submarines. We had finished the delicious duck confit she'd made and were embarking on the second or third bottle of wine when I found myself asking her questions in the hope of learning about her relationship with our father before he became my father. At that point, her husband Patricio, her daughter Luciana and Peruvian friend Arturo discreetly left the table and headed for the kitchen or the balcony overlooking the illuminated buildings of the financial district.

And so Melania began to revisit those years as if returning to an abandoned house after decades away, and as she moved deeper and deeper inside, clearing away cobwebs and blowing thick dust from every surface, she gradually recognised the shapes of the old pieces of furniture and remembered how she used to play among them. Then she explored rooms that had been shut up for ages, perhaps too long, poking around inside woodworm-riddled wardrobes, peering into chests of drawers, soot-stained chests, shelves strewn with dead insects – and suddenly the nostalgic trip down memory lane grew uncomfortable for her, as she noted presences stirring in the corners, slow-moving shadows that whispered something in her ear as they passed, something that at first she felt an urgent need to hear, but then didn't want to, whether out of fear or respect. Then it was as if she was trying to find her way out, but lost the trail, straying further into this labyrinth of suffering ghosts, stumbling into curtains that fell to reveal new sights, crossing rooms where the temperature suddenly plummeted, and when she finally found not an exit door but a window, she still had the strength to open it or break it and leap out, and then she opened her eyes and there I was, gathering up the pieces of her story, which had started out smooth and serene as a graceful bridge, but at some point lost its solidity and rigour before being smashed into smithereens.

And so Melania tells me about her parents' raging arguments, of how guilty she felt on the day of the separation because just weeks earlier, in the middle of one of those exhausting fights, she had told them it would be better if they weren't together anymore. She had said it without thinking, as a reaction, and when it came to pass, she believed that she had caused it. Melania talks about her mother, but also about mine, Cecilia, and remembers how one Sunday in the 1970s she answered the telephone at home and heard her voice, a voice as young as her own, and wondered then, and still wonders today, why his secretary had to call her father on a Sunday morning during the family breakfast. She remembers another phone call too, which she describes as wicked: all she heard was a baby crying at the other end of the line. She believes the baby was my new-born sister Valentina, and someone was deliberately making her cry into the telephone to send a clear message, a message along the lines of: don't forget that the Gaucho has another family, that another family exists. It could have been Cecilia's idea, or perhaps my grandmother Esperanza's, Melania now thinks, in Paris, surrounded by empty plates. Then she falls silent, searches in her memory and nods to herself, saying yes, Esperanza was behind that call. She says she went straight to the woman's house, determined to kick down the door with all her seventeen-year-old rage, to spit horrible words in her face, words she no longer recalls or doesn't wish to. Esperanza, she says, feigned ignorance and hypocritically cut her off. Then, not changing the subject but turning to a different character, she talks about the Gaucho, but as soon as she speaks his name she breaks down in tears. I'd never imagined she could cry like this. Not Melania, not my intellectual sister, the scholar, the politician, the socialist, the fighter, the lover of all things French. Now she's weeping like a lost little girl as she talks about the man who was her father during the time when he wasn't yet my father but was on his way to becoming so, and she confesses that she could never, ever forgive him for how he treated her mother, Lucila Mendiola. She says she cannot understand why he never said anything about what he felt for this other woman, why the fuck did he stay silent, why the fuck did he wait for the situation to get so unbearable before saying something. It's then that I ask Melania another question, and she looks at me with an improbable mixture of resentment, fondness, tenderness, insolence and sympathy, and she says 'Oh, little brother, of course your parents were lovers, they had been for a long time.' And I clench my fists, holding myself in so as not to explode, because I know what she says is true but no one has ever put it to me this way, and some things, when they're put this way, when someone finally gives voice to them, can be devastating. Which these words are, and all I can do is take them in, bite my lip and keep listening. And what I hear is Melania judging my parents' behaviour, and her words are daggers, daggers I've travelled all this way in search of, because in the end I didn't really want to eat duck or drink wine or look at the lit-up buildings of Nanterre. What I wanted was to bleed alongside my older sister, the one who fled everything for France, the one who has built a whole world here in an attempt to forget about the abandonment and breakup, the desperation and the helplessness.

When the storm passes, Melania regains her usual composure and tone of voice and recounts isolated snippets of information that build up a single canvas. Things like: she never supported her mother's position regarding the divorce; that it was uncle Juvenal and not our dad who paid her university fees; that when she informed Dad of her decision to study in France, he advised her she'd be better off going to the United States. 'What are you going to do over there, in France?' the Gaucho had asked her. And he was so controlling that he sent an ostentatious committee of diplomats and military attachés to receive her as she descended from the aeroplane. She recalls this with a smile, taking off her glasses to wipe her face with a handkerchief, and at that point I realise that Melania chose to leave because she couldn't or didn't want to deal with a family separation that involved divorcing her own father. Because both with her and later with Valentina, the Gaucho maintained a relationship of mutual understanding but also of reciprocal courtship, with a physical closeness that extended to pecks on the lips, romantic embraces, occasional slaps on the bottom and cuddling that, when it came to Valentina, I always found disagreeable and overly carnal. My father was such a womaniser that he even seduced his own daughters.

As a result, Melania was the worst affected by the Gaucho's departure from the Chorrillos house, and in response to this tragedy she decided, consciously or not, to declare war on him. To attack him where it would hurt the most. Not a domestic war, but a social one. She wouldn't go to scream inanities in the street outside his house, like her mother. Instead, she would plot something more brilliant, more intricate; something like organising political activism by the students at her school, the University of the Pacific, to challenge the military government. A government of which her father, Brigadier General Cisneros Vizquerra, was not only a part, but a key part, first as head of the National System for Supporting the Social Movement (SINAMOS), and later as Minister of the Interior, the most hard-line minister in those years that were already very hard.

We speak of 1975, of 1976. Melania is twenty-two, plays revolutionary ballads by Silvio Rodríguez on her guitar, and sympathises with the left, or with certain leaders on the left. One day she joins the FREN, the National Revolutionary Student Front, which brings together students from many universities: San Marcos, Garcilaso, the UNI, La Cantuta and the Catholic University. She enrols first as a member and then gradually climbs the hierarchy as activist, leader and finally spokeswoman. The FREN had just taken part in the protests that followed the historic police strike of February 1975, which was severely repressed by the Army.

As a result of this and other clashes with the regime, the Front issues monthly declarations demanding the liberation of imprisoned students, the restitution of frozen employee benefits and the resignation of, among other military leaders, the head of SINAMOS for his 'ineffectiveness, abusive response and inability to negotiate with grassroots organisations'. Melania drafts several of these declarations and uses them to send messages to her father. The FREN communiqués, with Melania's name among the signatories, reach the desk of General Cisneros, who finds it intolerable that his own daughter has adopted such dangerous and radical ideas and that she is publicly challenging him to resign. He secretly admires her valour and her leadership, but he doesn't yield. The general confronts the conflict with his daughter without ever showing weakness, keeping his paternal fondness firmly in check. He begins by issuing over-the-top warnings down the telephone, urging her to sever her links with the agitators. Then when he realises the uselessness of his exhortations, he expounds on the risks of engaging in violent resistance, and sets out the serious punishments applicable to acting outside the law. These calls are music to Melania's ears, who does the precise opposite of everything her father suggests and involves herself more deeply in her political activism: she becomes the leader of the Revolutionary Front at the University of the Pacific, coordinates actions with other university groups and each week plasters the walls of her department with posters calling for revolution, social justice and a government by the people, for the people.

In August 1975, General Francisco Morales Bermúdez leads a coup d'état against Velasco Alvarado, with the support of the Army, Navy and Air Force. Velasco – who had lost a leg and all his credibility within the armed forces – leaves the Palace of Government for his country residence and Morales declares himself president of the so-called second phase of the military government. This was a continuation of the dictatorship, but with a supposedly more democratic face.

In early 1976 General Cisneros, newly installed as Minister of the Interior, takes charge of monitoring and repressing the street agitators. The national mood is very heated following the Morales-led coup, and the trade unions are ratcheting up their demands, with daily calls not only for fairer working conditions but also for a return to democracy. Dozens of leaders break the orders of the Joint Command and call strikes and stoppages; many end up arrested, imprisoned or deported. By mid-1976 the student front has expanded and become more bellicose. There are daily confrontations in the streets, and a number of university students find themselves in the holding cells of the courts and the dungeons of the State Security forces.

One day at noon the Gaucho invites Melania to his office to propose a truce, an armistice. After speaking with her fellow protestors, she accepts. When she enters the Ministry she presents herself not as the Minister's daughter, but as a student leader. 'You have to stop demonstrating! If they want to demonstrate, let them, but not you!' the Gaucho barks at her in the presence of the other military officials standing behind him, immobile and inexpressive as a set of dummies from a previous century. 'If you want me to leave the Front, if you want me to stop protesting against this unelected government, then release our companions and tomorrow I'm out,' Melania replies, firmly, handing over a list with the names of thirty detained students, including Patricio Laguna, who will later become her boyfriend and then her husband. The General feels he is being blackmailed in his own office. Looking over the list of names, he knows he cannot accept any such conditions.

'I can't let them go,' he declares.

'Let them go, Dad!'

'Why? So they can start with their racket again half an hour later? Forget about it!'

'They're just students, but they're being treated like guerrillas.'

'I'm not convinced they aren't.'

'Dad, they're being tortured! They're being forced to be photographed holding weapons! That's a crime!'

'That's a lie! You're talking just like those dumb journalists.'

'You know they're being tortured! The Bureau of Investigation and State Security are in charge of that.' Melania gets agitated, her cheeks hot.

'If you can't prove what you're saying, you'll be held responsible for this slander, Melania!'

'I'm not lying! You are!'

'You're leaving me no choice than to…'

'Than what? Are you going to lock me up, too?'

'Yes! If you keep organising these uprisings and supporting these vermin, I'll put you in prison. It's over!'

The only ensuing sound is a lengthy exhalation on the part of the general, a cloud of smoke that expands until it disappears into the charged atmosphere in the room.

'You just dare!' Melania screams at him, withstanding this affront, staring at him insolently, wanting to offend him, to contradict him, to demean him in some way before his subordinates, his assistants, wanting to throw herself at him, tear that filthy authoritarian mask off his face and tell him all the hurtful things that are passing through her head but that she can't articulate in time.

That was the last time they ever discussed politics. Melania determined that voluntary exile was the only way to avoid going to prison, engaging with her father or having anything more to do with the dictatorship. She went to Paris with Patricio Laguna and they studied there, had a daughter and established a new life, or rather a newly mended life. When the Gaucho flew to visit her a year later in hopes of soothing the tensions, a turbulent atmosphere settled around them that thwarted the attempt at reconciliation. Perhaps it was the general's intermittent arrogance: he'd often act boorishly, as if he couldn't leave off being Minister of the Interior for even a moment, as if he liked being Minister above all else, as if it hadn't really sunk in that his daughter, the daughter standing in front of him, had moved to another country because of his actions. Melania remembers him inspecting her bookshelves, reading the titles on the spines and declaring proudly, pleased with himself: 'Here in Paris you read the books that in Lima I send to be burned.'

★ ★ ★

Whether to imitate his sister and to continue her legacy, or because one of the three older children had to settle the score with their father – and he had no shortage of desire to do so – Fermín too joined the social struggle, and crossed more boundaries in doing so than even Melania had.

In 1982, the Gaucho was again a minister: the Minister of War. During this truly dark period, when the terrorist offensive was taking lives every day and the government response had descended into a dirty war, when anyone could go out to the corner shop and wind up shot in the head without knowing who had fired the gun, Fermín began to collaborate with the People's Schools run by the Shining Path. In particular, with one school in the settlement of Villa El Salvador where he taught primary-level courses to children who were being raised to one day join a bloody revolution. When the Minister of War learned that his own son was on the list of teachers who were training future guerrillas – which implied he had become a follower of Maoist thought – he went straight to the Catholic University to look for him and didn't stop until he crossed the glass doors of the Sociology Faculty, where Fermín was in his fifth semester. His presence on the campus – his green uniform, dark glasses, thick moustache, a fat cigar in his mouth – intimidated faculty, students and staff alike. The brutish figure of General Cisneros ignoring the entrance protocol, marching through the campus, striding over the lawns it was forbidden to tread on, and angrily banging on the door of a classroom in session, provided the most shocking possible image of the militarism that still believed it ruled Peru. Fermín emerged from the classroom and found himself face to face with this man whose thuggish air turned him into a distorted version of his father.

No one heard precisely what the general said during those two or three minutes that he confronted his son in this rash and malicious way. But everyone knew it wasn't to wish him luck in the upcoming exams. Despite the tears that betrayed him, despite the sweat on his clenched palms, Fermín was brave enough to bear the gaze of his father undaunted – or perhaps he had no reaction at all and remained paralysed as he felt a torrent of rage or disgust rise through his veins. When it was his turn to speak, his nerves disappeared, a nausea accumulated over months or years surfaced, and from his throat there first emerged a convulsive howl, followed by a gobbet of explosive words, which burst in all directions upon contact with the air.

'Let's hope – let's hope it's not me pulling the trigger on the day the revolution comes for you!'

When Fermín recounts this moment, I don't know if I pity him or envy him for being the sole male child to have sparred with General Cisneros, to have challenged the omnipotent power he deployed, to have won or at least contested an argument, to have mocked his megalomania by joining the ranks of the opposition. I admire or envy this in Fermín: that he had full-blown and lasting reason to despise the Gaucho, reasons I have only found fleetingly. I admire or envy this enmity, as well as the harmony the two of them achieved years later. Because theirs was an adult friendship, one that perhaps had debts to pay, but no longer roles to fulfil. On several occasions his father – who is also mine, but at this point in the story is basically his alone – asked his forgiveness for having left the Chorrillos house, and would call him up of a night to talk and drink beer, as men of a certain age talk and drink beer. They met up sometimes in bars in Barranco, in tango clubs in Miraflores, or in Fermín's yellow Volkswagen, which had a good engine and could slip away from Dad's bodyguards through the side streets of Chorrillos. Once they'd left the guards behind, they'd stop by the boardwalk with the lights off, and they could both celebrate their getaway and feel they were on the same side at last.

'I would have loved', Fermín told me on his terrace that long, cold evening, 'I would have loved to enjoy the heights of our father's political career as you did; I would have loved to have been mentioned as the son of General Cisneros in his obituary, as you were.' I hear him say these words and realise they're hard for me to take in. I thought they would bounce off my armour, but instead they penetrate it, painfully. They are words that reveal, with their pain, that my relationship with Fermín will always be touched by conflict, like a choppy sea that drives away swimmers with its dangerous, inescapable currents. 'We never accepted your mother.' 'Your presence, and that of your sister and brother, was an imposition on my life.' 'I cannot love the uncles and aunts you love because they mistreated my mother and allied themselves with yours.' That's how Fermín talks. There's no aggression about him, just a starkness in his speech that I myself sought from him. 'This time I don't want you to treat me like a little brother, I don't want you to protect me, I don't want you to look after me, I don't want you to keep anything from me that I need to know. Go ahead, speak.' That's what I'd asked him to do. And he did. And I had to deal with the consequences.

* * *

Another day, I go to visit my sister Estrella. She has invited me to her apartment in La Molina for breakfast that morning. As soon as I walk in I note the aromatic candles placed in strategic spots, an abundance of incense sticks, a small army of elephants with their trunks pointing towards the door, owls for good luck, and a cup with four limes that, my sister would later explain, absorb any negative vibrations that might enter the house. Though I know nothing about *feng shui*, I have a suspicion that the furniture is arranged in accordance with the holistic order it prescribes. On one wall hangs an image of Hunab Ku, the Mayan god of creation. My sister believes in this deity and can read the Mayan calendar, which she uses to detect the energies that govern our universe. She taught my brother Facundo to read it too. Thanks to them both, I know that my Mayan sun sign is Storm, which means I am restless, free-spirited, friendly and energetic, though this may sound more like the description of a rabbit. I used to mock their beliefs in silence, judging them to be crass and esoteric. Now I've come to take an occasional – or expedient – interest in them. When I feel that things aren't working out, I'll call them to ask when the cycle of the next sign begins – the Hand, the Serpent, the Warrior, and so on – and what kind of attitude it will demand. Just as people turn to the weatherman to plan their weekends, sometimes I consult my mystical siblings for their spiritual forecasts, so I can know what to expect. Estrella is loquacious and expansive. She's like a slow-moving river, one tired of its course. She lacks Fermín's analytical acuity and Melania's intellectual spirit, but this means her version of events is infused with magnificent sentimental details. For moments at a time, I disassociate myself from what she's saying and look at her eyes, two expressive green rays over which a glaze of sadness has set, and I think about how there are pairs of eyes in the world – like hers, like my father's, perhaps mine too – that fail to hide their melancholy. All human eyes fail at some point, but some fail more often. Estrella's eyes are among them. I hear her recount her parents' relationship through scenes from her childhood and domestic life. It feels like she's talking about a film, not about her own life, or about life in those rare moments when it resembles a movie. Though her narration

135

is clearly biased and comes accompanied with opinions I find somewhat irritating, I believe what she says, because she too is the second sibling of three, and shares with me – or I share with her – that same angle of vision from which events can be observed from a distance and in hindsight. She too is from the middle. To be from the middle is to witness the spectacle of family life from a privileged perch. I'm also fond of her because we share a teeming history of illness: from viral chickenpox, mumps, measles and asthma to claustrophobia and somnambulism. It unites us. We are united by our father, by our talent at getting ill and because our births were emergencies: we were both entangled in our umbilical cords. When her mother, Lucila Mendiola, arrived at the maternity ward, the shift doctor took one look and said breezily: 'I can guarantee the mother's life, though I can't say the same about the baby.' My father stared at him stonily and responded: 'If you don't guarantee me both, then I won't guarantee yours.'

That morning my sister shows me letters, photographs, notes, a whole stationers' worth of documents supporting her version of her parents' mutual adoration. She describes them as a man and woman who were born to be together. By contrast, when she describes the relationship between her father and my mother, she portrays a story filled with mistakes, short-sighted and immature decisions, deceit, conspiracies and nefarious blockades imposed by third parties. It hurts me that Estrella leaves no possible room for love between my parents, that she doesn't consider the possibility that her father and my mother simply fell in love. Her compartmentalisation is understandable, she has the right to tell things this way, but I cannot avoid feeling a bit humiliated when I realise that, in her reading, what happened between the Gaucho Cisneros and Cecilia Zaldívar was the product of a chain of blunders that could or should have been halted. I ask myself how many friends of hers must have heard only her telling of the story, and I wonder too how many sources we really need to disentangle the morass of private stories that surround us.

After our dad died, Estrella tells me, many injustices were committed. 'Like what?' I ask, lighting another incense stick. 'The sabre of dad's that they gave you at the funeral should have gone to Fermín, as the oldest son,' she says. Her words transport me to the morning of the burial, to the moment when an Army officer presented me with my father's military cap and sabre. Holding these objects, I remember, meant that my hands were full when all I wanted was to cover my pain-crumpled face. 'And in the newspaper reports on the funeral', Estrella continues, 'they named your mother as if she was the widow, when we all know that the true widow was really my mother.' Yes, I think later, perhaps those obituaries should have been more specific and reasonable and legally accurate, and declared the truth: that Lucila Mendiola was the official widow of General Cisneros and that Cecilia Zaldívar was just the woman he loved until his death, the woman to whom he entrusted his last words, the woman who closed his eyes.

* * *

The day after I visited Melania in Paris, with her words still rattling around in my head, I went to look for the building where we lived for almost two years, on the steep, tree-lined streets of Saint-Cloud, in the west of Paris, near the Seine.

My parents, my sister Valentina and I moved there in June 1978 when my father was made military attaché at the Peruvian embassy. He was already a lieutenant general, and having been Minister of the Interior, he would have expected to be promoted to a senior post in the Joint Command, or perhaps another political position. However, following a personal conflict with President Morales Bermúdez, he was put up against the wall and told: either he retired from the Army, or he accepted the military attaché position in France – a position intended for brigadier generals – or one as Peruvian representative at the Inter-American Defense Board in Washington. Morales Bermúdez, influenced by advisors with their own interests, believed that a triumvirate composed of General Cisneros, General Arboleda and Admiral Cantoni wanted to overthrow him. He was told they conspired against him every night in the Gaucho's car, and it was Cisneros who intended to anoint himself president.

Morales was under pressure from both sides. The political parties were demanding he call elections immediately, while military circles had no desire to hasten the return to civil government. As a result, he felt insecure, remembering that my father had collaborated with him in overthrowing Velasco when the communists had infiltrated the government; remembering too the rebellion against him led by General Centurión just two years earlier. This fear led him to doubt the Gaucho's loyalty and to believe the best option was to keep him far from his circle of influence for a while. Friends of my father claim that he was the victim of a cowardly conspiracy led by General Omar Merino Panucci, a troublemaker and vampire-faced miser who had earned the nickname of Two-Bit among his college cohort.

These accounts, which portray my father as maligned and conspired-against, contrast with what I was told by 'El Zambo' Garcés on New Year's Eve when I finally persuaded him to talk about what he knew. El Zambo worked for years at our house, grew up with us and spent many a late night talking with my father – as well as listening to the drink-fuelled monologues in which he hawked up secrets from the Ministry of the Interior as if under the effects of a truth serum. My father held the rookie soldier, who was of mixed black and indigenous ancestry, in high esteem and had asked him to come to my grandmother Esperanza's house to help out with household chores. El Zambo quickly showed himself to be hard-working and willing and won the trust of the whole family. Over the years we adopted him almost as an older brother and confidant: Valentina and I asked him to sign our failed exams so our parents wouldn't see them, to lie on our behalf, or to accompany us to places we weren't allowed to go by ourselves.

My father told El Zambo a lot of things he may not have shared with anyone else. He did so because he needed to speak them out loud, give them voice, and because he knew that in his ready, friendly ears, all compromising information would automatically disintegrate. El Zambo's ears were like shredding machines that converted the most top-secret documents into tiny strips of paper.

Years later, at my mother's house, I find myself seated beside El Zambo on New Year's Eve. We eat turkey and have a drink, though he only drinks tea since his conversion to Mormonism, leaving behind his hard-drinking lifestyle, and he makes no exceptions for holidays. El Zambo tells me that one night, arriving home late from the Ministry of the Interior, my father confessed to him that he ordered wiretaps on the leading politicians of the day, and that he had a constant tail on the president himself, Morales Bermúdez.

'I have that bastard Morales by the balls,' my father said to El Zambo Garcés one night in 1977, as he administered himself a whisky, or it might have been cognac, or wine, or even just a cup of black coffee. But this expression, 'I have him by the balls' – perhaps because it led him reflexively to imagine the grotesque image of a naked Morales, his testicles in my father's grip, is crystal clear in Garcés' memory. He is restrained as he tells me all this, as if he still harbours information he will never reveal, hard and weighty facts that he himself, even after all these years, has not fully processed or understood. When I go to bed, with the sound of distant fireworks becoming ever more intermittent, it is with the bitter feeling of never having fully known my father. The feeling that for all the years we spent in close proximity, his darkest, densest and most fearsome areas were always far out of reach, completely inaccessible, exceeding my adolescent understanding of the world.

My father agreed to go to France so as not to satisfy his adversaries in the military who wanted to see his career hit the buffers. 'Don't fall into their trap,' his closest colleagues advised. He listened, and left for Paris, taking us with him. His anger with the president, however, took time to dissipate. My father felt that he'd been sent to the scrapyard, into an involuntary exile, and he made this very clear to everyone who sought him out in his small office inside the Consulate General of Peru, on Rue de l'Arcade. One such visitor was the writer Julio Ramón Ribeyro, drawn by curiosity to meet this general who had arrived from Peru with a reputation for speaking loud and clear. He and Ribeyro shared many coffees in the bustling *brasseries* along Kleber Ave., and many walks up Rue Copernic to Place Victor Hugo.

Today I'm walking the streets of Saint-Cloud with a knot in my stomach, because I want to see the house where I spent that period with my parents and sister. My niece Luciana offered to come with me, and here we are now, walking, stopping to check the map, sharing one and then two joints. We climb a set of stone steps, and a couple of minutes later, there it is in front of us: number 17, Rue

Dantan. This is the apartment building where we lived in 1978-1979. Peering through the gate I can just about recognise the flat we occupied. Everything looks smaller.

I've brought along a photograph of my mother, that shows her waving from the bedroom window. It's a wide-angle shot, most likely taken by my father a few days after moving in. My mother is barely a dot, a tiny silhouette. She is separated from the camera lens by a cluster of stark trees, a wire mesh fence, a carpet of dried leaves and a sliver of sky. The trees, the leaves and the sky are all still there. The window too. The wire fence has been replaced by a more modern and robust railing.

'There's no one around,' I say to Luciana. 'It'll be hard to get in.' Noting the tranquillity, the type of railing, the general orderliness, I remark that it seems a very conservative neighbourhood. Luciana nods and corroborates my impression. 'This is the most far-right district in all of Paris. Two blocks from here, on Rue Vauguyon, is the headquarters of the filthy National Front, and five streets further on is the house of its founder, the disgusting old Jean-Marie Le Pen. Know who I'm talking about?' 'Sort of,' I reply. 'He's a fascist, a Neanderthal who wants us all to go back to colonial times.' 'That bad?' I wonder.

'You have no idea who Le Pen is!' Luciana fumes. 'He's against immigrants, against communists, against Jews, against gays, against contraception, against abortion, against equality, against the prohibition of the burka in public places, against globalisation and even against the euro!'

I listen to her rising indignation and think about how Luciana is just as political and socialist as her mother, my sister Melania. I imagine her rapping onstage about incendiary issues in the dimly lit bars of the Paris underground scene, where she already has a certain reputation. I feel proud of her, even though I've had no influence whatsoever on her worldview and much less on her talent.

Having seen the reserved character of the neighbourhood, I can't imagine that anyone would let us wander around the building, and so I resign myself to gazing at our flat from the street. Luciana, calmer now, asks me why I keep on talking about it as 'our flat', as if we still lived there, as if it were 1978 and not 2012. In silence I travel down the tunnel through time and visualise my family emerging from the building, newly arrived from Peru, so young and full of optimism, so impeccably happy, so determined to get through each day despite their terrible French. I imagine that married couple passing by my side, imagine following them through the neighbourhood, treading on the fallen leaves along Rue Eugénie, as they take their two children to the park that's practically a nature reserve, or the Église Saint-Clodoald opposite the Town Hall, or the Le Chapelin Fretz flower shop, or the boarding school. I imagine watching the children as they ask to stop so they can gaze at the window displays of Le Bon Marché, with the shiny metal cars on sale, or to look at the market stalls set up around the square. I imagine the family spending their Saturday wandering the fountains and gardens of the Palace of Versailles, visiting the Museum of Man on the Trocadero or driving the five miles of roads around the safari park at Thoiry under the alternately cautious and ferocious gaze of monkeys, giraffes and lions. I imagine this family at different places all across Paris and I wonder what would happen if I approached them. How would I introduce myself? Would I tell them that I'm their son from the future? Would it be right to tell them what will come to pass? To tell them, for example, that they'll have a third child called Facundo who will become a pianist? Would it be a good idea to tell the father – my father – that he will retire from the Army within five years and will be mercilessly killed by cancer on

142

the morning of 15 July 1995? Would it be a good idea to tell the mother – my mother – that in six years' time she'll be living in a house with a garden in Monterrico, Lima, where she'll grow old magnificently among her plants, her dogs and her grandchildren? Would they believe me? And what would happen if I approached the girl in plaits, my sister Valentina, and informed her that she will grow up to study law, that she'll ride horses behind her father's back and will marry military men not once but twice: one from the Army and one from the Air Force? Would she take me seriously? Above all, I'm intrigued by the face that the gap-toothed little boy dressed up like a snowman would make – that little cry-baby, me, who doesn't want to sleep at boarding school and yells that he wants to go play on the swings. What face would he make if I told him that he'll someday end up bearded and alone in a room, writing down the concentric memories of this fictitious encounter? He'd probably throw a nut or a pebble at me, and run to hide behind those tree-like columns that are the legs of the Peruvian military attaché who is his father. Perhaps it would be wiser not to approach at all, just to watch them with a benevolent gaze. Better for them not to know how badly life will treat them.

My mental digression is cut off by Luciana's shout when a white-haired, aquiline-featured watchman finally appears. No matter how much we plead, he refuses us entry to the condominium. All we want to do is take a look, we call to him, but he ignores us as if we were a couple of squirrels, or rats. He is unmoved by my family history and doesn't even glance towards the photograph of my mother I hold out. Luciana asks him for the names of the current occupants of the flat and he just snorts. His reserve is disproportionate, absurd. He's like a former secret service agent who's been punished for some misdemeanour and been sent to patrol apartment buildings on the other side of the river. 'All we want to know is the surname so we can leave a note,' Luciana says in impeccable, formal French. '*Oui, oui,*' I chorus. The man barely separates his lips to enunciate three syllables. Ma-rre-cau. The Marrecau family. And so Luciana and I sit down on the kerb to write a note telling Monsieur Marrecau who we are, why we're there and how we wished we could have met in person to tell him that a Peruvian family lived in his apartment thirty years earlier, and were happy there. We try to hand it to the guard but he refuses to take it, insisting that he couldn't be responsible for ensuring it reaches its destination. Luciana reproaches him for his lack of consideration and goodwill, and now the man – who we are sure must be a follower of Le Pen – is rudely insisting we leave and insulting us with words I don't understand but which sound racist, when suddenly a taxi comes to a halt in the street and a blond man emerges who heads for the building. Luciana intercepts him and asks if he could please deliver our note to Monsieur Marrecau, and the blond man takes the piece of paper, reads it, smiles and tells us, his tone both gentle and surprised, that he is Philippe Marrecau. And so we laugh and cry at the coincidence, and to his bemusement we hug him like an old friend. Though he takes a quizzical look at our video camera and our (or rather my) tourist attire, Philippe seems persuaded by our Latin passion and allows us to come in. As we proceed towards the building entrance Luciana raises her middle finger in the direction of the guard, and I hurl a '*conchatumadre*' at him, knowing he won't understand, with the euphoria of someone experiencing a rare miracle. A few minutes later, when Philippe opens the door to the flat, I am overcome. My mind begins to violently release memories I had no idea were even there, memories that emerge as anxious and excited as if they'd been waiting all these years for the right trigger: the view of the balcony with its flowerpots, the layout of the bedrooms, the texture along the edge of a wall, the light on the kitchen tiles. I'm overwhelmed and swallow tears like saliva. At Luciana's request, Philippe Marrecau tells us a little about his life – he works as an aeroplane engineer, he's married, has two children – but I can barely hear him, my senses are confused, cancelling out or overlapping each other. Then he remarks on the previous occupants, who followed us in the early 1980s, and among their names he mentions the trumpet player Georges Jouvin – whose melodies I'm listening to now, as I write these words – and suddenly I feel that the flat, like every home in the world, has a history that deserves to be told, because its rooms were occupied at different times by three men who never met, who form something like a cosmic fraternity that is strange and wonderful to imagine: an aeronautical engineer, a military attaché, a celebrated trumpet player. They have nothing in common but the fact of having lived in these rooms where they ate, slept, made love, made plans, saw their children grow up, had hopes and dreams, missed people and left a part of themselves behind. And so I feel that I've come to collect the part left here by my father, and I accept it as a mission that cannot wait any longer, and head to the balcony to breathe deeply and look at the gardens from this height. Luciana goes downstairs and out into the cluster of stark trees, and from there she takes a photograph of me to match the one of my mother. With that, I bring the visit to a close, offer my thanks to Monsieur Marrecau in deplorable French and bid him farewell in the universal language of an embrace.

Emerging from the condominium, I suggest to Luciana we walk around the neighbourhood and share another joint. As we wander through these rediscovered streets, this disinterred neighbourhood, I feel reconciled with my father. During my conversation with Melania the day before I'd hated him for how he'd gone about it all, for how long it took him to make his romance with Cecilia public, for the silences that sharpened my older siblings' resentment towards my mother and towards us. But today I feel like I shouldn't judge him, that I am in no position to judge him, and I'm moved to value the life he gave us in Paris, and to thank him for having swallowed his pride and accepted a posting below his station, for being smart enough to leave the country. As I think about him I fervently wish I could have him beside me again, or that I could just see him alive once more, crossing the street, disappearing among the blurred silhouettes of the cold passers-by in Saint-Cloud.

Chapter 7

My great-grandfather was a bastard. My grandfather was an exile. My father was a foreigner. Three illegitimate, uprooted men. Three public men who defended their reputations and idiosyncrasies but privately, when alone with themselves, railed against their silence-filled origins. First ignoring and later burying the thornier details of their pasts, they turned their backs on the intrigues of their shared history, embarking on a course of permanent disorientation from which each tried, in his own way, to escape.

The three were careful to guard their centre. They protected themselves. They revealed little. The noise and fuss they made in public was simply a tactic to keep people from asking about the silence that filled them like a black liquid someone had poured into them long ago. All three, in addition, played different characters. Luis Benjamín was the accomplished poet. Fernán, the precocious editor of *La Prensa*. And my father, the hard-line, authoritarian minister of state. These were their roles and their alibis. And all three employed them with the unconscious aim of distracting attention from their family biography. They constantly raised their voices, but this was just another way of remaining silent. Their sense of illegitimacy, their unease, their rootlessness, made them jostle to stand out from the rest, to seek recognition. Their insecurity was so great, and so little did they do to accept the underlying realities of their lives, that they became public men to compensate this centuries-long solitude. All three were men of renown in their fields who never let themselves be known. All three were condemned to leave. All three underwent sudden changes, and then could not or would not – save for moments at a time – be the men they once were. All three became divided men, forced to harden their skins. And perhaps this is the source of the pattern that conceals the answer I'm not looking for. Perhaps it's about trying to be someone in a different place, in a foreign land, somewhere uncomfortable. Perhaps it's about leaving for distant shores. Erasing and exiling yourself. Or maybe not. Maybe it's just about writing. Maybe writing means exiling yourself. Maybe this book is a discreet form of exile.

My father, I realise today, became territorial to stop himself from going crazy. It was the only way he knew how to protect himself from the trauma that hounded him. He had come into existence deprived of any geographical reference point that could grant him a place in the world. He was Peruvian and also Argentinian, and he bore his foreignness like a fly trapped in a glass heart. When, at the age of twenty-one, he was the first of his siblings to make the decisive journey to Peru, he trembled not with excitement but with fear. In the letter he wrote to his brother Juvenal as soon as he arrived in Lima, on 11 September 1947, he tells him: 'You know, brother, because you already guessed, how scared I was of coming to Peru.'

His dual nationality or his indefinite nationality, his umbilical cord split in two, intensified by the exile of his father and the obscure genesis of his surname, caused irreversible damage to any sense of belonging. My father dealt with this from the most solid ground he could find, and from there tried to break the bonds that tied him to this uneasy inheritance he never knew how to name, to judge, or to face. To avoid being dragged down by these burdens, he decided to look only inward. I'm not lying when I say that my father only believed in himself, in the superman he believed himself to be, and that he automatically mistrusted everything that lay outside the scope of his understanding. Like science, for example. That's why he shunned doctors and medical treatments. Every time my mother pestered him to take the pills the doctors prescribed him, Amoxil, Benerva, Rivotril, he'd say, 'Leave them on the bedside table, I'll get to it later.' And when it came to the cancer, he disregarded chemotherapy with an unthinking disdain that would only hasten his decline.

He didn't believe in science, or in religion. He never prayed, and the few times he attended church he did so with military discipline, refusing to open his mouth to repeat the words of the liturgy, or to sing or take communion. He went to mass like someone accepting a punishment and stoically endured my mother's staunch Catholicism, as if by doing so he might shake off some unspeakable sin or error. Properly speaking he was neither agnostic nor atheist, simply a rock immune to the warmth of faith; his proverb was 'I am my own god.' What could there be, then, behind a man like my father, who believed in nothing and no one, who so rationally and obsessively set the boundaries of his domain, who rigorously established landmarks and borders, who jealously oversaw his territory, who controlled and manipulated his wife and his children? What could there be but the marks of an absence, an abandonment, that was not only a geographical abyss, but a bloody wound that had scarred over at an early age?

As far as I could see, my father wanted something for his children, at least for us younger ones, something that he'd never had. A specific dominion. A redoubt barricaded against the racket of the world. A bunker protected from everything going on outside, untouched by the distant sounds or terrifying explosions of the war that was shaking the country. To furnish us with this territory he got heavily into debt, but it was the only way to build that grand house in Monterrico, the most emblematic of all those we lived in. We had occupied a rented apartment on Aljovín St. and a house allocated by the Army on Grau de Piura Ave., and we'd sometimes stayed at my grandma's house on La Paz St. in Miraflores, near the ravines of Barranco. But the Monterrico house was our real home, the only one we ever owned, the one with the big garden, trees and palms, the pool, the double terrace, the grotto with its waterfall, the patios, the glass atriums. It was the winter barracks that my father erected for his Army retirement and for us to enjoy our own private world, a miniature country where we lacked for nothing.

We shared this house with him for eleven years. There he fell ill, there he suffered his heart attack, there he died, there his wake was held, there he seems to wander still. He had never before spent so long at a single address. Throughout his life in Buenos Aires and his military career, he'd done nothing but flit from one house to the next, always travelling, always on the move, always ready to leave wherever he'd just arrived. With Lucila Mendiola and their children he lived in the north, in Sullana, Las Lomas, Chocope, Querecotillo, and then in Chorrillos – all military postings. When my father walked out on his family after his relationship with Lucila became impossible, he lived for a while at his mother's house. Lucila then moved to a house on a street called Berlin, near the sea. From then on, Berlin St. would become another emblem, another name charged with meaning. Whenever my father left for his weekly lunch with my older brother and sisters, my mother would tell us, 'He's gone to Berlin,' and that was enough for us to understand the situation. They were waiting for him on Berlin St., but so was Lucila Mendiola, who in those days surpassed herself in her table decorations, paying him every attention, sending flowers to herself to see if she could awaken, if not jealousy, then at least the curiosity of her ex-husband. Other times, when my mother argued about my father's timorousness in response to Lucila's repeated pretences designed to stave off the divorce, she would reproach him for his supposed favouritism 'towards Berlin'. 'So why don't you go ahead and move to Berlin?' she'd say on some tense nights, leaving me unable to sleep, worrying that the argument would end with my father leaving our house too and going to Berlin, or to another house and another woman to have children I would surely despise. Berlin was Lucila and my older siblings. Monterrico was my mother and us, the three younger ones. My father struggled to make his six children all feel like part of a single clan. For my part, I make an effort to see Melania, Estrella and Fermín as my real siblings. Sometimes I feel that we manage it, that our affection flows like a deep river. And yet, because of decisions we didn't make and words we didn't say, a vast sea still separates us. A sea that pulls us in different directions and demands our loyalty – not to that shared ocean that is our father, but to the river mouths that are our mothers, the ones we saw go over the precipice in different epochs, different ways, different bedrooms. One ruled over Monterrico. The other over Berlin.

My father's other home was the Army. Yet even within the Army he was an outsider. A rare bird even in that cage for exotic birds. Unlike the Peruvian officers, who had absorbed the French *esprit de corps* that has guided Peru's military since its origins, my father was educated by the German-inspired Argentinian army. This provenance helped determine the toughness of the public figure he became when he began to occupy high-ranking positions. He had spent his years as a cadet in Buenos Aires with men who, decades later, would become the leaders of the dictatorship in Argentina, and subsequently grotesque celebrities, sentenced in public for torturing and killing. Long before they became murderers, these men were his friends. Afterwards, too.

* * *

My father possessed a refined and persuasive rhetorical ability that went well with his vocation as a teacher: he always sought to instil in the soldiers under his command a mystique that was entirely natural to him, rather than inundating them with technical lessons. This he may have inherited from General Pedro Cisneros, the beloved brother of his great-grandmother Nicolasa, a military man with long sideburns who lost his right thumb in the battle of La Palma, in Miraflores, in 1855. Though he barely seemed aware of his great-uncle's existence. Once when a journalist asked him if military service ran in the family he answered: 'No. I'm the only soldier in my family. There are stories about a General Cisneros in the Wars of Independence, but that's all.' Brief comments like these express my father's near complete lack of interest in tracing his genes or his ancestors. He knew the cracks he'd crawled out of, but had no desire to explore them.

His professional qualities, on the other hand, reveal a side of him that was an awkward fit with his personal cosmos. His military persona was formed of other traits, other intents. Among the many papers I found rooting through his file that time at the Little Pentagon were the annual performance reports written by his immediate superiors. They described him in the following terms: independent in his actions, a well-defined personality, irreproachable conduct, professional knowledge, exemplary in his integrity and discipline, sincere, loyal, affable, trustworthy, of excellent morality, of unblemished honesty, self-sacrificing in service, logical in his thinking, practical in spirit, strong sense of justice, marked spirit of collaboration, punctuality and accuracy, exceptional civility, high level of general culture, remarkable intelligence, great rigour in his work, resistance to fatigue, good sense of taste, neatness in dress, virile, healthy, discreet, strong, suitable for the campaign. These documents were signed by some of the most respected or feared figures in the Peruvian Army in the late 60s and 70s. Generals such as Nicolás Lindley, Tomás Berenguel, Gastón Ibáñez O'Brien, Armando Artola Azcárate, Víctor Helguera, Ernesto Montagne and Francisco Morales Bermúdez, who would later become president.

As I read the reports I thought about how little any of these descriptions could be applied to me. No one would describe me using these categorical concepts, these combinations of adjectives. I was struck by the term 'well-defined personality'. Perhaps because, unlike my father, I had never had a defined way of being. Long past adolescence, I continued to imitate other people's personalities: gestures, words, different ways of laughing, of walking, of thinking. For over thirty years I have been the sum of my fears, my desires, my envies, my longing to stand out. I never felt any sense of self-certainty. As soon as a more confident person appeared, I would adopt his manner, his pet phrases, everything that made him what he was. What for him may have been a useless imper-fection I recycled as a virtue. This gave me a provisional outer strength, while inside my insecurity expanded like grimy foam on a beach. Sometimes I wish I had – apart from all my innate characteristics – a personality like the one his superiors saw in my father. A 'well-defined' one.

* * *

After my father died, my uncle Reynaldo collected all the newspaper cuttings about his public life and organised them into ten binders.

There are the articles from newspapers and magazines that preserve what the Gaucho Cisneros said and what they said about him. There are hundreds of cuttings, dating back to 1970, which briefly mention his earliest appearances as general inspector at the Treasury, up until the obituaries of 1995. Twenty-five years summarised in these binders that smell of damp and whose metal rings are stained with rust after years buried in a trunk in the basement at the Monterrico house, where they slowly filled with mildew and those agile, shiny little insects called silverfish, which scutter through the pages of old books with their long antennae.

Reading today the news articles featuring my father, I realise how little I knew of the affairs he was involved in. I only had the most general idea of his actions during the governments of Morales Bermúdez and Fernando Belaúnde, and I was unacquainted with most of the countless statements and actions that led him to become such a controversial figure, and to acquire fame, power, admirers and enemies. He was a man who spoke directly in a society accustomed to evasion and digression. He was full-on, firm, bold, lucid, sometimes even prophetic, but also crude, irresponsible, obstinate, negligent and loud-mouthed.

Reviewing this immensity of yellowed cuttings is to imagine my father speeding through successive periods in fast-forward, and to recognise some of his indelible characteristics: his wit, for example, which invariably surfaced as soon as someone challenged him. On one occasion, a certain General Sánchez, who went by the nickname 'El

Loco' Sánchez, was determined to enter a military building on horseback, even though he knew it was prohibited. My father was in charge of the guard post, and when he saw the general's insistence, he stood in front of the gate and reminded him of the regulation.

'Forgive me, General, but you must dismount. You can't come in like this.'

'Don't you know who I am? I'm El Loco Sánchez, so open the gate!'

'You might be El Loco Sánchez, but I'm El Loco Cisneros and I'm in charge, so get off that horse!'

He earned himself a week's suspension for disobeying a superior. But such punishments had no impact on his provocative character. In 1973, at a crowded military meeting in the Palace of Government, the dictator Velasco asked him – either to unsettle him or to openly mock him – whether he was any relation of that Cisneros Mattos whose name had appeared on a list of suspected guerrillas who had been captured. The president's question was met by copious laughter. My father responded: 'I don't know, General, but I'm sure you agree that families are like de facto governments: we don't choose them, we accept them.' Velasco responded with a tight-lipped smile that barely concealed his fury and issued the order that Colonel Cisneros was not to set foot in the Palace again while he was president.

Still, it wasn't this incident, or the recollection of this incident, that led my father to conspire against Velasco many years later. It was the firm belief that his mandate was unacceptable because of Velasco's affiliation with communist sympathisers.

In 1975, a sector of the Army anxiously watched the government's growing instability after the widespread police strikes in February; the ruthless response to the strikes resulted in deaths, injuries, protest demonstrations and a wave of vandalism and looting of shops, markets and public buildings. The city hadn't seen such chaos for many years. The political discontent continued and neither Velasco nor his ministers could guarantee the disturbances wouldn't recur. Faced with this situation, a group of generals, admirals and Air Force chiefs, my father among them, met to overthrow the regime. They spent weeks working over the details of the plot in cars, cafés, restaurants, hotels, bars and even cinemas. The coup was carefully prepared between March and July, and launched in Tacna in August. Velasco was deposed and General Francisco Morales Bermúdez assumed the presidency. This did little to calm the widespread uncertainty: to the contrary, it only increased the unease of millions of Peruvians who were tired of military governments. They didn't know they would have to endure five more years of them.

By September 1975, my father has become the right-hand man of Morales, the new dictator. I can tell from the newspaper cuttings. He takes charge of the National System for Supporting the Social Movement (SINAMOS), and meets with young leaders, appearing to establish a dialogue with the sectors least satisfied by the new government's first economic measures. This role as mediator doesn't last long. The following year, when he is designated Minister of the Interior, his transformation begins: he leaves behind the prominent but anodyne general he had been and becomes *El Gaucho Cisneros*. His public metamorphosis coincides with my appearance in the world. What might my birth have meant to him? An impetus, an obstacle, a headache, a hope? My presence must have brought out in him some compassion or tenderness he found unsuitable for the controlling character he had begun to shape. Did he see any trace of himself in me? Any gesture that might have reminded him of his own father?

With the blessing of the president, who gives him carte blanche to take action and restore peace in the country, the Gaucho orders a state of emergency in several cities and imposes a curfew in Lima, preventing people from going out after midnight. Strikes are also prohibited, and a dozen newspapers shut down on the grounds that their editorial line clashes with the aims of the military government's Second Phase. Since this gives rise to union protests, he has hundreds of workers and leaders detained, and orders the deportation of those whose presence in the country is deemed toxic.

Amid this climate of vigilance and suspicion, a visit by US Secretary of State Henry Kissinger is announced. President Morales fears an attack on him and puts the Gaucho in charge of receiving him at the airport and chaperoning him during his stay in the city. For General Cisneros this is not a burden but an honour; he has long admired Kissinger, who together with Margaret Thatcher forms part of his international Olympus. The Gaucho has great respect for Kissinger's direction of US foreign policy and boasts that no one has followed as closely as he the Secretary's cunning moves on the Cold War chessboard. He holds Kissinger to be the real brain behind Richard Nixon and Gerald Ford, and even welcomes his direct intervention in Latin American politics, such as in Chile, where Kissinger supports the dictatorship of Augusto Pinochet, another of my father's heroes and idols.

On that 1976 visit, my father attends to Kissinger, taking him for lunch at the Swiss restaurant in La Herradura and to drink pisco sours at the bar in Salto del Fraile. A few days later, the Secretary of State travels on to Chile to meet with Pinochet at La Moneda, where he declares: 'In the United States, as you know, we are sympathetic with what you're trying to do here. Allende was heading the country towards communism, and I don't see why we need to stand by and watch a country go communist due to the irresponsibility of its own people. We want to help you, not undermine you.'

In the same period, the Gaucho also travels to Santiago to meet Pinochet. At home I have the black-and-white photographs from that day. One is a close-up of the two of them, Pinochet the taller, looking at each other, smiling, establishing a mute complicity as military men. The other photographs are wider shots, and show them in conversation on the velvet sofas at La Moneda. On the next day's cover of the Chilean newspaper *Las Últimas Noticias*, there are three headlines: the hunger strikes by the families of the detained and disappeared; the Chilean government's decision to prohibit imports of books by Gabriel García Márquez, Mario Vargas Llosa and Julio Cortázar; and the presence there of Peru's Minister of the Interior, General Cisneros Vizquerra, who 'declined to discuss the topics he addressed during his meeting with General Augusto Pinochet'.

It isn't easy to know or say or write that my father admired men like these. In Kissinger's case, he went further: he imitated him, celebrating his modus operandi and his whole conspiratorial, egotistic and manipulative persona. Kissinger, like my father – or my father, like Kissinger – loved secrets, acted under cover, tapped the telephones of politicians, journalists and even his own assistants, to check if he was being infiltrated. Power is the ultimate aphrodisiac, Kissinger used to say. My father never said this, but he might as well have.

If my father were still alive to witness Kissinger's fall from grace, after the declassification of documents proving US involvement in the massacres and torture in Chile, I'm sure he would have publicly condemned the widely held view of his old friend Henry as a war criminal. Likewise, he would have criticised Pinochet's arrest in London by Scotland Yard, repeating the words I so often heard: 'Chile is the way it is thanks to General Pinochet.'

* * *

In the late summer of 1976, with his attention re-focused on internal struggles, Minister Cisneros removes the editors of several newspapers and, having made their successors sign a good behaviour agreement, allows the weekly paper *El Tiempo* and the magazines *Oiga, Caretas, Equis* and *Opinión Libre* to circulate freely once more. Rumours begin to surface about the closure of the country's most left-wing magazine, *Marka*, but he denies them on television. 'If I wanted to shut down *Marka*, I'd have done it already. In any case, we don't want to silence anyone. Communists have the right to work too.' At that press conference, as in so many of his media appearances, he fires off expressions that seem startlingly brazen even in the turbulent context of a hard-line government like that of Morales Bermúdez.

If I were to release detainees every time someone asked, everybody would be set free. As journalists, you know that gatherings and strikes are prohibited without permission from the authorities. Whoever breaks the law will pay the price. That's why we imposed the curfew. The curfew is beneficial because the population needs to be disciplined. What's more, it's a measure that has been welcomed by women, because their husbands have to be home early from their shenanigans… I've heard it said that there have been more than a thousand deaths since the curfew began. This is completely false. There can't have been more than a dozen.

The ease with which my father speaks of arrests and deaths – a facility I still find infuriating, though it no longer surprises me – was what drove the radical left-wing of the 1970s to rail against him and hold him up as the central figure in an axis of evil. In the photos that accompany these press reports, General Cisneros is visibly conscious of his own power. His gestures and behaviour give him away. He receives journalists at the airport or at the end of public ceremonies with a cigar in one hand, the other in his pocket, with dark glasses and his chin held high. He answers the toughest questions bluntly, sometimes with pedantic coldness, sometimes with elegant irony. He speaks of the government's fair hand and foresight, denounces the infiltration of workplaces by extreme leftist agitators and demands that freedom of expression not be confused with subversive action.

Around this time, the unrest on the streets grows, with my sister Melania and university leaders at the helm. Around this time, following claims that students have been tortured, the minister and his eldest daughter argue heatedly in his office at the Ministry of the Interior; she will then take the next flight to Paris to escape Peru and her father. Around this time, I spend my days in a cot in the apartment on Aljovín St., where I live with my mother and my two-year-old sister Valentina. Every night, we await the arrival of my father, that uniformed figure who appears on the television; every morning, after kissing us goodbye, he crosses the threshold to become a supervillain.

There are groups who benefit from stoking unrest, my father explains to the government-approved journalists. It is a lie, he stresses, that the government tortures detainees. To calm the unions, he also announces that amnesties and humanitarian pardons will be granted to some of those arrested, and the trials of others will be suspended. The discord between the administration and the opposition press, however, remains raw. The Gaucho orders a second wave of closures, shutting down the magazines *Caretas*, *Oiga*, *Gente* and *La Palabra del Pueblo* for breaking their commitment not to insult the regime. For the same reason, he suppresses the circulation of *Momento*, *Opinión Libre*, *Equis*, *ABC*, *Amauta del Mar*, *El Periodista*, *Unidad* and even the weekly satirical publication *Monos y Monadas*, this latter because it 'harms the values of the people'. Some editors seek asylum in embassies, followed by exile in Panama, Mexico or Venezuela. They are tired of being persecuted by State Security and military intelligence agents, and of being punished in ways never seen before in Peru: the kidnapping of family members who have nothing to do with politics and who suddenly disappear for two or three days, taken to gloomy holding cells in the depths of buildings belonging to the Bureau of Investigation.

A few months ago, I looked up one of those former newspaper editors and asked if we could meet in a café so he could tell me what he remembered about those years. Beyond his own account of events, I was struck by how the signs of trauma expressed themselves: he was constantly glancing around us as if someone was observing from a nearby table, he scrutinised the waiters suspiciously and jumped at the sound of a dropped knife.

'These gentlemen seek asylum because their consciences weigh heavy on them,' the Gaucho declares, eliding the selective harassment that he himself was commanding. One afternoon, the journalist Enrique Zileri doesn't come home after facing down my father at a press conference and reproaching him for his abuse of the press. 'Where is Zileri?' the headlines interrogate my father from the newsstands. Seven days later, he reappears. General Cisneros had been reading these headlines from his Ministry office, while in a dark basement several floors below, locked up in one of the three cages built for this purpose, Zileri hoarsely yelled for freedom.

In the second half of 1976, the General stops harassing the press in the face of a greater threat: the appearance of a terrorist organisation calling itself the Peruvian People's Army, with links to university groups. Spokespeople on the left claim that this is an invention by Minister Cisneros to justify ideological persecution, and to distract public opinion from the rampant economic crisis and the brutality of the regime. The General silences these accusations by displaying the propaganda material confiscated from universities, including notebooks setting out plans to kidnap military and civil figures, and even dates for attacks on public and private institutions. Following a second raid on university campuses to break up the remainder of the supposed embryonic guerrilla group, the minister orders the arrest of a hundred student leaders and the same number of politicians.

'Cisneros following in the steps of Pinochet,' the headlines blare. 'There is an emergency law in place. I will arrest those who fail to comply with this law, simple as that. If you want to talk about repression in Peru, we could say that there's a selective repression,' my father acknowledges in an interview. He also advises parents to keep a close eye on their kids, without specifying who they should be protecting them from: the new urban terrorism or the military government.

These are troubled days and not even the Army is immune to internal conflict. A cohort of officers loyal to ex-president Velasco is being promoted up the ranks to occupy the highest levels of command, a cause for alarm among the more conservative wing of the Armed Forces. Early one morning, General Centurión, sworn enemy of the Velasco faction, occupies a barracks and declares his repudiation of the communist-leaning officers who are on the verge of taking over the institution. During the forty-eight hours the insurrection lasts, rumours of civil war take Lima by storm. Along the avenues of the Chorrillos district, green and brown tanks trundle back and forth like a slow herd of armoured rhinoceroses. The lack of information leads the city's residents to believe that it's a coup against Morales Bermúdez. General Centurión gives himself up only after negotiating the definitive retirement of the left-leaning generals in the Army. The Gaucho forms part of the delegation that intercedes to dampen the uprising as swiftly as possible, and avoid jeopardising the continuity of the military revolution.

One week after this mutiny, my father grants a telephone interview to the Mexican newspaper *Excélsior*. 'Our plan of government is for six years. Only then will we begin to consider the transfer of power,' he tells the reporter. He also reveals that the military leaders intend to form a political movement, a platform that brings together businessmen and professionals to participate in future elections. 'How can the people of Peru be certain that you will keep your word and hand over power?' the Mexican journalist asks. 'No one need worry. We won't stay a day longer than is strictly necessary.'

A copy of *Excélsior* reaches President Morales Bermúdez, who sees the two-page spread accompanied by an enormous photo of my father in profile, wreathed in the cigar smoke that curls from his mouth, and throws it down on his desk. He walks the eight paces to the mobile bar in his office, pulls the cork out of a Red Label and tilts the bottle over a glass until it measures three fingers of whisky. His next decision is to wrest all talk of revolutions away from Cisneros and drag him out of the media spotlight where he has found himself. At an end-of-year meeting, Morales tells his Minister of the Interior to turn down all interview requests and stick to private conversations with party leaders, in order to firm up the terrain ahead of the eventual elections.

During the summer of 1977, we spend weekends at an uncle's hacienda, running through the sugar cane and carob trees, watching packs of Dobermans and German Shepherds viciously fight over the scraps of food tossed to them by the house staff, and learning to swim in a dank pool whose murky, bottomless depths we were sure contained strange, poisonous creatures. Meanwhile, my father the minister would leave behind his own car, take one of my uncle's pick-ups to throw the journalists off the scent and drive through the countryside to the bucolic villas and mansions where the top leaders of Peru's right-wing parties would be waiting for him: APRA (Partido Aprista Peruano), Acción Popular and the Partido Popular Cristiano.

My father repeats this operation several times that summer. But that's not all. He also takes time to meet with one of his greatest friends from Argentina, Roberto Viola, a white-whiskered general who was then serving as Chief of the General Staff of his country's Army, and had come to Lima on an official visit. My father invites his old friend to lunch at the elegant Santa María spa, and secures exclusive use of the Esmeralda club for about forty people, including senior officers in the Peruvian Army and State Security agents.

My father and Viola stroll in the sun in their white suits, chat by the edge of a pool, raise toasts to their respective governments. Those were the months – the years, really – when terrorism and military repression were at their peak in Argentina. Together, my father and his guest tour four or five cities across the country, review the troops at different garrisons, eat and drink together. During the pauses on these trips they plan the most important event: the arrival of another old friend of my father's, Lieutenant General Jorge Rafael Videla, who plans to come to Peru as soon as he takes over the presidency so he can make direct contact with Morales Bermúdez.

'Videla and Morales must be able to talk in private. Just the two of them, a handful of officials. You too, of course. Any problems?' Viola asks my father as they fly back from Arequipa.

'None, Roberto, leave it to me. I'll talk to Pancho Morales. We'll coordinate the agenda and set a date.'

'You can assure us Videla won't face any trouble? We know there are Montonero guerrillas hiding out in Lima, and there's always one son of a bitch who wants to cause a ruckus.'

'Don't worry. We know who they are and where they are.'

'You'll take care of it, then?'

'I'll take care of it.'

And so he does. To avoid any risk of protests at Videla's presence in Peru, General Cisneros orders Ministerial agents to locate and arrest Carlos Alberto Maguid, an Argentinian connected to the Montonero movement who had sought refuge in Lima from the surveillance he'd been subjected to at home by paramilitaries of the Triple A, the Argentinian Anti-communist Alliance. Maguid is seized on his way out of the Catholic University, where he lectured, and taken to a tiny cell under the control of the State Security division. There he encounters a score of left-wing activists and student leaders who've been served with preventive detention during the period of the Argentinian President's visit to the city.

Videla arrives in Lima in the first week of March. My

father welcomes him with an embrace at the military air base and places an armoured car at his disposal; it leaves the airport via an emergency gate, evading the journalists who are awaiting a statement. He sets him up in a room on the ninth floor of the Sheraton hotel, and sends over a cellophane-wrapped hamper full of liquor, cigarettes and chocolates. The next day, Videla meets with Morales Bermúdez, first in a private room at the Sheraton, and later that afternoon at the Palace of Government. They shake hands before the press cameras, having signed a joint declaration that emphasises their firm rejection of 'the phenomenon of guerrilla violence'. 'What other issues did you address at your meeting, Mr President?' comes the first question. Videla steps up to answer, slender in his uniform, his hair meticulously arranged, a luxuriant moustache and grey-blue eyes reminiscent of passion fruit seeds. His deep, solemn voice and impeccable diction echo around the walls of the Túpac Amaru Hall. 'This meeting has served to bring a regional presence to the Peruvian military regime and to consolidate an agreement on nuclear issues that is aimed at the construction and equipping of the Nuclear Research Centre of Peru.'

Videla wasn't lying. There was a serious interest on the part of the Argentinians to mine and refine Peruvian uranium, since they were vying for regional leadership on nuclear energy with Brazil.

But what he did not and could not say was that he had also – or above all – come to request assistance from the Peruvian military in the clandestine arrest and deportation of Argentinian citizens in Lima whom he considered dangerous. Peru's military responded to this request with unusual alacrity. Once Videla returned to Buenos Aires, they released those they had detained, but continued to keep a close watch on Carlos Alberto Maguid.

Nearly a month later, after receiving instructions from Buenos Aires, Minister Cisneros ordered his kidnapping. Two secret policemen followed Maguid along Petit Thouars Ave., and before he could reach the junction with Javier Prado where he would take his bus for the university, they violently assaulted him. Maguid was never seen again. His disappearance gave rise to endless political and media speculation. When the case was reported, lengthy articles tried to resolve the enigma of what had occurred. Most of them name my father as the key actor. In addition to the kidnapping, they accuse General Cisneros of preventing the publication of the letters written by Maguid's wife, demanding that the Peruvian government explain what they had done with her husband. In a later interview, someone brought up the case and the Gaucho responded: 'I don't know where Maguid is now, but we're looking for him.' By then, Maguid was certainly not in Lima, and most likely was not anywhere at all.

A while ago I sent an 8mm film that belonged to my father to be digitised. It was a video of my sister Valentina's fourth birthday, celebrated on Sunday 17 April 1977. Grainy as they are, the images show around a hundred grown-ups mingling in the gardens of the Real Club de San Isidro, watching their children as they enjoy a clown show, dance to a band and take turns whacking a piñata with a plastic stick. Everything is decorated with balloons and streamers with the colours and textures of the period. A banner reads ¡Que viva la fiesta! My father appears in one shot, together with relatives and friends. He wears a sky blue suit, dark glasses, and holds the obligatory cigar and a glass of whisky. But he isn't aloof from the party: he takes part in the games organised by the clowns and smiles and does the limbo and guzzles a fizzy drink from a baby's bottle and slices up my sister's birthday cake and sings 'Happy Birthday' with an enthusiasm and joy I almost never saw in him. There's no doubt that he was a fond father that 17 April. Five days earlier, he had made Maguid disappear.

★ ★ ★

The Maguid mystery fades before the repeated shocks of the internal crisis. Communists and students face off with the police and find themselves in and out of prison. There's a new wave of closures of newspapers and magazines, especially the most critical ones, those that delved deepest to find out what had happened to the Argentinian refugee. 'I see arrogance, insolence and conceit on the part of the press media, who break their gentlemen's agreement and distort events. I'm troubled by how poorly freedom of expression is understood in this country. They leave us with no other alternative than to shut them down,' he declares to a reporter from *Caretas*, one of the few publications still allowed to circulate. In this interview – 'Ping Pong with Cisneros' – he speaks of the claims of human rights violations made by the families of many detainees. 'Strict directives have been issued, urging members of the police forces to comply with the regulations. I have personally distributed booklets on humanistic principles among the police corps.'

Trade unionists and workers, tired of the layoffs and the economic situation, declare the First General Workers' Strike for Tuesday 19 July. The left-wing press promise it will be a historic day. The government is on guard. The Sunday before the strike, General Cisneros appears on national television and radio, reading a message to the nation. My father's voice is multiplied across all the loudspeakers in Peru as he pronounces a speech that is little more than an arrogant ultimatum. Far from pacifying the workers' anger, the minister's warnings only serve to inflame it.

The day of the 19th, Red Tuesday, is drizzly. An unprecedented mass of people pours onto the streets. By noon, almost 100% of industry in Lima has shut down. The uprising is reproduced in Huancayo, Cusco, Tacna and Trujillo, and is soon beset by violence. In every city, the strikers throw stones at buses, light fires in the streets, form picket lines to cut off the centres. The government orders the disturbances to be crushed, but they prove too much for the police to deal with. Military patrols head for the squares, carry out raids, close union offices and open pitched battles with the mobs.

The next day, the newspapers chronicle the workers' victory over the government, the 700 strikers arrested and the need to call a constitutive assembly. The dictatorship senses the tremor and prepares a counter-strike. In a cabinet session, the Gaucho Cisneros proposes a purge to punish the workers. A few hours later, an emergency law is activated to dismiss those who promoted the general strike and the leading activists. Five thousand union leaders, among them miners, fishermen, textile workers and others, are thrown out of work for causing political trouble. They blame my father for the loss of their jobs and seek the support of the press, which becomes an echo chamber for their anger. Suddenly not only the left-wing press is criticising the government. In indignant opinion pieces, newspapers and magazines from across the spectrum complain that the dismissals are arbitrary. Faced with this torrent of criticism, the government decides to apply a little journalistic incentive: prior censorship. From this moment on, all publications would have to cross the Minister of the Interior's desk before going on sale.

Towards the end of 1977, my father spends every night in his office, evaluating the content of these publications, crossing things out and making emendations, tossing entire editions into the wastepaper basket. 'There was an agreement and it hasn't been respected. What we're doing is reviewing the content of publications before their release, to make sure they comply with the rules. No one can call this censorship. As the son of a journalist, brother of a journalist and cousin of a journalist, I am well aware of the limits of the media,' he says one night on a television channel.

'The People Demand Your Resignation, General,' is the front-page headline in the newspaper *Marka* one day. It continues: 'The Minister of the Interior possesses disproportionate political power: it is he and he alone who refuses to concede any amnesty to workers or political activists, or to rehire the workers and cadres who have been arbitrarily dismissed.' My father notes the criticism from *Marka*, and next morning a squad of soldiers turns up at the editor's office to carry out a requisition.

At this point, my father is at his most contemptible. Following the general strike he is determined to show his firm grip on the reins of national power, and his control over almost all areas. To do this, he ups the number of arrests with the support of every police department, even the funeral agency of the Bureau of Investigation; as a result, detainees spend days and nights on the floor alongside coffins whose contents it is best not to examine. The news items and photographs from 1977 make it clear: at the age of fifty-one, my father is running the country. His pals in the Army and the police entertain him at every chance, organising lunches and parties in his honour. They invite him to their leisure activities, compliment him and above all visit him in his Ministry office. Some of them truly admire him, while others merely flatter him with accolades and gifts of bottles of pisco and fighting cocks. They are all present in those photographs. 'El Gordo' Mejía. 'El Chato' Vinatea. 'El Cholo' Balta. 'El Coche' Miranda. 'El Cholo' Noriega. 'El

Gringo' Correa. 'El Coto' Arrisueño. 'El Mono' Zapata. The members of the Military Junta and the heads of the Bureau of Investigation of 1977 are gathered around my father at the Hacienda Villa or in the clubs of Chosica, posed on a balcony watching folk dances, horse riding displays, exclusive concerts by Los Morunos and other similarly rumpled and aged performers. Recently I discovered a video from that period. The film shows a horse ride led by my father, who is mounted on Tetchy, his blond-maned Isabelline horse. The Gaucho spurs the animal through the forests of Huachipa. It's a long ride marked by different stages, first trotting, then galloping through farmland and along stony paths. It's a sunny Saturday and all the riders are heading for the barracks at Potao, adjacent to the Acho bullring in Rímac. They cross a river and pass through thick vegetation near the peak of San Cristóbal. They traverse a shantytown with glimpses of old buses, billboards reading *Coca-Cola, It's the Real Thing*. And that's what is most striking about the first shots of the video: they are the real thing. My father leading the pack, like in a 70s western, all-powerful, hearing the trumpets of the mounted police who receive him like the last equestrian emperor.

★ ★ ★

In trying to explain the actions of the Minister of the Interior, various analysts warn that Cisneros may be planning a coup d'état against Morales Bermúdez. His search for the spotlight, they say, is part of a campaign that must be aimed at his laying claim to the presidency. Morales is left unsettled. Over the following months their relationship is so decisively undermined that their differences are exposed in the press whenever controversies arise, such as the infil-tration of the unions in Ilo, La Oroya and Chimbote by

171

communist agitators. While President Morales seeks reconciliation, Minister Cisneros sticks to the tough talk that the media now treat as congenital. Phrases like 'I like to take the bull by the horns' or 'Punishing subversives is a tough responsibility, but one I enjoy' are an invitation for the press to pursue their theory of a coup. The president cannot control his minister. His advisers at the Palace beg Morales Bermúdez to get rid of him. There are days when Cisneros acts as if he were president, and some media outlets are encouraged to project him as an alternative. One pens this editorial in *Oiga*:

> Amid the prevailing national climate of unrest and violence, Minister Cisneros is the natural replacement for Morales Bermúdez. If he were to take over power in a third phase of the military government, he would satisfy the desires of the right as well as those of the International Monetary Fund. He has an excellent relationship with the United States Embassy, and family members in key places: his brother Juvenal is editor of *La Prensa*, while his brother Gustavo is the top man at the Association of Exporters.

If there was ever a moment at which my father might have been catapulted into the presidency, it was this one. But his own decisions work against him once more, some of them grim and radical, such as the clandestine deportation of political activists for ideological motives. Declarations like 'There will be no transfer of power until civilians learn to behave,' or 'I don't imprison people out of malice, but out of firmness,' or 'No one will break me' all become newspaper headlines that finally send Morales Bermúdez off the rails: he comes to understand that if he doesn't act soon, one fine morning the Gaucho Cisneros will come knocking on his door with a line of tanks to remove him from the Palace of Government. That is when he decides to remove him from his post and send him as military attaché to Paris for a year.

My father returns from France in May 1979 as Chief of Staff of the Joint Command. In his first week in this new role, he receives an invitation to attend the anniversary of the creation of the Argentinian Army. He travels to Buenos Aires and meets Videla and Viola again, and the next day, in the Libertador building, receives decorations from all of them. A photograph appears in the Argentinian newspaper *Clarín* with an excerpt from my father's speech: 'Born in Buenos Aires and educated in Argentina, trained as a soldier at the National Military College, for the past thirty-two years I have been absent in person, but ever-present in spirit.'

This is the decisive trip on which he sees Beatriz Abdulá again. First, the appointment at the Plaza Hotel, and later, on a Saturday, he takes her to the Susana Rinaldi tango show in a dance hall in San Telmo. The day before, he had been to the same dance hall with his military friends. He hadn't intended to mention this to Beatriz, but when a waiter approaches the table to ask him to put out his cigarette, as smoking was forbidden, the Gaucho replies in a loud voice, 'How strange that it's forbidden. Just last night I was sitting at this same table smoking with my friend Lieutenant General Videla and no one said a word to us.' The waiter turns white, opens his eyes wide like he's seen a ghost, and makes a solicitous gesture as if to say the Gaucho can smoke all the cigarettes he likes, at any table in the hall.

The following night, at the Palermo racecourse, he meets another group of old friends, among them Leopoldo Fortunato Galtieri, with whom he'd been close when they were both cadets aged 19 or 20. There too was Guillermo Suárez Mason, nicknamed 'Pajarito' or Little Bird, and Antonio Domingo Bussi, whom he had already reencountered four years earlier in San Francisco, while taking the training course he exploited to stage his marriage to Cecilia Zaldívar for the second time. Indeed, Bussi was the witness at that symbolic union. Years later, on the day I discussed this episode with my mother, she spoke warmly of Bussi and the other military men, unaware or feigning ignorance of the monsters they really were. They were the Argentinian dictatorship's most brutal repressors, and were later found guilty of torture, disappearances and crimes against humanity. Several were sentenced to life in prison, and died there.

'Once, your father hid one of them in our house,' my mother said to me one afternoon, as we were eating at a restaurant.

It came out of the blue. We were alone. As usual, I'd dragged the conversation towards the past, and as always, she had made dramatic refusals while still following my lead.

'Which house? The Monterrico house?'

'Yes, Monterrico. Just for two or three days,' she said, her eyes on her plate, her fork toying with her ravioli.

'Which of them did he hide?'

She hesitated for a few seconds. 'Pajarito Suárez.' She looked uncomfortable, but she kept speaking.

'You don't remember his full name?' I asked, while I Googled the words 'Suárez', 'Argentina' and 'military' on my phone. Three seconds later, she no longer needed to strain her memory. 'Mum, are you talking about Guillermo Suárez Mason?'

'Yes, him! Pajarito Suárez Mason!' she replied, relieved to overcome the impasse in her mind.

'Well, I have news for you. This guy's nickname wasn't Little Bird, but the Butcher of El Olimpo'.

'Seriously? What does the Internet say?'

'You really want to know?'

174

'Yes.'

'Here it says that he was the Commander of the First Army Corps between 1976 and 1980. That he was known as the Butcher of El Olimpo because he was in charge of the El Olimpo garage, one of the biggest detention centres. During the dictatorship, he was also responsible for the torture centres hidden at Automotores Orletti, the Pozo de Bánfield and La Cacha. It says that he commanded the Army's 601st Intelligence Battalion, too, which specialised in kidnappings. That he was appointed Director of the state oil concern, YPF, and accused of pirating fuel to finance intelligence operations and supporting the Contras in Central America, as part of Operation Condor. That when the dictatorship collapsed he fled Argentina, and by 1984 was living in California. That in 1988 he was put on trial, but before the sentence was passed he was granted a pardon by President Carlos Menem. That in 1998 the Supreme Court ruled that, in spite of the pardon, his actions during the dictatorship must be investigated to clarify "information about the fate of the detainees". He was also accused of stealing the children of the disappeared who had been born in captivity. He was imprisoned in the Villa Devoto jail, and died on 21 June 2005 at the age of eighty-one. That's what it says.'

This recital left us in stunned silence.

'What year was this guy in our house?' I asked, nauseated.

'I don't know, around 1990 or 1991. They were after him.'

It was enough for her to mention the year for my memory to produce an image: my father standing at the door of my bedroom, warning my brother and me that no one was to go out to the back terrace for a few days. 'They're going to do some electrical work,' he said by way of explanation, before either of us could ask. 'Stick to this side of the house, OK,' he said with the tone he always used when giving orders. This prohibition was enough for the back terrace to become the focus of my attention for the subsequent hours and days. My fear of my father's chastisement was such that I didn't dare disobey, but I do remember that one afternoon I saw the shadow of a man on the other side of a curtain, moving slowly among the tables and sofas I knew so well. I thought it must be the electrician, so didn't investigate further. I can no longer recall anything about his appearance, apart from the silhouette. It was dense, elongated.

As I was trying to bring this silhouette into greater definition in my mind's eye, my mother interrupted me with a question:

'Let's see, tell me what it says about Antonio Bussi.'

'The witness at your marriage?' I typed the name into my phone.

She sensed my irony and put a forkful of ravioli into her mouth.

'Here we go,' I said, silently scanning the first lines. 'Listen carefully; this one's worse.'

'What does it say, what does it say?'

'It says here that your dear Antonio Domingo Bussi was removed from his post for crimes against humanity committed during the military dictatorship in Argentina, during which he was de facto governor of the province of Tucumán, between 1976 and 1978. He was tried and found guilty of kidnapping, murder and embezzlement. It says that the report of the bicameral investigative commission on human rights violations in Tucumán described Bussi's rule as "a vast apparatus of repression that oriented its real actions towards the elimination of trade union, political and student leaders, who had nothing to do with the injurious actions of the guerrillas". It says that during the period he was governor of Tucumán, numerous lawyers, doctors, trade unionists and politicians were murdered, kidnapped, imprisoned, tortured, mistreated. It says that Bussi was responsible for the disappearances in that province. That he was seen executing some of them with his own hands, throwing them into a pit after shooting them in the head. That he killed other detainees during interrogations. That he tortured them by beating them with a hose for hours until they died. And that…'

'That's enough, stop.' My mother's hands were covering her mouth. 'No wonder his wife always carried a pistol in her purse and wanted to teach me to fire it.'

I don't know if we changed the subject, but we certainly hastened to finish our lunch. Neither of us spoke in the car on the way home. Classical music on the radio filled in for words. The chords of Schubert or Brahms or Vivaldi occupied the empty space. In her head and mine, the same thoughts turned over like weightless bodies, the same disturbing images, the same discomfort grating on us like chalk on a blackboard. I didn't know then and I don't know now which is worse: for a murderer to have been witness to my parents' fictitious marriage, or for a murderer to have stayed in my house without any of us knowing, touching with his criminal hands the doors, walls and windows that I had touched before and would touch after that.

Every time I hear those names – Videla, Viola, Galtieri, Bussi, Suárez Mason – every time I think about the fact they formed part of my father's military circles when he was a cadet, I wonder what might have occurred if the Gaucho hadn't come to Peru at the age of twenty-one and instead had stayed in the Argentinian officers' school. What role he might have played in that dictatorship, what dirty activities he would have taken charge of, and to what extent his name would be marked today, perhaps linked to those

177

massacres, those kidnappings, those atrocious and indelible tortures that ranged from the application of electric cattle prods, the mutilation of limbs, the flaying of victims' faces, to the depraved, sadistic, barbaric practice of raping women before forcing live rats into their vaginas and stopping up the genital orifice to drive the animal crazy, causing it to gnaw its way through the victim's insides. On other occasions, they disappeared detainees on 'death flights': putting them onto aeroplanes in order to throw them into the sea, but only after torturing them, forcing them to put their heads into buckets of boiling water or containers of excrement, then sedating them with Pentothal to ensure they were unconscious when they hit the water and would drown.

One night I discovered a photo album in one of the trunks where we kept my father's belongings after his death. A red, leather-bound album with golden letters on the cover reading 'Gift of Brigadier General Don Ramón Juan Alberto Camps' contains black-and-white photographs of an Army dinner held in Buenos Aires during that 1979 trip. These images show all or almost all of the military officers who would be tried years later for genocide, and among them is my father, being fêted, receiving commemorative plates, diplomas, handshakes. In these photos my father is just another man in the group. He's one of them. He's wearing a dark three-piece suit, just like them, and smiles like they do, and in his gaze is a particular, sinister shine just like the gleam in the others' eyes. When I found this album I wanted to know who the host of this dinner was, this Don Camps. The information on the Internet was overwhelming. Camps was a professional torturer, a child abductor, a confessed mastermind of the elimination of troublesome journalists and the disappearance of thousands of people supposedly linked to subversive movements. He was in charge of nine police departments that were converted into clandestine centres where detainees were subject to all kinds of agonies and torments. Together these centres became known as the Camps Circuit. This is the individual who so thoughtfully gifted my father this velvet-lined, leather-bound album with its gilded lettering. When I travelled to Buenos Aires to meet Beatriz Abdulá's daughter and sister, I took this album with me, together with other photographs I found in the trunk that had been torn up and placed in a bag. When I reassembled them, they showed my father in the company of different men dressed in civilian clothing, with faces that suggested they bore the weight of many deaths on their backs. I became obsessed with these photos. I wanted to know the names of everyone who appeared in them. One afternoon, in a bookshop on Güemes St. in Mar del Plata, as I was looking for books on the dictatorship, I decided to show the album to the bookseller. I had overheard him talking to other customers and he seemed to be well-informed.

'I'd like to show you some photographs and for you to tell me if you can identify anyone,' I said as I produced the album from my backpack.

'Sure, go ahead,' he agreed from the other side of the counter.

As soon as he saw the faces, his eyes widened.

'But… how did you get your hands on this?' he asked in astonishment, glancing to either side as if we were looking at prohibited material, something obscene or subversive.

'Do you recognise them?' I persisted, focusing on the objective. I sensed that this young man, not much older than I was, was about to provide me with the answers I was looking for.

'Of course I recognise them,' he sighed with sorrow, or anger. 'This is the whole mob of torturers. The biggest sons of bitches in the history of the country. This one here

179

is Viola, this is Camps, this is Cristino Nicolaides, this is Reynaldo Bignone, this must be Miguel Etchecolatz.' As he named them he passed his index finger over the static faces of the men in the photographs. 'Where'd you get this from, man?' He fixed me with a stare.

'It was given to my father. He studied here with them in the Army, before he left for Peru'.

'Is your old man still alive?'

'No, he's dead.'

'Can I give you a piece of advice?'

'Sure.'

'Hide this piece of shit. Don't let anyone see it. Don't go showing it around, seriously.'

His words made me feel like an accomplice, that I too was contaminated. When I emerged onto the street I felt as if the backpack carried an explosive charge, as if the people around me could perceive my discomfort. I walked faster, anxious not to cross paths with some perceptive police officer who might notice my nervousness, which I felt as obvious as if I were wearing outlandish clothing. They might stop me, I thought. They might ask me questions and. hearing my foreign accent, insist I open the rucksack. Then I'd have to show them the red album – or rather the black album – of Brigadier General Camps, and tell the officers who my father was and how I was connected to the dictatorship in Argentina.

I didn't tell the bookseller nor any of the other people who later saw the photographs what my father thought of the torturers. After all, it wasn't just that he knew them; he studied with them for almost five years and adopted the same lessons and ideas. That's why, when the famous trials of the military juntas took place in Buenos Aires and La Plata in 1984 and 1985, my father wrote in his fortnightly column in the newspaper *Espreso* a fiery defence of the repressors:

The sentencing of the Argentinian generals, far from converting the victors into the defeated, has exalted them into a privileged position, for they will live to see their names – Videla, Massera, Viola, Galtieri and the rest – transcend, expanding and multiplying beyond the boundaries of their homeland to echo wherever there are men ready to follow their example and save their nations from the international plague of subversion. We all want to live in peace and freedom. But if we also want to be masters of our own destiny, we cannot accept a peace that is not grounded in freedom. And freedom is not a privilege: it is a right that people must know how to defend, and for which we fight without first asking ourselves the price of victory. Thank you, friends, for setting an example.

Similarly, in 1992, after paramilitaries kidnapped and murdered ten students from La Cantuta University in Lima, whose militancy in terrorist groups was far from clear, my father recalled in an interview his great fondness for his Argentinian comrades:

I am a friend of Argentinian Generals Videla, Viola and Galtieri, and today I admire them more than ever, not because they have committed excesses, but because they were courageous enough to tell the courts: we bear sole responsibility as commanders-in-chief. Everyone else was just obeying orders. I would be proud to occupy their place, because they saved their country from subversion. It is a great source of regret that I am retired. If I were still in active service and bore any responsibility in the La Cantuta case, you can be sure I would find myself seated in the dock, because I would have asked for it myself, and because that is the only way to teach subordinates what it means to have moral authority at any level of command.

*   *   *

The Gaucho's trip to Buenos Aires in 1979 did not go unnoticed in Lima. An editorial appeared in the magazine *Equis* that deduced the supposed purpose of the visit: 'The right-wing authoritarian current is represented by General Cisneros, who favours a Brazilian-style political regime and an Argentinian-style repressive approach. From his recent trip to Argentina he must have brought back the system perfected by Videla's men for the elimination of the left.'

It was mainly the left-leaning newspapers and magazines – though not exclusively – that connected Cisneros to all the incarcerations and disappearances that were happening at the time in Peru. Just as his name was linked to the kidnapping of the Argentinian citizen Maguid in 1977, so too was he implicated in that of three more Argentinians in June 1980. My father was no longer a minister of state by that point, but Chief of Staff of the Joint Command, and was closer to the dictatorship in Argentina than any other Peruvian official. Which meant it was impossible he didn't know about Plan Motel, the macabre international operation later known as Operation Condor, which aimed to eliminate communism from certain South American countries using the harshest criminal methods. My father and his successor as Minister of the Interior, Pedro Richter – my uncle Pedro, who as a boy I hugged countless times when he came to our house and stayed until late, always so well dressed, with a cravat around his neck – coordinated the actions that many years later were blamed on the government of Morales Bermúdez.

(As I write this in 2014, I learn – indeed, it falls to me to read the news story on the television channel where I work – that Italian courts have decided to put on trial some twenty members of military juntas from the 1970s and 1980s in Chile, Bolivia, Paraguay, Uruguay and Peru. The producer of the news programme passes me a piece of paper and indicates that I should read out the names of the Peruvian military personnel who are included in the trial. Something in me trembles. The cable mentions four officers. I know two of them: one is former president Morales Bermúdez. The other is my uncle, Pedro Richter. Both had been summoned to appear before an Italian court within five months, according to the cable. After reading this, I look at the camera and call a commercial break. Only then can I breathe again and shake my head to try and clear it of the single thought that has overwhelmed me: that if my father had been alive, he too would have been on that list.)

In June 1980, just weeks before the Morales Bermúdez regime came to an end, a new request for cooperation arrived from the Argentinian military. They had information that an attack was being planned on President Videla – who had already announced he would travel to Lima for the swearing-in of the newly elected president of Peru, the architect Fernando Belaúnde – and they had identified the leading members of the Montoneros who intended to carry it out. The list included Noemí Giannotti de Molfino, María Inés Raverta and Julio César Ramírez. The three were kidnapped close to Miraflores Park in broad daylight by a team comprising both Peruvian and Argentinian agents. They were taken to a house north of Lima, on the Playa Hondable military base. There, the Argentinian agents stripped, blindfolded and tortured them, applying cattle prods to their genitals and beating them with hoses. After a few days the Peruvian government deported them as criminals to Bolivia, where they were handed over to the Argentinian Army. Of the three, only Noemí Giannotti was ever seen again: a few weeks later her body was discovered face down in an apartment building in Madrid, Spain.

Since these disappearances took some time to come to light, the press was focused on Fernando Belaúnde's electoral victory and on the fresh democratic airs that were coming to blow away the thick military fog that had smothered Peru for so many years.

We had spent the first half of 1980 in Piura, where my father was responsible for the First Military Region. We lived for a few wonderful months at that magnificent house I have never returned to, the one where the photograph was taken of my father and I forming a human pyramid at the edge of the pool, on the verge of an acrobatic dive.

During this period, the newspapers centre their attention on the breakdown in relations between General Cisneros and President Morales Bermúdez, and demand that elections be called. It is imperative that the military finally return power to a civilian government. In the final months of the dictatorship, the magazine *Equis* speculates that Morales Bermúdez will instead be replaced, and insinuates that the new president could be General Cisneros.

It is said that the commission responsible for communicating to President Morales that he must leave office has already been established, and that General Cisneros will be at its head. There is no doubt that Cisneros is the most cultured, the most intelligent and the most powerful among the prominent military figures, but if he were to become president it would be a backward step for the country: he would seek continuity in order to achieve the Third Phase of the military government.

The predictions of *Equis* prove mistaken: Morales Bermúdez governs unhindered until the end, and hands the sash of office to Belaúnde. My father is named Inspector General of the Army. In the eyes of *Equis*, nevertheless, the

Gaucho remains sceptical of the new civilian government and is probably already plotting to overthrow Belaúnde. Left-wing Senator Enrique Bernales is one who supports this view. 'There is but a short step from repression to the overthrow of a president, and General Cisneros, one of the greatest violators of human rights in Peru, is fully capable of taking it.'

My father, however, attempts no coup nor even displays hostility towards the government. Quite the contrary: he lowers his profile, focuses his attention on his new role at the Inspectorate, supports the cabinet and stays out of the headlines for a few months. At this time he was probably also distracted by household affairs: we had moved in with my grandmother Esperanza, and work needed done on the second floor. My sister Valentina and I had recently entered primary school, and my father – who in my memory of these days appears and disappears like a flickering presence – may have been thinking about our education.

In June 1981, however, my father's name is back on the front pages, after a helicopter crash causes the death of the Commander-in-Chief, General Hoyos Rubio. The top position in the Army is left vacant as a result, and on account of his seniority General Cisneros is among those called upon to fill it.

Some media outlets refuse to believe the official account of the accident. Even though my father personally takes charge of the rescue work and spends entire days searching tirelessly for his friend, climbing on foot to the peak of the steep mountain where the helicopter came down – smashed like a toy with eleven burnt bodies scattered around it, including that of Hoyos, who is recognisable only by his wedding ring – and even though my father returns by aeroplane together with the coffins and, in tears, delivers her husband's remains to Hoyos' widow, a number of tabloids persist in insinuating that the Gaucho Cisneros had some involvement in the death of the Commander-in-Chief.

> The restless General Cisneros, whose military career has been stalled, has suddenly found his prospects brighter. With the death of Hoyos, he is the only beneficiary, returned to the military and the political forefront. We know there are financial and business circles interested in Cisneros becoming Commander-in-Chief so that he would put an end to the subversion and bring the country to order before it goes under. This would mean the Gaucho once again becoming the strongman at the head of the Army, and we would have to put up with his insatiable appetite for power, as well as the tangos he loves to croon at midnight, tone-deaf as he may be.

By October 1981, the press is treating his ascendance to the top position as a done deal. Once again the calculations are off. After lengthy military conclaves and tense negotiations between the government and the armed forces, my father is declared not Commander-in-Chief, but Minister of War. President Belaúnde is immediately criticised for this nomination. It is unconstitutional, they say. Military personnel cannot be ministers in a democratic administration. The president will be sleeping with the wolf inside the Palace of Government, they say. The more optimistic among the left-wing pundits suggest Belaúnde has nominated him precisely to hold him close, where he can keep an eye on him. The newspapers cry: 'The repression is coming!' 'Here comes Cisneros!' 'A dictator in the cabinet!'

In our house, no one notices these headlines. We don't even understand them. My mother, sister and I only have eyes and ears for one event: the arrival of my little brother Facundo. That's what really matters. I remember the copy of the newspaper *El Observador* of 23 October folded on the night table of room 208 in the maternity hospital. 'Cisneros Vizquerra to be a minister again.' For us, the news was that Cisneros Vizquerra was to be a father again. When the Gaucho reaches the clinic, he quickly updates my mother on what's happening outside. 'They've just named me minister.' Cecilia Zaldívar smiles because she sees how happy he is, and jokes that Facundo is his lucky charm, an angel who arrived with a blessing. And my father looks at her, nods, smiles and drops onto the visitors' armchair. Suddenly the sanitised, immaculate, impeccable atmosphere of the maternity clinic envelops him, relieves him of the impurity of the world he's come from, that grotto made of rumours, conspiracies, jealousies and denials. And I see my parents kissing, my sister Valentina playing with the sky blue balloons scattered everywhere, and Facundo with his huge eyes on the other side of the incubator glass, and I make a silent wish that nothing will ever change.

The swearing-in of the ministers takes place one week later. Perhaps it was a Tuesday, at half past three in the afternoon. I remember the golden hall of the Palace of Government. The great crucifix. My father kneeling at the feet of a bloodied Christ. My father kneeling, for the first time. I remember the family being introduced later on and President Belaúnde turning to me: 'You must be the Little Gaucho.' I remember my grandmother Esperanza, eighty-five years old, dressed in black, congratulating her son by blowing a kiss, causing a buzz among the journalists. I remember the celebratory lunch in the house on La Paz St., and a photographer from the magazine *Oiga* who turns up to take a portrait of the new Minister of War for the front cover of the next day's edition. My father takes up a position in the corner of the room and says something to the reporter, a phrase whose meaning I don't under-stand, but is clear to all the adults. 'Wait, let me take off my glasses, otherwise they'll confuse me with Pinochet.' A cartoon published two days later shows a lady leading her son around an aquarium. They stop before a huge fish tank with two piranhas separated by a glass wall. The mother explains that they can't share the tank because their murderous nature would lead them to eat each other. The child pipes up: 'That's not true, mother, haven't you seen how well Cisneros and Pinochet get on?'

* * *

My father becomes Minister Cisneros once more, and the old fears are reawakened. 'Martín Fierro, the iconic *gaucho* literary character, would be downright inspired by the terrors provoked by this Gaucho,' jokes a columnist. The left-wing press attack him, hounding him over the dismissal of workers in 1977, the murder of villagers, the torture of students, the disappearances of Montoneros, the tailing of radical leaders and the shutting down of newspapers. Meanwhile, the right-wing press talk of an 'anti-Cisneros campaign' and describe him as a military nationalist and decisive minister.

As if seeking a truce, the general sends a letter to all media outlets inviting them to take a more collaborative approach with the government. But the left doesn't fall for this and throws more fuel on the fire. 'President Belaúnde is digging his own grave by keeping Cisneros so close,' writes Ricardo Letts, a communist senator who took my father's nomination as Minister of War to the courts. Years later, when I'd begun to write political commentary for *El Comercio*, he filed a lawsuit against me for an article in which I jokingly summarised his involvement in the 1977 General Strike, where he'd wound up wringing out his socks at the door of the Palace of Government after being soaked by the water cannon.

The left cannot stand my father being back in government. They call a public rally to protest against his inclusion in the cabinet. They organise a solidarity march on which a banner can be read proclaiming 'Down with Cisneros, oppressor, sell-out and murderer!' To counter these attacks, the right-wing magazines seek to remind people that my father is the son of a diplomat, journalist and romantic poet who was deported by the dictator Leguía, as if the lyrical virtues and personal circumstances of my grandfather Fernán could somehow guarantee the good behaviour of the new Minister Cisneros. My uncle Juvenal also sticks his neck out for his younger brother and, in an attempt to calm the waters and give the general the benefit of the doubt in the face of left-wing scepticism, writes a column in *El Observador* entitled 'The Gaucho is also a lefty,' revealing that my father's best hand is actually his left.

But Minister Cisneros' cordiality towards the media is soon exhausted. The Shining Path terrorist group, led by Abimael Guzmán, has been established in the mountains for over two years. Their descent to the cities along the coast is only a matter of time: this threat demands a harsh response.

'Do you believe in democracy, General?' he is asked in his first press conference as Minister of War. 'Yes, I do believe in democracy,' he responds, 'but in a strong, presidential, almost authoritarian democracy. We shouldn't assume the right to live in a democracy; instead we should learn to live in one and not confuse it with licentiousness.' 'How do you believe we should deal with terrorism?' another reporter asks. 'Terrorism', the Gaucho responds, 'is no longer a myth but a reality. Many friendly countries are facing situations like ours. Terrorism must be confronted decisively and with drastic measures, so that society can live without fear.'

His opinions acquire sudden prominence with the subsequent spate of attacks perpetrated by the Shining Path.

A bomb on Angamos Avenue. Another in the municipality of Rímac. Another that plunges almost the entire capital into darkness. There is a public debate about the need to involve the army in the conflict against the insurgents, which so far has mobilised only the police. The majority are opposed, arguing that it risks a bloodbath. For my father, everything is perfectly clear. 'It's the president who has to decide whether or not the Army intervenes. As far as we're concerned, we are ready to act without a second thought.'

The next year, 1982, is a fraught one. From the tranquillity of primary school, I was blissfully unaware of the troubles that plagued my father. I saw him smoking cigars, drinking thick black coffees with haste or exasperation, always talking on the phone. I liked knowing that he was a minister, but I didn't like him having to be one all the time.

He talks constantly to the media. The radio, newspapers, magazines, television. *Oiga*, *El Peruano*, *Perspectiva*, *Correo*, Canal 4, Radio Programas del Perú. He receives journalists at home and at his office in the Little Pentagon. I answer some of these calls and get used to shouting 'Dad, they're calling from Canal 5,' or 'Dad, they're calling from *La República*.' The minister answers the journalists' questions as if he were angry. Or perhaps he really is. We need to fast-track the terrorist trials, he proposes. We need to put them up against the wall, he suggests. Another day – after a Shining Path raid on a Navy base and the theft of a large quantity of arms – he makes a furious statement on television: 'Don't mess with the Armed Forces, because we do know how to use our weapons.' I see this programme at home with my mother, brother and sister, and for the first time we fear the repercussions of his words. We don't say anything, but we sense it.

The left-wing press reproach him for his way of thinking and for describing as 'terrorism' what they consider 'isolated acts of sabotage by a few radicals'. The general ignores them with Olympian arrogance. In response to the increasing attacks, the bombings and the nightmarish news arriving in particular from the city of Ayacucho, he warns that the Armed Forces must respond as soon as possible. At a meeting of the Defence Council, in the presence of President Belaúnde and all the ministers, he makes no bones about it: 'The Armed Forces must intervene in Ayacucho before it is too late.'

The opposition media judge the minister's statement to be over the top and treat his position as a clumsy strategy to justify a coup d'état that would take him to power. 'With all his imperfections, we prefer Belaúnde a thousand times over the sight of you, General Cisneros, seated on the chair of Pizarro,' declares an editorial in the weekly *Kausa Popular*. Nevertheless, the situation worsens week by week.

In the early days of March 1982, a Shining Path column attacks Huamanga prison in Ayacucho and, following an exchange of fire with the police, succeeds in freeing a large number of subversives. Three police officers are shot dead. Three wounded terrorists find their way to the city hospital, where one night they are strangled and riddled with bullets by undercover police agents, in revenge for their fallen comrades. The event leaks to the press and becomes a scandal: it is claimed that two of those murdered were innocent. Leaflets appear bearing slogans and the hammer and sickle symbol, in which the guerrillas threaten that they will seize the city of Huamanga after Easter. They are now ready, they declare, to take over as the de facto authority in the region. On Easter Saturday, Minister Cisneros arrives in Huamanga by helicopter and immediately heads for the Los Cabitos military garrison. The soldiers anxiously await their orders to go and hunt the Shining Path guerrillas. A journalist notes down brief statements by the Gaucho. With his combat

191

fatigues, three-star military cap and trimmed moustache, he growls: 'We await our orders from the president. Our engines are running and we're ready to intervene.'

★ ★ ★

Only an event as disturbing to the international order as the Falklands War between the United Kingdom and Argentina could distract Minister Cisneros from insisting on what looked like the Army's imminent participation in armed struggle against the guerrillas.

My father had plenty of reasons for feeling personally affected by the Falklands War: he was born in Buenos Aires and had trained at the National Military College. As if that weren't enough, on the morning of 22 April 1982 a yellow notice arrived on his desk, issued by the Recruitment Office of the Argentinian Army's 3rd Division, advising him that the Territorial Forces reserves had been called up and ordering him to present himself immediately in Buenos Aires for military service. 'You will occupy, with the rank of Lieutenant of the Territorial Force, post 467 of the Argentina-Bolivia border, at the head of a platoon of soldiers,' the notice said. It was, of course, an adminis-trative error – the name Cisneros must have remained on an out-of-date list by mistake – but nevertheless my father, or the impatient soldier that lived inside him, stirred by the memory of his life in Argentina, felt like more of a Gaucho than ever and immediately telephoned his friend, President Leopoldo Fortunato Galtieri, to place himself at his disposition.

There was a further reason, perhaps even the main one, why the Falklands conflict so fired him up. A couple of days after the outbreak of war, Beatriz Abdulá, his unforget-table Beatriz, wrote him a letter to say that Matías – Mati

– her youngest son, now a twenty-one-year-old soldier, had been sent to Puerto Argentino, one of the combat zones. My father had met Mati in 1979 and chatted with him in Beatriz's house. He had been taken with this young man who was not his son but who could have been, and was proud of his military vocation, one that none of his own sons had followed.

On the morning of 5 May 1982, without advising President Belaúnde, Minister Cisneros calls a press conference in the Little Pentagon to declare that Peru 'must not only make statements of solidarity, but must demonstrate this solidarity with action'. He goes on to claim that the military is in a position to support Argentina with troops, ships, submarines, aeroplanes, helicopters, anti-aircraft systems, tanks, supplies and everything the sister country requires. *Caretas* puts him on its front cover. My father stands in his office, unsheathing the sword given to him by General Perón when he graduated as a second lieutenant. The headline: 'Let Me Go to the Falklands!'

President Belaúnde is appalled at the Minister of War once again becoming the spokesman for the whole Executive, and his personal concerns again interfering with the interests of the government. But it's already too late. The declarations by Minister Cisneros have resounded all over the world. The international press point to the minister as the architect of a possible agreement between the Peruvian Army and the Argentinian Army. These front pages sideline Belaúnde: the president prefers to support the mediation efforts of the United States, whose consuls and dignitaries are trying at all costs to avoid open war between the United Kingdom and Argentina. Before the press pack at the Palace of Government, Belaúnde asks for neutrality and support for the US government, and demands that no one speak of 'military assistance' while the diplomatic negotiations continue. 'Peru's sole mission is to serve as a peacemaker,' he underlines, with the measured and solemn tone of a cardinal. For his part, Minister Cisneros keeps nothing to himself: whenever reporters call the house, he doesn't hesitate to disobey the president and insist that Peru should pursue military intervention.

From Washington, through the ambassador to Peru, the US government begins to pressure Belaúnde to remove the vexatious Cisneros from the cabinet. 'His statements are inopportune and fuel a regional current of military support for Argentina that is jeopardising American mediation. If that support takes root, it is we who will look like the saboteurs,' the ambassador says by telephone. President Belaúnde understands the message and at the next council of ministers – among the most tense of all such meetings held in 1982 – announces the government's decision not to pursue any belligerent course of action with regard to the Falklands. To the surprise of all those present, and the Gaucho above all, the president argues that if Peru supports Argentina with war materiel it would be failing to attend to its own borders, particularly those with Chile and Ecuador. 'They have stayed on the sidelines of this dispute, waiting for us to make a mistake. They could take advantage of our weakness,' he observes, looking at the stern faces of his ministers one after the other.

'As for you, General', he says, turning to look directly at Cisneros, 'I would be grateful if you would put less passion into your statements when discussing military assistance for Argentina.'

The general stands up. A shudder runs around the room.

'Forgive me, Mr President, but I don't put passion into my statements. I put passion into my ideas, especially when they are just.'

'You forget, General, that I am the one who takes the

decisions here, not you.'

'May I remind you, Mr President, that it was you, not me, who signed the Ministry of Defence documents saying that we should offer military support to Argentina. My statements seek only to be consistent with your actions.'

In the days following this bitter exchange of views, my father is ready to throw in the towel. But when he hears of the pressure from the Americans, he swallows his pride and rejects the idea of leaving the Ministry. He won't give the gringos that pleasure. If they want to see him out of government, they can sit and wait for it. And if Belaúnde demands his resignation, he will denounce him for allowing a foreign government to meddle in internal affairs. In the end, his intransigence wins over the diplomatic chicanery. The United States abandons its unsuccessful attempt at mediation and Belaúnde, after receiving two emissaries from President Galtieri, decides to send ten Mirage fighter jets with full tanks, as well as ground-to-air and surface-to-air missiles, howitzers, bombs and ammunition. The planes, whose Peruvian flags were erased and replaced with Argentinian ones to deceive the neighbouring countries, leave in formation in the middle of the night, flying silently and using a special route to avoid detection by Chile's radar stations in Iquique and Antofagasta.

Peru's support is not enough to prevent Argentina from losing the war, but it serves to tighten the bonds between the Gaucho and the leaders of the dictatorship, who send him countless honours in gratitude. None of them compare, though, to the letter Beatriz Abdulá writes to let him know that Mati has returned safely from the conflict, psychologically traumatised, but alive. 'My son is young, he will recover,' Beatriz says. She had learned from the media that the Gaucho Cisneros was the one who had insisted on helping Argentina from the outset. 'I felt very proud of you,' she confesses. My father will hide this letter in the locked second drawer of his desk, inside a manila envelope labelled 'Personal'.

★ ★ ★

In July 1982, with the Falklands chapter behind them, terrorism remains the number one problem for the Belaúnde government, which refuses to let the Army enter the town of Ayacucho, now virtually a staging post for the Shining Path. The Minister of War, in one of his last actions before he retires from active military service, visits all the military bases across the country, from north to south. The left-wing press believe that this farewell tour must conceal the coordination of an attempt to overthrow the democratic regime. 'Watch out! Cisneros is planning a coup,' the headline reads in *Kausa Popular*.

That month of July must have been unbearable for my father. On the 22nd, he formally takes his military retirement, in a ceremony captured in a photograph that shows him downcast, with that regal solemnity that always came across him when he was sad, as he bends to kiss the Peruvian flag. One week later, on the 28th, his mother Esperanza dies from advanced leukaemia. My grandmother's death occurs in the early morning. When the phone call comes, my father is getting dressed in preparation for the National Day military parade. I can still picture his crumpled face on the television, seated beside President Belaúnde on the podium. The camera shows him in close up: he is a mass of clumsy gestures. Throughout the parade he thinks of his mother or the corpse of his mother. Hours later, he arrives at the house on La Paz St., where the wake is being held, and from there we go together to the Presbítero Maestro cemetery to bury her. During this journey, sitting beside me in the car, my father doesn't say a word. He is an orphan disguised as a minister of state. A few days earlier he had ceased to be an active soldier; now he has ceased to be a son. First the institution, then the mother. By the time August arrived, he was no longer the same man.

Although retired military personnel have no reason to wear their uniforms, he insisted on using his as soon as he returned to work after the mourning period. 'I'm still a minister,' he says to his reflection in the mirror, adjusting his cap. It is true. He is still Minister of War, and is ready to show just how much the Belaúnde government still needs him. He knows that his self-esteem depends on his remaining a part of the cabinet, and that he will sink into depression if removed. For this reason, to preserve his share of power, to hold onto his office, he determines not to further damage his relationship with the president, but to follow his instructions and be less energetic and categorical during his interviews with the press.

He sticks carefully to these intentions for several weeks, until the first of September arrives. On that day he is scheduled to take a helicopter ride to Andahuaylas, where the presence of a group of Shining Path guerrillas has been reported. There are twenty, perhaps thirty of them. In order to win an advantage, and to prevent other terrorist columns moving from neighbouring provinces to Andahuaylas and reinforcing the exposed contingent, General Cisneros travels to Umaca and coordinates the surveillance missions in situ, drawing up Operation Deadbolt, aimed at encircling this small detachment of rebels. At his side, the Minister of the Interior, Lieutenant General Agustín Gallardo, follows his orders. Even when the police move with stealth, the guerrillas sniff out their presence in the steep hills. On day three, a patrol is attacked by a terrorist platoon: the police react, shots are fired back and forth, there is no let up in the exchange of ammunition. From the base, the Minister of War issues instructions over the radio for a helicopter to support the patrol. By the end of the day, seven militants are dead and three captured. One of the dead is Edith Lagos, the youngest Shining Path leader and a poet from Ayacucho, tiny and fragile in appearance but courageous in combat, who had soon abandoned her law degree in Lima to join the forces of Abimael Guzmán.

> *Life has dealt me blows*
> *and these blows have sharpened my hearing.*
> *My ears have heard so much.*
> *My eyes have seen so many things.*
> *My eyes have shed tears at so much pain*
> *and all this pain*
> *has become a cry on my lips.*

So writes Edith Lagos. When she falls, the Army issues an official account stating that she died in the course of the military confrontation. A few days later, however, her elder sister Norma Lagos claims that she was captured and tortured before being executed, and accuses the Minister of War, General Cisneros, of giving this order. 'They tortured her, they brutally beat her, they cut her on the stomach while the minister was there. They shot her later, when she was already dead. The account of the confrontation is an invention,' Norma relates to a magazine. A few days later, speaking at a press conference in Andahuaylas, General Cisneros responds to this accusation: 'I saw Lagos' body myself, but I saw no signs of beating or torture. She did have several bullet holes in the back and lower stomach, and a piece of intestine was sticking out.'

Returning to Lima, my father seems less sure that the Army should take up the fight against terrorism. He changes his mind from one day to the next. 'We are ready physically, psychologically and technically to intervene as soon as President Belaúnde calls on the support of all the Armed Forces, not only the Army,' he declares to *Expreso*. 'I don't think the process has reached the stage where the men of the Armed Forces can take action,' he states to *Oiga*. 'It isn't the right moment for the Army to act against terrorism. Our intervention would unfortunately be far more drastic, and we must avoid the social cost to the country,' he tells *El Observador*.

The journalists who despise him believe his expressions of doubt to be strategic. 'The General wants to hold onto the Ministry, and so he cools his rhetoric to stay in Belaúnde's good graces,' speculate his enemies. As soon as my father reads these fanciful statements in the newspapers he returns to his original point of view and defends the Army's presence in Ayacucho, as if to leave no one in any doubt about how tough and bold he can be. As if to ensure no one suspects him of being one of the brown-nosers swarming around the president. 'Let there be no doubt: on the day we intervene, terrorism will end in this country,' he tells *El Comercio*.

On the morning that headline hits the streets, the police receive an anonymous phone call: a bomb threat made against the home of the Minister of War. 'Tell Cisneros to watch out. That motherfucking dog's going to die,' a disguised voice says. That day my sister Valentina and I don't go to school, but stay in the house with our uniforms, satchels and lunch boxes. From the second floor of the house on La Paz St. we watch the police as they come and go: unknown men and women with special jackets and devices, meticulously checking every corner of the building, inside every plant pot, beneath every doormat. Not since my grandmother's wake have I seen so many people at the house. So much for us living on the 'street of peace'.

On Wednesday 22 December, the Minister of War presents himself before the Defence Committee of the Chamber of Deputies and warns that if the Army goes into Ayacucho there will be an indiscriminate massacre. The same day, the magazine *Quehacer* publishes an interview he had given a few days earlier. The cover shows an extreme close-up of the Gaucho: his pupils glassy and his eyes with no lashes behind gold-framed glasses, his mouth covered by his left hand, which holds a burning cigarette between his middle and index fingers. The camera is focused on the black pearl of his ring. What he said in this interview would mark the rest of his life. Mine, too.

What we are seeing in Ayacucho, General Cisneros, is a kind of 'control' by the Shining Path: a feeling that unseen eyes are following us, watching us, hunting us.

That's one of the major problems. We don't know who or where they are. They all look like anyone else living in the mountains...

How can this problem be approached?

If the attacks take place at night, I would impose a curfew in Ayacucho. Anything that moves at night gets shot.

If this is necessary, doesn't it mean that the Shining Path are effectively organised, and are achieving their objectives? Is that not the case?

I don't believe they've had any success. They have imposed themselves through terror.

Their success lies in the fact the police forces have been unable to stamp them out...

Well, the police forces are acting effectively within the limitations imposed on them...

And what are those limitations?

First, the lack of adequate equipment. Second, the unequal conditions in which they have to confront the Shining Path.

The terrorists know exactly where the lookout towers are, where the posts are, how many men are in each one and what their movements are. The police forces don't know where the insurgents are, how many there are, or when they're going to attack. For the police forces to succeed, they would have to start shooting guerrillas and non-guerrillas alike because that's the only way to be sure. If they kill sixty people they might get three from the Shining Path... and the police would probably say that all sixty were terrorists.

And what do you think about this option, General? Does it appeal to you?

I think it would be the worst possible option and that's why I'm opposed to the Armed Forces entering this struggle until it's strictly necessary. We don't want this confrontation and neither do the Shining Path. Not because we fear confronting them, but because we're trained and hardened to fight. But ordering Peruvians to kill Peruvians, without being sure that those who will die are even the ones responsible for the terror, is a very hard decision to take, though it's easy to ask for. The involvement of the Army must be the last resort for the government to impose order in the country. I believe it's necessary to attempt every other solution before sending in the Armed Forces, because we will take control of the zone and we will act. We are professionals in the art of war and we are prepared to kill.

No one, or almost no one in the years to come, would notice the Gaucho's precision when stating that he believed an indiscriminate massacre to be 'the worst possible option'. Almost everyone – politicians, priests, sociologists, journalists, poets – condemned the 'for the police forces to succeed they would have to start shooting guerrillas and non-guerrillas alike' and the 'we are prepared to kill'. In 2007, twelve years after my father's death, in response to the emergence of views that sought to associate him with the creation of a theory of collective annihilation, I published an article aimed at defending him. I titled it 'Against a Black Legend'. In a few stark, solemn paragraphs I put my hands to the fire for my father, staunchly defending his democratic spirit:

As his son, it angers me (and as a journalist, it troubles me) that for so many years his responses in the *Quehacer* interview have been taken out of context to suggest that he drew up and patented an extermination manual, or that he spread ideas in the barracks worthy of a murderous dictator. He held a decisive political position in that armed conflict, and due to his geopolitical knowledge and his objective reading of the Shining Path issue, he was among those responsible for determining the strategic positions of the military commandos. There is a massive leap from there to saying that it was he who organised the indeterminate massacre of the Shining Path militants and innocent victims, but a leap that some have not hesitated to take in recent days.

For me – as no doubt for many readers – it is difficult to understand the military philosophy that 'in war there are no human rights', but I admit that as civilians we do not deal in the same concepts as the military and this affects our ability to understand each other. The military is trained to go to war; we, as civilians, are educated to avoid it.

My father never shunned responsibility for his actions as minister, or as a military general. That's why he earned a reputation as a tough and uncompromising soldier. Now that he is no longer here, I allow myself to write these few lines to preserve the dignity of his name and to safeguard the serenity of his memory.

'Preserve'. 'Safeguard'. I wince now at the candour of those words or of the person I was when I wrote them. It's not something I would do today. It was a naïve defence that no one had asked me to launch, but which I felt was my right to set out, moved by what forces I do not know. Was I driven by an authentic desire for justice or a suppressed hunger to capitalise on my father's name and stress that I was not only his son but also his public defender? Sometimes I have the impression that not even the Gaucho himself would have publicly defended himself this way, because he was the primary engine of his own reputation. In later interviews, whenever he had the opportunity to rectify or contextualise his statements in *Quehacer*, he refused to do so, or did so only half-heartedly, allowing people to hold onto the terrible image of him. He had to be the bad guy. He had laboured for years to achieve this. No other military general or politician could wrest the role away from him. What in hell's name was I thinking, depriving him of his aura?

In December 1982 President Belaúnde issues an ultimatum to the Shining Path to surrender. Abimael Guzmán rejects it. In response, the government gives the green light for intervention by the Army, which sends 520 soldiers to the Ayacucho jungle and orders the arrest of anyone suspected of involvement with subversive activities. Journalists, who know that the Minister of War is behind these measures, call him continually to ask for his views. The minister – who knows or intuits that he won't remain in the cabinet for long, that his declarations in *Quehacer* will be used to force him out, that these are his final days in power – gives himself full rein, unleashing another torrent of fierce, thunderous, unbridled words. 'I can assure you that 1983 will be a year of order and peace. Ayacucho will be calm. The days of the Shining Path are numbered. The Army will respond to the bloodbath begun by the terrorists.

We are awaiting orders for the first attack,' he says, as if he could guarantee an outcome that was no longer going to depend on him.

The next day, his words appear as headlines on the newsstands: 'Cisneros announces extermination of Shining Path by end of year.' This is his final statement as minister. Although spokespeople on the right support him publicly and claim that President Belaúnde has confidence in his Minister of War, the General leaves the cabinet in mid-January. 'The Gaucho falls at last!' cries *Última Hora*. The pundits accuse him of an 'unstoppable thirst for power', of having woven his 'own anti-guerrilla strategy', or simply of being 'too tough for a democratic government'.

★ ★ ★

We spend that summer, the first summer of his retirement, at Punta Negra, in a house we'd rented at the top of a hill. General Cisneros' ranch by the beach, the left-wing press call it. To this beach house there come and go a constant stream of soldiers dressed as civilians and politicians dressed as politicians. Even Alan García, who would become president of Peru two years later, shows up a couple of times. My sister Valentina and I stay clear of my father's conversations with these people on the terrace. Only my mother intervenes from time to time and is thoroughly bored by their conspiratorial murmurs. For our part, we're having too much fun in the pools of the Club Punta Negra, or riding our bikes around the resort, or playing near the intimidating rock outcrops, or invading the houses of the Gamio, the Cerruti, or the Souza families, or dancing to B52 songs at our first parties, or embarking on expeditions to the dangerous El Revés beach, where the current betrays the most daring swimmers, some of whom are swallowed up by that sea with its yellowish foam that we're forbidden to approach, and which we approach for that very reason, if only to feel the temperature of its dark waters.

And so the summer days go by. My father up there, on the terrace in the sun, planning his political future and analysing the situation of the country in the company of old friends, guzzling aged whisky, imported vodka, cold beers, eating banquets to the tunes played by local groups or even mariachi bands, hired to sing their endless repertoires until the early hours of the morning. Down below, in the shingly sand, when not playing with my twelve- and thirteen-year-old buddies – who at the time seemed my closest friends but who in fact I would never meet again – I was building my own universe. A universe with time and space for a secret hobby I don't share with anyone: hunting lizards. That's what I spend the summer doing. When no one can see me, I am a lizard hunter. Armed with a stick, creeping through the weeds that sprout from the rocks above a nearly secluded beach, I track these swift little reptiles. Once I catch them, I knock them out with a blow, I immobilise them somehow on a brick from a nearby building site and then I torture them, burning their scaly skin with one of my father's cigarette lighters, applying the flame to their stomachs, and the poor lizards wriggle desperately, trying to get away, emitting shrieks inaudible to human ears. Before they're completely charred – acting with a cruelty, a sadism and a brutality that wells up in me from some source I've never brought myself to understand – I mutilate their limbs, their five-toed legs and their tails, which begin to jump around of their own accord, leaving tracks of greenish blood as they zigzag away from the lifeless body of the mutilated animal. This is something I do not once but several times that summer of 1983. Always alone, always on that same beach, without any witnesses who might question the violence that overtakes me.

***

The Gaucho's departure from the cabinet doesn't keep him out of the headlines. There is no shortage of reasons for his name to stay in the front-page news, and they are never good reasons. In mid-March, *Marka* accuses him of being behind an allegedly irregular purchase of over 100,000 Argentinian rifles during his time as Minister of War. FAL rifles, which supposedly proved to be defective. *Marka* claims the operation implicates an arms seller by the name of Schneider. Reading these articles years later, the name sounds familiar. After a few minutes' thought it comes to me: my uncle Raúl, Raúl Schneider, and his pretty wife Irene, accompanying my parents in photographs, strolling through gardens in Montevideo or posing on the viewpoint at Iguazú Falls.

'Everything points towards former minister Cisneros Vizquerra,' reads one of the *Marka* headlines. The newspaper *Clarín* takes up the story in Buenos Aires. Nevertheless, although new details appear each week, the allegation is poorly documented. General Cisneros responds with a furious public letter, dismissing it as an act of revenge against a former minister who shut down newspapers and expelled communists. The right-wing media support his position. The affair is put to bed when the Army and the Congressional Standing Committee endorse the purchase and declare themselves satisfied with the explanations offered by my father. In response, the editor of *Marka*, a seasoned journalist by the name of Juan Manuel Macedo, writes irate, libelous columns. As I read them now, I realise that he is the very same Juanma Macedo whom I greet every evening on the television set where we both work, and I can't help but wonder if his cordiality towards me is genuine or a pretence.

A few months after these allegations are cleared up, my father is mentioned as a potential candidate to head up the Ministry of the Interior again, or even as prime minister. The left-wing press are in no doubt that the source of these rumours is Cisneros himself: 'He is nostalgic for power and wants to return to the Belaúnde government by any means possible.' There is some truth behind the speculation: the Gaucho does miss being in office, though there is also an appeal to being able to offer his political views without restriction. If his opinions on how to deal with the Shining Path were forceful before, now – no longer part of the regime, answerable to no boss or mandate – his words are devastating. 'If the judges have qualms, then the terrorists should be subject to military trials,' he tells *Oiga*. 'If terrorism reaches the levels it did in Argentina in the 1970s, the Armed Forces will be obliged to take power again,' he warns Canal 4. 'Telephone lines and postal communications must be intercepted, as I did in the past,' he reveals in *Expreso*. 'This is a dirty war because the leaders of the rebellion exploit people's hope and naïveté,' he remarks in *La República*. 'The death penalty should be imposed. That would make Shining Path sympathisers think twice about fighting to the death. It won't solve the problem of the rebellion, but at least the criminals we sentence won't kill again,' he says in *Perspectiva*. 'If more guerrillas are dying, it's because our men have better aim,' he jokes to *El Comercio*. 'We can't have a squeamish peacetime democracy when the country is experiencing a prolonged war,' he observes in *Caretas*. 'I don't see how the rule of law can be upheld in a warzone. We order the Armed Forces to eliminate the Shining Path, and just as we're about to pull the trigger the prosecutor general appears to check if we're going to shoot the guy head-on or from the side, and then the lawyer turns up, followed by the journalist, the photographer, the priest.

What the hell is going on?' he complains in *El Nacional*.

My father keeps nothing to himself, and refuses to exercise more self-restraint. Every time a reporter rouses him, fishing for some controversial statement that will spark debate and provide journalistic material for the rest of the week, he plays along and resumes the role that had begun to soften in retirement, a mixture of vigilante and repressor:

What recommendations would you offer, General, to halt the advance of the Shining Path?

We have to counterattack and cut off the space still left to the guerrillas. Anyone showing support for the Shining Path must be eliminated from public service. For example, if a teacher is found to have connections to the Path, is an activist, they must be eliminated from the teaching profession.

Only from the profession, I imagine…

That's what I said, from the profession. The other thing, even if I think it I don't say it.

And do you think it?

No.

Are you sure, General?

I don't think it today.

This is the tone of his declarations over the following years. The further he is from power, the more emphatic his words, as if he feels the need to make himself noticed in order to stay relevant within the political sphere, or just so he wouldn't seem like any old retired military officer. His impudence rekindles old hatreds on the left and creates new antipathies.

'With what authority does General Cisneros talk about how to wage war on the Shining Path if he never did so when he had the chance? The only battles this Gaucho wins are around tables in the Miraflores Casino.' So writes

Salomón Bautista in his magazine. He is a fifty-something journalist, obese, big-nosed, who wears light jackets he can't close properly and ties that look too short above his prominent belly, and who suffers from arthritic feet, which he drags around the bars of Lima. He favours Miraflores and San Isidro, where he is often seen limping delicately to ease the suffering in his inflamed heels. He sits at the bar and orders beers that he tops up with Coca-Cola, and eats green tamales all night until he is finally satiated. Grotesque, greedy, he converses with the locals, gathering rumours and political gossip that he decants into his celebrated opinion columns, which are steeped in this foul-mouthed, bar-crawling air. Having spent most of the military government in Panama, Salomón Bautista – the oldest son of a former communist who sought refuge there as soon as Velasco fell – returned to Peru and founded his magazine, *Cuestionario*. Despite its sober name, the publication specialises in long articles filled with reckless lies and fallacies, in addition to its main attraction: the relentless and incendiary outpourings of its editor.

Between 1985 and 1990, the five-year duration of the Alan García government, General Cisneros is nothing short of a regular in *Cuestionario*. The magazine criticises every single one of his proposals, from the imposition of the state of emergency throughout the country, to the Armed Forces' entry into San Marcos University to 'clear out' subversives, to the mobilisation of military reservists to confront terrorism. 'We retired officers should be fighting the Shining Path,' the general declares.

But these aren't the statements that most exasperate Salomón Bautista. Those would come later, once the terrorist attacks have become bloodier still and the bodies begin to pile up in the hundreds on both sides. Statements like those in which the Gaucho obstinately defends second lieutenant

Telmo Hurtado, nicknamed the 'Curse of Accomarca' for the massacres he perpetrated there and in the nearby zones of Llocllapampa, Pitecc, Huancayocc, Umaru and Bellavista. 'Don't you realise that Second Lieutenant Hurtado has spent a long time in Ayacucho risking his life for Peru every minute of every day?' Years later, Hurtado himself confesses his responsibility in the indiscriminate murder of these innocent townspeople who had nothing to do with the Shining Path, or at least not enough to deserve being cut into pieces or burned alive.

The Gaucho also declares himself in favour of the military and police operation that leads to the deaths of hundreds of prisoners in the riots sweeping the El Frontón, Lurigancho and Santa Bárbara jails. His words make an even more indignant critic of Salomón Bautista.

Days before the riots break out, the press reveal that the terrorists imprisoned in El Frontón are refusing to be trans-ferred to the Canto Grande jail because they believe the conditions there to be inhuman. In a three-page interview with *Oiga*, my father protests: 'This little group of subver-sives has imposed its own rules on the state, which has expended a huge amount of resources to build a secure prison like Canto Grande, but lacks the authority to move them there. Who's in charge? The government or the terrorists?' A few hours after this edition of *Oiga* appears on the newsstands, Shining Path delegates, in what seems to be a direct riposte to General Cisneros, issue a communiqué saying 'We'd rather die than go to Canto Grande.'

'What do you think of that, General?' they ask my father on Canal 5, who speaks via a direct link from the Monterrico house.

'If the rebels prefer to die, then I think we should give them their wish. That's one of the few pleasures that the state can provide. If they like, they can sign a letter and we'll go right ahead. The state will fulfil their request. And if they prefer not to surrender, then we'll finish them off anyway.'

My father replies as if he was still in charge of the operation, using plural conjugations and pronouns that were nothing but a symptom of his longing to exercise real power.

Working together with the Marines, the Armed Forces quash the riot and kill eighty per cent of the terrorists held prisoner in El Frontón. The same occurs in Lurigancho and Santa Bárbara, where the ordinary prisoners have joined forces with the protest leaders. General Cisneros arrives at the studios of Canal 5 to discuss the outcome of the military actions along with a panel of experts. 'There is only one goal in war: to win. And while we're at war, the ones responsible for defending society are the professionals. We're not blood-thirsty, just professional. We know how to kill. These are the results.' This is his first contribution to the debate, speaking once again as if he had been part of the outcome, as if he had been physically present among the soldiers shooting at the prisoners, shooting at those with their hands above their heads, sunk to their knees in surrender.

At the time, if any of his children, siblings or friends committed the mistake of suggesting he not be so critical, or reminded him that he was no longer in active service, the Gaucho would react violently, his eyes motionless behind his glasses, his moustache bristling. Brandishing any object within reach – a pencil, a spoon, a pipe – he'd raise his voice to explain to anyone within earshot that he had never felt like he was retired. 'I may no longer have political respon-sibilities', he'd shout, 'but I still have a military vocation and no one is going to take that away from me, damn it. That's something I'm going to die with. I will die a soldier, and I want my gravestone to read that here lies an honourable soldier, here lies a true soldier!'

While the right-wing press promotes the 'Cisnerist doctrine' and the need to 'Cisnerise' the Army, praising the former minister's analysis of the terrorist problem and the solutions he puts forward in his interviews, their left-wing counterparts treat him with scorn. As always, Salomón Bautista is to the fore. 'Cisneros is the most ardent defender of the dirty war,' writes Bautista in his *Cuestionario* column after the prison killings. Over the course of 1987, the general continues to make regular media appearances. He begins by criticising President Alan García's closeness to the Cuban government. Then he denounces García's ideological proximity to the Túpac Amaru revolutionary movement, the new guerrilla group that has recently emerged in the mountains. He still blames President García for having destroyed the unity within APRA and for bringing the ruling party closer to Marx than to its founder, Víctor Raúl Haya de la Torre. Finally, he warns of a possible coup d'état by the generals, which could remedy the whole thing. In response to the Gaucho's statements, Salomón Bautista – who has since become a close friend of Alan García, trading his beer/Coca-Cola mixture in the bars of Miraflores and San Isidro for Pantagruelesque private lunches at the table the President has permanently reserved at the El Cordano bar – returns to the charge again, regretting 'the ideological narrowness and dogmatic stubbornness of Cisneros'. Then he pours petrol on the fire by writing nothing less than this: 'God save Peru from both Abimael Guzmán and the Gaucho, that bull dog with dark designs who dreams of a far-right military coup.'

Without responding directly to Bautista's attacks but taking them into consideration, the general defends himself in the trenches offered by *El Nacional*, *Misión* and *Expreso*. He asks: 'If this country permits such a defence of terrorism, then why am I not allowed to defend the coup?' Cisneros criticises the government for accepting or permitting or supporting political coexistence with Marxism, and not daring to put a definitive end to subversion, becoming its 'involuntary ally'. He also rejects the merging of the Ministries of War, Navy and Air Force into the Ministry of Defence; accuses Alan García of being weak, erratic, personalist, polarising; and warns that worn-out governments like this one only lead to power vacuums. 'This vacuum will be filled either by anarchy or by the Armed Forces. Of these two options, I prefer the Armed Forces,' declares the general.

Igor Meléndez, an established reporter for *Misión*, asks him what should be done with the Shining Path prisoners:

I would order the execution of all the top ranks of the Shining Path.

But… what about human rights, General?

Look, Meléndez, if this is a war, we can't send a priest to talk to them before we kill them, nor a lawyer to read them their rights.

Are you proposing unconstitutional methods, General Cisneros…?

Let me give you an example, Igor. When a relative is seriously ill and you place them in a doctor's hands, you don't tell him where to make the incision, do you?

Of course not.

Well, it's the same with the Armed Forces. They're ready to put an end to the subversion, not to discuss their methods.

What you're telling me is that our military are in fact acting against the law and the international treaties Peru has signed?

No, I am not. What I'm telling you is that I teach a soldier to kill, that's what I prepare him for. Later I teach him to defend himself, but first and foremost to kill.

That's very tough talk, General Cisneros.

I may be tough, but I'm also pragmatic. I say what I think, while politicians think too carefully about what they say. I'm a soldier, Meléndez, and I've been trained to kill. I've been trained to lead a group of men who kill and fight to keep from getting killed themselves. If we're assigned a mission, people must know that this is how we think.

So, you're not concerned about killing innocent people...

In a war it's not always only the guilty who die.

Do you mean to say the state is killing the innocent?

Listen to me, Meléndez. If the rebels win, we'll become a communist country and you'll see me and many other military men hanging from the trees. It's certainly unfortunate that innocent people have to die today, but that's preferable to the massacre that may come tomorrow.

What you're proposing is that we follow the example of Argentina...

In 1982, President Belaúnde told me: 'I don't want an Argentina-style solution.' 'Me neither,' I replied, and I pointed out that if we embarked on a war right then and there, the outcome would be fifteen hundred dead bodies. I told him: 'The longer you take to make a decision, the more people will have committed themselves to the rebellion.'

Wouldn't it be better to seek dialogue with the guerrilla leaders?

Don't be so damn naïve! Terrorists must be put down, killed without mercy! Then we can prise information from the ones taken prisoner, by any means necessary. If they decide to open their mouths once we've got them, then and only then can we talk about dialogue.

The morning after this interview, an elected representative from the ruling party, and another on the left, propose a motion to Congress that seeks to charge General Cisneros with 'sedition, disturbance of public order, threatening national security, inciting coups d'état, rebellion and murder'.

Reproaches rain down on the Gaucho from all sides, even from the circle of retired military officers. Former colleagues now distance themselves from him, stating publicly that Cisneros 'is no longer relevant or important'. Only a few rightist media outlets and politicians applaud his iron fist. The left-wing press, meanwhile, have a field day with his statements. 'It's time for Cisneros to lay down his sword like the old warrior he is,' jokes *Kausa Popular*, while 'All mouth and no trousers' is the headline in *Última Hora*. 'Bolivia had its García Meza, in Peru we have Cisneros Vizquerra,' exclaims *Equis*, in allusion to General Luis García Meza Tejada, who had overthrown Lidia Gueiler Tejada, Bolivia's first and only female president – who was also his cousin.

None of these criticisms come anywhere near the level of extravagance and recklessness achieved by Salomón Bautista, who dedicates an entire issue of *Cuestionario* to a verbal lynching.

This is a short-arse general of puny moral and physical stature, who has Napoleonic appetites and longs to recover the power he lost when he retired, who believes himself to be bold and influential when in truth he is all bark and no bite. At home, for instance, he rules over no one; he is not even obeyed by his youthful second wife, at whose feet he fell after conspiring to get rid of the first one. The readers of *Cuestionario* must know that this jumped-up general punished his subordinates for breaking their conjugal vows and drinking themselves into oblivion, only to engage in the very same depravities himself.

I can picture tubby Salomón Bautista now, gleefully bashing away at his typewriter's clunky keys, whether in the slum-like magazine office on the top floor of a building on Junín St., or in his shabby room in the Barrios Altos district, on the second floor of a house taken over by prostitutes, junkies, low-lives and other unfortunates who socialised with Bautista as if he was one of their own, speaking to him in liquor-soaked voices from out of the uniform darkness that rendered them unrecognisable. I can see him hunched by a window or skylight, drinking his beer cut with Coca-Cola, chain-smoking cigarettes, probably barefoot to ease the arthritic aches of his already-deformed feet. I see him cackling as he considers how to punish General Cisneros, stirring up the same old allegations and printing all kinds of wild claims he has dreamt up. 'Let's not forget that General Cisneros once ordered the assault on the offices of the National Agrarian Confederation; that he personally pursued union leaders over rooftops and through yards; that with his own hands he tried to kidnap the sacred coffin of General Velasco Alvarado, and that he set free a score of drug traffickers who paid him millions of dollars in exchange for their liberty.' Salomón Bautista types on, by now without jacket or shirt or trousers, his pale carcass covered only by a string vest and over-stretched pants, doused in that sweat-soaked night, and he decides to liquidate Cisneros once and for all with a tirade of epithets, insults and name-calling that will overwhelm readers with their unforgettable genius. Bewitched by his own prose, drugged by his dark virtuosity and his hatred, selecting virulent adjectives as if they were deadly pins for a voodoo doll, he hits the caps lock key of his clanking machine:

GENERAL CISNEROS IS THE BLACK POPE OF FASCISM! THE HIGH PRIEST OF REPRESSION! SCOUNDREL OF THE FATHERLAND! SLUM HOODLUM! COUP-STIRRING TANGO AFICIONADO! THE GRAND INQUISITOR! COUP-CUCKOO! THE ABIMAEL GUZMÁN OF THE RIGHT! DEVIL OF THE PAMPAS! CLUB-WIELDING TURK! BIG BAD WOLF OF THE CAVERNS! VIDELA'S PET! WANNABE PINOCHET! FRIEND TO

THE GENOCIDES! GESTAPO NOSTALGIST! CERBERUS OF THE UPRISING! SCARECROW OF TORQUEMADA! GENGHIS KHAN OF BUENOS AIRES! FLAG-BEARER OF THE DICTATORSHIP! COLD-BLODDED APOLOGIST! INCORRIGIBLE BUTCHER! ATTILA THE GAUCHO! FEARFUL COMMANDANT! SCOURGE OF THE LEFT! IDEOLOGUE OF REPRESSION! GRIM HUSSAR OF THE NIGHT!

I can see Salomón Bautista now, already overcome as he places the final exclamation mark, collapsing onto his desk, which is covered with crumpled papers and dried crusts of bread, and banging his head against the typewriter as he falls asleep or slips into a stupor or drops dead from a rage-induced heart-attack.

I remember that issue of *Cuestionario* well. I read it many years later. A sideboard in the house was stuffed with magazines from the 1970s and 80s, hundreds of large tomes bound in green leather, their spines bearing the name of the journal stamped in gold letters. When we got bored of the TV, my sister Valentina and I liked to spend hours leafing through these volumes. I particularly enjoyed the old-fashioned adverts, the fashions, the happy young faces gazing out of the society pages, alongside politicians and actors whose stars had clearly faded. My sister, by contrast, liked to pause over the pages that featured my father and read them out loud with relish, so we'd learn a little more about who he was or who that man in a blue tracksuit had been – the same man who was sitting outside at the patio table under the parasol, drinking a Bloody Mary for breakfast and snacking on salted beetroot. When we came across that issue of *Cuestionario*, Valentina broke into tears at the first article and marched out to the patio, demanding to know if what they said in the magazine was true or not. I found all this very funny and of little importance, though I was intrigued

217

by the name of Salomón Bautista, which made me think of the grotesque biblical characters with the hairy faces that appeared in outdated books and movies about Easter.

* * *

How strange that November of 1987 looks now. I could have sworn it was a period worth reliving, but now I'm not so sure. While my father is producing these explosive statements, I'm struggling to get through my first year of secondary school. This is a time when I hate everything about myself: my glasses, my fragility, the Olympian indifference I am treated with by Mariela Arboleda, the girl I've loved or desired or simply longed for since the end of primary school. I also hate the fact my mother isn't with us because of a lung disease that keeps her in the military hospital for three months, unable to escape the bed with its broken springs, the drips, the trays of tasteless food.

Only with the passage of the years – and multiple conversations along the way – have I been able to reconstruct this period and understand how hard she took her hospitalization. Not only because of the chest pains from the pleurisy, or the jabs she receives to calm them, but because she feel abandoned. My father goes to see her twice a week for a few minutes, and then he leaves again without saying where to. Is he still deceiving Cecilia with that former air hostess who lives somewhere by San Borja Park, or does he have another lover by now? My father's few and fleeting visits to the military hospital are a cause of concern for Doctor Puch too, who speaks to my mother every day, and has perhaps fallen in love with her over these many weeks. At first they only talk about her treatment, but Puch gradually begins to touch on her emotional life, to explore that solitude that appears to be the true cause of her

218

ills. Whenever he takes Cecilia's wrist, the doctor strokes her hand, seeking to provide the tranquillity my father does not, afflicting her with his absences, escapades and undoubted infidelities. Months later, Puch goes to visit Cecilia at the Monterrico house, taking her some medicines. He says he wants to see how her recovery is coming along. When he leaves, my father – who has sensed a warmth between his wife and the doctor that is alien to him – tells Cecilia in one of his few outbursts of jealousy: 'What did that timewaster want? Why does he need to bring the medicines here? Do him a favour and make sure he doesn't come back. I don't want to have to tell him myself.'

★ ★ ★

The final stretch of the 1980s are a hellish time. On top of the ferocity of the Shining Path and the MRTA, who kill civilians, police and soldiers alike, the country has to endure President Alan García, who accumulates blunders at a dizzying rate. His plan to nationalise the banks and financial institutions causes such a ruckus that people pour onto the streets chanting 'He's going to fall, he's going to fall, Crazy Horse is going to fall!' The slogan alludes to the mental instability of someone who, well-placed sources claim, needs a regular dose of lithium to keep himself on an even keel and stave off attacks of mania or depression.

Although they had been introduced at Punta Negra years earlier by a mutual acquaintance, my uncle Sergio Ramírez Ronceros, and had spent an apparently amiable evening together, the reality is that my father cannot stand García. The feeling is mutual. That's why from 1987 until the end of the Aprista government, my father is not only García's harshest military critic, but also the first to applaud and support any attempt to unseat him.

The most ambitious such attempt is the so-called Green Plan, devised by elements within the Army in consultation with former military officers, General Cisneros among them.

The mission of the Green Plan, according to the first paragraph of the final document, is as follows:

> To evaluate future national scenarios in order to choose the most suitable among them, overthrow the civil government and dissolve the executive and legislative powers so that the Armed Forces can take command of the state, in order to revert the current political, social and economic situation, which threatens to destroy the system and institutions that safeguard the integrity of the Peruvian Republic.

For the military – the 'Greens' – García represents a profound failure, a tragedy, a threat. His administration sows widespread evils that can only be corrected with an authoritarian response: hyperinflation, flight of capital, hypertrophy of the state, expansion of bureaucracy, a huge increase in foreign debt, recession, violence, unemployment. In the streets, when people manage to overcome their fear of leaving the house, they grow old on street corners, queuing interminably for basic goods. If a car bomb doesn't explode on their way home, they can bring their kids milk in plastic bags and a few rolls of People's Bread to make up the frugal breakfasts Peruvians endured in the 1980s. The Green Plan proposes to put an end to all this and establish an 'efficient mentality' with the support of business leaders, a model that future president Alberto Fujimori will eventually adopt in place of the government plan he so sorely lacked.

In 1988 my father predicts that García won't see out the end of his term 'if the rebellion, lack of confidence and economic crisis continue'. A Univisión TV report to mark the thousandth day of the Aprista government includes an interview with him, filmed at home, that lasts one minute and twenty seconds. The reporter introduces him with the words: 'In Lima the latest statements by General Luis Cisneros have caused an uproar. Although exaggerated by the press, he retains close links with serving military officers.' The shot cuts to the Gaucho, who is wearing a brown cotton jacket, his gold watch on his left wrist, a Rothmans in his mouth, his breathing rather laboured:

> This is no longer a presidential government but a personalist one. A government in which the president forces ministers to say what he wants, and the parliament to approve what he wants. At this very moment he is engaged in a struggle with the judiciary to impose his personal designs. As a result, if a coup should occur, it will be entirely and solely the responsibility of President García.

The horizontal panning of the camera reveals, to one side, the brown briefcase whose five-digit code I always wanted to work out; the radio-television set – a great novelty in its time – that I would ask to borrow to watch my favourite series, *Hammer House of Horror*, the sculpture of a rearing black horse; the commemorative plates and all those other desk items that today – scattered, smashed, defunct, buried, forgotten, sold, lost – can no longer bring anyone back to life.

One morning, Mariella Balbi, the lead reporter for *La República*, arrives at my father's office in the basement of the Monterrico house. She expresses an interest in the three- and four-hour-long meetings he is holding in the San Isidro Country Club, where he has often been seen in recent weeks in confabulation with other retired military officers until late at night. Trying to conceal his surprise, the general confines himself to saying that they are strictly personal appointments. 'Yet there is a strong rumour, General, about a group of officials planning a coup. Do you know anything about this?' Balbi insists. 'Absolutely nothing,' Cisneros replies curtly, wondering whether his answer is best accompanied by a puff on the Hamilton resting in the ashtray, or a sip from the cup of black coffee that stands steaming at a corner of the desk. He opts for the coffee.

I'm asking you because you are renowned as a plotter of coups. If an uprising were being planned, you would surely know about it.

Now hang on a moment. Let me tell you, Ms Balbi, that over the course of my career, sometimes in fulfilment of orders and sometimes of my own will, I have conspired against military governments. As a second-lieutenant I conspired against Bustamante. As a lieutenant against General Odría. As a captain I was part of the plot led by General Zenón Noriega. As a major I intervened in the coup that took out President Prado. As a lieutenant colonel I participated in Velasco's coup against Belaúnde. As a colonel I conspired against Velasco, and as a brigadier general, well, I'm sure there'll have been some conspiring. So, if you are going to tell me I am a coup-plotter, at least say that I am a coup-plotter with democratic principles.

But that's a contradiction!

Let me repeat myself. I've never plotted against a democratic government. Not to date.

Not to date? That sounds like a threat to President García.

Well, President García is doing his very best to convince me to break with my tradition.'

The Green Plan against Alan García is revealed by the international press. One day in January 1989 the *Washington Post* headlines its international news pages: 'Presumed military coup in Peru frustrated by US opposition.'

The article describes the meetings among military officers in the Country Club, as well as those they or their emissaries have held with officials from the US Embassy in Lima to request that country's support should the uprising occur. 'The Peruvian officers had a date planned, even the exact time the tanks would roll out onto the street. They were going to carry out a Pinochet-style coup to ensure they were firmly embedded in power,' claims the *Post*.

I never would have known the depth of my father's involvement in these lengthy – and fruitless – negotiations if I hadn't met Major General Jaime Monsante Barchelli around noon on 23 January 2013, in the changing room of the club where I went to swim and he went to play Basque pelota or pétanque or simply to pass the time.

'I bet you don't know who I am!' he said as he approached the metal locker I was just closing, his arms wide open.

I could only summon a look of confusion.

'I'm Jaime Monsante, a friend of your father's!' he introduced himself, embracing me warmly.

In 1987, as part of the manoeuvres orchestrated by the faction of the Armed Forces that intended to overthrow García, Monsante had ordered three fighter jets to carry out a flyover of the Palace of Government. This was a message from the military to warn García that he should take seriously the discontent in the barracks, and to be ready for anything. 'That day, I thought we were going to bomb the Palace, but they only wanted to scare Alan or perhaps to warn him,' Monsante later confesses to me, as we enjoy fillet of seared beef in one of the club's restaurants, watching the huge waves hitting the Chorrillos breakwater, their spray scattering the pigeons and seagulls that gather there in search of food. After swearing me to total discretion

223

with theatrical displays of distress, as if he secretly hoped I would someday reveal what he is about to share, Monsante relates to me that at the end of 1987 my father, through his contacts, hired two hitmen in the United States to eliminate Alan García.

These were the exact words he used: hired, hitmen, eliminate. 'This wasn't something we arranged in the Country Club. It was in the Sheraton Hotel. We met there in the middle of the night. A group of businessmen put up money for the operation and paid in advance for the hitmen to come to Lima. Your father got them aboard, but no one had reckoned with the fact that the same plane was carrying none other than Luis Alberto Sánchez!' In 1987, Sánchez was the oldest and most respected leader of the APRA party, and a large security contingent was waiting to receive him at Lima airport. 'The quick-thinking hitmen', Monsante continues, 'were very professional. On arrival, they put their cases through security together with Sánchez's, collecting them from the belt when the Aprista people were looking the other way. As far as I recall, they spent a few days in Lima, staking out García, but then the businessmen got cold feet and asked the Gaucho to abort the mission. He put them on the next plane out of the country. That's how the assassination of the president was halted.'

García doesn't need to know such details to place my father among his detractors and enemies. Despite the president's animosity toward General Cisneros, he reads the articles he writes for *Expreso* in which he criticises the government's failings and the abysmal lack of intelligence in its anti-dissident strategy. One morning in late 1987 García summons General Belisario Schwartz, the most experienced advisor to the intelligence services, to the Palace of Government. He demands explanations for the allegations made by Cisneros. He could have called on his Minister of War, the Aprista-supporting General Coco Flores, but doubts his abilities and views him as an ornament in the cabinet, placed there to mollify the party.

'Listen, Schwartz, what's going on? Where are the intelligence reports? Is anyone doing any work over there or are you all just scratching your balls?' García challenges the general, leaning back in his leather chair, his feet propped up on his desk, a copy of *Expreso* lying open at the opinion pages.

'Mr President, these reports exist. I send them to you every week. You receive them.'

'Yes, yes, but there's nothing on what to do about terrorism.'

'What needs to be done is not a matter for the intelligence services. It's a question of your own political decisions.'

'Dammit, are you trying to tell me how to govern?'

'Not at all, sir. You are the president. But let me tell you one thing: you're surrounded by the wrong people. You believe the music they whisper in your ears.'

'You refer to the Minister of War?'

'Yes, but not only him…'

'You think I don't know Coco Flores is a useless minister?'

'You said it, sir.'

'Listen, Schwartz, since we're talking about it, why don't you tell me who you'd put in his place.'

'The person I'd recommend won't please you at all.'

'Who do you mean? Speak, dammit!'

'I'd replace him with General Cisneros.' Schwartz raises a finger and motions to the newspaper.

'Cisneros?' García dismisses the suggestion with a gesture of annoyance, tosses the newspaper to the floor and returns his gaze to the vast window that overlooks a corner of the Plaza de Armas. 'You may leave, Schwartz. Don't forget to sharpen up those reports.'

Criticism of the Gaucho intensifies when in November 1989 the Shining Path calls an armed strike in Junín, Huánuco, Ayacucho, Huancavelica, Cerro de Pasco, Puno, Cañete, Huaral and Lima, in an attempt to sabotage the upcoming municipal elections. The terrorists – who have already crept up on the outskirts of Lima, infiltrated the poor suburbs and even marched down the city's main avenues and highways with their balaclavas removed – are seeking to penetrate still further into the capital. In his *Expreso* column and in interviews, General Cisneros insists on the death penalty for terrorist leaders and again proposes military tribunals for captured guerrilla fighters. He misses no opportunity to blame Alan García for permitting the chaos with his failure to act: 'President García lacks the willpower either to resign or to take responsibility for what is going on. He is the main problem facing this country today. He doesn't realise that Peru is on fire. All he cares about are his barbecues, palace cocktails and parties.'

Earlier that year, on 29 July, the Gaucho and García had met at the Peruvian Independence Day parade. My father had recently accused the president not only of permitting the advance of the rebels, but also of setting up death squads to get rid of his political enemies. 'The Armed Forces must not allow García to finish his term in office. If the country is sunk, we have the President of the Republic to thank,' he tells Ricardo Müller, host of a Canal 2 programme.

Days later, Müller has the opportunity to ask the question of the president himself, in a live interview broadcast from the Palace:

Don't you think the criticisms of General Cisneros represent a signif-icant sector of the Army?'

I do not believe that Cisneros represents anyone in the Army. What's more, I don't think he ever did. Too bad for him.

Well, he was Minister of the Interior and would have become Commander-in-Chief if he hadn't accepted the War Ministry portfolio.

And he was also responsible for the expansion of the Shining Path. For that reason, he has little moral authority to be talking about things he failed to do.

The day of the military parade, my father climbs onto the central podium and, following the protocol in place every year, greets the ministers and dignitaries assembled there on the way to his seat. The line is long and slow-moving. The television cameras broadcast proceedings across the nation. Gradually the Gaucho draws closer to García, who has already spotted him. Then they are face to face.

'Good morning, sir,' García says, looking down at him from his full six foot four height.

Those to either side can sense the tension between them.

'Good morning, sir,' the Gaucho responds.

'You address me as Mr President!' García grips his hand. The line falls silent.

'And you address me as General!' Cisneros grips even tighter.

This was the last time their paths crossed.

* * *

The following year, 1990, is not short of incidents. In January, the Tupac Amaru Revolutionary Movement (MRTA) assassinates the former Minister of Defence,

General López Albújar, a friend of my father's. 'Selective terrorism has commenced,' the Gaucho says when they call for his reaction.

I can still recall the grim images of the bullet-riddled General López Albújar, his eyes blank forever, his bloodied body dripping into the seat of the car he was driving when his assassins surprised him. At the time, I was convinced that if my father didn't fall to a terrorist ambush, he would be executed by APRA paramilitaries who'd had enough of his criticism. Every time the news showed the images of the dead López Albújar in his three-piece suit, being gathered up by his assistants from among the shattered windscreen glass, I would automatically swap the general's face for my father's. We were deeply afraid that something similar would happen to him, or maybe to one of us. Beginning in 1988, I had a recurring nightmare in which a column of a hundred terrorists wearing balaclavas or red scarves on their heads descended from the hills in front of us, encircling our house and shooting until they'd killed us all. Similar dreams tormented my sister Valentina, my brother Facundo and my mother too. By the early 90s, we were all experts in dealing with telephone threats. My mother answered the phone on numerous occasions to hear distorted voices warning her that her children would be kidnapped as they left school or that our house would be blown up that very night. She would fly into a state of panic and not calm down until my father swore that nothing would happen to us.

During this period, we would use different routes to get to school each day. If one day we took Angamos Ave. followed by Benavides, the next we'd go by the Primavera bridge and then down Tomás Marsano, or head up Javier Prado and meander through San Borja Norte. Inside the car, we sat as follows: my father beside the driver in the front, and two bodyguards in the back, sitting on each side of my siblings and me. Five or six streets before we reached the school, my father would give the order for us to crouch down and cover ourselves with our schoolbags. I'd always try to hold my breath as we crossed those last blocks. This was the routine every day for a year and a half.

We also got used to reporting the full names of any new friends we made, together with their addresses and the professions of their parents. We resigned ourselves to only inviting home those approved by my father after days of analysing this information. My sister Valentina and I considered this a paranoid irritation, but we acquiesced so we could avoid having to listen to my father's explanations, which included the dramatic but veridical story of an Argentinian general who was blown up after a terrorist infiltrated his home as a friend of his daughter, and having patiently won the trust of the family, left a bomb under his car or his bed. Some years later I came across a film that recounts these events: *Garage Olimpo* (1999). Every time my father told the story he altered the scenario in which the general was killed instantly. 'In war, a man must suspect everyone, and check under his bed for bombs before he goes to sleep at night,' he once said in an interview. I had friends who never entered my house because one of their parents had belonged to the far left, or simply because their details didn't fit. Valentina suffered most: it took her months to organise a party because it depended on my father approving the guest list, which was meticulously examined and usually ended up reduced to one-third its size. Grand soirées my sister planned for fifty ended up as tea parties for her dolls.

The thing that most terrified me – and at the same time morbidly fascinated me – was the possibility of being kidnapped by the Shining Path or MRTA. One night, I saw a TV news report about the kidnapping of a famous motocross rider, the son of a wealthy businessman. I remember his name: Heriberto Scavia. To strike fear into his family, who refused to pay the ransom, the terrorists cut off his ear and sent it to his father in a pizza box. The TV showed the images. As well as shocking me to such an extent that I spent weeks dreaming about Scavia's ear – I even remember thinking, absurdly, that at least if he got out alive he would be able to hide the amputated ear under his motorcycle helmet – the case made me wonder if my parents would pay the ransom in the event I was kidnapped. Then I imagined what it would be like to live with the kidnappers while the negotiations went on. Would they feed me? How often would they let me go to the toilet? Would they beat me so I'd talk and tell them how much money my dad had? Would they keep me tied up? Would I be able to eat with my hands bound? How would I keep clean? I saw myself sleeping on a mattress without sheets, in a room stinking of piss, where the only light came from a bare bulb hanging from the ceiling. I imagined that one of the kidnappers, the weakest of the bunch, the least well-trained, would take pity on me one night and help me escape through one of the windows, and I'd get away and return safe and sound to my house, with only a few cuts and bruises, and my parents would welcome me with open arms, while at school they would give me a standing ovation. That's what I imagined: that I'd be on the front page of all the newspapers, that I'd win everyone's attention. Some of those mornings on the way to school, as I ducked my head under my backpack I wished that someone would kidnap me.

Some of my family's fears come into sharper focus when in April 1990 my father decides to stand for the Senate. A friend had invited him to join the list of candidates for Somos Libres, a minority grouping on the right wing. In truth, it doesn't have much of a following in the country. The slogan is something like 'A truly independent force' and the symbol is a light bulb, like the light bulb of ideas, the only light that doesn't go dark despite the terrorist attacks. My father is number two on the list. At home, we're all excited about the campaign, which is very low-budget indeed, and we put our shoulders to the wheel. I remember taking leaflets and posters to school that read: 'For the Senate, choose the light bulb, and put your cross by number 2 for a Gaucho in Congress!' One afternoon, at the end of the lunch break, friends help me tape the posters around the walls of the courtyard. The supervisor, Valdivia the Mole, catches us at it. Furiously blowing his whistle, he orders us to take everything back down immediately. I don't know if this is because political propaganda is banned at school or because he's an APRA supporter and the Apristas hate my father. But my friends, instead of obeying the Mole, hoist me onto their shoulders in triumph, as if I were the candidate in the Senate, as if they too want my father to win, as if they too care about the campaign, and they begin to march round the courtyard shouting 'Cisneros for President!' and while the Mole blows his whistle indignantly, trying to break up the spontaneous demonstration, still more students join the improvised rally, and from up there on their shoulders I laugh and think that perhaps being a candidate and gathering a crowd and being adored by the masses isn't such a bad thing after all.

As a candidate, the Gaucho once again proposes the death penalty, not only for terrorists but also for corrupt officials and for drug traffickers. 'But our main targets are the terrorist leaders, who are never going to be convicted by our current laws, who will never be caught red-handed, but who are the masterminds of the attacks.' A journalist from *Oiga* asks him:

Don't you think the cure is worse than the sickness? Isn't it a win for the terrorists if we offer them martyrs?

I prefer a dead 'hero' to a living terrorist leader. It's unconscionable that 18,000 lives have been lost in the country because of the decisions of one man, Abimael Guzmán. It's unthinkable that our country, poor as it is, has suffered billions of dollars of damage due to the decisions of that one man. And now they say he shouldn't suffer the death penalty? What is treason if not that?

But surely the death penalty is a flagrant violation of human rights in a democratic system?

If it's a matter of conscience, then I would demand constitutional reform.

Such as?

I'd call a referendum! Let's see what the people think. Since everyone wants to wash their hands in order to be at peace with their conscience, let's hold a referendum! Then we'll see what the parents, children, brothers and sisters of the victims of terrorism think. We'll see what everyone who has been kidnapped and threatened with death by terrorists think! This is a democratic regime, is it not? So, let's see what the majority of the population thinks about it. I have no doubt whatsoever that they favour the death penalty.

Don't you think that life imprisonment would be a worse punishment for Abimael Guzmán?

No. And I hope to live long enough to see Guzmán face a firing squad. Sincerely, that would give me great pleasure.

Although his ideas do have a lot of acolytes, and when we go out to the supermarket or to a restaurant people are always coming up to greet him and say they're going to put their cross by his name, my father receives a percentage well below what he needed to win a seat: just 3,000 votes. He doesn't like losing, but he doesn't lose heart. He keeps doing his thing: working with his fellow Army retirees as security consultants for companies, and discussing politics with friends, family or with El Zambo Garcés. What's more, something is happening in the country that has journalists calling him up. They know the Gaucho speaks his mind and that's why they seek him out. Whenever he goes to give television interviews, my mother asks him to tone down his statements. If not for yourself, then at least for the children, she begs him, standing by the front door and watching as he gets the Chevrolet out of the garage.

In July 1990, before Alan García completes his term in office, my father appears on the programme hosted by Jaime Bayly on Canal 4, to discuss the scandalous escape of Víctor Polay Campos, an MRTA leader, and 47 of his followers from the Castro Castro prison. My father is convinced the APRA party facilitated their escape. 'To start with,' he points out to Bayly, 'Polay is the child of Aprista militants. The Minister of Health is his brother-in-law. What's more, he and García were buddies in the 70s, when they both rattled around Paris playing guitars in the Latin Quarter.' In any case, the escape is undoubtedly suspicious. According to a congressional investigation that would be cut short, it happened at three in the morning, taking advantage of the shift change. The prisoners escaped through a tunnel, reinforced with props and even equipped with electricity, which had been under construction for months while the police turned a blind eye. Polay escaped from his own cell because someone provided him with the keys to the main gate of his building, together with a plan of the tunnel.

'So what do you think about Polay's tunnel, General?' Bayly asks him that night in the Canal 4 studio.

At home we follow every detail of the conversation. My mother opens and closes her hands in front of the screen, sending vibes to the Gaucho so that he'll speak calmly and not say anything too outrageous.

'This tunnel, Jaime, is such a technically accomplished work of engineering that the Aprista government was able to give it an official inauguration.'

Bayly laughs. 'That's true, very true. Tell me something, General. What would you say to Polay if he were in front of you now?' The journalist's tone of voice turns serious.

The question is like bait for my father. We can see it in his face from the other side of the TV set. We're certain he will unleash a furious response.

'Don't ask me that, Jaime, because I might say something foolish,' the Gaucho replies, and lights up a cigarette right there, the smoke clouding the camera's view of him.

My mother breathes more easily at this evasion, thinking he has remembered her words on parting. 'Don't answer, don't answer,' she begs the television.

'Go on, General. That's what this programme is for, to say foolish things,' Bayly goads him.

At home, we begin to pray. In the studio, my father sucks on the cigarette as if mulling over his best reply, one that he can stand by without putting his family at risk. Or so it seems.

'If I had Polay in front of me right now, I wouldn't say anything,' my father answers. We're already celebrating his restraint, when suddenly we hear his voice again: 'I would put a bullet in his head.'

* * *

Things don't change much after that. At the outset my father seems to agree with some of the more radical decisions of the new government, led by Alberto Fujimori, and even with the dissolution of Congress in 1992. However he gradually loses patience with how easily the ethnically

Japanese president, who has come to power almost by a miracle, is manipulated.

The Gaucho is concerned above all by the pernicious presence of the intelligence agent Vladimiro Montesinos in the president's inner circle. In columns written for *Caretas*, *Expreso* and *La República*, my father reminds people that when Montesinos was in the Army he was accused of treason and dismissed for abandoning his post at a frontier garrison and fleeing to the United States with false papers. 'A man of that moral character cannot be an adviser to the president, let alone a deputy chief of the SIN, the National Intelligence System,' declares General Cisneros, adding that the SIN is becoming a kind of Gestapo with ties to the CIA and international drug trafficking. 'Someday Montesinos will have to pay in court for the abuses he is committing,' he says in mid-1992, when Vladimiro's shadow seems to be expanding in all directions.

Throughout this period, terrorist attacks continue to afflict cities across the country, including Lima, which wakes each day to find dogs hanging from the electricity poles, dried out, having bled to death. These uncertain times are exploited by secret service agents, who carry out bloody raids in search of suspects, or attack the regime's political enemies by planting bombs. They do this in the office of the APRA leader Mercedes Cabanillas, and in the residence of the opposition congressman Manuel Moreyra.

And they also did it in the Monterrico house.

I still get goosebumps when I think of it now. On 5 June 1992, a bomb had detonated in a Navy vehicle parked outside the Canal 2 television station. Three people died and many more were injured. The attack was attributed to the Shining Path, although some time later the owner of the channel, Baruch Ivcher, would say that 'It was planted by the Shining Path, but planned by the SIN.' Canal 2 had gone from supporting the Fujimori government to confronting it with constant allegations. The bombing, in Ivcher's view, was punishment for the change of position in the editorial line.

That night, we go to bed still shocked by the horrifying scenes we had seen on TV. The night passes in a silent dance of shadows until, at five in the morning, the house is shaken by a boom. A short, incredibly loud, atomic noise. The noise that marks the end of the world. I jump out of bed and run to my parents' room to find Valentina and Facundo already there. We all hide under the blanket, perplexed and frightened. Except my father. He sits on the bed, turning the dial on the radio to try and find some information. For a moment we wonder if the Shining Path has attacked the racecourse, just a few streets away, where a major horse race is soon to be held. My sister Valentina tries to make a phone call, and discovers that there is no dial tone. Then smoke drifts into the room, followed by the penetrating smell of gunpowder. It appears to come from our front hall. Stunned, we advance down the corridor like mistrustful sleepwalkers. 'The television must have exploded,' our mother muses on the way. Her naïveté is revealed when we reach the front door and see the atrocious spectacle. Only then do we understand what is happening: someone has just thrown dynamite at our house. 'We could be dead,' exclaims Valentina. My father tells us to go to our rooms, but we convince him it's better to stay together. We begin to survey the damage. There is a great pit in the garden, as if a meteorite had fallen during the night. The windows are broken, the frames hanging loose, the metal door is bent, the walls separating the garden from the street have collapsed. There is glass and earth and pieces of tile everywhere.

We stare at this new landscape in astonishment and anger. My mother bursts into tears and hits my father several times in the chest, as if blaming him for what could have happened to us, as if to emphasise that we are innocent, that we shouldn't have to bear the consequences of his declarations against the government. I, however, don't feel so innocent, because I consider myself indebted to my father's remarks: if only recently I benefited from them in a public speaking contest that won me a certain prestige in high school, then now I must be loyal to his words and also accept the devastation they have wrought. Outside, there is fresh graffiti on the pavement: MRTA. My father looks at it thoughtfully, and swiftly concludes: 'Terrorists don't threaten you, they kill you without warning. This is Montesinos' doing.' No more than twenty minutes pass before officers from the Police Bomb Squad arrive, quickly followed by a crowd of journalists, friends, relatives and curious neighbours. My father appears disconcerted, but is convinced that they only intended to frighten him. Just days earlier, he had criticised Fujimori in a number of news media, and attacked Montesinos and General Hermoza Ríos in particular for the much-discussed crimes of La Cantuta and Barrios Altos. My father didn't condemn the crimes themselves ('They're better off dead, but it was poorly done' he said of the victims, who were suspected of collaborating with the Shining Path), but rather the cowardice of those who ordered the operations and didn't dare to take responsibility for them. His statements echoed as far away as the *Wall Street Journal*. As a result, we started to receive threatening telephone calls again at the Monterrico house. My father dismissed this harassment and further toughened his media remarks on Montesinos, never imagining that they would throw an explosive package at his front door. 'Montesinos behind Cisneros bomb?' is the headline in *La República* the next day. 'Bombs thrown at residence of retired general Cisneros Vizquerra,' reads the *Expreso*. 'Mysterious attack:

bomb at house of the Gaucho Cisneros not Shining Path. Montesinos paramilitaries suspected,' considers *Caretas*.

One month later a large-scale attack shakes the city, this time clearly the work of the Shining Path. A car bomb with 400 kilos of dynamite inside blows up in the narrow street of Tarata, in Miraflores. Twenty-four people die, five are never found, and more than 200 are injured. The survivors are traumatised, never able to forget the brutal images of the scattered bodies, the plumes of smoke, the intense light of the explosion.

Two days later, a seventy-year-old man, the father of a dentist who died in a building on Tarata St. and who was seen on television crying 'my son, my son!' amid the flames, becomes the symbol of the marches for peace that proliferate in Miraflores. One night, that man appears on Canal 4 to speak to audiences across the country. 'This is the moment', my father says, sitting beside me at home, 'to send a direct message to the terrorists. This is how we start to push back against those sons of bitches.' Seconds later, he watches as the man pulls a rosary from his pocket and says in a broken voice that he forgives the people who planted the bomb because 'we are all children of God and deserve mercy'. My father, outraged, leaps up and thumps the wall, yelling 'You old fool!' at the screen.

His reaction is one of total impotence. Peru is trapped between a terrorist group that kills openly and a dictatorship that kills in secret, and he, who can no longer do anything, who has no more power than that afforded by his media statements and his fortnightly columns, cannot bear the fact that the citizens, represented on this occasion by this old believer, should waste such a magnificent opportunity to demand respect.

* * *

Although the capture of Abimael Guzmán in September 1992 is a logical moment for national reconciliation, unease persists in a sector of the Armed Forces at the way Fujimori and Montesinos decree the promotion of generals according to their personal preferences, without respecting the internal hierarchy or the usual meritocratic process. This discontent boils over in November with a failed coup attempt. With their plans discovered, the implicated military personnel are taken to a regular jail filled with common criminals, which leads to a public protest by nineteen retired generals, Cisneros at their head. The protest takes the form of a letter addressed to General Hermoza Ríos, about whom the Gaucho has a very clear opinion, which he sets out in an interview with *Debate*:

General Hermoza Ríos must not be ratified as commander-in-chief, because he is the primary disruptive and divisive element that seeks to polarise our institution. The current struggles in the Army are the direct result of his presence.

Won't you give him credit for the capture of Abimael?

Just a moment: Abimael was captured as the result of intelligence work by the police. Hermoza Ríos had nothing to do with it. In any case, I can't understand why the government hasn't put an end to Guzmán's miserable life. Keeping him alive costs us a lot of money that could be spent on better things. We've no idea what will happen in the future, and you know very well that politicians in this country love handing out pardons to all and sundry. Guzmán has to pay with his life. He is incapable of remorse.

General, how do you view the role of the Army at this juncture?

The Army is totally under the heel of the politicians, and Hermoza Ríos has a lot to do with that. He has lost respect and leadership, he has allowed the Armed Forces to be manipulated, he has divided the institution. He lacks both the character and the circumstances to remain at the helm.

Not five days pass after making these declarations before a military court opens a case against my father for a made-up, unheard-of crime: 'offending the Nation and insulting a superior'. This isn't the only piece of news he struggles to take in. One week earlier, his family doctor, Silvio Albán, had delivered the results of the tests he had forced him to undergo. He has cancer. Cystic cancer in the prostate that, although operable, requires a long and painful treatment.

The Gaucho decides to keep the diagnosis a secret in order to focus on his legal situation. In the government-controlled newspapers, Fujimori and Hermoza Ríos wage war against him, dragging up and distorting what he said in *Quehacer* back in 1983 about how to fight terrorism in Ayacucho. And in an article in the official newspaper *El Peruano*, entitled 'What does the general want?', an anonymous editor describes my father's criticisms as 'contrary to the discipline that characterises the military institution' and speculates on the scenario that may await him: 'Be careful, General Cisneros Vizquerra. You don't want to end your life in jail like your esteemed friend General Videla, imprisoned for genocide.'

His friends and his siblings recommend that he seek political asylum in Argentina or in Spain, as other military personnel have done when they became political targets of the dictatorship. My mother asks him to do this too. Seated on the back terrace, the dog at his feet, swathed in cigarette smoke, he weighs it up, but takes the decision to stay in Peru and submit to the legal process. He presents his position in a typewritten letter that he sends to the few newspapers and magazines not under the sway of the government.

With the full peace of my conscience granted by my faith in God and my unwavering conduct; with my pride in coming from a home that bears an unblemished name, where I discovered my love for truth and justice at a young age, where I suffered the consequences of the imprisonment and exile of my father; and with the conviction that, during my time in the Army, I learned from my teachers the principles underpinning institutional life, principles I endeavoured to spread among the men who were my colleagues and whose continued relevance I shall seek to demonstrate, I have determined to publicly express my gratitude for all the invitations I have received to seek asylum in different embassies, under the current circumstances

My decision to remain in the country should not be compared to the decisions taken by others, which are equally deserving of respect.

It is because I have faith in military justice and because I trust the men in uniform who administer this justice that I choose not to leave Peru, and I shall submit myself to the ruling of this court.

In the end, the circumstances in which I find myself offer an opportunity for me to offer one more lesson to my children and my institution. Upholding one's principles is the only thing that makes all life's troubles worthwhile.

★ ★ ★

On Wednesday 25 January 1993 the Gaucho attends the Supreme Council of Military Justice for the first time. Two days earlier he had celebrated his sixty-seventh birthday. A newspaper headline declares: 'Cisneros to be detained after hearing.' I read this on the minibus taking me to the academy where I am preparing for my third attempt to enter university. I am shaken up, twisting and turning in my seat, roiling with helplessness. Once I reach the academy I am completely unable to focus in class. All I can think about is that when I get home my dad might not be there anymore, but in prison. After the hearing, which lasts three hours and ten minutes, the judge accepts the request of the prosecutor and sentences him to thirty days of suspended military imprisonment. In his plea, without having first discussed it with his lawyer, my father demands that the court remove the suspension: 'I accept the decision but I do not share it, because I have the right to comment on the conduct of any general of less seniority than myself. I am a retired military officer, and I do not have superiors. If the punishment for expressing my views is prison, Your Honour, then I ask to be imprisoned. I have my suitcase ready here.' His lawyer listens to him, wide-eyed with incredulity.

Leaving the court, my father is surrounded by a swarm of journalists. The sun is fierce. The reporters wear huge sunglasses and short-sleeve shirts. They record the Gaucho's statements in notebooks and voice recorders that look like Walkmans. There too are the microphones and cameras of America, Radio Cadena, Canal 2, Eco, Global, laying siege to my father, a man who no longer hears very well, who asks them to repeat their questions from behind his thick-lensed glasses; a man who frowns and wrinkles his nose at the interrogation, perhaps in exhaustion or in pain from the cancer. But he reaffirms what he has just told the judge. 'I will not go into exile.' 'I will attend court whenever I am asked.' 'I have committed no crime.' 'I take responsibility for everything I have said.' 'I have no fears.' These are the words my father is uttering that day in January 1993 when Enrique suddenly appears behind him, 'Quique', the chauffeur who worked for us at that time and whose loyalty to my father was iron clad. Quique takes over, rescues my father from the horde of reporters – who are unaware they are talking to a very sick general – and deposits him in the back seat of the second-hand red Toyota that was my father's final purchase.

Two months later, despite the judge's explicit assertion that he is prohibited from commenting publicly on the trial or on the persons who gave rise to the trial – 'You must abstain from offending superiors verbally or by means of publications in the media or of any other nature, under penalty of the sentence being made effective' – my father gives an interview to a Brazilian newspaper in which, stubborn, foolish and irresponsible, he offloads his opinions on Fujimori, Montesinos and Hermoza Ríos, and warns that there are still decent officers in the Army who may be ready to conspire against the government:

What we have in Peru is a situation of misrule that has led to the destruction of our institutions, especially the Armed Forces, who have lost their professionalism to the point of renouncing their codes of camaraderie and loyalty. If Alan García has gone down in posterity as the worst president of Peru, Alberto Fujimori will be remembered as the most ineffective civilian dictator of all time. I would not be surprised if the solution to this situation is found in the few worthy individuals who still survive in the barracks.

He would never have shut up even if his lips were sewn together with barbed wire. His bravura costs him dearly. The military court summons him back and increases his suspended sentence to ninety days. Three months of jail. The lawyer explains to the journalists that there is no possibility of appeal. It's *res judicata*, he says. Upon leaving the Supreme Council, the journalists again swamp my father, who answers them all at once with one of his epic tirades, heavy with stoicism, which at least allows him to reaffirm what he believed to be his most genuine values. 'The coming battle, gentlemen, will be a harsh one, but it's reserved for men who have the courage to accept it, the tenacity to wage it and the firm will to win it.'

The opposition newspapers and politicians, including some figures who had attacked my father decades prior, reject the punishment imposed, describing it as an outrage, as a gag, as harassment. Once the ninety days have passed, my father cannot stand the forced silence any longer and once again writes articles railing against the government, and so the government seeks out subtler but more hurtful ways to intimidate him. In January 1994 he asks for medical treatment abroad, invoking the health insurance plan to which all lieutenant generals with at least thirty-five years' service have a right, but General Hermoza Ríos refuses to let him leave the country, and as if this were not enough, does all he can to hinder his access to the medicines he needs.

But my father is a tough old dog. Despite his illness and the sentence, he gathers the necessary strength and spirit to wage what would be his final political battle: a second attempt at entering Congress. The presidential candidate for the Unión Por el Perú party, the UPP, is the prestigious diplomat Javier Pérez de Cuéllar, a former secretary-general of the UN. He invites him to take number six on the parliamentary list. Posters with the slogan 'The Gaucho Cisneros, a brave man for Congress' appear within hours.

This time, unlike his first attempt, my father is working with a more robust political platform and with a greater number of people determined to support him. If we felt we had been committed to the 1990 campaign with the Somos Libres light bulb, we now redouble our efforts and get fully stuck in to the endeavour. We already know that my father is ill, and we don't even want to imagine what a new electoral failure will do to him.

To finish the design for one of the posters, my father asks me to draft some rhyming couplets. I'm no longer a

fan of rhymes and only write prose poems that my father
doesn't understand, but I have no hesitation in knocking
something up for him. I had completely forgotten what I
wrote until recently, rummaging in the drawers and chests
that were forbidden to me for years, I rediscovered these
artless quatrains.

Because he's a natural leader,
because he's a simple fellow,
because he was always a caudillo
in the military sphere.
Because he fears no one,
because he's a soldier first,
when you vote, mark the one
and write a six to the side.
And no matter who it bothers,
with your sovereign ballot
the Peruvian military
will have the place it deserves.
With work until the year 2000,
on the ninth of April,
vote, vote, vote:
The Gaucho for Congress!

What hit me when I found this piece of paper, what
really left me curled up in pain, was recalling and feeling
the conviction and certainty with which I'd written 'until
the year 2000', even though I knew my father's body
was already racked with cancer. It was as if I'd wanted to
persuade myself that if he won the election, if his spirit was
restored, then he could defeat the illness and stay with us
for a few more years. I remember the days of March and
April 1995, remember seeing how old my father looked,
grey-haired, the skin hanging from his arms, but still garbed

in the vitality of his speech, in the strength that always braced his words. I see him on the campaign trail, returning to the links between Montesinos and the drug traffickers, tenaciously opposing Fujimori's re-election, denouncing corruption in the Army. 'The president can buy up the Army if he wishes, but it doesn't belong to him, it belongs to Peru. Re-electing Fujimori will only bring us a more autocratic government,' he tells the reporters who come to visit.

On the Sunday of the election the Monterrico house takes on a party atmosphere. Or at least the anticipation of a party. From early in the morning we get everything ready to receive friends and family. Everyone comes to lunch and to hear the first projections, which come in at four in the afternoon. The most recent polls clearly suggest that the UPP will win between sixteen and eighteen seats in parliament. *Caretas* has published an article with the names of those most likely to occupy these seats. Although the preferential voting system may work against my father, his position as number 6 on the list operates strongly in his favour. Indeed, *Caretas* describes him as a sure winner, together with the top thirteen UPP candidates. That is why on the morning of the election, while remaining cautious, we can barely conceal our excitement and optimism. This is going to be the comeback, my father's great comeback, I think to myself.

After breakfast we organise ourselves into groups to go and vote. I am particularly active and animated that day. I've recently turned eighteen and I'm ready to visit the polling booth for the first time. As will never again be the case, I have absolutely no doubt about how I'll vote: I will put my X by the symbol of the UPP and in the adjacent boxes write a '6', for the Gaucho Cisneros, and an '11' for Grados Bertorini, a politician and journalist I like because of the stories he writes in *Expreso* under the pseudonym Toribio Gol.

Upon returning from the vote we have a hectic lunch. There are many more people than usual, what with uncles and aunts, cousins and friends, and the house is filled with a pleasant uproar – the perfect prelude to a long afternoon that can only end auspiciously. The hustle and bustle feels strange to me, alien. After all, it was only recently that all this furniture, these walls and bedrooms had seemed to be impregnated with a silent, corrosive grime, sullied by my father's trial and the dreadful news of his illness. One public and one private event that had marred the appearance of the house itself. The trial and the cancer. But none of that matters now. The twenty-somethings in attendance are gathered around the television, hanging on every word of Humberto Martínez Morosini, the host on the Panamericana channel. My father, enthroned on a wicker chair, looks on, laughing or mocking as we crowd around him. As four o'clock approaches we count backwards from ten as if it were New Year, and then fall silent to stare at the screen, trusting in the good news the announcer will bring. Then we see and hear the numbers. Although the presidential result was a foregone conclusion, the margin of Fujimori's victory is galling. The 64.4% in favour of the sitting president is decisive, against the 21.8% for Pérez de Cuéllar. The re-election of Fujimori is not in question. But the real blow for us is still to come, with the congressional vote predictions. Dumbstruck, we watch as the names of the UPP favourites mentioned in *Caretas* appear, one after another. All the names are there except my father's. There are the principal numbers on the list, from 1 to 18. Only number 6 is missing. Estrada, Fernández Baca, Grados Bertorini, Pease, Choque, Avendaño, Mohme, Pardo, Donayre, Townsend, Cerro Moral, Lozano Lozano,

Forsyth, Guerra García, García Sayán, Massa Gálvez, Moya Bendezú and Chipoco. The sole surname that does not appear on the screen in Cisneros. We are immobile. My father switches off the television and sits back down amid a heavy, cold silence, an Antarctic silence, abrasive, cosmic and absolute. Gradually some voices emerge from the silence to question the newsflash, to question what is self-evident, and to encourage my father, telling him not to worry, that we have to wait for the official figures to be approved by the National Electoral Court. But he doesn't hear them. He doesn't hear us. I have my eyes fixed on him and I know he can't hear a single one of the words emerging from the mouths of the friends and relatives who suddenly sense the need to disappear, to abandon this uncomfortable scene. My father has the fierce, indecipherable expression of an Inca sacrificial knife and his mind is elsewhere, perhaps recalling – too late – the advice offered to him days earlier by his few real friends on the list of candidates: 'Make sure you have a couple of electoral observers keeping an eye on your votes.' 'This government is capable of anything: don't give Montesinos an inch.' 'Even the UPP people might sabotage you in order to secure a seat.'

He hadn't taken enough precautions, had trusted in his luck, in the polls, in the list published by *Caretas*, in the rumours, in the fact he held number 6. He'd believed he was a sure thing. It was unquestionably very strange that he was the only one among the UPP favourites not to enter Congress – as the official results later confirmed – but it was too late to do anything. Nothing but rant in public and condemn the whole process, in the hope that some international body, some entity with an impressive name would do something in the name of regional democracy. And that's exactly what the Gaucho did: protest out loud. It was the final card he had to play and he played it, knowing that if he didn't win the round, unemployment and illness were lying in wait to swallow him whole.

If something gave us hope it was seeing that my father wasn't alone in his protest. Some dozen candidates from other parties, who had been favourites and ended up sidelined, join him at a press conference in a room at the Miraflores Casino. The Gaucho takes the microphone before anyone else and looks directly at the few cameras present:

Vladimiro Montesinos, the true head of the intelligence services, has obstructed the election to Congress of figures considered dangerous for the re-elected government. This is a scandal that must be investigated and those responsible for the fraud must be punished for their wanton distortion of the people's will.

The next day the headlines flood in: 'Electoral scandal.' 'The Electoral Court conceals electronic fraud.' 'Candidates demand recount of preferential voting slips.' 'Candidates to Congress join forces to demand Electoral Court take responsibility.' Some editorial writers who had never shown any sympathy for my father briefly set aside their personal hatred to call out the obvious manipulation of the ballots. 'There are retired generals who failed to win a seat despite receiving a high number of preferential votes, among them Luis Cisneros. He is on the blacklist of the intelligence services, which is in charge of the computerised voting system,' writes Enrique Zileri in *Caretas*. The same journalist who years earlier had spent a week in a basement cell of the Ministry of the Interior on the orders of the man he is now defending.

In the days prior to the final ruling of the Electoral Court, the phone rings off the hook in our house. Friends of my father call him to offer encouragement and remind him that millions of ballots still need to be counted, that the names of the winning candidates can still change, that he shouldn't give up yet. But my father has already given up. By this point he already knows or senses that he won't win the battle. And he suspects that it wasn't exactly Montesinos who stole his votes: his sources tell him of strange movements carried out by one of the officials hired by another UPP candidate. Although I have no proof, I've never doubted that some such shenanigans took place. It no longer matters. The concrete result was that this stab in the back drove my father into a depression, and invigorated the cancer that was creeping through the conduits of his body. This defeat, which had wounded his pride and clouded his future, catapulted him into the wheelchair in which, just one month later, he entered the cancer ward for the first time.

★ ★ ★

Much later, in early 2000, I crossed the threshold of Congress on my first day working as a copy editor at the Chief Clerk's Office, and I felt that destiny or chance had finally cleared the air in a room long abandoned, and in some way remedied a long-standing family injury. 'At least you made it into Congress,' my sister Valentina remarked, when I told her about my new job. That first day, as soon as I had a moment free from my tasks, I sneaked into the empty debating chamber and sat for no more than a minute in the seat that would have belonged to my father. It was one of those useless, poetic acts you believe can mend the bitter fissures of the past – only to realise later that the crack has only deepened, that nothing has been fixed, that nothing is ever fixed.

In April 1995, before his illness became more aggressive, in what would turn out to be his final interview, the Gaucho still has enough air in his lungs to condemn the reach of the government's tentacles in *La República*. The title 'I accuse' leads to two full pages scattered with ideas and hypotheses such as: 'The democratic spring was but the breeze of a day,' 'We don't accomplish anything by staying silent,' 'The Fujimori, Hermoza Ríos and Montesinos Brotherhood controls absolutely everything,' 'They are the ones who manipulate the military in order to prosecute and imprison retired officers.'

Aren't you worried about going to prison, General?
When you know you aren't protecting interests of any kind, then you can and should keep talking, even if you must pay a high price for doing so. That's why we chose this profession, why we still belong to the military. When we die, we'll be buried in dress uniform, and if we intend to wear that uniform with honour on our final journey, we must continue to offer our opinions and confront those who seek to silence us.

This was his final newspaper interview. Three months later he appeared in the headlines once more, but would no longer be there to read them.

Chapter 8

In the early years of writing this novel, when I still lacked a lot of information, the military side of my father's identity gave rise to questions I became obsessed with answering. I wanted to know, above all, whether my father had ever killed anyone. I don't mean killing blindly in combat, as he was never involved in an armed engagement; I mean selecting a victim for disappearance with a bullet to the head. There were days when it seemed so obvious, so true to the logic of his temperament and of his time. On other days, though, I preferred to be more sceptical. Everything became clearer when I asked the question of General Belisario Schwartz, one of his closest friends in the Army. Both had been second lieutenants in 1948, a year after my father arrived from Buenos Aires, and they worked together very closely during his Ministry of the Interior period, when the Gaucho was Minister and Schwartz the head of the intelligence service. I can imagine – no: I actually can't – the things they talked about and plotted when they found themselves alone in the ministerial office of the San Borja high-rise building. In the Army, Schwartz was known as El Mocho, or 'Stubby', because when he was a cadet in Tumbes he once accidentally fired a bullet as he was field-stripping his Mauser pistol, shredding the finger he'd placed at the end of the barrel. His right index finger. He could have killed himself that day: the shot made him drop the weapon and, as it fell to the ground, it released another bullet that ricocheted off the ceiling and grazed him on the rebound. I still remember Schwartz's mangled hand: his finger-stump provoked a mixture of fascination and repugnance in my childhood self. The left-wing journalists didn't call him El Mocho; their nickname for him was El Malo, or the Evil One, because they claimed he was behind several of the kidnappings, bomb attacks and disappearances used by the military government to harass its opponents or simply to dispose of them.

The day I went to pick him up at his home on Porta St. in Miraflores, I was struck by how much he had aged. He no longer walked upright, but with the help of a stick, advancing more slowly than might be expected even for a man of eighty-six. A leather cap covered his hairless head. He was lucid, but he sometimes embarked on rambling detours, eventually finding his way back unaided. As I drove, I thought about how this vulnerable old man sitting beside me, gazing out the window at the street like a child travelling in a car for the first time, had once been a feared military leader. If my father were still alive, I thought, this is how he'd look, or worse, and I silently felt a kind of relief that he was dead. I spoiled old Schwartz that afternoon, taking him to an excellent restaurant in Barranco where I plied him with gourmet dishes. I accompanied him to the bathroom every time he needed to go, leading him by his right arm – the missing finger still repelled and fascinated me – and above all I listened to him chatter. First, I let him regale me with accounts of his time as head honcho of the intelligence services. 'I took care of everything', he recalled, spearing a crispy grilled octopus tentacle with his fork, 'from the psychological intimidation to the beatings, and sometimes right up to the end.' 'The end?' I enquired, naïvely. 'Elimination,' Schwartz replied, sucking on the straw in his glass of lemonade. And then he confessed to me, or acted as if he were confessing, that he once discovered two Chilean spies in the Locumba barracks – 'two strong-willed lieutenants' – who had infiltrated the Peruvian Army. Once identified, they were arrested and transported to Lima, where they were held in an old SIN facility in Chorrillos. 'And what happened to them?' I wanted to know. 'We made them disappear, of course,' he said, struggling to chew an asparagus stalk. 'When President Morales Bermúdez asked me where the Chileans were, I replied: "Three metres underground, General".' He smiled, revealing his false teeth.

'Did my dad know about this?'

'Yes, of course. He backed me up.'

'And do you know if he eliminated anyone himself, or ordered anyone to be eliminated?' I asked, spreading butter on a piece of olive bread, as if to alleviate for myself the weight of my question.

His face fell.

General Belisario Schwartz looked at me and took a few seconds before answering, realising that his questioner was no longer the timid, quiet boy he'd met years earlier, but a man who spoke from out of the depths into which he had descended without anyone's help, from a place where there was no point in speaking with anything other than the truth, even if the truth was no more than a short-lived flame, soon to be snuffed out.

'I wouldn't rule it out,' he said, raising the last piece of octopus to his mouth.

'But, do you know if he did?' I persisted.

'Look, my boy, if he did, then he did it so well that no one found out.'

He then went on to extol the Gaucho's humanity, how courteous and firm he was, what a good and honest friend he'd been. 'When he was Minister of the Interior, he was offered a huge amount of money by business owners to raise the motel rates. They even offered him a helicopter. He always refused,' he mumbled before wiping his mouth with a napkin. He abruptly picked up his cap and stick. 'Shall we go?'

It wasn't hard to work out what was behind Schwartz's evasiveness. Unintentionally, the old general, El Malo, El Mocho, had helped me to calm, or cure, or extirpate the question that had been hounding me for years. My persistent doubts had led me, for example, to read the entirety of the final report published in 2003 by the Truth and Reconciliation Commission, the balance sheet of the war against subversion – in particular the chapters dedicated to the leading figures in the Armed Forces – to see what it said about my father and how the commissioners evaluated his management, his opinions, his ministerial decisions, his statements about how the Shining Path should be dealt with. I was surprised and relieved to read in one paragraph:

Many confused Cisneros' terrible warnings with threats. They charged him with malevolence, rather than weighing the seriousness of his words.

The view of the Commission – which had comprised four priests, just one military official and eight civilians, several of them former left-wing militants – earned me only temporary relief. My relief was suspended, diluted or destroyed altogether when I discovered the photographs of my father in the company of Pinochet, of Uruguayan dictator Juan María Bordaberry, of Kissinger and Videla. Or when I returned to the newspaper cuttings that summarised his time at the Ministry of the Interior, that epoch of persecutions, wiretaps, deaths in strikes, disappearances during the curfew, and mass extrajudicial arrests, or the political articles in which he expressed his solidarity with the Argentinian dictatorship, or the historical articles in which he praised the dictator Manuel Odría, a former de facto president who was not only a repressor and a populist, but stupid too.

I'm seized with exasperation whenever I think about the kind of figures my father held in such high esteem. When I learn that he secretly received advice at Hacienda Pariachi from Esparza Zañartu, the Machiavellian figure Odría entrusted with the liquidation of communists and APRA party members, the figure who Mario Vargas Llosa recreated in *Conversation in The Cathedral* as Cayo Bermúdez. When articles or opinion pieces appear in which someone recalls the time of 'the iron fist of Cisneros'. When someone turns up claiming that my father ordered the torture of a relative. I feel overcome by a sense of weariness or saturation, as if I'll never resolve the great paradox that was my father, I'll never free myself from the weight of the stone that's been crushing my shoulders all this time, deforming them. When I receive online messages saying things like 'So you're the son of the butcher Cisneros Vizquerra, huh?', when they try to pit me against him, when some opinion-peddler brings him up in some twisted way only for the sake of backing up an argument, I wonder how many people this man must have damaged, intentionally or otherwise – this man who, among other things, was my father; this man I've now known for more years dead than I knew him alive; this man who lives inside me, yet remains so far out of reach.

One day, as a way of reducing the distance between us, I decided to look through the manuscripts of the articles he published in *Expreso* between 1986 and 1993. Right up to the end, he'd signed as Lieutenant General, never specifying that he was retired, as an allegorical way of continuing to wear his uniform. I wanted to study the tension and rhythm revealed by his orderly, left-handed script. I found the drafts of articles railing against communism, against the presidential re-election, against the creation of the Ministry of Defence, against García Pérez, against Fujimori, against Montesinos, against Vargas Llosa, against the maligning of the Armed Forces. The last one he wrote, the last one in this archive, is a detailed analysis of the Gulf War, which includes a table of comparisons he himself had drawn up of the military might unleashed by both the coalition forces and the Iraqi army during Operation Desert Storm. It's the strangest feeling to read such lively analysis now of a war long finished by a man long gone. When he started writing for *Expreso*, the communist press mocked him. In a section of *Kausa Popular* dedicated to sketches and cartoons, a headline blared 'NEWSFLASH! TYPEWRITING GORILLA DISCOVERED!' accompanied by a caricature depicting my father as an ape, dressed in a military cape, banging at a typewriter with two fingers. What these communist critics didn't know was that, before typing them up, this gorilla wrote his articles out neatly by hand, and called on his wife and children to hear him reading the draft aloud, and measured their reactions and accepted their comments with humility. I remember my father addressing us, his glasses held between his fingers, transforming the TV room into a conference hall with the gravity of his voice alone, pausing in the right places to suit the flow of his rhythmic prose, free of barrack-room slang. Naturally, we were an already adoring audience, hanging on his every word, incapable of objecting to his arguments, and always ready to applaud even when we didn't understand what we were applauding. His articles revealed a side of him that no other activity succeeded in bringing out. Only I know how many nights I've spent – ever since I began to write opinion pieces in newspapers – trying to write like him, calling a spade a spade, then re-reading what I've written and realising how lukewarm I sound. Both of us wrote, but we never talked about what writing meant to us. Or about so many other things. We left millions of topics untouched. Your father never shut up, people who remember him still say today. Perhaps he didn't shut up in front of others, but he did in front of me. And perhaps that's what drives this exhausting, useless quest of mine: to find among his remains, among the chasms of abandonment, the scattered messages that General Cisneros left for his fifth child.

In his political articles, my father is a man who never falters, who always expresses his opinions with conviction. The same can't be said of his letters, at least not the letters from his youth, where his doubts waver and expand and reveal how fearful and insecure he once was. When I read these letters, after my uncle Gustavo entrusted them to me just a few years ago, I loved my father more, because I felt that we shared the raw material of uncertainty, and for the first time it occurred to me that this was a legacy he had handed down to me. If he had written a will, he might have been specific about it: 'I leave all my doubts to my fifth-born son.' It was my bad luck that my father's early reticence didn't endure, or was suppressed by the arrogant and insensitive figure he became or pretended to be until the end of his days.

I have also said that my father was a prescriptive man who got us all to obey him. At home, this was a constant. No one else was capable of making the dogs – the untamed, long-fanged German Shepherds that were our pets – flatten their ears and crouch down before him. He needed only shout their names once – Courage! Lightning! Goofy! – to transform them into trembling puppies. My father even had an effect on inanimate objects: certain corners and rooms of the Monterrico house only acquired meaning, light and substance when he moved through them. Every time he went on a trip, the mansion took on the inscrutable aspect of a house for sale. As soon as he returned, its soul, activity and movement were restored. My father's mood decreed the indoor temperature: this was one of the many powers I attributed to him as a child. And for this and other skills I was proud of him. I liked showing off my pride, like someone riding a particularly fine horse. When a school friend invited me to his house for the first time, I looked forward to the moment when his parents asked me about mine. Specifically, about my father. I actually waited for it, like an actor waits in the wings for his cue to walk onstage and recite his piece. My father is a military man. Military? Are you connected to General Cisneros? This question followed like clockwork. Yes, he's my father. Boastfully. I loved that moment, loved how confident I felt as the attitude of these previously unknown parents changed towards me. Suddenly they respected me, they liked the idea that I should be friends with their son. If a moment earlier they'd seen me – or I'd seen myself – as an accessory, an intruder, as soon as I revealed my identity, revealed myself as the son of the Gaucho Cisneros, I felt the eyes of my hosts rest more cordially on me. I felt that I'd fully mastered the situation, that I was at their level, that I gained in stature – so much so that my friend of the moment began to shrink, to seem insignificant, and I might even have suggested he go play in the park with the other kids while I discussed weighty matters of national importance with his parents. Indeed, when I'd visit my friends' houses, I'd bring along the topics that my father addressed in his conversations and interviews, and I'd sit at these unfamiliar tables to set out his ideas and theories on the latest drama shaking the country, and when I noted the close attention my friends' parents paid me, I felt my body fill with power, as if imbued with a kind of radiance. If the parents in question had been distant, they quickly became friendly. If they were wealthy, upper-class people, they dropped their haughtiness. If they were middle- or lower-class, they began to treat me with respect, as if honoured to have the son of such an influential former minister seated in their dining room. Some of these parents even congratulated me. They congratulated me for being his son: the mere mention of his name distinguished me. What they didn't know was that I felt more comfortable and sure of myself telling them about him than I did with the man himself. They had no idea just how different we really were.

Later, when I was fifteen or sixteen, the tide of feeling began to flow in the other direction and I began to tire of his name constantly surfacing in my conversations. I felt I could never free myself of him. It was gratifying, of course, that other people praised my father's character, but his popularity began to exhaust me. His popularity distanced him from me. I didn't want to have a popular father. I wanted one who would talk to me more, who would ask me things. I wanted him to raise me, but especially to spoil me. I wanted a father who paid more attention to what might be going on inside my head. Though to be that father, perhaps he needed a different son, one who clung less to his mother's skirts, a son who was less timid, or less lacklustre. We were friends, but the kind of friends who don't express their feelings to each other. I loved him because he was my father, but I could come to hate him when he treated me as a subordinate, or when he displayed those fucking mannerisms of his, those ridiculous, vain gestures that revealed the self-satisfied braggart he really was, gloating over the international repercussions of some opinion he had expressed, or how he'd been the most applauded speaker on some panel.

The fact that I appeared late in his life – two weeks before his fiftieth birthday – limited the possibilities of making our relationship a more affectionate one. I wish I'd been older during his military career, so we could have celebrated his promotions together, his swearings-in as a minister; so we could have discussed his statements, and shared a beer without it having to feel like some momentous occasion. In fact, I only remember drinking a beer with my dad twice. Once, the day I turned seventeen, at a party: a down-in-one that was more for the benefit of those present than for ourselves; and another on the cruise we took to the Bahamas in 1994. I was still underage, but he ordered two cans of Heineken from the bar and we drank them up on deck, staring out over the Caribbean in silence. It was the only time we broke the law together. It was the only time we looked at the sea together. I would have liked to get drunk with my father – if not with beer then with the vodka-and-oranges he so loved – instead of just seeing him return drunk late at night from one of his 'lunches'. He would arrive belting out 'Somos los mozos de Caba' at the top of his voice, that cavalry hymn sung to the same tune as John Philip Sousa's 'Stars and Stripes Forever', the king of American military marches. The words, still sung by officers today, boast of the 'scores of ladies' they get when they 'go on the hunt', the thousand-sol bills that 'rule our pockets' and the bottles of rum that 'rule our hearts'. One night in 2010, my car was pulled over by a patrolman. I was over the limit. The officer approached, asked for my papers and told me to breathe on his face. He informed me that we had to go to the station. With all my protestations falling on deaf ears, I played my last card and told him I was the son of General Cisneros, as if General Cisneros were still alive and could come riding to my rescue if I dialled his number. By way of proof, I showed him an old Ministry of Defence ID. The cop peered at the blurred photo dubiously, and asked me what regiment he belonged to. The cavalry, I replied. Just like mine, he responded. And so, in an alcohol-influenced act of brio, I began to sing 'Somos los mozos de Caba', just like my father did when he came home drunk, and to my surprise, the official knew it by heart. Drive carefully, he said to me when I'd finished, and as I drove carefully home I thought about how, even fifteen years after his death, my father's name could still do things for me. Save me from a night in the cells, for example.

Learning that cavalry song may be the closest I've ever come to adopting a military spirit. I was never interested in following in my father's footsteps, but nor was he interested in my doing so. Indeed, when my high school grades began to plummet in an abrupt and troubling fashion, he threatened to send me to the Pedro Ruiz Gallo military college, making it sound more like a punishment than an incentive. Several of my teenage nightmares took place in that college, with older students beating me and forcing me to man up, as my father demanded. Even Kafka's father, the merchant Hermann Kafka, whom the writer describes as a despotic being who obliterated his son's very presence, once encouraged him to become a soldier upon seeing how well he marched. My father never encouraged me to do so. Nor did he go through with his threat to send me to military college. And a good thing too. Perhaps he saw signs from early on that my temperament wasn't suited for the barracks. Or perhaps he wanted to compensate for the decision of his own parents, who had sent him to the military college in Argentina to discipline him, extinguishing the artist in him, the magician, the dancer. Or perhaps he simply saw I wasn't made of stern enough stuff to be a cadet. My mother and sister never stop reminding me of the day I pulled one of my father's military caps over my ears, climbed onto the back of the sofa and launched myself onto the cushions: I was imitating the hero Alfonso Ugarte, who spurred his horse off the Rock of Arica, clutching the Peruvian flag, refusing to surrender to the Chileans. That day, my horse was a broomstick and we both pitched down the precipice of the sofa. Some metal protrusion struck my forehead and the epic scene abruptly transformed into one of me bent over the bathroom sink, wailing as I saw in the mirror the rivulets of blood running down my face. I never had even a speck of soldier in me. Nor a leader, a chief, a commando. My vocation is so unlike his that I still shiver when someone exclaims, in response to some turn of phrase or spontaneous gesture, 'You're just like your father.'

I didn't like his vocation, but I did like his weapons. Or at least the opportunity to fire them. Or even just touching them. Sometimes, when my parents went out, if the game I was playing required it, I would lift down one of his decorative rifles – I still remember a long-barrelled black one with relief lettering on the butt – and creep into the dense bushes of the garden, firing silent shots at the terrorists lurking in dark corners of my imagination. My father never found out that I borrowed his guns. If I even motioned as if to pick one up he would get angry. When I was older, after his retirement and during the period of the anonymous telephone threats, I acquired a renewed interest in his weapons in light of the possibility of having to use them in an attack on the family. He kept a 6.35 mm Browning in one of the drawers of his dressing table; an Iver Johnson Safety Automatic revolver in his night table; a Remington semi-automatic rifle in his closet; a small Ingram machine gun in a secret compartment in his desk; and two rifles, one a Winchester and the other a special two-barrelled one, hidden behind his bookcase. I always associated these weapons with his virility, with his role as domestic hero and his ability to keep us safe. Although I was terrified by the idea of being attacked in our own home – not only by terrorists but by any ordinary burglar or an emissary of the dictatorship – something inside me was excited by the thought of seeing my father in such desperate circumstances, grabbing the Safety with both hands, aiming at the bad guy, taking him out, leaving him sprawled on our stone steps. There were also two black Magnum .44s with brown grips, kept in holsters by the rear doors of the blue Chevy. I don't remember anyone using them, but on many trips to school, on those mornings when we had to crouch down and cover our heads with our school bags, I imagined a terrorist ambush or a kidnapping attempt at a red light, and I saw myself pulling one of the weighty pistols from its holster, aiming and firing heroically at the attackers. Although, if such a situation were to have arisen, it's more likely that I would have lacked the strength or pluck to pull the trigger.

I only learned to shoot many years later, at a military training ground, after my father was dead. I went with two friends. I remember how each time I discharged the weapon the recoil would push me backwards, more readily than the other trainees, which caused some tittering among the staff in charge of the session. My aim was a total disaster too. Without question, war was not my favourite pastime. It never had been, except when I'd play in the garden with the armies of plastic soldiers I bought at the Surquillo market: miniature green commandos that fired and died and spied the enemy hidden in the plant pots, and that could even bravely launch themselves from the roof with parachutes made from rubbish bags or nylon stockings. I played at these make-believe wars while my country was going through a real one. A war that seemed very far off in the bunker-like Monterrico house. I knew that people were going hungry outside, and dying at the hands of terrorists, and I saw it happening on television at night, but I was never really aware that this problem had anything to do with me. In the 80s and 90s I never suffered the shortages everyone else did. Unlike most of my generation, I enjoyed security, good food, comforts and the freedom I longed for, however carefully circumscribed by my father. I never had to queue at a supermarket. I never feared a police officer. No member of my family was ever disappeared. I experienced moments of intense fright in response to the menacing phone calls, the threats of kidnapping, the possibility of a bomb attack, but I remained absolutely convinced that we would emerge unharmed, that our four bodyguards would take care of keeping us alive. I don't remember all of their names, but I do remember our nicknames for them: 'Petete' Herrera, 'El Negro' Alonso, 'El Pollo' and 'El Flaco' Sarmiento. They slept in Army cars outside and came into the house for specific things: to eat lunch, to use the toilet in the basement, to play ping-pong with me. Herrera was the most experienced of the four: he was from Tocache, in the jungle, and was proud of the fact that he not only worked for the Army intelligence services but was also studying law at university. He was a fan of Rambo, Bruce Lee, Chuck Norris; he could recite entire passages from *Enter the Dragon* and *The Delta Force*. We called him 'Petete', like the know-it-all cartoon character, because he was always ready with an explanation or a maxim. After working for my father, he engaged in secret operations for the intelligence service. In 1992 his name appeared in the newspapers as one of the agents involved in the Barrios Altos massacre. My blood turned cold to read that the man who had taken care of us for so many months, who had shown us such affection, had been capable of firing at the men, women and children who died there. Of El Negro I recall his tropical mane of hair, his salsa music tapes stuffed in the glove box and his warm smile, unsuited to someone carrying a machine gun at all times. With that same smile, that same machine gun and that same unaffectedness, he once came to pick me up from school, provoking hysteria among a group of teachers whose racist stereotypes led them to imagine he was a terrorist or assailant and began screaming like magpies. El Pollo was the youngest, the most lethargic, the one who kept crumpled porn magazines in the boot, the one who took longest to leave the car to carry out the nightly patrols, the one who cocked his weapon every five minutes to catch the attention of passers-by. I can still see El Pollo with his teeth chattering, his hair standing on end, wrapped in blankets, drinking hot tea directly from a thermos flask to try and keep warm. And what can I say about El Flaco Sarmiento other than that he was as mad as a hatter, though his madness seemed to be the result of some disturbing experience in one of the emergency zones where he said he'd served. Sarmiento was tall, with small green eyes like marbles, his ribs and collarbone showing beneath his shirt, and he had a bristly moustache that covered the mark of a cleft lip. Although his behaviour was strange and many of the things he said were incomprehensible, he made me laugh when he spoke like a stern officer, giving me orders as if I were an undercover spy. One of the things I most liked about the detective novels I read at the time was that the characters behaved just like these men who took care of my house: glancing around furtively all the time, making notes in tiny copybooks, pretending to read newspapers while observing the passers-by, talking in code, using hand signals, or refusing to talk at all. They and my father took care to ensure our peaceful little island was never breached by the hatred from outside: the hatred of the political class, of inequality, of repression. They and my father managed to make the worst years of Peru the best years of my life, years in which I felt, to paraphrase Nabokov, 'that everything was as it should be, nothing would ever change, no one would ever die'.

When my father died in 1995, all that security died with him. Then came fear, shortages, vulnerability, the need to work things out on our own. I experienced not only a slow internal collapse, but also a change in my relationship with my wider surroundings. From 1995 onwards I directed my discontent towards Lima, towards Peru and above all towards the government. Those were years as bad as or worse than the previous ones. At university we marched the streets twice a week to protest the Fujimori dictatorship, and it was on one such demonstration in the city centre, after hours of breathing tear gas and dodging police batons, that I felt rage – the rage of those who had been suffering and complaining for years – begin to stir in me for the first time. Only then did I start to understand that my country was a backward, unequal shithole, where thousands of people resented each other and fought over the few available opportunities to get ahead. In a sense, my father's death cast me into the world, grounded me, made me appreciate the gravity of what had happened and was continuing to happen around me. That awareness arrived in tandem with a powerful sense of guilt. For although my father safeguarded the tranquillity of our family, he never avoided telling us what was going on in Peru. His information may have been sparing, but he did tell us. I was the one who didn't want to hear it, the one who privately scoffed at his concern for the levels of violence in the country.

Not even in 1990, when he helped me with the school public speaking contest, did I understand what he was trying to say. He prepared a didactic, emotional speech for me, entitled 'Peruvian Youth and Subversion'. I was nothing but a talking parrot who had carefully memorised the words he dictated to me. I was fourteen, old enough to understand what was going on around us, but I didn't understand. Caught up in my feelings of reproach towards my father, I ignored his warnings about the state of affairs and selfishly satisfied myself with knowing that we lacked for nothing at home, that nothing bad was going to happen to us. Only very occasionally, when my sister Valentina got talking about politics at the dinner table, did I pay attention to what my father said. I can see him now, leaning back in his chair, criticising the Alan García administration for its profligate spending instead of channelling more resources to the Army and putting an end to the Shining Path once and for all. I can see him illustrating the topic with a fable or analogy he would later include in one of his *Expreso* articles. 'Imagine you have a tumbledown house that someone's trying to take off you,' he would say. 'Imagine the pipes are kaput, the windows are broken, there are holes in the roof. What would you do? Would you defend it from the invaders, or would you fix it up first, to get it all shiny and new for them?' My sister and I would answer in unison: "We'd defend it!' And then he would rise to his feet, take the last sip from his cup and conclude: 'Always defend your home. Even if it's in ruins, it's still yours. No one can take it from you.'

Chapter 9

My father spawned a constellation of identities. He was baptised as Luis Federico, but his parents called him 'Chucho' and his siblings 'Fredy'. To Beatriz Abdulá and his Argentinian friends in the 30s and 40s, he was always 'the Gaucho', while Lucila Mendiola, his first wife, and their friends and family in Sullana knew him as 'Lucho'. His companions in the Army, even after his retirement, always addressed him as General, while the bodyguards referred to him with an impersonal but totalising alias: the Man. My mother called him 'dear' under all circumstances, whether to summon him affectionately from some distant corner of the house, or to admonish him for arriving late or saying something rude. I called him 'Dad' but since his death I refer to him as 'my Father'. Each one of these names or pseudonyms has its own personality, its particular secrets. The very essence of my father is scattered among them. If there was anything real about him, it was probably to be found where these multiple selves overlapped: the centre of a Venn diagram.

I wonder now what nickname Aurelia Pasquel might have used for him. She was the retired air stewardess my father got involved with when we moved to the Monterrico house, or perhaps before then. I knew of her existence, but I didn't know her name. It was my mother Cecilia Zaldívar who brought it up one afternoon just a year ago, during one of those revelation-filled, therapeutic lunches of ours.

'Your father swore to me that it was just a fling, nothing serious,' she said. But I never believed my father, and I'm sure she didn't believe him either. I spent days scouring Facebook for this mysterious woman's name and didn't rest until I found her. It had to be Aurelia Pasquel. Although she quickly accepted my 'friend' request – perhaps consumed by the same curiosity that had driven me to trace her – and responded to my initial messages in an amicable tone, she then seemed to become discouraged or regretful and never answered my requests to meet for coffee. Perhaps someone persuaded her not to dig up a past she had worked hard to overcome. I can't deny there was something strange or morbid in seeking to meet my father's lover (is that even the right term?), to ask her face-to-face all the questions that had piled up inside me, between my head and my throat. But this concern was overcome by my need to explore my father's hidden facets, his multiple personalities, and to learn more about the person who had driven such a rift between him and my mother. Had he stopped loving Cecilia Zaldívar as he had stopped loving Lucila Mendiola before her? When and where had he met Aurelia Pasquel? Was it merely a few nights of romance or a parallel relationship? Was she married when he came into her life? Did my father ever consider leaving the Monterrico house, leaving us? And if so, did he only discard the idea in order to avoid another nightmare like the one he went through with my older siblings when he abandoned chalet 69 in Chorrillos on 11 September 1971? How did he talk about us in his conversations with Aurelia? Did we exist to her? Did my mother? Was it true that my father visited her in an apartment in San Borja, in a development named Mariscal Ramón Castilla – after the former president whose own lover, incidentally, betrayed him with my great-grandfather? One morning, looking through Aurelia Pasquel's photos on

Facebook, I recognised someone I believed to be her older son, Julián. He had been introduced to me years earlier at a barbecue somewhere on the outskirts of Lima. That day, unlike most of the guests, we were both single, and perhaps for that reason we were drawn to each other's company, laughing at the others, toasting with a certain complicity, completely unaware that his mother and my father had been lovers in the past. We could easily have brought up the names of our parents, and perhaps this would have led us to put two and two together, to draw silent conclusions, but nothing of the sort occurred. Julián and I were simply brief acquaintances. Our parents' forbidden story was there the whole time, right in front of our eyes and ears, enveloping us like a mist, or like a fine veil that was never pulled aside.

My sister Valentina has erased this scene from her memory, but I can't. The two of us are in the dining room, interrogating the Gaucho, who's smoking and staring straight ahead, unresponsive as a stone. This was probably 1987. I don't remember how, but we know that he has an anonymous lover, and we're demanding that he leave her – or else leave our house. I now imagine this must have been Aurelia Pasquel. It's odd that Valentina doesn't remember this moment, because she was the one who spoke for both of us throughout, emphasising our annoyance and disappointment, and staunchly defending our mother, who was roaming around the house shifting erratically from depression to bad-temperedness, then from bad-temperedness to an exasperating silence. She would spend hours watering the garden until it flooded, or unexpectedly taking her car on long drives to nowhere, furious outings from which she would return with her makeup running, enveloped in an aroma of cigarettes and sorrow I can still smell today. Valentina was only fourteen at the time, but she was fully capable of putting my father up against the ropes. If he listened to anyone in the house, it was to her. In that dining-room scene, I am merely a decorative figure who nods along with my sister's cutting words. Leave that woman or get out. My father opens his mouth, expels a smoke ring that fades into the air and mumbles something indefinite like 'I promise it's going to end.' Nothing more. Silent, I gaze at him without understanding what his words really mean.

There is a cartoon, published in the satirical fortnightly *Monos y Monadas* in the late 70s, that shows my father flustered as he rummages around in his wardrobe, shouting to his wife: 'I must get to Congress and can't find the democratic convictions I left in this drawer!' As a kid this cartoon – which now hangs in a frame above my desk – perturbed me for reasons that had nothing to do with political critique. It was the woman in the drawing that interested and puzzled me most. I wondered who the artist was trying to depict: my father's first or second wife. The figure had Lucila Mendiola's hair, but the nose was clearly Cecilia Zaldívar's. Did the cartoonist know them? Did he know my father had married twice? When in 1987 I learned he had a mistress, and since I didn't yet know her name, my imagination reached for the face of the woman in the caricature in an attempt to make her, in some sense or other, real.

According to my uncle Reynaldo, my father's entanglement with Aurelia Pasquel was a bona fide love affair, not just a fling. When he told me this, I felt a resentful, and resigned, rancour towards the Gaucho. Yet why should I be surprised if, ever since Beatriz Abdulá, my father's relationships with women had ranged almost exclusively from tortuous romance to long-suffering passion, by way of melodramatic tangos? Wherever there were obstacles and prohibitions he found an excuse to obsess over someone, following the examples of lovesickness that his father and his grandfather, Fernán and Luis Benjamín, had set in earlier epochs and centuries. Like them, as if he were incapable of cultivating platonic friendships with women, my father fell in love – or acted as if he was in love – with an extravagance that was rarely reciprocated. 'I was a seducer. When I came to Peru from Argentina I was madly in love, even if I later got dumped,' he told a reporter from *VEA* magazine a few years before he died.

My father was not a collector of women, nor one of those macho men who boast of their conquests and belch out anecdotes, often greatly embellished, of their escapades as insatiable sexual predators. No. My father was a selective seducer, a patient hunter, a Don Juan, a strategic narcissist – yet he was also erratic and sentimental. If I had known anything about this in my early teens, if we had ever spoken of his disappointments and mine with even a jot of honesty, perhaps I would have suffered less in my tendency to go off the rails every time a girl started to mean something to me. When I finally had the chance to read my father's ardent letters to Beatriz, the tender cards he sent Lucila, his overblown poems for Cecilia, I felt discovered, exposed. His solemn words, so full of hope and resolve, have also been my own. As a teenager, I too had fallen in love in this way: melodramatically, copiously, desperately, as if at bottom I was in love not with the women who received my letters and poems, but rather with the very fact of being able to write or tell them all those things. Just like my father, I loved becoming a broadcaster of shameless, all-encompassing oaths that were impossible to retract, oaths that sent me down marvellous but inhospitable paths, oaths that led me into dense, dark forests with luxuriant trees, where it was hard to make out the clearings and the pathways home. Yes, women were the excuse, the name, the pretext; the poor, transient muses. The really exciting thing wasn't love; it was losing my head about someone, abandoning myself to floods of sensual language, the drive to say everything, promise everything, flay myself, burn myself, set fire to the world, a burnt offering for an utterly unpredictable future.

★ ★ ★

Around the time I moved up to high school I got used to sleeping with the radio on. To send me to sleep quickly, I would tune in to a station playing Spanish ballads. The radio stayed on until my father got home, and he would come into my room to unplug it. Countless times, I pretended to be asleep just so I could listen to his ritual as he entered the house: the sound of the Chevy parking; the metallic creak of the front door or the sliding door from the garden; a brief exchange of words with my mother if she was still up; the click of the light in my room; the radio knob; the plug being pulled out of the wall.

My school class once took an overnight trip to Chosica. It was a kind of spiritual away day plus camping. The second-year students set up tents on a riverbank, lit fires and played guitars, singing Spanish-language rock songs and ballads. Our teachers had asked all the parents to write a letter to their children. At my mother's insistence, my father had acquiesced. That night I opened it, expecting little. I was surprised, moved and also embarrassed to read a line referring to 'that person' whom I 'surely thought about' every night while I listened to my radio ballads. As I re-read the paragraph I glanced around to make sure no one was watching me. It seemed impossible that my father, who had never touched on such intimate subjects in conversation with me, could have written such a personal letter. I was in love with a girl, Lorena Antúnez, but I had never breathed a word to my parents about her. Reading this letter I felt trapped, caught. Without a doubt, I now understood, my father didn't just switch off the radio when he came into my room at night, but he also looked at me; there must have been some gesture in my sleeping face that he recognised, that immediately prompted him to make a mental note he would express in this letter, the only one I remember of the two or three he ever wrote to me.

I'm not sure what happened in my adolescence that made me lose this ability to love so vehemently, torrentially – or at least to temper it with a healthy, protective scepticism. Not my father. He always liked loving this way, hurling all of himself into it. Ever since that Army regulation prevented him from consecrating his love for Beatriz Abdulá in 1947, he decided to love against the rules, even if this would later mean betraying his official partners. If the Gaucho could have seen what transpired at his own wake, he'd have preferred to remain in his coffin. There was Aurelia Pasquel, incognito, seated two rows behind Lucila Mendiola, and thirty paces from Cecilia Zaldívar. From their respective places, each pondered her own words, brought together in their love for the man who lay behind the glass in the box, with his military trappings.

It's not that my father couldn't stop falling in love with women. Evidently he could. In different epochs, both single and married, he had a series of short-lived adventures, flirtations or affairs with women as varied as Carmen Monteagudo, a lady who managed investments and property; Sofía Barreda, a tall, slender, dark-skinned woman who sold high-end handicrafts in a Conquistadores Ave. store; and Glenda Zarina, a famous writer who had authored a series of self-help books featuring a charismatic green-skinned alien child who lived on the banks of the Amazon and transmitted telepathic messages of love. I never

277

met Carmen Monteagudo or Sofía Barreda. I did once meet Glenda Zarina, when I had to interview her for a literature programme I used to present. I didn't know that she had known my father during the military government, let alone that she'd slept with him at a hotel off Central Highway, as recounted to me by a faithless mutual friend. During the interview I asked her why she'd chosen the Amazon jungle as the backdrop for her stories. 'Because green is my favourite colour,' she explained, in an involuntary nod to the green of military uniforms.

★ ★ ★

My father never spoke to me of sex or women. All sex-related matters were an electric fence that kept us at bay. I didn't look to him for advice, nor did he seek to offer any when my sexual awakening began to trouble me. Several school friends had already lost their virginity with an older cousin, a more experienced neighbour or even a maid. Others had waited until they were fifteen and asked their fathers to take them to a brothel, or at least to give them enough money to pick up a whore on Arequipa or Javier Prado avenues. 'Your old man's in the military – tell him to take you to the knocking shop. That's what they all do, it's normal. My grandpa was in the Marines and he took my old man to La Nené del Callao to get his rocks off,' my friend Alex Aldana told me one day as we were leaving school. He was already frequenting the red light districts of San Isidro and Barranco. I nodded as I listened to his advice, but in reality I didn't even consider the possibility of talking to my father in such terms. Terrified of his reaction and determined to avoid it, I kept quiet and stuck to the petty pleasures of masturbation. I would only discover actual sex after eighteen, a few months after my father died.

278

Even to become a man in that sense, to acquire that kind of manliness, I needed him to disappear. His only gesture I might describe as educational was to hide a condom in one of my shoes. I think he could have done more. He could, for example, have told me if not about his own experiences then about those of his soldiers. In 1967, when he was in charge of the 15th cavalry regiment in the Las Lomas district, a vast open space near the border with Ecuador, he ordered three tents to be set up some distance from the main encampment so that, in the best style described by Mario Vargas Llosa in *Captain Pantoja and the Special Service*, a group of prostitutes could attend to the soldiers. Every two weeks he would go down to the city of Catacaos with his number two, Captain Calandria, 'El Gringo' Calandria, and they'd visit dodgy night clubs and pick out the girls together and send them for medical check-ups before their official recruitment. The squadrons formed queues behind the tents, anxiously waiting their turn, desperate for release after weeks without any female contact. 'And you and my father,' I asked El Gringo Calandria the afternoon we walked along the shoreline of Chorrillos bay, talking about my father, 'did you enter the tents, too?' 'No. We'd go down to Sullana some evenings, where there were more decent places with nicer girls, but we wouldn't always score. Sometimes we'd just go to watch, to mess around, and then we'd head off to the bar run by 'La Negra' Delia. We pretty much owned her place. We'd leave our caps on hooks with our names on them, and we'd throw dice and drink beer until eleven o'clock or midnight.'

The prostitutes offered their services to the soldiers of the 15th for months, until one day the camp doctor sent a letter to Lieutenant Colonel Cisneros informing him that two soldiers had caught gonorrhoea. My father immediately suspended all sexual services and ordered an exhaustive investigation, which produced the surprising conclusion that the prostitutes hadn't introduced the disease, but rather the town priest, Father Ekberg, and his sacristan. They visited every week to provide the troops with spiritual support, in exchange, it would appear, for the soldiers assuaging their carnal debts with martial vigour.

At first, the religious men refused to undergo any kind of examination, declaring it an affront to their dignity, but they were forced to yield before the intervention of the Archbishop of Piura, who arrived at the camp one day on Lieutenant Colonel Cisneros' request. 'Only then did we learn', El Gringo Calandria recounted, 'that the faggot Ekberg and his altar boy were getting the soldiers to take them up the ass on the other side of a hill.'

If heterosexual sex was an uncomfortable subject at home, then mentioning homosexuality was simply out of the question. It was a taboo subject for my father, despite the fact that – or precisely because – two of his brothers, my uncles Reynaldo and Adrián, were bisexual. As a kid I had no idea, for example, that the young men my uncle Reynaldo put up at my grandmother's house – Heinz, Johnny, Cipriano – were in fact his lovers. And I befriended them without understanding my mother's warnings that I shouldn't be left alone with any of them. How could I imagine that Reynaldo was involved with these young men sexually when he was always the Casanova uncle, the one who had been with more women in his youth than his brothers and cousins put together? Every time Reynaldo saw me arriving from school he'd ask me: 'How many girls do you have on the go now, or are you still spanking the monkey?' This left me deeply ashamed, because I felt incapable of winning a sweetheart or conquering anyone at all. Indeed, I hoped to learn from them, my youngest uncles, Reynaldo and Adrián: the ones who got the most girls, the handsome bohemians who sang in Portuguese, played the guitar, wore leather boots and jackets, drove sports cars and stayed in bed until after ten. I could never have imagined that they both shared – though they didn't even mention it to each other – a silent weakness for other men.

While we lived on the second floor of the house on La Paz St., my uncle Reynaldo had affairs with twenty- and thirty-something men, some of whom fell in love with him and fled in tears when the feeling wasn't reciprocated. The only sentiment my uncle showed towards these lovers was a generous paternalism with a dash of sexual fervour. Nothing more. No one ever awoke in him the madness, desire and both carnal and emotional dependence he'd felt for Manolo de Gorostiaga, an older man, a well-known television game show host, likewise a closeted homosexual, who had changed Reynaldo's life and worldview many years before.

They had met at an embassy cocktail party, talked all night and within a few weeks had gone to bed together. The discreet conduct they upheld in Lima went out the window on their regular getaways to Madrid or Lisbon, where they shut themselves up in luxury hotel rooms with huge windows, loving and laughing at the world, surrounded by bottles of Cointreau. When Manolo's wife Gina tracked them down and called the room telephone, Reynaldo would answer, and she would feel greatly relieved that he wasn't gallivanting around with one of the female models who pursued him for his looks, his money and his fame. If my uncle Reynaldo had only one true love, if there was ever anyone who drove him wild, it was Manolo, whom he kept seeing until the very end, and at whose wake he remained until every last funeral rite had been performed. My father knew about the relationship, but never recriminated his brother; indeed, he sought to protect him with his silence.

My uncle Adrián, meanwhile, was constantly falling for boys barely over the age of consent. Even though he became involved with a neighbour he almost married – they had a daughter together – he would not or could not abandon his trysts with these tender lads, sexual partners he protected both emotionally and financially. 'I'd like to marry you, but I can't: I catch sight of a teenage beauty and can't take my eyes off him,' Adrián confessed one night to Irene, the neighbour, his face red with tears and shame. He was once arrested for harassing a boy of sixteen, and my father had to get up in the middle of the night to get him out of jail – after he'd made his brother swear never to do anything like that again. Adrián kept his promise. He became more prudent in his crushes, and had a beach house built at Pulpos where he could hold his orgiastic parties without anyone bothering him.

My father always took great care never to make even the slightest allusion to the sexual preferences of his two younger brothers, whom he respected, loved and cared for, despite his avowed homophobia. 'If any son of mine turns out a queer, I'll string him up by his balls,' he warned me one day in the garden, without my having said or done a thing. His vehemence jarred with the circumstances and was perhaps his way of unburdening himself of the unease he felt about my uncles' way of life.

On another occasion he became unreasonably furious when he saw I'd allowed a little rattail to grow at the nape of my neck. It was a fashion among my school friends, probably copied from Italian football player Roberto Baggio. One night, my father summoned me and insisted I cut it off, claiming that long hair threatened my virility. I refused and went to bed. From my room, I could hear my parents arguing, my mother defending me. When I awoke next morning, upon scratching my neck I found the Baggio tail was gone. My father had snipped it off as I slept. When I went to demand why, he replied, not raising his eyes from the newspapers: 'I won't have poofters in my own home.'

I don't believe he would have been happy with my literary career either. I'm sure he would have disapproved of my novels. Even though his father and grandfather had been writers, his judgement of male behaviour led him to associate literature with some salacious universe teeming with vices, homosexuality among them.

He thought this of Mario Vargas Llosa, for example. 'Everyone knows that Vargas Llosa wrote *The Time of the Hero* because he was angry at being thrown out of the Leoncio Prado military college for being homosexual,' he once declared in a magazine interview.

★ ★ ★

In the final years of high school I took a deep interest in religion, to the extent that I attended mass twice a week, speaking every day with the school's American priests, who lent me books on their vocation and encouraged me to consider taking vows. When my father discovered these books, he was deeply suspicious. 'That boy's not turning into a poof, is he?' he asked my older brother Fermín, who'd graduated in psychology, one of those nights they spent pub crawling around Barranco in a yellow Volkswagen. My brother laughed and told him that his fears suggested a deep phobia he should examine more closely. Nothing Fermín said, however, served to relieve his suspicions. My father never said anything to me about my interest in becoming a priest, but a latent anxiety remained. One night I invited a friend to stay over at the Monterrico house because it had got too late for him to take the bus home. He was a friend who also conversed with the school priests, attended weekend retreats with me and was also considering the seminary. 'It's no problem for me to stay over, right?' he asked. I assured him it was fine and started to unfold a camp bed beside my own. Minutes later my father came down the corridor and abruptly opened the door to find us laughing as we extended the sheets. The scene must have looked dangerously gay to him. 'Dammit, how many times have I told you to leave the door open!' he bellowed. My father hated us shutting our doors. He hated us having privacy, the idea that we could do things behind his back. He wanted to have visual control over what was happening in our bedrooms; if he could have placed cameras in each one, as he had once installed intercoms, he would have done. Sometimes I felt my room was like a cell with an open door. On the few occasions I was able to push it closed and press the metal button on the handle that locked it, whether because my father was away or too caught up in his many activities, I was immediately filled with a sense of relief. I felt at ease hidden away inside, alone, but this comfort would soon shatter when he reappeared to rap on the door with his knuckles once, twice, three times, demanding I open up. I found it deeply unfair that he demanded this transparency from us when he kept himself so literally and symbolically closed off. That night, following the scene with the sheets, he called me into his bedroom. I told my friend to make himself comfortable. Entering my father's room, he received me with a blow. A hard and unanticipated smack across the face that tumbled me to the floor. I'll never forget it. My mother would later spend hours trying to explain that it was a reaction to the cancer medicines he was taking at the time, that they were affecting his nervous system. Maybe. Perhaps she was right. But I think it was something else. I think that my father exploded at the thought that his second male child was a homosexual or was on his way to becoming one, just like his own beloved brothers. Perhaps he was trying to punish them through me. Perhaps beating me was the only way he could approach the matter. That night my friend slept peacefully, but I could not. I was kept awake by the fear that my father was going to burst in and send him packing. And although the next day he begged my forgiveness with genuine tears, the blow remained inside me like a blood clot. Today, if I catch myself acting violently or aggressively, it's as if that blow has come to the surface again and taken control of me. Then I'm flooded by an ancient rage, a fury I struggle to temper or channel somewhere it won't harm anyone, as if it were a powerful explosive that must be carried far out to sea for safe disposal.

* * *

It may be that my father became more conservative over the years, or that his machismo led him to flaunt a rigid mindset of moderation that clashed with many of his own most fundamental life experiences. When he claimed in an April 1995 interview with *VEA* that 'I'm not in favour of sex before marriage because it spoils the surprise,' it seemed like a joke in poor taste, though I can only interpret it as an indirect warning to my sister Valentina and her boyfriend of the time, rather than a moral precept he followed himself. Of course my father believed in sex before marriage: he had engaged in it for years. Naturally, it suited him to alter his true ideology and make such declarations to buff up his image as an upstanding man before the elections – and in passing to safeguard the supposed virginity of his one unmarried daughter, or to chastise her if she had lost it.

My father protected Valentina from the boys who hovered around her, as he had done in the past with his older daughters Melania and Estrella. With all three daughters he was re-afflicted by the sick jealousy he had suffered long ago with Beatriz Abdulá's friends in Buenos Aires, with Lucila Mendiola's in Sullana, and with Cecilia Zaldívar's in Lima. Over time, he had become a less possessive husband, but when Melania and Estrella started going to parties, my father would secretly follow them in his car, park on the corner and spend the whole night there, peering through his binoculars to make sure they didn't emerge in the company of some undesirable. Or perhaps even willing this to happen, so he could get out the car, puff himself up and give the boy a well-deserved bawling-out. The night Valentina celebrated her fifteenth birthday, my father came home to find a pack of teenagers dancing on his terrace, vomiting in his garden, finishing all the liquor in his drinks cabinet and probing his youngest daughter's miniskirt with their eyes. He switched off the lights, killed the music and herded the drunks out of the house until just one remained, who he threatened with his revolver until the boy crawled out the front gate on all fours.

The general said in public that he opposed both sex before marriage and abortion. 'Only permissible in cases of rape', he argued. Years earlier, however, he had encouraged or permitted Cecilia Zaldívar to abort on two occasions. The first time, in 1972, the circumstances were undoubtedly difficult: they'd only been together a few months and he still lived with Lucila Mendiola and their children at the chalet in Chorrillos. The news of the pregnancy must have caused them shock rather than excitement. A secret child born out of wedlock would not only have been a scandal for the Cisneros side of the family – even if it did honour their lineage – but above all an offence to Cecilia's parents, Eduviges and Eleuterio, and in the long run a cause for separation. It may have been, then, that they both agreed on the abortion, which ended up saving their relationship, perhaps even strengthening it. But by 1980, on the second occasion, the scenario was very different. My parents were already living together as a married couple – even if the marriage had never been formalised – had two children, Valentina and me, and the support of both their families. Why then did Cecilia decide to abort again?

We had just returned from Piura and my father had high expectations of the new government, led by President Fernando Belaúnde. He was sure they would offer him a cabinet position and was wholly prepared to accept; after all, his political future depended on it. When my mother announced she was pregnant – this time proud, eager, determined and willing to have the child, their third – the Gaucho tried to dissuade her. Perhaps he was influenced by friends who told him his career was at a crucial turning point and it would be unwise to take on new family obligations. Or perhaps it was just his own political ego. In any case, he asked her to end the pregnancy. He would take care of everything, he said. Cecilia refused, but eventually gave in. So my father called on Pepe Caicedo, Lima's most prominent gynaecologist, the same one who had helped Cecilia with her first abortion and delivered her first two babies, to do the dirty work again.

Two years later, when she miraculously fell pregnant with my brother Facundo, although both the political horizon and the Gaucho's own future remained uncertain, Cecilia fought tooth and nail to defend her pregnancy, and warned my father that nothing would stop her having that baby. My father accepted. Facundo's arrival somehow compensated for the previous losses, but they would always weigh on my mother. Throughout my adolescence I tended to believe that my parents' fights were due to the naturally bad temper of my mother, who would fly into rages for the most idiotic, absurd and capricious reasons. For years

I pitied my father who, poor man, was forced to put up with Cecilia Zaldívar's yelling and reproaches, patient as a saint. If my parents ever get divorced, I thought, it'll be her fault. Only once I learned about the abortions did I come to understand the whole story. I realised that my mother was never crazy, just wounded; that if she lost her rag and yelled and wept in these sudden outbursts, the root cause was the frustration of motherhood denied. 'I could have had five little angels,' my mother would sometimes say in a low voice, and I failed to understand, mocking her delirious chatter. But now I do understand her, and I regret thinking she was crazy. Instead, late though I may be, I admire her for having put up with everything she had to put up with. Not only the terminated pregnancies, but all the rest, too: the rude glares and the stuck-up faces of the other women at the Military Club; my father's brutal selfishness, his affair with Aurelia Pasquel, his passivity and cowardice when it came to divorcing Lucila Mendiola, and even how he let himself die – refusing to get treatment when he needed to, expecting that she, my mother, would be the one sitting at his bedside, holding his hand until the end, until he was nothing but a bundle in need of burying.

Chapter 10

There is something dangerous about doubling back to retrace those years of tame, well-structured family life. Years when we took for granted that nothing would ever change enough to become a threat, at least within the island kingdom that was the Monterrico house. Years when it was even possible to dream of becoming a poet. If my mother had had her way about it, I would have dreamt of becoming a diplomat or lawyer, or some other decorous profession that obliged me to shave and wear a suit and tie in exchange for a monthly salary. One night, during one of her famous fits of pragmatism in which she proclaimed her views on my future, she embarked on a speech in front of the whole family to try and dissuade me from taking up poetry, assuring me I would end up in obscurity – or worse, in poverty, which she herself had escaped from – and lose the social standing won by my father's hard work. To my surprise, he thumped the table with indignation and cut her off. 'Don't ruin his dreams,' he barked before withdrawing to his room, leaving us all open-mouthed.

My father liked my first poems – rhyming ditties that sound amateurish, distant and disingenuous today. He applauded them not because they revealed some effervescent creative spirit on my part but because the rhyme suggested order, discipline, restraint, an enchanting but rigid music that never strayed from its course. My father wanted me to write like his father and his grandfather, and not to abandon the furrow they'd carved out: those centuries of steady erosion that had determined so many lives. I spent years forcing myself to fill notebooks with countless rhymes in an attempt to resemble my grandfather as much as possible, to see if that way I could win my father's admiration at last, to see if he would capitulate to me just once in his life. I think that in some sense I succeeded. Poetry was the only subject I was sure I knew more about than he did. In every other field of knowledge, I was defeated by his intelligence and wolfish acumen. But poetry made me superior, helped me expose something rudimentary in my father, the poverty of his literary knowledge, his potted artistic learning cobbled together out of reproductions, imitations of famous still lifes, Capodimonte porcelains, a few insipid lines by Amado Nervo, and tangos by Gardel.

It is contradictory yet symptomatic that my father should defend my dreams to my mother without ever speaking of his own. He talked about his plans, not his dreams. He was a dreamer who didn't dream, or who didn't recount his dreams. He belonged so fully to the physical world, and believed so little in the oneiric dimension of existence, that I wouldn't have been surprised to learn that some mental reflex had blocked the pathway of dreams in his brain. Perhaps his subconscious dictator had closed it by decree.

My father didn't talk about what he did, either. At work he didn't talk about home, and at home he didn't talk about work. He wasn't just reserved: he was cryptic. His mouth wasn't just a tomb, but a whole mausoleum. Perhaps the natural indiscretion I would later indulge, freely revealing my private life in newspaper columns, on the radio or in books, was a belated reaction to – or revenge for – my father's infuriating silences.

His was a selective silence, it's true, because when it

came to discussing politics or instructing us on topics of general culture – geography, history, arithmetic – he suffered from extreme logorrhoea. No one could shut him up. In any case, it was always amusing to listen to him because he seasoned his lessons and opinions with anecdotes that brought out his sense of humour. He did have a great sense of humour, even if it was marked by a double standard. He'd laugh, for example, at the inane, predictable sketches about Otto and Fritz (those naïve characters whose lives mocked the square, slow-witted thinking of German immigrants to the Peruvian countryside in the early 1900s), but in ordinary life, in situations demanding swift responses, he was capable of startling ripostes that sparkled with intelligent irony. It was odd: on the one hand he'd rail against the tacky humour of TV programmes he considered painfully cheesy, like *Laughter and Salsa* – 'Do me a favour and switch off that nonsense' he'd say when he found us watching it – but on the other hand he never missed the political parodies of *Camotillo el Tinterillo*, starring the comedian Tulio Loza, who, now that I think about it, delivered his monologues in rhyming verse.

His severity and self-control were sometimes disarmed by a joke of mine or by a film I'd suggested, and at such moments I felt a warm glow of pride. I'd conclude that this self-assured, dominating man that was my father did have unprotected cracks, fissures I could slip through. It was at my insistence that we watched several episodes of *Cine Pícaro*, which was like a vulgar version of Laurel and Hardy – an Argentinian series with 'Fatty' Jorge Porcel and 'Skinny' Alberto Olmedo broadcast on Canal 9 on Saturday nights. I liked to see my father chortling at the adventures of the clumsy duo; it sometimes made me giggle just to see him doubled up in laughter. I liked to share this show with him not because of its sexual allusions, which only caused uncomfortable silences (as I've said, sex had no place in our conversations), but because of the Argentinian slang used by Porcel and Olmedo, and the way their dialogues sparked my father's recollections of Buenos Aires. Perhaps if he entered a kind of nostalgic trance, I thought, I could encourage him to talk about the city where he was born, grew up and was happy at my age, when he was perhaps more like me. His guffaws at these films or at the mocking rhymes I'd compose to slander political figures – Alan García was a favourite target – pierced my father's armour. His military mask would slip, he'd show his false teeth when he smiled, he'd emerge from out of the character he had created, and he'd cough and sputter and roar and then I'd feel that my father really existed, that we could laugh at the same stupidities, that there was room for unimportant things in his life, and the power of comedy made us friends. As a result I hated the adverts that interrupted the films, which inserted banal pauses into these moments of glory when our roles were erased, and then his laughter would fade, he'd turn back into my father again and I his son, and it would be time to switch off the TV, for it was late and we all had to get up early the next day and do the shopping for Sunday brunch.

* * *

In those years my need for attention, for people to notice me, was so great that my mind would invent strange forms of self-torture. I'd spend long minutes staring at the ceiling fan in the kitchen, with its green blades and four speeds, asking myself what would happen if I turned it up to the highest speed and stuck my finger in the air: how quickly would the fan slice my finger to pieces? There'd be blood everywhere. There'd be pain. It would cause collective

292

trauma and oblige everyone to take care of me. That's how I thought sometimes. But I was never brave enough to act. Unlike my father, I'd never have cut open my palm with a knife to prove my virility. Or perhaps I had no need to prove it. Or perhaps I had no virility.

There was another period when I'd threaten everyone that I was going to run away from home. My mother and Valentina would fly into a state of panic. I liked to scare them. My father, on the hand, wouldn't even react. Let him go ahead, let him, just see if he dares, he'd say, without even glancing up from whatever he was doing at that moment: reading the paper, watching television. He knew I wouldn't have the nerve to step out onto the street. Rooted to his wicker chair, crossing his legs, eating olives, not even looking at me, my father could get inside my head, see my thoughts and tie them up in knots like snakes. Let him, just see if he dares. His words, so charged with conviction, subdued and paralysed me.

And I never did dare. All I wanted to do was go out, take a few turns around the block, pretend to disappear and see if that way, even just in this one pathetic way, my father would be at all perturbed by my absence. Because that's how I felt at the time: that he would be absolutely fine without me, that my disappearance from the world wouldn't affect him in the least. This made me mad at myself. I'd get mad and then I'd hate myself because my anger wasn't enough to carry out a single memorable act of rebellion. Perhaps a strange wisdom illuminated me then and told me to stay where I was. For if I did leave, then I might have corroborated just how little my father cared, how quickly he got used to my absence, and that's something I would never have recovered from.

The only thing that awoke his interest at home was the TV news. The ten o'clock news was sacred. No one could interrupt him while he was watching. I grew up hating the news and all those starched news anchors of the 80s and 90s. Martínez Morosini, Aldo Morzán, Arturo Pomar. They could talk through the glass and capture my father's attention. Now that I work as a news presenter, I like to imagine how my father would see me. If he were alive, I think, I'd be the one reading him the news at night and I would at last hold his attention. Or perhaps not. Perhaps he would change the channel so that someone else could read him the news, someone other than his son. Someone else whose head wasn't so easy to get into.

When the news ended, he'd get up, move through the house and reassert his air of authority. He was always the centre of everything that occurred at the Monterrico house. If there was a gathering or a party, he was the star. It wasn't something he necessarily intended: it just happened, and then there was no way to get him out of the box others seemed to put him in, partly out of flattery and partly because my father really was a genial, unstoppable chatterbox. Nobody could overshadow him; his character did not allow competition. And if his children did a dance or recited a poem by their grandfather or performed some artistic show with our aunts' encouragement, he'd treat it as a brief recess, an intermission, a break before returning to the central activity of the gathering: listening to him talking about politics.

One Sunday afternoon, so many years ago now that it seems a lifetime away, he revealed the secret of the magic trick I was performing in front of the entire extended family. Perhaps he couldn't bear me holding everyone's attention instead of him. Eighty people were watching – or I believed them to be watching – as I manipulated a deck of cards and passed my wand over it, trying not to drop my plastic top hat. From somewhere in the background, leaning against a wall, a glass of whisky in his hand, a cigarette dangling from his lips, my father shouted out the number and suit of the card that gave away the whole show. The seven of spades. Even though everyone knew I was a hopeless magician and were just playing along with my childish performance, they would still pretend to be astonished. Until he ruined it. Even though he had called himself Mandrake Cisneros at my age, even though he understood what it meant for a child of ten to feel like a magician, he couldn't bear being ignored. Giving away the trick from his spot by the back wall was his ungainly way of reminding everyone else, especially me, that he was the only one in this house who could cast a spell on the crowd, even if he had to humiliate his own child to achieve it.

It was experiences like these – which sound so silly and self-absorbed to me today, but which at the time felt like unforgiveable betrayals – that shaped my sense of insularity. One of the first manifestations of this isolation was my covetousness, my obsession with amassing possessions and protecting what I had amassed. Being greedy, stingy, miserly, not spending the pocket money I received, or collecting objects and not sharing them, was an unhappy way of owning something, of gaining presence, of materialising myself, as if the packets of biscuits that came into my hands, or the coins and notes I managed to save, or the toys, the books, the clothes I was given, were my only real possessions, as if I *was* them or was made of them. I found it very difficult to spend my money or lend my belongings: I wasn't sure I possessed anything else. Keeping control over my things was a way to make myself visible, to assert myself in that clan where I felt affection was so unevenly distributed. Every time one of my possessions disappeared because someone had borrowed it, I would fly into a rage, feeling that I'd been sent back to that middle-ground nothingness, that temperate centre, that second place that did me so much damage at the time – yet which was ultimately the most profitable, the only position possible for the man writing this book. Were I the oldest or youngest child I would never have needed to write. Not this way. Not this book.

I must clarify that this avarice was a trait all my own, something personal and not inherited. My parents were fair with money, and generous when they were able. Never profligate, but never petty. I'd say equitable. I'd say Solomonic. I'd also say prudent. My parents filled stacks of notebooks with budgets and flow charts to keep track of their income, expenditures, contingencies, the various expenses demanded by the Monterrico house. They made up a very efficient administrative pair. When I saw them working on those notebooks, drawing lines with a ruler and inserting figures, I thought that was what they must have been like during their years at the Treasury, when he was the minister's advisor and she the office secretary. There they were together again, cross-checking numbers, erasing digits, perhaps falling in love – if not with each other then at least with the team they formed. It's a strange thing: my father was a genius with numbers, but a disaster with business. His facility with multiplication, division and square roots did him no good whatsoever when it came to improving his finances once he found himself trapped by the reality of his Army pension. Perhaps he should have been more astute, or crafty, or cynical, like several of his military and civilian acquaintances in high positions who made piles of money by snaffling funds from public institutions. It had never occurred to him to steal, so he was forced to replace his regular income with a new-found entrepreneurial spirit. First, he set up an import business that went bust the day his partner disappeared with most of the capital. Then he opened a security company that failed to secure regular clients. Finally, he attempted to establish, together with his brothers, a private university where each of them would teach one subject; his was military life and defence. The idea was well received and was on the point of becoming a reality when they decided not to go ahead with it. None of these efforts prospered, and soon the household bills and the school and university fees weren't being paid with the usual punctuality. His general's pension was just enough to cover the expenses of the Monterrico house and the house on Berlin St., where Lucila Mendiola still lived, though she was starting to ail. And so the lean years began. One by one the house staff left, the drivers, the helpers, the bodyguards. Club memberships were suspended until further notice. The two cars, the Chevrolet and the Nissan, were put up for sale. The family wardrobes saw few changes for a long time. 'God will provide,' said my mother. My father said nothing: God's plans were no concern of his.

Another effect of this austerity was the immediate distancing of many close friends who, year after year, and more because it suited them than out of real affection, would send cellophane-wrapped Christmas hampers stuffed with imported goods impossible to get hold of in Lima: packages, cans and bottles of liquor that filled our cupboards and lasted until the end of the summer. Suddenly, these baskets ceased to arrive and were replaced by simple postcards that we pinned around the staircase and to the door and window frames. My mother, my siblings and myself took a number of measures. We decided to take turns with the domestic chores. On Wednesdays, for example, I had to lay the table, wash the dishes, sweep, mop and wax the wooden floors. On Fridays it was my task to vacuum the carpets, tidy the garden, clean the outdoor spaces and maintain the pool.

One day my father said he couldn't take it any more: he was going to rent out the house. To avoid this dreadful outcome, we all set about finding any possible form of paid work available. My father accepted our decision with great reluctance, his face grim with impotence, sadness or fallen pride. And so my mother started to sell package tours at a friend's travel agency, my sister Valentina put her university degree on hold to promote Coca-Cola in a shopping centre, and I began part-time work at a Kentucky Fried Chicken.

The golden age was officially over. Only when my father was hired as inspector of the racecourse could we breathe freely once more. But for the year and a half he spent out of work, living only off his pension, we all became experts in rationing everything. At the KFC, even though the pay was miserable, I found a certain satisfaction in my autonomy and even took a peculiar pleasure in the heavy labour. I had to sweep the dried leaves from the huge playground, clean the toilets, open the rubbish bags and count the pieces of food that the customers had left half-eaten. That was when I was working front-of-house. The days when I was on the kitchen rota were no better: I had to open up the raw chicken corpses, remove all the viscera and impurities from their bellies, marinate them in a special liquid and then put them in the cooler until the next day. I worked there for five months, from five in the afternoon to eleven at night. I used to walk home, devouring soggy potato chips and pieces of reheated chicken the supervisors gave me, and I felt incomprehensibly proud of this shitty job and my exploitative bosses. When I ended my shift so exhausted that my legs would carry me no more, I'd take one of the green buses that left me a few blocks from home, buses that advanced so slowly I'd get off feeling like an old man, like I'd aged during the journey. I would have stayed at the KFC for longer if my father hadn't forced me to give it up, horrified after I recounted my working day to him. 'No,' I told him, 'I want to carry on, I want to work!' 'Hand in your notice or I'll come and drag you out of there in front of everyone!' I begged him to let me stay, but he yelled at me, leaving me no alternative: 'I didn't raise my children to pluck chickens!'

My brief tenure at KFC allowed me to save a bit of cash and experience for the first time the sensation of buying books, comics and collectible figures with my own money. I wanted to have my own things, things that no one else could touch. In that I resembled my father, and I still do. He never let me play with his ornaments, and so when he'd go out, the first thing I'd do was sneak into his office and play with his things for the simple pleasure of disobeying him. But not only for that. Caressing these objects also meant caressing his world, walking through his inner walls and exploring inaccessible parts of him with my hands, investigating the cave that was always so hard to reach with my other senses. His study was a fascinating museum of solemnity and I couldn't help but want to handle the bronze miniatures on his desk: the tanks, cannon, helicopters with movable doors and rotors, the horses with huge teeth, hieratic soldiers, silver-plated bullets, severe busts of Francisco Bolognesi, Miguel Grau and José de San Martín, swords hanging on the wall, binoculars in their leather cases, the field canteens, the visored caps of the 'Junín Hussars' Cavalry Regiment, a wooden bar trunk on castors and – of progressively diminishing interest – souvenir plates, flags, wooden pencil holders, and heavy military figures serving as paperweights.

His prohibition, of course, wasn't limited to the objects in his study. In general, no one was allowed to touch anything of his if he wasn't there to keep watch, which reduced the fun enormously. I suppose he had good reason to impose these rules on me, considering I had broken his record player, his radio, his Walkman and his two portable TVs, but even so I found it excessive that he forbade me from entering his domain. So I took advantage of his work trips to rifle through his drawers, smell his clothes, peruse his papers, handle the Basque pelota and tennis rackets he never used, but still refused to let us touch. I can still picture myself rooting around his wardrobe with a little torch, penetrating the intimate nooks and crannies of his innermost realms with the self-imposed mission to discover something new about him.

Some of the old military items that belonged to my father are now inside a large glass display case at the Gold Museum in Lima. It shook me up to see them there the first time I visited. There were the weapons, miniature boats, tanks and helicopters I'd picked up hundreds of times without his permission, now gazing out at me from that aura of immortality acquired by objects in a museum. Every time I go and see them I think that the wax dummy that represents my father will suddenly come to life and start berating me for my disobedience.

When today, at the age of nearly forty, I'm asked why I still collect action figures and lead soldiers, I say it's because they remind me of films and series that were important to me as a teenager. It's not true. At bottom I think it's because they compensate for my dad's prohibitions. The bad thing is that I've developed a possessive neurosis just like his: every time someone visits me and picks up one of those miniatures, I suffer just as stupidly as he did.

The fact that he didn't allow me into his world wasn't the worst of it. The worst was when he got angry. He tended to be reasonable, patient, to practice self-control and defuse tense situations that were veering toward arguments. But when he'd lose his temper over some defiance of mine, he'd fly into a rage that radiated fear for miles around. He didn't even need to raise his voice: all he had to do was open his eyes wide like an enraged animal and I'd start to shake. Any spark of rebellion would be stamped out as soon as he fixed me with the hypnotic gun barrels of his eyes. If I started to protest out of stubbornness or naïveté, I would always lose. 'Because I feel like it' was the final resort in his reasoning, an inviolable border, an impenetrable wall before which all arguments surrendered, five words that shattered the desire not so much to argue as to understand why certain freedoms were forbidden to me. 'I don't care what your friends' parents say. I'm your father,' he'd growl crossly, utterly uninterested in explaining why he found it so important to impose the same disciplinary whims that had comprised his own upbringing. No matter what I said, I couldn't change his mind. Even if I was in the right, he'd subject me to his view, prompting a spiral of frustration and impotence around an ember of smouldering charcoal that, instead of being consumed, grew larger every year.

There was a kind of closed-offness in my father that I could never get through: an indecipherable hieroglyphic, a safe box with a combination I felt I'd need centuries to crack. For just as he'd display his vehemence and drive me away with his bellowing, he could also suddenly be overcome with tears in specific situations. 'I can be moved watching a film, reading a book or at the antics of my son. I am a man of flesh and blood. I also have a genetic aptitude for tears,' he told the reporter from *VEA* in his penultimate interview.

I'm left uneasy by that 'genetic aptitude for tears', as if crying were a kind of natural talent, a virtue handed down through generations of blood. What he didn't mention in that interview was that he wept most of all when he thought about his own father. At the memory of some lesson he'd taught him, or some verse he wrote. That was a moment when the name of Fernán Cisneros Bustamante sprang to life. It was touching to glimpse, under the ogre's skin, the presence of someone who could be gentle, who had parts that were shattered. His recollections of his long-dead father slipped through the few cracks left unprotected by his military rigour; once inside him, they disordered everything. That's what my grandfather's ghost could do. My father was proud of the public life of his exiled father, yet I can't recall a single occasion on which he referred to the doubts his father suffered as a man. He didn't say these things, but he expressed them through tears, and I had to figure out when that weeping was nostalgia and when it was reproach – and I couldn't ask, because to ask was to reopen a wound, and the Gaucho Cisneros wouldn't tolerate anyone touching his wounds. Wounds, he maintained, heal themselves.

★ ★ ★

My dear son Federico: cultivate your perspective today, because it's shaped by your ability to take charge of life and to love your family!

Your father, Fernán

Buenos Aires, 5 February 1947

My grandfather wrote this dedication to my father under a photograph I'm looking at now. There is Fernán, impeccably dressed, a corner of a white handkerchief deliberately peering from his front pocket, a lit cigar between the index and middle fingers of his right hand. The photograph is a portrait of my grandfather's aplomb. A languid aplomb. The cylindrical head, the unlined forehead, the bushy eyebrows, one drooping eyelid, one sleepy eye, the satellite-dish ears, the left side of the nose more prominent than the right, the mouth tilted in an undefinable expression halfway between a smile and a pout, the dark, staggered, untouchable circles around the eyes, the sparse hair scrupulously arranged across the vast globe of his cranium. 'Your ability to take charge of life' is surely the most symbolic expression in this message, penned over seventy years ago now. What does it mean to take charge of life? Doesn't it mean twisting its natural course, rebelling against its order and refusing its temptations? Taking charge of life means preventing it from setting the rules of the game and defining the perimeter of our movements. Taking charge of life means cornering it, subduing it, dodging its traps, distrusting its charm, reluctantly enjoying its rewards. It means necessarily mistrusting its apparent harmony, doubting its definitions and its stereotypes. If you let life surround you and overwhelm you, like a seductive, calm-looking sea that suddenly turns rough and swallows everything within its reach, then you will have lost perspective, distance, horizon. If you can't outsmart life, if you're unable to see past its representations, then you cannot imagine the future, you become paralysed, you become incapable of love. Did my father cultivate his perspective? Did he take charge of life? We know, at least, that he didn't take charge of death.

* * *

The Gaucho knew or sensed the murkiness of his origin, but never wanted to dig up those disagreeable or disturbing remains. In general, he preferred to bury things. Hence his apprehension and his silence. By not speaking, by not taking responsibility for the archaeology demanded by generation after generation without anyone ever finishing the job, he delegated. Some of that legacy, I suppose, has fallen to me. In November 1988, seven years before he died, he wrote this dedication in my copy of his only book, *Dialogues on the Military Vocation*:

With hope for your aptitude today, and your responsibility tomorrow.

My father was sixty-two when he wrote that. I was just twelve. Twelve, and vastly anxious in the face of words like 'aptitude', 'responsibility' and 'hope'. Now I understand what he meant. He – or the part of him that was never able to flourish – commended the writing of this book to me. It is his commission. It is my responsibility.

★ ★ ★

As a kid I didn't really understand who my father was to others, or his political importance or influence in Peru. I didn't treat his popularity as an acquired or added value because I grew up with him as a public man, meaning it was normal (or more or less normal) to see him surrounded by cameras, to have journalists coming in and out of the house, people greeting him in shops and in supermarket aisles. This changed one day when my mother asked me to go down to the basement to tell him that lunch was ready. He was in the middle of giving a TV interview. There were studio lights, cables, cameras, cameramen, tripods, a microphone, a very heavily made-up journalist and two people who seemed to be her assistants. I stood behind the door, peeping in, and after a few minutes of watching and listening I realised that my father was someone important to these people, that his opinions carried special weight. I silently gloated to think that this military and political celebrity would, in just a few minutes' time, be sitting beside me at the dining table, eating his beef with cabbage or carrots, or pork cutlets or slices of ham with mango. I wondered how much those journalists would give to know what I knew, to see him as I saw him: walking around the house in vest and underpants; sunbathing in the garden in his only swimming costume; dancing a tip-toe *milonga* across the blue kitchen tiles; singing *ranchera* songs during those Saturday lunches that ran on into dinner and then descended into riotous parties, which left him stretched out snoring in the corridor, interrupted by alcohol-befuddled snorts that were more like the death throes of a captured animal. As I spied on the interview that afternoon I understood that behind this figure who spoke and declaimed and smoked with the mannerisms of a little king there was an ordinary man, and it was a question of paying close attention until he appeared and I could make him mine.

With the onset of adolescence, however, I became contradictory. I wanted to get closer to him, but at the same time I developed a kind of repulsion towards him. His age began to annoy me. I despised his grey hair, his sixty-some-thing years. Today I'm embarrassed by my judgmental attitude, and it strikes me as worthy of an imbecile with no personality of his own, but that's how I thought at the time. I loved him, I respected him, I continued to consider him a hero, my hero, but I found his age distasteful and I didn't like the fact that he was the oldest among all the parents of my classmates. When I was picked up from school, there was no shortage of cruel jokes about his grandfatherly appearance (which was, in any case, wholly appropriate, since he already had four grandchildren from my older siblings). I couldn't stand him turning up for the activities I was involved in, as it soon made me the target for cruel comments by taller and stronger boys than me. I could do nothing in revenge. But even if I could have got revenge, it wouldn't have altered the underlying source of my anger: his age, his distance from my own generation. My father was totally unaware of contemporary trends, of the latest films, the latest music, the latest artists, the latest rock bands – of rock in general. He knew nothing of slang or of the latest haircuts, and even if he did, he rejected them out of hand. Everything about him was old-fashioned. The youngest thing about him was my mother, and at the age of thirteen, fourteen or fifteen that really pissed me off.

Which is why I preferred not to tell him anything the day I made the final of the school public speaking competition, even though it was only thanks to the speech he had dictated to me on 'Peruvian Youth and Subversion'. All I did was memorise it and perform it with a certain dramatic flair in the first rounds. I should have invited him to the final. He deserved to come, but his age embarrassed me. That night, when I was scheduled to compete with older boys from the fourth and fifth years, I went alone to the auditorium on Reducto Avenue. There were some two hundred people in the audience. When it was my turn to step onto the stage, I acted as if each word emerging from my mouth had first been created in my mind, with great conviction and unnecessary but authoritatively histrionic gestures. There I was, talking in a language that wasn't mine, but my father's; I was being my father, just as my grandfather Fernán had imagined himself when he recited the poems written by his father Luis Benjamín before an audience at the 1897 Expo, with words that both were and weren't his. Luis Benjamín, by then suffering from Parkinson's, had composed a poem called 'The Supreme Moment' especially for the occasion, but on the day of the ceremony he took a turn for the worse and decided not to go. Instead he asked the fifteen-year-old Fernán to go in his stead. That night was a watershed moment. The boy nervously climbed the steps onto the stage, stood on a stool to gain height and gradually grew more confident as he recited his father's poem. He spoke with his father's virtuosity, making use of his youth and his deep voice to share the words with the audience. When Fernán reached the end, when the final line emerged from his dry mouth, he was met with thunderous applause, and he didn't know if they were applauding him or his sick father, and he believed for a moment that he was his father, believed his father had taken over his body. And so his life's mission revealed itself to him: the inescapable mission of embodying his father, of following him like an idol, of extending the dying man's life through his own. For a few minutes, Fernán was Luis Benjamín. The body was the son's, the poetry the father's, and the confusion ended with the wild ovation from the hundreds of people in the hall, watching him wide-eyed from below, while my grandfather stared back with his eyes dazzled by the lights. That's exactly how I found myself on the night of the public speaking contest, usurping my father's words, delivering a speech on the Marxist-Leninist-Maoist ideology promulgated by the Shining Path – what the hell could I know about that? – and exhorting the youth of Peru to examine their patriotic consciences and put an end to this scourge. I was in the middle of the speech when I clearly heard from the back of the hall a noise that was intimately familiar to me. My father's cough. His tobacco-filled cough, his gravelly smoker's cough, his addict's cough, that cough issuing from bronchial tubes irritated by nicotine and damaged by tar, that unmistakable cough, his alone, that lonely man's cough bursting now in my ears, leaving me paralysed in a nebula that was only torn or broken by the applause.

That night I won the public speaking competition. Or he won it through me. I don't know exactly how to put it, but I felt from that point on that I'd grown stronger somehow, and I became the high school orator, the little fellow in class 3B and then 4C who opened assemblies with reflections on diverse topics. What nobody ever knew was that I simply repeated the lines my father wrote down for me the night before. He was the scriptwriter for all those inspired disquisitions. He was the ventriloquist and I was his puppet. Every time I had to give a speech, I'd ask for his help and he'd take to it as if it were his own homework, and we'd practice every night until I learned the text from start to finish. Several months after winning the public speaking contest, perhaps tired of being an impostor, a would-be actor who read from another's script, I entered an essay competition for International Water Day, submitting a text I'd written without his help. Everyone had high expectations of me following my triumph over the older students. I didn't show anyone my composition, but I was proud of having written it alone, of having organised the words according to my judgment, my intuition, my own good sense. When the results were pinned up on a noticeboard, reality hit me hard. My name didn't even figure among the honourable mentions. Without my father, I thought, I'd never win anything.

That same year, I opted not to ask him to be my confirmation sponsor. I didn't want to walk down the aisle of the church alongside an old man. In any case, he hardly met the requirements, or so I wanted to believe. 'Sponsors must be adults who lead lives in accordance with the Christian faith, as they will bear witness and offer their support to the candidate,' read the letter handed out by the Religious Studies teacher. In the end I chose Enrique Martínez, a distant relative, an honorary uncle who lived between Lima and Boston, where he worked in computer programming. My uncle Enrique didn't lead a life particularly in accordance with the Christian faith either, but he was young, modern, played electric guitar and looked healthy. That's what I needed: a sponsor who was a handsome rocker. A photogenic sponsor who'd draw positive remarks. I was very tense on the evening of the confirmation: every time I looked round to see if my uncle Enrique had arrived, his seat was still empty. The ceremony continued until it was time for the climatic moment: all of the candidates had to stand up and walk in a row towards the altar, where Monsignor Albano Quinn Wilson was waiting to anoint our foreheads with the chrism. All were escorted by their sponsors, who placed their right hands on their shoulders. All but me. When my turn came I advanced towards the large crucifix with a face of defeat, looking up at the priest from the depths of my despair. I was going to be the only one who would be confirmed without a sponsor. I would be falsely confirmed, or 'illegitimate', to use a word more suited to my biography. But just as the Monsignor was about to smear the oil on my forehead, I felt a hand fall heavily on my right shoulder, and my anguish vanished in an instant. I turned to grin at uncle Enrique for having arrived just in time, but in his place I found the round, noble, jowly face of my father. The old man of sixty-four, whose appearance I found so hateful, had got to his feet when he realised that uncle Enrique was never going to turn up, setting aside his agnosticism to race down the aisle because it was unjust or inappropriate for his son to be left unprotected at the altar. There is a photo of this moment. My head is bowed, my hands together and one foot turned out – a longstanding tic that was an expression of insecurity. Monsignor Albano Quinn Wilson is anointing my head, having made the sign of the cross. My father stands behind me. We are both wearing three-piece suits, and our eyes are closed, joined in a silence charged with everything there is to say.

But no one should be tempted to think he overflowed with noble acts. My father could be cruel too when he chose. If I was bothered by how old he looked, he was equally annoyed by my appearance. You have to fix those teeth, he'd say in front of guests. I'd stand there with my mouth fastened shut, longing to mock him by telling everyone that he had false teeth. Other times he'd refer condescendingly to my height, forgetting that his father was a five-foot-three midget. (A midget, it's true, without complexes; a brilliant midget. On one occasion, following a meeting of international diplomats, my grandfather Fernán was struggling to retrieve his jacket from the hat stand: some valet had hung it from the highest hook. A Dutch delegate noticed and passed it down to him. My grandfather looked up at him and said: 'Thank you very much, sir. If you happen to drop something, do let me know.')

I can only recall a single occasion when my father said something positive about my appearance. I'd put on a three-piece suit to go to a friend's fifteenth birthday party and went into his room to say goodbye. 'This little fellow has his charm,' he said from his bed, as I rearranged my fringe in the mirror. It was the poorest kind of compliment, almost a generous insult, but it made me feel attractive for the first time. Even in this way, my father's interventions were substantive. He could be harsh, but there was more certainty or truthfulness in his opinions than in those of my mother, who told her children we were beautiful even on our worst days. My father never dispensed praise or flattery for free. And that night, however meagre the compliment, it felt like he'd noted something handsome in me.

My desire to be like him was so great that when I needed new clothes, instead of going to the stores in Miraflores or San Isidro, I'd ask my mother to take me to Mirales, the tailor who made my father's clothes for him.

Mirales lived and worked in a two-storey house in Surquillo and kept an ancient ledger in which he noted down his clients' names together with the annual evolution of their physical dimensions and volume. I knew I'd never reach my father's height or girth, but I liked to look at those numbers in that book, check his measurements against mine, as if it were a register of the comparative scores of our bodies. And even though Mirales insisted on making up suits for me with innovative cuts, leafing through magazines to help me choose models suited to my age, I wanted my trousers and jackets to be the same kind my father wore. Even though I thought he was an unfashionable old man, he had something I didn't: a style, a way of wearing clothes and inhabiting them that made him seem both imposing and magnetic.

Before going out to a party in my teenage years – perhaps I still do it today – I'd shut myself up in the bathroom and repeat, step by step, my father's method for getting ready. He'd always take as long as he needed to feel comfortable with what he saw in the mirror. First he'd comb his damp hair by parting it to the left side of his head with a precision so geometric that the comb was more like a compass or set square in his hand. Then he'd shave. I loved to watch him shaving. I longed to have a beard and moustache just so I could imitate this ritual. He'd smother his face in foam, then he'd sweep it with the razor, sector by sector, before passing it from bottom to top around the chin and neck, and at the end, after rinsing, he'd strike the razor against the sink to shake off the tiny hairs trapped between the blades. I remember the residue of his beard scattered over the yellow porcelain of his sink. It looked like the cigarette ash he left wherever he went. As soon as I think of that ash I feel the urge to talk about my father's cigarette smoking. The cigarettes of the nicotine addict he was. The cigarettes of that anxious man who fretted about his continued relevance, about being seen as a public hero. My father was always smoking. There is not a single photo, video or memory of him without a cigarette. When he was a minister, he smoked five packets per day, one hundred cigarettes per day, seven hundred per week, three thousand per month, thirty-six thousand per year. 'How much do you smoke, General?' a journalist asked him in 1990 for *Perspectiva*. 'While I was at the Ministry of the Interior I smoked five packets a day and drank twenty cups of black coffee. And here I am, alive and kicking. Now I smoke three packets and drink half as much coffee. In twenty years' time I'll only be smoking one packet,' he buoyantly declared. His calculations were out. He only lived five more years. Not twenty. Five years that, naturally, he spent smoking wherever he went. He even took his fags into the hospital and probably worked out a way to sneak some inside his coffin. He smoked right up until his final days, behind everyone's back, maybe with the complicity of some nurse, maybe without anyone's complicity at all. When he died and I was given the excruciating task of returning to the clinic to collect his belongings, I found a packet of Hamilton cigarettes in the pocket of his dressing gown. It was open.

My father always boasted that his chest X-rays depicted his lungs as two limpid reservoirs. Although they weren't the direct cause of his death, the cigarettes exacerbated the damage to his respiratory tract. 'Kill yourself if you want, but not my children,' Cecilia Zaldívar would say when she found him smoking inside the house. So my father would go out into the garden surrounded by that silky sheen of smoke that escorted him everywhere like a docile shadow. I'd watch him from the window and admire his relationship with cigarettes, or the intellectual or contemplative air it conferred on him. In fact, I too attempted to embark on a smoking career one day, but within seconds I was choking, and desisted. Then my asthma appeared and this illness soon tempered my eagerness to imitate him. It was as if my body was sending me a message I would only understand much later: don't seek to follow your father's example.

Every time I got back home from school, the smell of cigarettes was the unmistakable sign my father was somewhere nearby, pacing, trying to sort out the country. How could I forget that smell, when everything was saturated with it. It's a smell I still associate with all the smoking paraphernalia: the lighters, the filters, the boxes of cigars, the cartons hidden in the wardrobe, the smuggled packs and tins, the Rothmans, the John Player Specials, the Dunhills. About a year ago, during a trip to Brazil, aboard a boat crossing Todos los Santos Bay off the coast of Bahía, I saw a man smoking and flicking the ash from his cigarette into the sea. I immediately thought of my father. My father and his ashtrays. The constantly overflowing ashtrays all around the house. The ashtrays made of metal, of ceramic, of plastic, of glass. The car ashtrays. The shells brought back from the beach to be used as ashtrays. The whole garden as a great ashtray. The loo and the sink as ashtrays. The throwaway jelly cups that, filled with that ash, looked like receptacles for some primitive, bitter dessert. I played with the piles of ash as if they were dunes of moon dust, as if the stubbed-out butts with their white filters were bent-over astronauts that had perished in their attempt to colonise the Moon. I imagined some disaster had befallen the crew, an epidemic, an alien attack, the lack of air on the lunar surface or simply a cosmic madness produced by their distance from the Earth. I wandered around the house squishing the heaps of ash in the ashtrays with the butts, and inventing new chapters in the space saga. But my father's ashtrays weren't really a great place for playing anything. My father's ashtrays were the crematoria where he incinerated everything he preferred to keep silent.

★ ★ ★

My mother and my siblings describe my father differently. I did see the attributes they emphasise now, both the positive and the negative ones, but he had a different way of exercising his fatherliness towards me. A way that only I could perceive. The father I knew was a combination of the punisher, the disciplinarian, the teacher, the tutor. I owe my discovery of poetry and literature to my uncle Juvenal, but my father was the first person to take an interest in my education, to introduce me to the dictionary and to the vast fifteen-volume encyclopaedia that dominated his library. His attempts at domestic education could be unwieldy, but they were justified by the didactic ambition he put into them. Even if he was incapable of revealing our family's past to me, he at least made an effort to teach me about world history.

I was ten years old the afternoon he shut me up in my room under instructions to learn the definitions of the Pre-Incan cultures – the Mochica, Chavin and Tiwanaku civilisations – for an exam on Peruvian history. The agreement was the following: I had to learn everything in the book by rote, and then go to his room for him to test me on it. If I made a single error in my recitation, he would send me back to my cell to re-memorise every term, every proper name, every fact. Only when I could repeat it perfectly would he let me go out to play with my friends, who'd been waiting for me for hours. Yet when liberation arrived at last, I found that I no longer felt like playing with anyone; instead, I preferred to stay with him and repeat my lessons on other cultures or on anything else. In that back-and-forth between my room and his, though I hated him for forcing me to memorise everything word for word, a bond was forged that drew us together, however authoritarian it may have been. The basic notions I still have of the Mochica, Chavin and Tiwanaku civilisations were imbued in me on those afternoons when my father, with his clumsy didactic methods, made me feel like he was in charge of my upbringing, teaching me something of much greater importance: that I'd find my freedom not in playing, but in learning.

Unfortunately, I wasn't always so receptive to his attempts to rectify my ignorance. On days when I felt resentful or was simply blind, I failed to take advantage of exceptional opportunities. One day he took me to the Army Museum, located in the Real Felipe Fortress, that colossal citadel commissioned by the last viceroys of Peru in 1747 to protect the port of Callao from the avarice of the corsairs. Today I can imagine how epic such a visit with my father might have been, exploring by his side the labyrinthine military construction of stone and brick, the corners marked by turrets bearing the names of kings and saints. What really happened leaves me full of regret. After spending an hour dutifully looking at relics and wax models of military heroes, I slipped away to play in the vast central courtyard with some other kid, kicking a ball around among the mountain guns and tanks of the Artillery Park, while my father descended to the catacombs and the rusty-celled dungeons, where the skeletons are piled up in the hundreds and ghosts pass through the bars, silently trampling the heaps of bleached skulls.

Another way of getting to know him was through sports. His was not an especially muscular or sinewy body, though it was still evident that he'd been in excellent shape for many years. He was portly in the way of a retired military man, but his hairless body retained a certain taurine brawn. He liked horse-riding and fencing. Chess too, which he taught me over a series of afternoons, though he was overly insistent, fruitlessly trying to instil in me a love of the game. We must have played a hundred times, without me winning once. Not with the white pieces, nor with the black. He never let me. He wasn't one of those parents who stage dramatic defeats in order to inpire a false confidence in their offspring. He'd win swiftly, in a handful of moves, and punctiliously point out my strategic errors: how easily I left the queen unprotected, my too-quick deployment of the bishops, my failure to exploit the abilities of the knights, my sluggishness in bringing the rooks to the fore.

I was more interested in football. He cultivated my passion with a few key gestures: he tracked down a specific blue and red ball that I'd seen on a TV advert to give me as a birthday present. He joined me some Sundays to listen to football games on the radio that I knew he didn't really care about. He bought me special football boots I needed for a trial, an important trial that resulted in a resounding failure I didn't want to share with anyone, but which maybe I should have shared with him. He got his hands on two tickets for the manager's box so I could go to the National Stadium for the first time – not with him, but with El Zambo Garcés – to watch a friendly match between Peru's national team and Argentina's River Plate club, which Peru won 3-2. Together, we cheered on Argentina in the final of Mexico 86, and when they won we ran out euphorically into the garden to have a kick-about with that blue and red ball. It was the only time that I saw my father with a ball between his feet: he struggled to receive my passes and find his footing, tried to control the ball or kick it to me, and ended up falling on his back.

But what we didn't achieve with football we did with ping-pong, swimming, and walking. Especially ping-pong. In those years when I started to distance myself from home life and sought pretexts for avoiding my siblings and those Sunday family gatherings I found phony or simply boring, my father bought a ping-pong table. That table was a miracle. If ever there was a table around which I truly felt close to him and the rest of the family, it was that Corsa table we set up in the basement: easily folded away, divided by a professional net my parents purchased in the United States, I'd clean it every morning and cover it every night like an altar. One day, as we fought a lengthy match, my father – availing himself of the pauses that the pain in his hip forced him to take – told me how in the late 70s he and General Morales Bermúdez would shut themselves up in the Treasury office to play table tennis. It was comical to imagine the situation at that moment in the country's history: while the dictator Velasco Alvarado was rolling out the agrarian reform across the country, the Minister of the Treasury and his advisor were engaged in hard-fought sets across a table that undoubtedly matched the green of their uniforms.

For five summers running I organised family championships that encompassed not only my parents and siblings but also the drivers, house staff and bodyguards. The tournaments lasted three weeks and the winner lifted a plastic trophy. I kept a folder in which I meticulously noted down the statistics for each game, the scores and the ranking of the leading players, including extravagantly critical, amusing and mock-technical remarks on their performances that my father quickly dictated and I transcribed. We were such good friends when we played ping-pong. Rivals too. When he fell ill, he stopped playing because the pain in his waist prevented him reaching the faster balls and he switched to the role of umpire, from a chair. The tournaments lost their sparkle and weren't the same anymore. When the people who worked in the house started to leave because we couldn't afford to pay them any longer, it was the end. The unused table started to peel, and we folded it away in a corner. After my father died, my uncle Adrián bought the table off us, repaired it and set it up in his Pulpos beach house. Every time I went to visit I saw the table, but it was just any old table to me now and I began to feel like I'd imagined everything that had happened around it. Even today, though, the hollow sound of a plastic ball hitting a ping-pong table triggers images I associate with my father.

There was another period that preceded our table tennis era: our swimming period. The time of water. My father had taught me to swim as a kid with a method best described as martial. To teach me to hold my breath, he would grab me by the hair, plunge me below the surface of the swimming pool, and pull me up again only when I began to show signs of drowning. As soon as I started to get my usual colour back, he would repeat the operation. I was just five or six at the time, but he believed that those early exercises in survival were character-building. In reality, they achieved precisely the opposite: this water-based torture only added to my claustrophobia, my anxiety, my nervousness. But I can't complain: I did learn to swim. Very well. As a young boy and as a teenager I often swam by his side, in the pool at the Piura house but especially at the Monterrico house. The pool was the only place we could all enjoy him. In the pool, he wore no uniform. There my siblings and I could climb onto him, comb his hair, rock him in our arms and carry him around as if he were a weightless, sixty-year-old baby, a doll rather than a father. We could hold freestyle races, surprise him with aerial somersaults he complained were both too dangerous and imperfectly executed, dive behind him like baby dolphins. We could watch him swimming with his eyes shut without hitting the pool sides, without a care for the many insects – spiders, bees, grasshoppers, cockroaches – that fled the garden and drowned in the pool. Even dead, we found the insects so scary and disgusting that we'd splash the water to send them off to float together in a corner we all called 'the bug corner'. The water was the antidote to my father's thuggishness. The water calmed him.

The water was pleasure, not responsibility. With him, I was happier in the water than on land.

Even today, whenever I go swimming, each stroke stirs something in me, recalls my father's rhythm as he swam. During my research for this novel, when the process of assembling the story was at its knottiest, I'd go to swim in an Olympic-size pool, imagining that my forefathers were swimming alongside me. A dead relative in each lane. My father, my grandfather, my great-grandfather and my great-great-grandfather, Gregorio Cartagena, the priest with no face. I'd imagine them doing the same number of laps as me, all of us keeping pace with each other, and how as they went back and forth they'd think about their dilemmas as I thought about mine, trying to resolve them, taking a breath every three strokes, plunging their faces in the water, expelling air through their noses, kicking their feet, following the straight course of the black line at the bottom of the pool. Then when I realised just how much room there was in my head for crazy ideas, I'd stop and hang on to the lane dividers. I'd think about how awful it'd be to have to live with all my forebears in a world without death or bodily decay. How pathetic it'd be if we were all immortal and we remained, unageing, in the fullness of our intellect, at the peak of our courage. How tragic and dark life would be without death. How atrocious it would be to be deprived of losing our ancestors, to never understand this accumulated loss as the stuff we're made of: their ashes, their worms, their bones, their still-growing hair and nails. That is our clay. It would be unbearable to live in a world still inhabited by my forebears: reminding me incessantly of my condition as an epigone, as their debtor, a son of, grandson of, great-grandson of, great-great-grandson of, incapable of elaborating an independence, a name or even a solitude to call my own.

★ ★ ★

Though my father firmly believed it was impossible for a child of his not to be smart, my school grades certainly disappointed him. In primary school I'd had an unprecedented run at the top of the class, which bolstered his expectations. In the first years of high school, however, I'd rarely bring home a jotter that wasn't full of red pen. If my carelessness or mediocrity had been limited to the academic sphere, perhaps it wouldn't have made him so angry, but I soon showed signs of bad behaviour at school. The day I was punished with a disciplinary form and a three-day suspension, things got tough between us. It was the first year of high school, and I was eleven. If only the American priests had punished me for some rebellious or subordinate attitude that I could have remembered years later as something significant or worthwhile. Sadly, this wasn't the case. Around that time the TV series *The Addams Family* was in vogue, with its earworm theme tune that showed the characters clicking their fingers in unison. It was an innocent, stupid song that I rewrote in a pornographic version that alluded to Gomez's penis, Morticia's vulva and the lewd, unpredictable behaviour of the rest of the Addams clan. The perverted song caused great hilarity among classmates who usually paid me no attention. So at break time I had the whole class singing away and clicking their fingers. This was the most exciting thing ever. I was leading the chorus, singing at the top of my lungs – 'Gomez is a gigolo, Morticia a whore, Grandmama a harlot and Fester a fag' – when Father Patrick Sgarioto, a Canadian priest of Italian origin with the dour demeanour of a Doberman, appeared behind me. He waited for the end of the refrain to grab me by the ear and drag me to the principal's office. For forty minutes I waited in a side-room that resembled a cell.

When I was finally called through, I saw my father sitting there. They'd sent for him. The look on his face made me crumble and I threw myself into his arms in tears. I think he was more annoyed by this contemptible demonstration of weakness than by the 'obscenities' I'd sung in the school playground. The headmaster informed him of my suspension and let us go. He drove me home in the Chevrolet without a word. At first I thought perhaps his disapproval wasn't as great as I'd feared. After all, he swore shamelessly all the time. I felt an incipient sense of relief. Then we got out the car and he said: 'You're grounded for a month. You've completely disappointed me.' Staying at home for a month was the least of it. The real punishment was letting him down.

Years later, after I failed to pass my university entrance exams for the second time, he said something similar. It was 1992. I'd studied for months at the most expensive cramming school in Lima. My uncle Juvenal, who knew the owner, had wangled me a half-scholarship. When I got home from the second entrance exam, drunk and angry at myself for having failed once again, his words were the coup de grâce I needed to feel like the most miserable individual on the face of the planet. 'I'm disappointed in you,' he said without looking at me. What could I say? That I was paralysed by timed exams? That I hated competing? How do you say that to a soldier who's spent his life enduring the harshest possible range of physical and intellectual tests and who, what's more, won the sword of honour among his entire cohort? How could I explain my failure to a winner like him? The torment only increased when, quite rightly, he reminded me how little advantage I took of circumstances and opportunities that he would have longed for as a young man. This comparison between our abilities – which was hypothetical and counterfactual, but felt very real – was a recurring source of hurt. I often went to bed ruminating on that motto of General José de San Martín, liberator of South America, that my father so often repeated to us: 'You will be what you must be, or else you will be nothing.' I fell asleep with these words ringing in my mind, thinking that perhaps this was my destiny, this was what I deserved: to be Nothing and Nobody.

Today my father is the one who inhabits the Nothingness that I felt I was floating through then. Nothingness is the air he lives in, the wind that sometimes shakes the windows at the Monterrico house. Whenever I try to conjure him, I picture him in the same spaces around the house, starting with the breakfast nook where he'd fall asleep sipping hot soup at night. He'd tip his head back and start snoring with his mouth open. I'd hear those guttural reverberations from my room and emerge to contemplate him like someone gazing out at a muffled, sedated sea. He'd wake up with a start, see me standing there and say 'Don't do this at the table,' then grab his bowl with both hands and slurp down the rest of the soup. I'd ask him why he was allowed to do things we weren't, but instead of answering he'd fall back to sleep and his silence was a kind of boast, a way of reminding me that he was the one who called the shots in the kitchen. Which was ridiculous, because I never saw him cook a thing, let alone wield a brush, fix a pipe, change a tyre or even a light bulb.

Nevertheless, he did have a domestic side. Proof of this lies is the exacting methods he used to teach me to make my bed ('Smooth the wrinkles in the sheets with the palm of your hand until they disappear'; 'No corner of the pillow should be visible'; 'Make sure the folds in the quilt are parallel on each side'); to organise my wardrobe ('Shirts, T-shirts and sweaters are folded following the seams and are stacked by colour and texture in symmetrical and equidistant columns'; 'Trousers must be smoothed along the creases and the zip closed before you hang them up'; 'Shoes go on the first shelf, trainers on the second'); to set the table ('Knives are always turned to the same side'; 'Bread plates on the left, wine glasses on the right'; 'Napkins go with the design face up'); and even how to arrange banknotes in my wallet ('The lowest value notes to the front, the highest to the back'). My father... I complain that he never took me into account for serious discussions, that he never talked to me about politics or that he excluded me from adult conversations, but I forget that there were things he shared with me alone, and that he must have seen enough of something in me to entrust me with this domestic wisdom. When I remember those moments when I was his student or his recruit, I realise I lacked the time and intelligence to understand him, to absorb his symbolic language, to decipher what was behind those rudimentary gestures he made in his attempts to express himself.

I never saw him in the kitchen, just as I never saw him on a bus, in a stadium, a bar, a cinema, a theatre or at a concert. I do remember him in supermarkets, churches, restaurants, at beaches. Today, his ghost's natural habitat is the Monterrico house. There he is, there he always was, with his routines and his phrases, both borrowed and his own. 'I'm going to the loo to powder my nose.' 'I'm going to the loo to do what no one else can do for me.' 'This is how I am, nothing to be done; I was born for loving.' 'To stick to your brother is a good old law that'll help you in many dangers. Remember it boys, and hold together in fair as well as in stormy weather, when a family fight among themselves they're soon eaten up by strangers.' 'If you do what's easy as if it were difficult, you'll end up doing what's difficult as if it were easy.' 'Maybe, *quizás*, *peut-être*.' 'You're a nincompoop.' 'You're an ignoramus.' 'These are my crown jewels.' 'These are my babes.' 'Do you think I shit money?' 'Loves there are many, love only you.' 'There you go buying all the lottery tickets and all I'm raffling is a bonk on the head.'

There'll always be room in my head for these sayings. I also know many coined by others, by writers I admire; I've forgotten some and others I'll no doubt forget. But my father's trivial maxims are firmly embedded in me. Even when I'd rather make room for smarter, more famous or more literary adages, they won't budge. I can't erase those sayings from my head any more than I can expunge his signature from my hand. I sign things just like my father. I sign 'Cisneros', stretching out the C and finishing off the S with a flourish. Using his signature makes me feel secure. My self-esteem swells in the instant it takes me to complete it. My signature. His signature. When I think about it, I have the impression that I'm still being constructed by him. That I'm still following his dictates. That for the eighteen years we shared, he filled my mind with ideas, thoughts, orders that still govern me today. My father was a writer who didn't know he was a writer, and all the rest of us were characters wandering through that labyrinthine personal book of his that was the Monterrico house.

Chapter 11

That afternoon in 1992 when Doctor Silvio Albán came to visit my father, he was surprised to discover that his testicles were as dark and swollen as two fermented figs. My father never let himself be touched by anyone but Albán, who was his personal doctor and one of his oldest and most loyal Army friends. Albán was a large, hunchbacked man who always smelled of soap. His skin was blemished from the sun and he had prominent gums. He wore a white apron over his three-piece suit, his stethoscope around his neck like a collar, and carried a small black leather case which held his tiny torches for inspecting the ears and throats of his patients.

'Gaucho, I'm going to send you to the hospital. I want to take a lymph node biopsy,' Albán told my father that day, with a cordial brevity which suggested that it wasn't too serious. But it was. Very. The morning after the test, the doctor entered the spacious room of the military hospital, where my father had agreed to stay, accompanied by Doctor Zurita, the head of the Department of Oncology. My mother was there and heard every word that was spoken: at some point she felt the need to stand up, move over to my father's bed and take his hand. It was then that the two of them heard from Doctor Zurita's mouth the phrase that would determine the course of everything that was to come: 'General, you have cancer of the prostate.' Your father's eyes, Cecilia Zaldívar would tell me years later, were like those of a lost child.

Albán and Zurita recommended that he commence treatment immediately, but before they could elaborate my father had already decided not to commence anything at all. The fear or the shock barely lasted a few seconds. He didn't make his position explicit, but it was clear to him he wanted to carry on with the cancer inside him. He didn't want chemotherapy or injections or tubes or vomiting or surgery. He didn't want to lose his hair or arouse anyone's pity. He wanted to continue with his life, his routines: to drink his whiskies, smoke his cigarettes and his cigars, make statements that shook up public debates, and project an energy that would mask his real state of health. We shouldn't flaunt our afflictions, he'd say. As those days passed, he began to act as if he'd known beforehand what kind of disease was growing within him, as if he were wholly accustomed to the fact. A year before the diagnosis, my mother recalls, he turned up late at night, drunkenly singing 'Los mozos de Caba' as usual, and while she was giving him a dressing-down him for having overdone it again, he sat down on the bottom step in the hall of the Monterrico house and told her 'Don't worry, darling, soon you'll be free of me because I'm going to die and I know exactly what of.' My mother paid him no heed, writing it off as a drunkard's delirium, and went to make him some coffee in the kitchen. 'I'm going to die of prostate cancer!' he yelled, his tongue stumbling over the words. 'Shut up, you'll wake the children,' Cecilia replied.

Perhaps it was true. Perhaps he knew and that's why he neither sought a second opinion nor fell into depression when he was diagnosed. He didn't place himself in the hands of either science or religion, but accepted his destiny with martial dignity. The ones who didn't accept it were the rest of us, who couldn't understand his selfishness and were determined to wrest him off the rails of this tragedy, terrified he would abandon us before his time. I write 'we'

326

in plural, but as I think about it now, perhaps it was only my mother, my uncles and my older siblings who really understood the magnitude of events, the only ones to try to halt them. Not me. I didn't understand the gravity of my father's illness. I remember well the day he sat down beside me to tell me he had cancer. We were watching television. He did it as if he were the man delivering the weather forecast after the news. His voice monotonous, slightly scornful. I don't know if he was scared, but he succeeded in making sure I didn't pay much attention to that cancer; I was left with the firm impression that some doctor's pincers would get it out of there. His tone was so indifferent and dry that when I noted it down in the diary I kept at the time, I mentioned it with a coldness that seems pitiful now: 'Yesterday Dad told me he had cancer. But he says he's going to get better,' was all I wrote on that page whose other entries are dedicated to my academic disasters and the girls I was fruitlessly chasing. For so many years my father had made me feel that he was a superior being, so unbreakable, so incorruptible, that the idea of his dying or disappearing was inconceivable to me. My father couldn't die. He was immortal. He was the Gaucho Cisneros. He was bolted together from steel and titanium. Nothing could kill him. Not the terrorists' bullets nor the bombs of Montesinos. Least of all cancer. If he said he was going to get better, there was no reason to think differently.

Not long after the diagnosis, my sister Estrella, the second of my father's children with Lucila Mendiola, persuaded him to travel with her to my aunt Carlota's house in Cuernavaca, Mexico. There he underwent an alternative therapy invented by a Chinese guru. He ate only vegetables, slept a lot and was subjected to hot baths in natural tubs filled with an ancient healing clay. The treatment seemed to lift his spirits slightly, but did nothing to detain the progression of the cancer.

In January 1994 my mother convinced him to seek treatment in a hospital in the United States, but the commander-in-chief of the Army, General Hermoza Ríos, prevented him from using his military health insurance for the purpose. Only in July of that year – during the family trip we took to Miami – did my father have a check-up in the cancer centre of a hospital whose biblical name I've never forgotten: Mount Sinai Hospital. Just like the mountain where Moses received the commandments from God to save his people. There, the doctors confirmed the severity of the cancer. There, they told him he had a year and a half to live. There, they told him what he had to do if he wanted to enjoy a good quality of life in the time remaining to him. The doctors gave him these commandments. He didn't pay them any attention either. That day, while he and my mother spoke with the doctors in the hospital, Valentina, Facundo and I stayed outside in the car park, taking photographs among the palm trees to escape the infernal midday heat. I thought we were there because my father had to have a check-up for his myopia. I never linked the hospital to his cancer, and that's why I cursed how long they were taking and carried on with a contagious insolence that spread to my brother and sister, unaware that in an anonymous consulting room somewhere in that huge building, behind one of its hundreds of windows, my father had just received an ultimatum.

My father hadn't wanted to make that trip. He saw it as a superfluous, unnecessary and inappropriate expenditure, considering our financial situation. It was his friend Juan del Polo who insisted he go. 'Dammit, Gaucho, stop your bloody nonsense. You're ill, you don't know how long you've got. Go with Cecilia and the kids,' Juan told him, and handed over the tickets and itinerary. So it was thanks to Juan that we took that cruise through the Bahamas before spending a few days in Orlando, Florida to visit all the theme parks we could stand. Universal Studios, Magic Kingdom, Epcot, MGM, Wet'n Wild, Sea World, Disney World. I picture these places and remember my father struggling to walk, standing in those endless winding queues, climbing aboard roller-coasters, trying his best to keep up with us, while we called him a spoilsport every time he begged for a pause to alleviate the pain in his legs and waist. I see him in his Bermuda shorts, those glasses that made his eyes look bigger; a man far away from his years of military glory, a different man altogether. I see him standing quietly, whistling, glancing around with curiosity, half-understanding the instructions in English. My father: he could be bent over with agonising pains in his joints, his bones could creak, he could be dizzy – but he didn't complain, he didn't want to look like an old man, and he put on his best face for the photographs. Nevertheless, some nights in the darkness of the room all five of us shared in the hotel, I could hear his agitation and his mutterings of pain, and I'd wonder if the cancer might not be doing away with him after all.

That trip was or should have been our family valedictory. My bad attitude didn't help. I was seventeen and thought the world stank. I was seventeen and didn't know my father was dying. On the cruise ship, I thought the activities organised by the crew on deck were the dumbest things ever – choreographed dances, games and contests played to the rhythm of a tropical band – so instead of joining in with the others I found pretexts to go back to my cabin and shut myself up to read magazines, or sleep or just look at the ocean. And every time we disembarked at some island, port city or tourist resort, I fled the rest of the clan to improvise my own tours. My father grew tired of telling me off. After a few times he gave up and let me do whatever I wanted. My behaviour was deplorable. When he died a year later,

I was filled with remorse. Every time I saw the photos or the video of the cruise, I'd punish myself: they showed all too clearly that my attitude wasn't even rebellious, but simply offhand, apathetic. Many years later I joined my then girlfriend Marisela and her parents on a beautiful trip to the Riviera Maya, in Mexico. On the first night the hotel organised an event to welcome the new guests. The various activities and Hawaiian-style tunes took me back to that 1994 cruise. I was no longer a seventeen-year-old boy but a man of thirty-five. Marisela enthusiastically sat in the front row for the show. At the first opportunity, I went up on the stage as a volunteer and made a fool of myself. I danced, I jumped, I followed instructions, I smiled, I competed, I lost. Marisela and her family applauded from their seats. I don't know if I wanted to fix or amend the past, but whatever it was, it was completely useless.

★ ★ ★

Towards the end of 1994 the cancer began to manifest itself. My father had been unable to urinate comfortably for months. It caused him pain to piss. Every time we happened to go to a restaurant toilet together I'd see him out of the corner of my eye from the adjacent urinal, emptying his bladder drop by drop, staring impotently at the ceiling. Not long afterwards, I'm not sure exactly when, he simply began to piss his trousers and wet the bed like an incontinent child. The only one who became aware of these accidents was my mother, who tried to persuade him to use some adult nappies that she'd found. My father stared at her indignantly and threw the package into the corner, yelling that he wasn't some feeble old cripple and that he'd do himself in before using them. One evening, returning from a social event, my father refused to get out of the car. 'What's wrong, dear?' my mother asked him. He remained silent. He'd wet himself, but this time there was blood. 'I'm ashamed you have to wash my trousers,' he told her, and collapsed in tears over the steering wheel. My mother hugged him and told him not to worry, that they were together, they would get through the illness, everything would be the same as before. But my father knew that this wasn't true. He knew that his days on Earth were numbered and he wept disconsolately while we slept inside, oblivious to the fact that he was falling apart in a puddle of urine, buckled by a sorrow and a rage that would never go away, and which somehow linger here still, swathing these words that have spent years refusing to emerge, to be spat out.

From that night on my father got accustomed to carrying a metal bedpan under the car seat to relieve himself in case of emergency. That was how he spent the entire summer of 1995, during the exhausting campaign to enter Congress on the UPP ticket, the devastating results of which so demoralised him, flattened him, killing off his will to keep fighting. One night, the party leader, Javier Pérez de Cuéllar, organised a reception in his home to congratulate the newly elected members of Congress. My father didn't want to attend, but felt obliged out of a sense of duty and comradeship. The only thing Cecilia Zaldívar remembers of that night is that at one point my father got up from the table they'd been assigned and went off to the toilet. When he returned he was pale, sweating, close to fainting. 'My pressure's dropped,' he whispered in her ear. 'Let's go home, come on,' she said straight away, and discreetly took him out without saying goodbye to anyone.

Everything about him gradually changed. It wasn't just that he wet himself: he also sweated in excess, complained of unbearable pain in his right leg and twitched constantly. Then there was the disagreeable taste in his mouth left by the only pills my mother could persuade him to take. I was oblivious to these changes, most of them happening behind closed doors. From my perspective, my father was severely ill, but it was all under control and there was no visible reason to believe that it could become critical. Or so went my theory until the morning of the attack. The morning of 13 May 1995.

Like every Saturday, my father had got up to have his breakfast and had put on a blue tracksuit, a striped white flannel polo shirt and white slippers. He had woken us up on his way to the kitchen. He always did that: he couldn't bear us sleeping in even on weekends, and so he'd drag the sheets off us with the rough tenderness of a dog nipping without malice. My mother was at the sink, squeezing oranges, and glanced up as he came in. They greeted each other and my father sat down at the head of the table. The sun was shining brightly outside. Everything was as it always was. A few minutes later my father asked for the newspapers. They're right in front of you, dear, my mother said without turning around from the juicer. Where are they, I can't see them. There, on the table. But where. Beside you! I can't see them, everything's blurry. What's wrong, dear? I can't see properly. Dear! Dear! Oh, my dear!

I arrived just as my mother was approaching the table to help him, and what I saw left me frozen. My father's eyes were rolled back, his body was shaking with violent spasms and a white foam began to trickle from his mouth. His face was no longer his. I don't know at what moment Valentina, Facundo and El Zambo Garcés arrived. My father slid out of the chair onto the floor, still convulsing, amid a wave of cries and shouts of alarm and fear. No one knew what to do or who to turn to. We'd never seen anything like it. Valentina — wrapped in a towel, having leapt out of the shower upon hearing my mother's yelling — suffered a panic attack and began to bang her head on the floor. Even so, she was the first to reach the telephone and call an ambulance. My mother was praying and shrieking. El Zambo Garcés tried to subdue my father's shuddering body, fanned him with the newspapers, placed cushions under his head. My brother Facundo covered his eyes with his pyjama shirt. I was frozen to the spot. It was a horrific scene. It was as if all the historical illnesses of the Cisneros family had come together at once in my father's body. The phthisis of Nicolasa, the Parkinson's of Luis Benjamín, the heart arrhythmia of Fernán. When your father is convulsing, when his eyes are blank, when his body is possessed, what hurts isn't the experience of witnessing him like this, but knowing he won't be coming back. Not as the same man, at least. And so it was with my father. The ambulance arrived quickly, the paramedics took him away on a stretcher, and a few blocks later wheeled him through the emergency doors of the San Pablo hospital. Even though he was released just two days later, he wasn't the same when he returned to the Monterrico house. He came back damaged. Wounded. There are days when I think that my father did in fact die that morning, and the man who came back in the wheelchair, the one we still referred to as Dad, who talked incoherently and remained with us for two more months, was actually an imposter, a double, a fake. I don't know why, but for these past twenty years I've kept the striped polo shirt he was wearing on the day he started to die. I keep it in a drawer and it's almost like I've got him hidden in there. Sometimes I put it on and my chest starts to take on the shape of my father's. It's as if the funereal garment retained the memory – or the shape of the memory – of the body it once dressed, as if it were forever saddened by the knowledge that it won't be touched again by its original owner, the man who brought it to life.

The attack forced us to change how we saw our father, and how he saw himself. Once invincible, he was suddenly an old man defeated by illness. Two months earlier, he'd been one of the star candidates to Congress, and retained the sheen of his fame. Now he was just someone on his way out. He hadn't been chosen for Congress, but for cancer. He was destroyed by the loss of his independence, his senility, firing off sentences that no longer intimidated anyone, inspiring embarrassment and pity. We had depended on him in so many ways, and now were his only crutch, his only contact with reality. He seemed in better spirits the Sunday we celebrated what would be his final Father's Day. A lot of people came. Brothers and sisters, uncles and aunts, cousins. After lunch, we split up into three groups to play charades. When it was his turn to mime something to the circle, he found that he didn't know how to turn the words someone had whispered in his ear into gestures. He sat still for a moment, staring at the ground, and just when we started to fear he might have had a stroke or a heart attack, he started to laugh with all his might, with all the muscles in his jaw. A thunderous laugh that shook the walls, the doors, the windows and the trees in the garden. He laughed at himself in huge guffaws, both contagious and sad, the laughter of someone who knows that he'll probably never laugh again that way. A farewell laugh from a man who, in his wheel-chair, couldn't see the bleakness of the moment, because the bleakness was inside him.

The only beneficial or soothing aspect of those last weeks was that my father finally let go of the intransigent general's mask he always wore and brought out his gentle, peaceful and vulnerable side. It hurt me to see him incapac-itated, but at the same time there was something in his incapacitation that gave me relief. It was as if by losing his ferocity my father had stepped down from the imaginary pedestal he had always occupied and had finally become one of us. Every time he asked me to push his wheelchair down one of the corridors of the Monterrico house, I couldn't help feeling, deep inside, a certain pleasure that my father finally depended on me, even if it was only to transfer him from one room to another. The cancer tore off the shells, the layers of skin and the masks he'd used to construct his personality – whether for his institution, for the media, or for his family. My father would die on 15 July, but it was on the day of his attack that the Gaucho Cisneros Vizquerra truly died. Hearing that composite name still makes me shiver today, and will do for the rest of my life.

* * *

When he went back into hospital he had fractures in his hip and left leg. His femur was so weak that it could have broken if he sneezed. If I remember correctly, it broke in three when he bent down in the bathroom to pick up his talcum powder. Beside his hospital bed a pulley was set up that raised his leg in the air, with a bag of sand as the counterweight. I'd never seen him so hobbled.

My father only tolerated the presence of my mother in his room. He would barely let the rest of us in; he didn't want us to see him like that. Much less the former president Belaúnde, who came to visit him one morning. When he went into hospital my father asked to enter via the back door to avoid being photographed by the press. Two days later, however, he was on the front pages: 'General Cisneros in hospital for cancer treatment.' We were all ordered not to say anything about my father to any of the journalists who turned up asking for him each day. Nevertheless, updates continued to appear in *Expreso*, *El Comercio*, *El Mundo*, *Ojo*. 'Cisneros in intensive care.' 'Slight improvement in condition of General Cisneros.' 'Cisneros on oxygen.' 'General Cisneros undergoing cobalt treatment.' 'Hip fracture due to metastasis.' 'Embolism in the leg.' 'Gravely ill.'

The operation on his femur lasted seven or eight hours. At first it seemed successful. The doctor who came to check him over, a Doctor Castillo, told him: 'General, you can sit on the edge of the bed and try to stand.' My father was overjoyed at this, Cecilia Zaldívar tells me. But something happened as he tried to get up: his fingernails turned purple and his breathing became congested. He entered a state of asphyxia and began to suffocate, convulsing, a grimy foam seeping from his mouth. There was uproar in the room. A stampede of nurses entered and whisked him off to the Intensive Care Unit, while my older siblings blamed Doctor Castillo for asking him to make an effort he wasn't ready for. When I went to see him later in the ICU, it felt like entering a gloomy chapel. There was my father, intubated, surrounded by a trauma surgeon, a nephrologist and an oncologist. He's suffered a pulmonary embolism, one of them said. I paced back and forth, looking at the other two patients in the unit, each agonising in their own compartments, surrounded by weeping relatives or friends. Both would die in the next few days.

I don't remember my final conversation with my father. I don't remember if we managed to say anything much in those last days in hospital. In fact, I don't remember my father even speaking a word while he was there. My brother Facundo recalls a few sentences they exchanged. I don't. When my thoughts return to those scenes in the cancer ward, they're enveloped in spine-chilling silence. I can hear the steps of people in the corridors, the squeaking of the nurses' rubber-soled shoes, the squealing wheels of the cleaning trolleys, entire families sobbing. But I can't hear my father. I think I'd stopped hearing him much earlier. Our communication had withered away in the months before his relapse. What I do remember is that, when it was my turn to look after him, I watched him like someone gazes at a work of art in a gallery, trying to notice something that spoke to me alone. What was my father thinking about in that bed, surrounded by all that noisy equipment? All of his bodily effort was focused on breathing, on sucking up what little oxygen he could find and channelling it to his blood. And his mind? What was happening there? What was occupying it? Down what paths was it wandering? Was there space for serenity, or was it all a tidal surge of fear?

We were unable to talk, but I needed to communicate with him somehow, and that's how I began to sing softly into his ear on the last night. The night of Friday 14 July. Of all possible songs I chose 'How could I not believe in God', the only one sung at mass that moved him. At that time I held a robust Catholic faith that I cultivated by going to church every week and participating in the work of the parish. So I turned to that song, investing it with healing strength and singing it in the belief that it alone could save my father, convinced that all the prayers in the world couldn't be more powerful than those very words, certain that it could invoke a miracle. God won't be able to ignore me, I thought.

That night I sang in my father's ear like someone singing into a shell in the hope of talking to the sea. As I sang, I stroked his hair, which had begun to turn yellow. I sang as he breathed through a tube that looked like some kind of vacuum cleaner for sucking out his soul. I sang in the hope that one syllable would reach his dimmed consciousness and I believed in the power of that single syllable until 2:20 a.m. on the morning of the 15th, when my mother came in to relieve me. My father died a few hours later. The only result of that song was a newfound hatred of God. The last time I sang 'How could I not believe in God' was also the day I stopped believing in God forever.

On the morning of the 15th I left the cancer ward with a sense of relief. It had done me good to spend the night there. Before leaving the ICU, a doctor told me that my father had responded well to the blood dialysis they'd carried out the previous day after one of his kidneys failed. I took that piece of news with me to the gym at my club where I could let out all my rage, stress and panic. There I was, lying on a red bench, angrily raising a metal bar above my chest, hearing the clinking of the heavy black discs, wondering once again if there was still space in my father's mind for a calm thought in these tragic hours. And at that moment it felt like a cruel paradox, an unintentionally disrespectful act to be showing off my physical energy when he was barely strong enough to keep his heart beating. I let the barbell fall back onto the support with a clatter. The noise made people look round. Someone asked me if I needed help. I said I was fine. And then, multiplied over the loudspeakers, I heard the voice of a receptionist addressing me. 'Mr Cisneros Zaldívar, please go to the front desk to take an urgent call.' And that voice sounded black to me. And I felt weak. And suddenly it seemed to me that the whole club could hear the voice as I was hearing it. That indifferent voice announcing, as it might announce the day's programme of activities, that my father had ceased to exist.

While I drove as fast as I could back to the hospital, I thought about my father's end, how he'd have preferred a thousand times over to be attacked by a terrorist cell than by prostate cancer. He'd spent years preparing and provisioning himself for external assaults of all kinds. He had an armoured car, weapons, sensors, bodyguards, electric fences topping the walls around the house. What he could never anticipate was an enemy that lay within, that the ambush would come from inside his own body. In a number of interviews from 1992 onwards he referred to terrorism as a malignant cancer, the cells of which were propagating across the towns in the mountains. He said this without knowing that his illness was imitating them. My father's cancer, incubated in the prostate, advanced through his body with the stealth of a Shining Path column at night, scaling cliffs, fanning out, colonising organs as if they were villages where they had to dynamite a bridge, an electrical substation or a government building to threaten the authorities, or shoot a few peasants to sow fear. When my father's cancer metastasised, when his system surrendered to the cancerous siege, there was nothing to be done. The war was lost. The conquest of the territory was complete. And the only soldier defending it was dead.

I reached the hospital to find a great commotion. After several hours, tired of crying or seeing people cry, I sat down beside my uncle Adrián, who was in a corner apart from the rest. I saw that he wasn't just sad: he was angry. 'They killed your old man,' he muttered between clenched teeth. He had no way of proving what he said, but he was sure that agents of Montesinos had entered the ward during the night and switched off the machine delivering oxygen to my father. I thought he was crazy, but then my sister Estrella – who has a notable history of accurate premonitions – told me she'd dreamt the night before of a tall blonde nurse with her hair in a bun who injected my father with something deadly. Both theories sounded delirious, but there was one element that stood out: the infamous Doctor Castillo, whose first name we'd never learnt, the one who had involuntarily triggered the embolism that sent my father into intensive care, had suddenly disappeared, without even signing the death certificate. The black hand that some were searching for could have been his. But there was no point in giving credence to the possibility of a conspiracy against my father. I'd seen him the night before. He was a dying man. Life had already fallen away from him. There was no longer any need for him to be eliminated.

I was also able see his body when my mother told me to come in and say goodbye to him, as if the dead could momentarily come back to life to make their farewells. I entered with the intention of embracing him tightly, in a desperate attempt to absorb his erudition, his knowledge, his mettle, his patience, everything that was still warm but was disappearing with the rest of him. What was lying there, however, was not my father anymore. It was just a defeated body. I thought: where has he gone? And I gave him a perfunctory kiss on the forehead that served only to confirm he was as cold as ice.

I've returned to those corridors over the years, bearing witness to other losses I felt as keenly as if they were my own. In others' disconsolation I found my pain renewed. And I embraced the uncertainty that I felt at eighteen, and I again became – unfortunately for myself and for those I was accompanying and supposedly consoling – a stunned and wounded adolescent, incapable of reacting with maturity or decorum.

★ ★ ★

My father's wake was held at the Monterrico house, guarded by an entire squad of Junín Hussars. That was how he'd wished it. He wanted his death to be replete with symbols of military dignity. No one argued with him. No one contradicted him on anything, even on the days when the illness stopped him thinking clearly. Only now am I struck by the fact that we held the vigil at home – that we acceded to this last request, demonstrating a final authoritarian wish to keep ruling over his domestic territory. It was a macabre thing to have his dead body lying there for two days, just a few metres away from the rooms where we were trying to get some sleep, or something resembling sleep. Lying under my bed covers on the nights after his death, my head had room for one image only: my father, shut up in a box at the back of the house, rotting inside his gala uniform, his hands holding a rosary and a photograph, on the back of which I'd written a few verses, now impossible to recall. During the vigil, as his body fermented, I felt he wasn't altogether dead, that he continued to accompany us, that even in death he was able to protect us, and I imagined him singing and getting drunk on Bloody Marys beneath the equestrian paintings on the terrace. I had to make a great effort to tell myself that my father was no longer alive, that he was nothing but a decaying body inside a coffin – a body that had switched off like a domestic appliance worn out by years of use.

During the wake there were reporters and photographers from newspapers and TV channels. Some approached me for statements on the circumstances of my father's death and for information about the burial. I told them everything they wanted to know, going into irrelevant details. I couldn't hold back. I'd never had a microphone placed in front of me before, wanting to hear my views. No one had ever interviewed me. I'd never felt that my opinion or testimony was something worthy of being shared. I was deep in real grief, a frank and painful grief, but vanity still crept into my heart. I tried to stamp out this dark and at the same time intoxicating feeling. I thought it was selfish, offensive and unjust. I felt like a traitor. Yet the foul black thought stalked me like a vulture, like a voice in the middle of the hurly-burly, whispering in my ear: now that your father has died, people will finally notice you.

I can picture myself that day, not only giving statements to the press, but also laughing with friends, going out for pizza at the Chacarilla shopping centre. I see myself driving towards the centre, losing control of the car, ending up on the curb and apologising to the passengers, who must have thought I was on drugs or having a nervous breakdown. I see myself receiving an embrace from Lorena Antúnez, the girl I'd fallen in love with at the beginning of high school or maybe even before that. A long time had passed since then, but even so I was moved that she showed up at my house, beautiful in a black two-piece suit, and it stunned me to see her sitting with her sisters in the middle of my living room, weeping for my father; I remember that it caused me joy and shame, as I thought resignedly that this would be the greatest intimacy we'd ever share.

As I went back and forth, dealing with the countless things that needed doing, I was constantly aware that my mother, my siblings and I were the centre of attention. Not my father, but us, the widow and the newly fatherless children. The camera lights remained lit behind us like dragonflies. My pain was genuine, but a part of my subconscious was enjoying everything. I don't know why but I was excited by the fact that our pain was televised. And when later, at the burial, during the silence following the bugle call, an Army officer presented me with a cushion on which rested my father's military cap and sabre, I felt hundreds of eyes upon me. I felt the compassion of the people who had come, their desire to console me, their anguished laments. I liked being the point where all gazes converged. My tears were the most sincere I've ever spilled, and the bitterness of loss was like a corkscrew turning inside me, but for some mysterious reason I didn't want the sorrowful ceremony to end. It was a horrible feeling, and it's horrible to write it, but I wouldn't have minded if the burial of my father had lasted a few hours longer.

There is a video documenting moments from the two hours we spent at the cemetery that Sunday morning. It captures the light drizzle that was falling throughout. I don't know who recorded the scene – perhaps my cousin Pipo, who carried a video camera everywhere – but whoever it was produced some astonishing close-ups of those of us who were standing beside the grave. The recording still exists, digitised, but I've never wanted to watch it again. It's a brief, silent film; I know the script by heart. Yet it would be impossible for me to destroy it or throw it away. Instead, I keep it hidden in a corner, waiting for the mould to do to it what the worms did to my father.

I've returned to something else, though: the front pages from the day after the burial. 'Farewell, General,' reads *Expreso*. Below the headline it continues: 'He died poor, faithful to his ideas; his remains now rest in peace in his tomb.' When I read these yellowing newspaper cuttings today, they still seem so recent. The photographs show uncles and aunts who have died in the decades since, but who were there on that July morning in 1995, and suddenly the flood of memory transports me back to the graveside, next to my mother, and the fear and incredulity of that moment slip through the years and find me where I'm sitting now, clawing at me, reminding me that death continues to exercise its fearful dominion. The Monday 17 June headline in *La República* reads: 'The Gaucho Cisneros is dead.' *El Nacional*: 'The widow and six children of the deceased, greatly affected by the death of their father, received the condolences of those who attended the wake.' *El Comercio*: 'The penultimate of his children remarked that the funeral was postponed by one day because military honours cannot be paid on Sundays according to Army regulations.' I am my father's penultimate child. Or was.

In other reports I read: 'Remains of General Cisneros Vizquerra buried with military honours.' 'Cadets from the military college stood guard until the end.' 'There was a military band, troop of honour, a salvo of thirteen cannons and a minute's silence.' 'His remains were laid to rest in the Los Pinos section of the Jardines de la Paz cemetery.'

I look over these cuttings and realise that I had never contemplated my life without my father. As a boy, the world without him was unimaginable. When I grew up, I continued to feel that way. My father had made sure that all of us orbited around him, and our dependence was so absolute, so essential, that no one ever stopped to think about the disaster his disappearance would unleash. I associated my future with his physical presence and I had assumed that I'd carry on living with my parents and siblings in the Monterrico house until the end of time. But his death marked the end of time. And when it happened, when the blow fell, when we weren't ready for it, the pain came after the bewilderment. All we had to do was gaze into each others' faces upon returning from the burial, when all the relatives and friends had gone, to discover the same terrifying question reflected there: now what? Our world had crumbled and vanished, sweeping away all its accumulated sediment of certainties. Death carried him off, and took the life we knew with it. We ourselves disappeared, or rather mutated in record time. That's what death does to people: it instantly imposes the internal changes that might otherwise take a decade to evolve. We grow old in one go. Our features dim.

How my father's prestige has faded since 15 July 1995. Who knows how much I can really recover in this anxious and perhaps fruitless exercise of asking others what they know or remember. I will never have enough material to rebuild my father – and yet I keep looking for the scattered pieces, as if there were some way to restore the original model. Although more than 'restore', the word would perhaps be 'beget'. Here, I have begotten the Gaucho, bestowing his name on an imagined creature. And in this way I become his literary father. Literature is the biological process that has allowed me to bring him into the world, into my world, giving rise to his birth in fiction.

Chapter 12

Today you're not even a memory, but a fragment of a memory that assails me in gentle gusts. That falls on me like hailstones.

My mother sees you in dreams; she says she talks to you. I envy that communication. I haven't dreamt of you even once in all these years. If you appear before me, it's in the ideas that come to mind while I'm reading or watching a film. These books and movies are the dreams I can't dream.

You wanted to enter Congress, but you failed. I found myself working there by accident. You wanted to make a TV programme, but it didn't work out. I ended up presenting one without even intending to. You wanted to write about your life, but your life didn't leave you enough time. Here I am instead, writing about you. Did you transfer your outstanding desires to me? I never asked for this inheritance but it fell to me; it was implanted in me. Ever since I realised this, I've distrusted my own goals and objectives: so many of them are just your old ambitions in new clothing.

You liked to be recognised, to be popular. Behind your zeal for service, which led you to set your sights on Congress or television, was the desire to remain in the public eye, to hold some kind of power. That differentiates us. Power doesn't interest me. Not that sort of power. If I were moved by any kind of power at all, it would be the power of revealing absolutely everything about who we are.

There are people who insist that we looked like each other. I see no resemblance. Your nose was upturned. Your ears were large and doughy. Your brush-like moustache grew differently from mine. Your forehead was wide, your skull rounded. Our only shared trait is a mole on the cheek. That, and perhaps our eyes: not in their colour or temperature, but because of what happens inside them, in the pupils.

I look through old albums with my mother and with my sister Valentina. There is one photo in which you seem to be strangling me, but in most of them you evade physical contact. You lived for sixty-nine years. I was born before your fifty-first birthday. I only knew you – it's a figure of speech – for eighteen years of your life. I suppose I began to have an awareness of your presence very early on, but the photos can't help me figure out when we began to form a relationship. Some of them don't even provide proof of my existence.

The more hermetic you were, the more diabolically strong and sure of yourself you felt. Perhaps in opposition to that, I cleave to everything that seems weak, vulnerable, erratic, everything that seems destined to stumble.

My mother wasn't the problem. She was always there. Her love was guaranteed. She would never leave me. Not you. You were the mythical one. The utopian. The one who appeared in the newspapers. The one who wore a uniform that was also a disguise. You were the one I needed to conquer. My mother was real, flesh and blood. She didn't appear on television. She was a tangible piece of the world. A rock. You, meanwhile, were already a flickering light, swift and ungraspable.

My twelve-year tenure at the newspaper served as training for this book. What did I do from Monday to

Friday? Review old articles, select data, cross-reference, write down dates, look for subliminal information in photographs, interview sources face to face or by telephone, travel in search of people, record conversations, transcribe the recordings. I chose to be a journalist not because of journalism, but to be ready to cover the emergency I unconsciously knew would arrive: the day when I'd have to declassify your files.

Everything I know now comes from hundreds of hours of conversations with my mother, my brothers and sisters, my uncles and aunts and thirty or so other people who knew you. There were more people still to interview, but I stopped. One day I understood that I didn't want to write a profile or a biography or a documentary: what I needed to do was to fill the blank spaces with my imagination, because you are also – or above all – made of what I imagine you were, of what I'm unaware of and what will always remain a question mark. Literature penetrates the facts that affect us. That's what I needed: to get into your memory, to act on it like an organ that requires surgery.

When you died, we'd only just begun to get to know each other. Who have we become over the twenty years since your death? Why did it become so urgent for me to find it out, to write about it and to make this story into a kind of offering? Why do I write about you? Why do I read so much literature of mourning? Why all those books about dead fathers, all that underlining, all those annotations on the final pages? Why those films and documentaries on lost or abandoned children? Why travel to Buenos Aires, Mar del Plata or Paris, as if your real remains were to be found in those cities? Why go to Huácar, that village frozen in time where my great-great-grandmother fell in love with a priest? Why this pilgrimage to manufacture an epic? I've travelled to places where I know you were happy, seeking proof of that happiness, trying to imagine how you breathed in those climes, how you walked those streets, how you conversed with people, how you saw yourself facing the future. I've travelled into your past while knowing your future, and that has allowed me to weigh the successes and failures of the many decisions you made. Stay or return. Carry on or quit. And even though I've salvaged valuable fistfuls of the sand that you left behind, you still seem like a measureless beach to me.

★ ★ ★

I've also looked for my father in others. My uncle Juvenal, above all. When we'd leave his house on General Borgoño St. in Miraflores to walk along Pardo Ave. in search of some discreet restaurant, I'd feel like he was my father, or rather that I was his son, or should have been. Juvenal asked me how I felt, scrutinised my fears, talked to me like no one else did, told me about the importance of poetry as a way of easing the soul. Then we'd return to his house and sit in his library drinking tea, and when he disappeared for a siesta I'd stay there, picking out books from among the thousands on his shelves, and I'd feel like it was a kind of ship, or womb or vault or lost ark; and I'd think it was unfair that I wasn't his son. In the photographs hung on the walls of his library, Juvenal appeared next to Borges, García Márquez, Cortázar, Ribeyro, Vargas Llosa, Cabrera Infante. On our walls, my father, the Gaucho, appeared alongside Videla, Pinochet, Kissinger, Bordaberry.

For years I sought out substitutes for my father. Models that turned out to be opposites of the original. One of them was Guillermo Rosas, an Argentinian journalist who hired me to work alongside him at a radio station when he was already an idol and I was just a timid newcomer. We became great friends. Guillermo was born in Rosario, beside the Paraná River. He was a Peronist and came to Lima – or escaped Argentina – after seeing his friends, leaders in the Montonero movement, killed at the hands of the military. I can't count the times that Guillermo told me – his eyes hot with tears that forced him to pull his car over – about his experience during the dictatorship, about the repression led by my father's military pals. One morning in the radio booth he showed me how to knot my tie. It was such an intimate, teacherly and affectionate moment that later, returning home on the bus, I felt like I'd been unfaithful to my dead father.

That feeling, however, was nothing compared to the wave of betrayal I felt the time I agreed to judge a competition of poetry by imprisoned writers, and ended up giving the prizes to an MRTA terrorist and a former leader of the Shining Path. I even had photographs taken together with them at the end of the ceremony, and smiled at the camera, and only later, checking their names against my files, realised that both of them had been at the forefront of their respective criminal organizations when my father was Minister of War or in the years following his retirement from the military, when he was promoting the death penalty for terrorist leaders in his articles. I deduced that the name of the Gaucho Cisneros must have figured on their blacklists for kidnapping or extermination. I felt a sense of disloyalty for taking a decision in favour of these terrorists, for letting myself be carried away by the power of the poems they'd written in prison, for rewarding the poetry of people who had once sought to kill my father. My father would have strung them up. I hung medals around their necks.

* * *

Age, I believe, isn't determined by how many years you've lived, but by how many things have happened to you. It's events, not calendars, that determine growth. I turned eighteen in January 1995, six months before my father died, but I've always felt that the document that truly accredited my arrival to adulthood was not my new national identity card but his death certificate. Certificate number 040495. The coroner gave me that document the afternoon I had to return to the clinic for his belongings. If the death of a son numbs the father, the death of the father awakens the son. When my father died, I woke up, I felt bigger, older. I had no choice.

* * *

As a child I invented a game. I'd lift down the oval mirror in the guest WC and hold it out flat in front of me, the edge against my stomach, with the glass facing upwards, in such a way that if I was inside, it reflected the ceilings, and if I was playing in the garden it replicated the infinite skies.

Once I was in this position, I'd begin to walk, carrying the mirror like someone bearing a heavy tray of food or a newspaper that demanded total attention. With my gaze buried in the glass, I convinced myself that the floor was made of whatever appeared in the reflection: an expanse of white-painted cement, concrete structures, wooden beams, glass chandeliers hanging upwards, freed from gravity, and whatever else was found on the ceilings of the rooms. By contrast, if I played the game outside, I had to be careful not to tread on the clouds, the crowns of the trees spreading upside down like artichokes, not to crush the distant bird flitting past that, in the logic of the game, looked like some rapacious insect. It was a solitary, escapist pursuit; incongruous, inverted.

Persistent memories are not the symptom of a healthy memory, but of a damaged memory. The thing you remember most is what has most deeply affected you.

* * *

I want some of this immaterial thing you now are. I want to dream about you like my mother does, and hear what you have to say to me, or believe you still have something to say to me. I can't stand the indifference of your death. I feel like I'm less your son because I can't dream about you. I'm tired of probing your death from my place in life, while you do nothing for me from your place in death. Or if you do you don't show it, you don't say a thing about it, just like when you were alive.

Sometimes I wonder whether I'm idealising the time we shared. Would I really want you to be alive again? What would you have become? An unbearable old codger? Or someone more respectful of our choices? Today, you'd be eighty-nine years old. I can't fit the face you had when you died to the one you'd have in this alternative universe. You wouldn't have been able to endure getting older. That's why I don't believe you just died, but rather let yourself die. You took control even over your own death. You died at the right moment: when I still had time to discover my talents and reorient my own self. If you'd died later, perhaps I'd already have been firmly moulded in your image, and it would have been harder or impossible for me to break free of you. The things I've done that you never lived to see, things that define me today: would you have tolerated them? Would I have done them while you were still around? Would I have taken the same decisions if I'd first had to listen to your usually conservative and retrograde opinions? If you'd lived longer, your influence would have grown greater still. The best thing you did for me was to let yourself die.

Just as there is discomfort and pain in the accounts of the children of the persecuted, the deported and the disappeared, whose stories embody the frustration and defencelessness of millions and give rise to protests against impunity, so too there is discomfort and pain in the account of the son of a military man and repressor who issued groundshaking pronouncements and never hesitated to order the imprisonment or kidnapping or torture of people who would later tell their stories with the heroism they deserved. Although it may not seem like it, villains too are made of wounds. My father was a uniformed villain. His uniform was a scab. Below it were the sores that nobody saw, that he never displayed. If I reveal these sores here, it's in order to allow them to scar over once and for all. For my father is now a scar, not a wound. Not any more.

Just as a father is never prepared to bury his son, a son is never prepared to dig up his father. For most children who have lost a parent, it's no small task to dig them up, to sift through the remains. Turning over their tomb or raking through their biography seems an unforgivable sacrilege, a twisted, profane act, an ignoble betrayal of the peace demanded by the dead. If you've lost a parent, it's easy to forget that the living also deserve a certain peace, a peace that can often only be achieved at the expense of the peace of the dead. Perhaps it's a mistake to believe that the dead expect us to leave them in peace. Perhaps they hope for the opposite: for us to seek ways of interrogating them, of asking them what they never dared to tell us, of demanding that they finally release the essential information we've always unknowingly lacked. The information whose existence would have remained a mystery to us if we hadn't given timely credit to the suspicion and pain left behind. Perhaps, in order to rest, the dead need to speak, to offer details, to confess.

If your dead choose you, if they pursue you, it's because they're asking you to give them a voice, to fill in the blanks, the gaps. To gather, order and share their truths and their lies. Truths and lies that, at bottom, aren't so very different from your own.

Perhaps this is what it means to write: to invite the dead to speak through you.

Family Tree

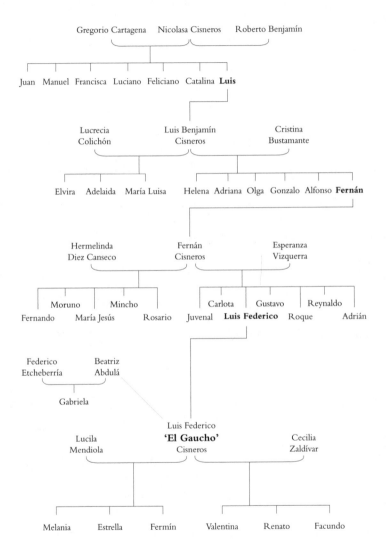

Translator's Note

There are points at which the work of the author and the translator overlap, and others where they diverge. One aspect of the process the translator need not worry about are such incidentals as plot, character and setting. All the focus is on the language, and in this sense translation has been called 'a purer form of writing'. One thing that does perhaps replicate the experience of the author is the doubts that arise when we are deeply immersed in the process. And this is, above all, a book about doubt. Translation happens at a very different speed to reading, and as a translator we doubt, among other things, our ability to calibrate the final text so that it achieves the same velocity as the original. A certain distance from the text is required to allow us to experience it again as a reader. A distance from the author, too. To an even greater extent than is usual for a work of translation this book demanded that I inhabit the author's voice, and feel the weight of the questions about his father that he describes as having crushed his shoulders for so long. Having corresponded with Renato Cisneros, who always answered my queries about the text swiftly and graciously, I was at one point seized by an urge to meet him in person, not to talk about the book but to observe how he moves, his bearing, how he holds his knife and fork, how he laughs. To see or imagine for myself the traces of the father in the son. But just as I was considering this, he had to leave Europe for Peru for an extended period and it was no longer feasible. And that is probably for the better. I might have felt inhibited by him stepping off the page, out of the uncertain realm he inhabits here between fiction and reality. Instead, the process has been more like the tango that his father apparently danced so well. One leading, the other following, mirroring each other's steps.

The day after I completed final corrections to the manuscript I met a Peruvian woman at a party in Berlin, who upon hearing the name Renato Cisneros laughed and told me that a relative of hers is married to a granddaughter of the Cisneros who was Minister of the Interior. At that moment, the Cisneros family finally entered the real world for me for the first time.

Written as it was for an audience familiar with Peruvian history, I took the liberty of making a handful of additions and clarifications, with Renato's blessing. A few words here and there, nothing more, nothing to alter the pace of the book. For the same reason I decided against adding notes.

I am grateful to English PEN for the faith they placed in me by granting the book a PEN Translates award. My warmest thanks to Carolina and Sam of Charco Press for an excellent and close working relationship. I would like to offer special appreciation to Robin Myers, who edited this translation. If there is any elegance in these lines, it is largely thanks to her. Thank you to Fiona Mackintosh for attentive proofreading. Another reader, the most perceptive one I know, declines to be acknowledged in case of accusations of doing the translator's homework for him. Any remaining mistakes are of course my own. I'd like to dedicate the translation to Rosario and Niamh Zoe, with apologies for the missed weekends.

Fionn Petch, 2018

CHARCO PRESS

Director/Editor: Carolina Orloff
Director: Samuel McDowell

www.charcopress.com

The Distance Between Us was published on
80gsm Munken Print Cream paper.

The text was designed using Bembo 11 and ITC Galliard Pro.

Printed July 2018 by Bell and Bain Ltd.
303 Burnfield Road, Thornliebank, Glasgow G46 7UQ

Printed using responsibly sourced paper and environmentally
friendly adhesive